I0608211

The Afflicted Saga
Deliverance
Tale of the Fallen: Book VI

Katika Schneider

ISBN: 978-1-952673-02-3

For Nessix and Mathias
Kol and Veed
Brant and Sazrah and Annin and Etha

You've been the best cast of characters an author could ever ask for, and grateful doesn't begin to describe what I feel for you.

Thank you for choosing me to bring your story to life.

ACKNOWLEDGMENTS

With this, the final book of Tale of the Fallen, I want to look at things a bit differently. The usual abundance of gratitude still goes out to the staples in my publishing journey—my beta readers, Sarah Miller for my cover, the authors and mentors who continue to help guide my path, my street team for putting up with middle-of-the-night questions, and always, *always* my readers—but I feel it's time that I also acknowledge… life.

The majority of the finished version of Deliverance was completed during a time of quite a bit of personal and worldwide turmoil. But here we are. Sharing a book together. Continuing to move forward. Doing what we can to create a more beautiful world.

So, for Deliverance's acknowledgements, I'd like to acknowledge *life* and all of the garbage and glory it throws at us.

May we all find beauty.
May we all find peace.
May we all find deliverance.

ONE

When Khin had told Mathias that she trusted Tristan, she'd meant it. When she'd assisted the vampire lord in locating and obtaining the items his god wanted, she'd meant it still. Even after Tristan had walked her through the silly ritual of placing that gross scrap of leather in the little box she'd found in the Citadel's repository and pricked her thumb to press her bloody fingerprint on its clasp, she hadn't questioned what he was doing. The box had warmed, the compass affixed to its lid spinning until it settled toward the north, and when Tristan asked her once more if she still trusted him, Khin had thought it a pointless question.

That was before he'd scooped her up to follow the compass's guidance.

Khin had been frightened when Mathias had forced her onto a horse to gallop toward her destroyed home all those weeks ago, intimidated by the animal's speed and size and unpredictable nature. That had been before she'd fallen in line with the immortal predator who clutched her close as he zipped across the countryside with smooth leaps which made their surroundings pass by in an indecipherable blur.

Unlike her trip on horseback, it wasn't fear which kept Khin from squirming, but the force of Tristan's' momentum. She sank against his torso, hair plastered to her face as the snaps of her skirt and his coat whipped in the wind stirred up by his movement. She gripped the sacred box close to her chest with her right hand, fingers of her left one latched onto the thick velvet of Tristan's collar, and she struggled to breathe past the violent lashing of the wind they raced through. Once her eyes had been moistened enough by tears, she peered them open to find Tristan's hazel eyes alight with a hungry anticipation, thin brows tipped in determination and delicate lips gently curving with a smug confidence. His focus was intense, certain he'd obtain the outcome he was hunting, and Khin saw for the first time hints of that danger Mathias had warned her about.

You trust him. He won't lead you to harm, only answers.

Khin appreciated the thought, whether or not she could believe it at the moment, and tightened her grip on the wooden box in a weak attempt to use its warmth to battle the wind's chill. She was past worrying about Mathias's doubts. He might have been Abaeloth's greatest champion, but he didn't know *everything*. And, armed with the magical device of Tristan's god, Khin was well on her way to finding the one answer Zeal had been tearing itself apart searching for before the paladin could find it himself.

For the first time in her life, Khin was confident she'd made the right decision, one which would leave her in control of the balance of her future. And it had been a vampire, not some gallant knight, who had shown her how to reach it. Basking in the comforting glow of this newfound purpose, it took the abrupt slowing of Tristan's speed and the tickle of her hair easing its grasp on her cheeks for Khin to remember the nature of the mission they were on. Tristan continued to decelerate until he stopped completely and carefully let Khin slide from his arms.

Legs unsure of their stability, Khin leaned into the support of Tristan's hands until she discovered her balance at last and was able to cast her attention at the open grassland around them. Hazy mountains stretched up in the distance, the only disruptions along the level horizon. Khin had come all this way because she trusted Tristan, and she would continue to do so. But that didn't mean she understood why they were here.

"I thought you said we were tracking a demon's soul," she said, wrinkling her nose as she tried to pull stray hairs off her tongue.

Tristan took the wooden box from her hand and studied the compass as he strode ahead. "We are."

Khin pressed her lips together in the first bout of uncertainty she'd felt all day, and hastily followed after him. "But there's nothing here." She continued to cast her gaze about, searching for anything that could be interpreted as a grave marker.

"Oh, there is something here." Tristan didn't lift his eyes from the compass as he marched on, a deepening determination settled across his face. "We just have to keep looking."

Khin frowned. That was the most Mathias-like answer she'd ever heard come out of Tristan, and she was absolutely terrified of the idea of losing her usefulness now. "Do you know where we are?"

"Haven't the faintest." He didn't sound concerned about that fact. "My family governed over regions in the east and my knowledge of current domains is rather out of date." The compass's needle tugged toward the west and Tristan followed its guidance. "I do know that we are where we need to be, and that is all that matters."

Khin glanced from the box to the focus which sharpened Tristan's face. "But…" When he flicked an eye at her timid debate, she drew in a deep breath and continued. "There is *nothing here*," she repeated. "No graveyard, no tombstones. *Nothing.*"

Tristan's smooth laughter plucked at what little irritation Khin was capable of feeling toward him. "You think the Order of the White Circle has ever been in the habit of burying the demons they kill?" Khin blushed at his open mockery of her ignorance and Tristan, still needing to preserve her obedience, tried a different approach. "Souls do not remain tied to their body after death, Khin. That is *how* one dies."

"Then what about all the ghost stories about the dead creeping through graveyards?" She shivered despite the sun's steady warmth, and crossed her arms tightly.

"You answered your own question. They're stories."

Khin shook her head, staggering a moment as a wave of dizziness passed through her with the motion. "That can't be right.

3

If ghosts are just stories, how had you been able to talk to my parents?"

The compass needle began a slow revolution, and Tristan stopped to contemplate its behavior, holding his free arm out across Khin's chest to keep her from wandering ahead of him. "It hadn't been their ghosts and I hadn't been within miles of their bodies." The needle's spinning picked up speed until the box started to vibrate in Tristan's hand. "Souls are far more complex than your—"

"T-Tristan...?"

Interruptions were terribly uncharacteristic for the girl, but Tristan couldn't even begin to feel irritated about it past the feeble whimper which had delivered his name.

"I don' feel... very..."

Khin's knees caved from beneath her, and Tristan barely caught her before she collapsed to the ground. As he eased her the rest of the way down, he glanced once more at the relic in his other hand. It had quit vibrating, the compass needle now ticking evenly back and forth like a metronome, and as Khin leaned against him, sweaty forehead pressed against the side of his neck and breath coming too fast and shallow to sustain consciousness much longer, Tristan knew they'd found what they'd been looking for. Loathing to release his god's artifact which had only so recently been recovered, Tristan nestled it into the grass at his side to grasp Khin's shoulders and gently push her back from him. Losing her would be far too devastating to Ceredulus's cause. Damn mortals and their fragility...

"You need to calm down," he told her evenly, all illusions of charm gone. *My lord, I need your aid.*

"I—" Khin gasped the word a few times, her head bobbing forward as though she was fighting exhaustion. "I can't."

"You must," Tristan insisted, pulling her back into his support as he stretched his senses into their surroundings. He felt no malice around them, though it was difficult to perceive much past the enticing and alarming flutter of Khin's panicked heartbeat. "We've found Berann's soul, and I suspect he's searching for a vessel. If you lose consciousness, that vessel will be you."

His rationale did nothing to calm Khin, and her fingers weakly clawed at the fine silk of his shirt as though she was trying to climb her way from the bottom of a well. "Help me, Tristan," she whimpered. "I can't... I don't want to..."

Tristan bared his fangs in a vicious snarl. He didn't want Khin to be taken by this demon, either. *Ceredulus, Berann is here and I need your help.*

Stall him.

Shock erased the dangerous look from Tristan's face. *Stall him? I can't even sense him!*

I've almost won.

Tristan had served Ceredulus unflinchingly in every waking moment, but this was the first time he'd ever felt abandoned by his god. They both knew Khin's value in the quest to restore Ceredulus's influence on Abaeloth, and the god was leaving Tristan without any sort of guidance? It had been lifetimes ago since the vampire had recognized the pathetic squirm of fear, but as he searched for a soul he couldn't locate with the ridiculous notion of convincing the impatient and powerful ancient oraku it had belonged to to leave the vulnerable human alone, Tristan was promptly reminded why he'd hated this humiliating emotion. In his arms, Khin continued to tremble.

Swallowing his modesty and lifting his searching gaze, Tristan attempted to follow his god's order. "I know you are here, Berann." Between his anger and creeping dread, Tristan's voice lacked its trademark smoothness. "And you will leave this child alone. She was the conduit which led me to you, and for that service, you will not harm her."

"I'm scared, Tristan," Khin murmured, the wind-tattered lace of his collar sticking to her balmy cheek as she tried to lift her head from his shoulder to bring her fevered gaze to his.

"No need to be afraid, Khin," he replied, though he pointedly kept his eyes raised to avoid witnessing the girl's rapidly paling flesh and the listing of her emptying eyes. "Julianna was wrong about you. You are so much more than a survivor. You are a hero, and you will persevere as one."

Tristan's desperate rallying couldn't cut through the screaming haze pounding through Khin's ears. Something cold and crushing wrapped around her heart, slowing its beating a little more by the second, but not in a manner which calmed her. She convulsed against the seizing sensation, caught by Tristan's firm hands to keep from sprawling to the ground.

"You are a fool!" Tristan shouted to the demon he could neither locate nor contend with. "You cannot return to this plane without the blessing of my god. He is fond of this young woman and if you harm her, he will ensure you never reach this realm again."

Khin leaned heavily into Tristan's arms, sinking lower toward the ground as though the life was draining from her. How was Tristan supposed to reason with this creature? Ceredulus hadn't even been born, much less a god, before Berann had been slain; the damn demon likely had no idea that the dead could even return to life. Not to mention the fact that Tristan didn't speak one word of the demons' tongue. Grasping at straws, he shifted his mindset from the dignified dialect of Eastern Gelthin and scratched up his knowledge of the languages more commonly spoken here in the west.

"You know not what—"

A fierce gale shot down from the heavens, striking the ground not more than two yards from Tristan. The force of the gust was enough to topple the vampire lord backwards and he barely closed his arms around Khin to keep her from being cast away. The tracking box rolled and bounced from its resting spot and the grass around the focus of this divine impact flattened out in a ring. Shaking the daze from his head, Tristan sprang up to hunch protectively over Khin, but as he got to his knees, he had to fight back his urge to sag in relief.

Mathias Sagewind had arrived, as timely as ever, and beside him, free after more than nine centuries of imprisonment, was Ceredulus.

The paladin wasted no time setting a righteous concern across his brows as he rushed ahead to Khin as she moaned on the ground, fingers digging into the earth as she fought a sensation she couldn't explain, and Ceredulus's lip curled as he stalked close behind.

"You son of a bitch," Mathias growled at Tristan as he knelt down beside Khin and swatted the vampire away. "What did you do to her?"

"He cannot be blamed for her status, Mathias," Ceredulus replied, too distracted by uncovering the faint whispers of Berann's soul to enjoy the opportunity to torment the paladin over the dire straits affecting his pet mortal. "The only way to locate a missing soul is to bind it to a living one."

Mathias slipped his fingers over Khin's wrist to gauge her weakening pulse and turned to fling his fury back at the god he never should have made any deals with. "You bound her to an ancient oraku? What did you *think* would happen to her?"

Ceredulus, confident Mathias wouldn't dare to take any action against him until Berann was properly managed, didn't give the paladin so much as a glance. "Oh, I was quite concerned about what would happen to her, and you know I always aim to look after my own. Why did you think I was in such a hurry to gain your compliance?"

Mathias's jaw ached from how hard he clenched his teeth and he searched out the warmth of Etha's blessing in earnest to siphon it into the suffering girl. "Well, you gained my compliance," he seethed. "Now stop whatever it is that's happening."

Ceredulus heaved an inconvenienced sigh and spared Mathias a withering glance. "Not even Etha could read the language this demon is fluent in and you expect me to rush this…"

"You are Abaeloth's specialist in manipulating souls and you claimed to know what was going on. Now do something before I fling you back into the Veil."

Ceredulus never should have agreed to stay by Mathias's side. Sifting away his irritation, acutely aware of Khin's rapidly disintegrating wellness, and desperate for a mortal servant to carry out his bidding, Ceredulus reached forward and grasped the wisp of the thread which probed for the girl's life, and gave it a stout tug. Khin gasped and rolled to her side, curling her knees to her chest, and Mathias held Tristan back with a firm glower. Ceredulus reacted to none of this.

You are the demon known as Berann? He sent the message straight from his cognizance down the soul's thread, speaking in the rawest capacity possible.

I am. The reply was low and cool, commanding the respect of the young god. *And who are you?*

I am Ceredulus, god of the undead, and—

Be gone, Berann ordered. *Never again will I serve your kind.*

Entitlement encouraged Ceredulus to strike back at Berann's curt dismissal, but the god had spent centuries priding himself on his self-control and superior intellect. *I am not asking you to serve me or my kind, but would trouble you to tell me who it is you do serve.*

Justice.

No amount of intelligence could keep Ceredulus from scoffing at that answer. Mathias had certainly found a demon after his own heart… *Justice for who?*

For the wrongs made against my kind. Release me, child, so I might fulfill my quest.

A faint smile played at the god's lips. Berann likely hadn't meant to imply it, but he was, in fact, helpless to continue trying to force his soul into the place occupied by Khin's as long as Ceredulus kept a hold of this thread. *I would be happy to aid in your efforts, but demand you leave the girl alone. She is my property and I will not have her damaged.*

Your property? sneered Berann's soul. *Have the divine learned nothing?*

Oh, we've learned much, which is how this child *is able to prevent you, mighty oraku, from weaving your own magic. I do not object to you returning, rather I'd been a significant part of facilitating it, but you will not harm this girl to do so.*

Abaeloth does not have time for the divine to have suddenly developed a conscience, Berann retorted. *After centuries waiting here, I am presented with three immortals and this girl. It is regrettable that I must choose myself over her innocence, but my mission is too vital. I can stop my kind from destroying Abaeloth.*

Ceredulus flung a glance at where Mathias doted over the gasping young woman. *We've got a dull sword and rusty old shield that's reliably held them at bay for some time now. I will not doubt that you know a great secret to render Abaeloth's current defenses unnecessary, but you will not take my servant to deliver it.*

And I will not deliver it to such a beast as yourself, so it seems we are at an impasse.

Ceredulus bit back his immediate response. Abaeloth, her demons chief among them, had valid reason to doubt the gods' integrity, and though Berann was being as difficult as the paladin who had brought him to Ceredulus's attention, he'd been cordial so far. Convincing Berann to trust him could take lifetimes which Khin didn't have and, judging by how she still pinched her eyes shut and writhed on the ground, either whatever foolishness Mathias had taken part in to handicap himself from Etha's grace had affected him more than Ceredulus had first thought, or Berann was more powerful than any of them had bargained for. Neither option pointed toward anything Ceredulus was pleased to accept.

You do not trust me, Ceredulus granted, *and that is fine, but you can't possibly think a scrawny frame like the one you're after will hold up against your brothers?*

I only need a scrawny frame to manipulate threads.

Berann had made a good point, one which Ceredulus had too much experience with to disregard. *And what threads do you plan to manipulate once you've found a body to inhabit?*

Any and all that I must. I do not wish to work through aggression, but I will not make the same mistake twice.

Ceredulus smirked. *You're referring to the Order?*

Are they still the predominant military force on Gelthin?

Unfortunately.

Then yes.

Ceredulus thought this over carefully, contemplative eyes drifting back to Mathias. He could feel the tremendous power Berann commanded through this single thread of his soul alone, and he had no doubt that the Order would continue to deny help to even the most civilized demon's cause. He knew better than to think Berann would be able to wipe out the entire organization, but if he hit the key players, made a large enough dent... Ceredulus may be able to escape the boundaries Zeal had placed him within. His gaze lowered to Khin, her mouth twisted in an agonized frown, sweat rolling down her forehead as her chest heaved… Ceredulus *had* her. He could easily train himself other mortal servants if he lost her and was free to do so, but few would be so pure or pliable, none so able to breach the suspicions of the rest of the world. Khin was the first follower he'd had whose motivations were innocent, and that was too valuable to lose.

I am Ceredulus, god of the undead, he repeated, *and this young woman is my priestess. Even with your power and insight, it could take you days' worth of your frustration and her suffering for you to fully integrate with her body.*

Then I have even less time to deal with your prattle.

A brief dysphoria flickered across the periphery of Ceredulus's consciousness as Berann's disembodied soul attempted an attack on him, and the god laughed. *I want to help you, Berann.*

That's what every god has said, the demon sneered.

Ceredulus allowed that disrespect to slide off him with the rest. *I could sew you back into a vessel and you could be a functioning oraku again moments later if you'll work with me.*

I work for no god.

This was beginning to grow tiresome. *Give me one day to find a more appropriate vessel for you and I will personally and permanently bind you to it and let you walk away from me to seek whatever justice you're after.*

Berann had answered everything else Ceredulus had thrown at him instantly, but this time, he hesitated before replying. *And what happens when you fail just as your peers had?*

If I fail—Ceredulus sent a pitying look at the gasping human girl then slowly raised his hardening gaze to Tristan—*you are welcome to possess my priestess. But give me one day of your patience.*

The thread's pulse of agitation slowed. *One day. And then the girl is mine.*

Just as the demon didn't entirely trust Ceredulus, the god wasn't without doubts about Berann's honesty. *If you choose to break these terms, I will bind you to a fly and smash you. Do you understand?*

You are assuming you'd be able to catch me.

There hadn't been malice in the reply, and that worked just as well as compliance for Ceredulus. Mostly certain he was making the right decision, the god loosened his hold on Berann's soul and let it slip free from his grasp. After several moments passed without

Khin's condition degrading any further, Ceredulus turned to face the little gathering.

"We will need a body," he said.

Tristan lifted his anxious gaze to Ceredulus, waiting for his orders, and Mathias turned to glare at the god.

"There will be no body," the paladin insisted.

"There will be if you want to see Khin rise as herself ever again," Ceredulus said. "Berann is reasonable, but he's already been bound to this realm and is eager to spread the message he tried to deliver before your men killed him. If we cannot provide him a more acceptable host within a day, he will take Khin."

At his feet, the girl whimpered.

Tristan stood. "A body should be easy to obtain."

Ceredulus held up a hand to stop Tristan from leaving quite yet, keeping his keen gaze fixed upon Mathias. "Not just any body will do. We need someone weak enough to take without a struggle that might damage it, with no local kin to worry about them when they go missing. Someone another demon wouldn't question poking about their affairs."

That was a rather specific list of requirements. Tristan turned his attention to Mathias to see if he might have any friends in Heiligate who might fit the bill when he caught an entirely different flavor of loathing etched between the human's brows. A devious smile lifted Tristan's lips.

"Sir Sagewind, have you thought of a likely candidate?"

Mathias gasped, ashamed of himself for wearing his emotions so plainly. He *had* thought of someone weak and without mortal connections, someone the demons actually wanted to get their hands on. Someone his subdued vengeful side didn't completely care about the fate of. One look into Tristan's glittering eyes reminded Mathias of the difference between his motivations and those of the disgusting creatures flanking him, and he turned his attention to Khin. "I do not condone this."

Tristan voiced a presumptuous snort. "I think it's safe to say no one expected you to; it would be completely against your standing as the White Paladin. Almost as much as you being part of raising a demon from the dead in the first place. You must care

11

about Nessix an awful lot."

As Mathias bristled at the vampire's goading, Ceredulus gave Tristan a nod of approval. The angrier Mathias got, the easier it would be to slip into his mind and harvest the information he needed for himself.

"My personal life is none of your business," Mathias muttered.

"Perhaps not," Tristan agreed. "All I'm doing is trying to help save the fates of two imperiled women you claim to be invested in. I'd thought we had the same objective here."

"Your objectives will never be—"

"That Afflicted boy?" Ceredulus asked.

Mathias threw his shoulders back, eyes widening as a guilty flush swept across his cheeks.

"Oh, yes." Ceredulus moved up beside Mathias and crossed his arms. "You've got some terrible thoughts regarding that unfortunate wretch. And you're right. He *is* the most ideal candidate for the honor of bearing Berann back into the world."

Mathias narrowed his eyes, scowling at Tristan since he was too reluctant to throw his anger at a god right now. "This was never part of our arrangement, Ceredulus."

"It was never a stipulation against it."

"You said you weren't after spreading your influence."

The god scoffed. "Obtaining the answers *you* were so desperate to find has nothing to do with spreading my influence. It's one demon, Mathias. One who has already made it quite clear that he resents that I'm a god. No influence to be spread there."

"I will take no part in killing a man for the purpose of raising a demon."

"Not even to secure your lover's safety?" Ceredulus waited a generous moment for Mathias to find his tongue, continuing when the paladin gave no answer. "Abaeloth has long relied on you, Mathias Sagewind, Etha's shield, to protect it from the darkest of evils. You've found light in such places in the past; let yourself acknowledge the one here. If you won't do it for Khin or Etha or Abaeloth, do it for your Nessix."

Khin had stabilized from her writhing but still kept her eyes pinched shut, and as Tristan and Ceredulus scrutinized his morality,

Mathias couldn't help but feel responsible for her condition, just the same as he felt responsible for being unable to keep Nessix out of Kol's hands. This was a valid solution to their problems, an action Mathias had entertained, unprompted, earlier. But that couldn't stop his desire to only do good, nor would it negate his hatred for Ceredulus.

"I…" His longing to put an end to his uncertainty poured over his ethics, slowly smothering him until all he could find was a vague impression of his moral code, and he had to try again. "I can't."

Ceredulus hissed his dissatisfaction with exaggerated disgust and flung his arms down to his sides. "Then let Berann take Khin. Let Nessix anguish in the hells."

"I *can't*!" Mathias cried, head threatening to burst with frustration.

"You need not dirty your hands over this, Sir Sagewind," Tristan offered. "Invite me back into the Citadel and I will take care of the rest."

"My hands may not be dirtied, but my conscience would be."

"Please, Mathias…" Ceredulus muttered. "Your conscience has already come up with far more vile, wasteful ways to deal with that traitorous little worm. If it's really so hard for you, consider it his redemption."

Mathias couldn't decide what was worse, that he'd had such thoughts in the first place or that Ceredulus had uncovered them. He could easily spare Talier's wretched life, make him suffer with the memories of what he'd done and the fate his actions had brought upon his brother, but in doing so, Mathias would sign Khin's fate. The girl, on the other hand, had strayed from the path he'd wanted for her and had caused an impressive swath of damage in doing so. Neither mortal was without flaws, but could Mathias truly sentence either of them to be possessed by a demon he could only hope had some grasp of virtue?

"Can you afford *not* to?"

An unsolicited shudder rippled across Mathias's shoulders as Ceredulus commented on his thoughts once again, and all he could see in his mind was Nes's tired eyes, resigned to her station and

13

fate, trusting that, somehow, they'd be able to overcome the impossibilities the demons had created. Mathias had vowed to stop at nothing, and he'd already come this far. Defeated, just as Ceredulus had planned for him to be, Mathias hung his head.

"Do it." His command was small and mumbled, but not missed by the keen ears waiting for it.

"That's not an invitation, Sir Sagewind."

Mathias sneered and flashed his glare up to Tristan, expecting the vampire's malicious humor. Instead, he met a stoic understanding, the resolve of urgency which Mathias had struggled with for the past several months. Sickened, but believing that hadn't been Tristan's intent, Mathias lowered his eyes once again.

"For the sole purpose of luring Talier Dalton outside, I invite you, Tristan Swift, to enter the Citadel."

There was no smugness in the manner which Tristan straightened his shoulders. "For that purpose alone, I accept your invitation."

Not waiting around for Mathias to revoke the permission he'd hastily granted, Tristan dashed off toward Zeal with all of the remaining strength he had, his elegant form blurring as he disappeared into the distance. A firm hand clapped down on Mathias's shoulder and the bold paladin hunched under its weight.

"You and I are both men of patience," Ceredulus said. "Your fight, and mine, is nearly through."

Mathias focused on Khin's anguished face as Berann kept his threads gently entwined with hers. If only he could believe that.

TWO

Nessix tried to be alarmed by the frantic shouting and the stampede of demons churning through the corridors, but her dream stop fueled drowsiness quelled her ability to react to any manner of chaos. She registered the strict orders being called out, to move faster, to get deeper into the tunnels. Kol's heart pounded rapidly as he pressed her closer against his chest, a tremble of fatigue and uncertainty woven into the strength of his arms. All the while, Nes's mind repelled her worries—for herself and Kol, for the mortal force outside which she was sure had been sent to recover her—an artificial calm assuring her that she was the safest one in this entire situation. It wasn't until Kol's gait abruptly jerked and he nearly dropped her that adrenaline spiked enough for Nessix to soak in the danger she was in.

"Is he—" Kol's voice rasped with exhaustion and a fear which reverberated in Nessix's bones.

"He's breathing. Secure the prisoner, sir."

Kol didn't move, and Nessix lifted her head from his shoulder to follow his forlorn gaze to where Annin slumped on the floor. The oraku's head hung limply between his shoulders, face pale and eyes closed, as the two winded alar supporting him adjusted their grips, and Nessix resented the fact that she was still bound by shackles and the residue of an overdose of dream stop. Unarmed and secured in Kol's grasp, there was no option for her to slit the oraku's throat in his time of weakness.

Grell's roar rebounded down the tunnel, and Kol tore his eyes from his suffering friend, baring his teeth at the very thought of the inoga. He closed his grip tighter over Nessix, and he turned back to the demons who grumbled and groaned as they hefted Annin's arms over their shoulders.

"If *anything* happens to him…" Kol growled.

"Yeah," the demon on the left grunted. "You told us."

Kol held his glare on the two alar a moment longer, conveying all of the appropriate threats of what would happen to them if Annin didn't see tomorrow, until a commotion at the entry point suggested Grell was on the move. Escaping the inoga, at least until his current round of battle lust wore off and while Annin was out of commission, was imperative for Kol's well-being. Trusting Annin would pull through as he always did, Kol hastened deeper into the maze of halls to bring Nessix to the holding cells. He'd have preferred to return her directly to her army so progress toward dominating the inoga could continue, but his objective now that Nessix was back in his hands, was to ensure he survived long enough to see this revolution through. Securing Nessix, as Grell expected him to do, was a necessary step in achieving that.

It was a beautiful irony, returning Nessix to the cell where she'd first tried to kill him now that she'd agreed to serve him, but Kol didn't have the time or energy to think about that. Chasing off the few loitering demons in the hall so there would be no witnesses to what was to come, Kol carried Nessix into the tiny room, kicked the door shut, and eased her onto the cot which bore age-faded streaks of her blood. After the grueling flight back to Elidae, his arms rejoiced at the chance to rest, shoulders aching as they were able to stretch into their full range of motion at last. But surpassing the euphoria of physical relief, Kol was struck with the chill that came from seating Nessix on the edge of the cot.

The heat of her body had warmed his chest in place of her soul vessel, and he defeated his urge to scoop her back into his arms to continue drawing on that comfort by turning to investigate the chamber for anything she could use as a weapon, just in case he wasn't the next person to visit her. Coherence had seeped back into her, evident by her ability to hold her head more erect than not as she slowly took in her surroundings and the memories contained in them. She was slow to do so, but she raised her eyes to Kol's, her firm brows all but demanding him to speak his mind. Kol shied from her presence, daunted by the unconscious pull Nessix had over him, and he paced past a blood stain on the floor which he'd been responsible for when she'd forced his hand to keep her from killing him. She waited on Kol to break through his discomfort more patiently than she'd ever waited on anything in her life, further muddling the alar's thoughts.

Grimacing as he swallowed down a dry throat, Kol returned to the cot and placed his hand atop Nessix's shackles, stopping himself before he reached for the key. The pressure of her gaze—benevolent and drowsy, but ever ready for action—drove into him, and Kol couldn't hide from the inconvenient truth of his fragility or gratitude any longer. He cast his eyes aside.

"You saved my life," he said gruffly.

"I did."

He frowned, still struggling with the notion that, after all he'd done and all he'd yet to do, he was worthy of such compassion from the woman he'd brought so much suffering to. "Why?"

Nessix's brows furrowed and she shook her head. "Because we made an agreement."

Kol's upper lip twitched at the outward simplicity of her reasoning, and he turned his eyes back to her to search for the absent mockery he'd have preferred to see. "You could have escaped while my men were crippled. You had reinforcements on the ground. And you spared me because I'd asked for your loyalty?"

"I spared you because I *gave* you my loyalty." When Kol voiced a sharp hiss and looked away, Nessix leaned forward. "How could I show you obedience if you were dead? How could I change the hells without your guidance? What is it demons think loyalty is, Kol?"

The truth was, Kol didn't remember what loyalty truly was anymore. The fact that he and Annin had worked toward the same goals for centuries now and that the oraku hadn't followed through on any of his cryptic threats of killing him yet had led Kol to believe they'd shared this virtue, but what it came down to was that demons were not a virtuous lot. On some level, Kol was quite aware that Annin had refrained from killing him, not out of the concept of friendship, but because he still had uses for him. And if Kol could shed that annoying veil of wistfulness which clouded his view of Annin, he could admit that his usefulness to the oraku had likely been the entirety of what their relationship had been built on all along. But the stance which Nessix had taken? This was different.

Nessix couldn't escape Kol, not permanently, and they both knew it. He'd dragged her into a torment she didn't deserve, bound her to the worst horrors he had to live with. He'd ruined her life in every regard, and he admitted as much freely, and Nessix, no matter what past behavior suggested, should have hated him for it. She'd submitted to his pleas that night in the field, and though Kol's delusional mind had ravenously soaked up her compliance, he hadn't believed her sincerity, not completely. There was so little honor left in Kol's life, so few selfless intentions, that he was certain if push came to shove, Nessix would do as everyone else in his life had done and look out for herself to get another step ahead.

But she hadn't taken that step, not without dragging him with her. He'd asked her for obedience. He'd asked for her loyalty. And in warning him against those archers' horns, she'd proven that she would stand beside him until he was through with her.

A blast of heat struck Kol's face, stinging his eyes and trembling his upper lip. He was a *demon*. How could anyone choose to show him such compassion? His fingers curled around Nessix's shackles and he lowered his head to hide the shame of what she had done to him.

"What does Zeal know?" he asked.

Nessix tried to draw her hands closer to herself, but they were held fast in place. "Zeal?" she asked, voice cracking. "I doubt they'd listen to anyone short of their goddess."

Kol's fingers clenched tighter and he peered up at the way Nessix's eyes avoided his the way her words avoided his question. "What about Mathias, then? What did you tell him?"

The feeling filtered out of Nessix's lips, excuses Kol would neither want nor tolerate rushing to her tongue. She looked away as she whispered her answer. "Everything I knew."

Kol slapped his hand on the shackles, but spoke softly. "Damn you, little one." He shook his head, trying to process how to remedy what Nessix had put into play. "How much progress did you make on the matter you were after?"

"We..." Nessix bowed her head and squirmed at the slow twist developing in her stomach. "We found a heading. A flimsy one, but..." She fell into a guilty silence.

"Mathias will pursue it," Kol confirmed for her.

"I suspect he will."

"*Damn* you, little one..." Kol had been a fool to not explain anything about Berann to her after she'd proven to know of his existence. He could have tailored what she knew to his own purposes, made her believe he was a mundane soldier of no renown—or even chosen to explain to her why he was so dangerous. But he hadn't trusted her enough to keep his secrets; it had taken her running away from him to establish that.

"I'm sorry." She whispered her apology, trying to twist her fingers around to grasp his. "I did what I had to within the limits of what I knew."

"I know you did," Kol spat, his bitterness directed at himself. "But that doesn't amend the peril you may have put us in."

Nessix had suspected as much, but what was done was done, and all she could do was keep marching forward. "So, what's next?"

Kol snapped his face up at Nessix's question. Though her brows drooped with residual drowsiness, there was a clarity in her eyes which expressed her regret for the anguish she'd caused him. A year ago, he would have slapped her for such pity. Today, it only made him adore her more, which made this inconvenient truth that much harder to deliver. Kol squeezed on the shackles until the metal bit into his palm, and then released his hold as he turned away to hide what other emotions may be waiting to express themselves.

"Grell will deliver your punishment," he said, "and there is nothing I will be able to do to stop it."

Nessix gulped down the tiny swell of terror which bubbled up her throat. She'd known from the moment she'd dropped that first guard on Elidae that this was coming once Kol found her, but she'd also expected her punishment to be delivered by his predictable and pliable hands. Not one part of her looked forward to whatever torture Grell would come up with for her. "Can you give me any idea of what to expect?"

Kol ran a hand through his hair, briefly grasping a fistful of his dark locks, and he couldn't stop himself from turning back to her. "Grell's goal is to break you. He will wait for the dream stop's influence to wear off so you'll feel all of the pain he wants to inflict, so your chaos will beg you to fight him. He will make a public spectacle of your humbling, and he doesn't tire from such attention quickly. Begin building your walls now, little one. I will need you strong on the other side of whatever he does to you."

A chill swept across Nessix and she lowered her eyes, curling her fingers into fists since she couldn't pick at her cuticles. "Will he…" Her voice trembled and she cleared her throat before lifting her timid gaze to Kol's. "Is there a chance he'll do to me what was done to Auden?"

That was the horrifying question Kol had been actively ignoring since that first time Nessix had attacked Grell in the chasm. If the inoga chose to end Nessix, all of Kol's plans would be over; at this point, his life would be over. He'd denied this possibility for so long but as Nessix sat there, tired eyes wide as she held her breath awaiting his answer, he had to admit it at last.

"It's a possibility," he said quietly, "but unlikely. He's expressed having too many uses for the akhuerai, ones which require you functioning at their head and—" He snipped his words into silence, eyes flashing with a loathing which blindsided Nessix, and he scoffed and stepped away.

"And what?" she pressed.

"And you're asking too many questions," Kol muttered.

"This is my fate we're discussing, Kol," Nessix said. "You asked me to trust you. You asked me to walk away from safety into this uncertainty not even you have a lead on. Prove to me I didn't make a mistake."

Kol spun back on Nessix, teeth bared in a fury she didn't balk at. "He needs you controllable."

Nessix relaxed a bit with a gentle laugh and shake of her head. Hadn't they just discussed this? "I don't take my vows lightly. I swore to you my—"

He pinched his eyes shut in frustration and silenced her reassurance with the firm pressing of his lips as he gathered his nerve to face the most recent error he'd made. "Not controllable by me. Controllable by him."

Nessix watched the alar's developing anxiety and was snared by a sharp vein of fear when he opened his eyes. Annin knew of the ruse Kol had created regarding his influence over her, but she doubted Grell was sharp enough to make any solid connection about it on his own. But if he did… Nessix hadn't lied; she did not take her vows lightly and, while she still could not put a name to the bizarre fondness she shared with Kol, it had even driven her to speak in his defense to Mathias. Grell didn't frighten her. She shook her head deliberately.

"If he does anything to you to achieve this, controlling me won't—"

Kol winced at the strictness building steam behind Nessix's warning, too uncomfortable hearing her voice her intention to defend him—when he knew in all likelihood the nature of the fate awaiting him—to let her finish speaking. "I've already accepted that I'll pay for your disobedience. That has little to do with my concerns."

Nessix swept her gaze up and down Kol's tense body before meeting his eyes and holding them against his will. "Then what are you worried about?"

"I'm not—" The hells had conditioned demons to hide their weaknesses and it had taken Nessix's unintended influence on Kol to draw his out. He had no reason to hide the truth from her, not now and not while they were in private, but that didn't stop him from wanting to hide it from himself. Nessix continued to stare at him, patient but unyielding. She needed to know the truth.

Kol lowered his head and strode up to her, kneeling and resting a hand once more on her shackles. When he spoke, it was with a lowered voice, as though he suspected eavesdroppers to be hiding in the corners of the room. "I no longer have the other half of your soul."

Of all the confessions Nessix had imagined Kol would give her, this had not been among them, and the gravity of what it meant was not lost on her. There was still much she didn't know about the akhuerai and the workings of souls in general, but she was quite aware of a soul's role in sustaining life. She'd been comfortable with Kol possessing half of her soul, trusting him with it early on. The thought that it was missing, and the limited number of people who would think—or dare—to take it from him... Nessix's adrenaline spiked, rousing her past the dream stop's last soporific effects.

"Who has it?"

Kol accepted her demand without correction, hanging his head to avoid falling victim to the brewing panic in her eyes as he shook it. "Annin convinced me to leave it with a surface-bound connection of ours before we marched on Zeal."

Nessix wheezed in a shallow breath. The other half of what kept her alive wasn't even in the hells? "And Grell's intervention on the road..."

"Kept me from retrieving it, yes." Kol swallowed the lump pressing up his throat as the dread of his initial revelation snuck up on him once more. "And I am quite confident that he killed the demon who had it."

Nessix paled, feeding off Kol's apprehension. "So does Grell have it now?"

Kol frowned. "I don't know. I don't believe he does, as I'm sure he'd have flaunted it to me if he did. But I can't be sure."

Nessix couldn't remember a time when Kol had been uncertain about anything she asked him. Evasive, yes, but never unable to settle on an answer for himself. When he'd asked her for her help, she'd known he was frightened. She hadn't imagined this had been part of that reason. "What does this mean?"

Kol shook his head and left his face pointed away from her. "If we're lucky, it means I'll sneak back to the surface and find it once you get settled in with your army."

Nessix frowned at Kol's tight tone and continued avoidance of her eyes. "And if we're unlucky?"

"I don't know." His answer came instantly, delivered as a response to the exact same question he'd just asked himself. "I haven't had a chance to talk it over with Annin yet."

Nessix scoffed and rolled her eyes. Just as Annin resented Kol's affection for Nessix, Nessix resented the alar's dependency on Annin. She accepted it more gracefully than Annin accepted her role in Kol's life, but she didn't have an ounce of trust in the oraku. "He told me to stay away from you, you know," she said quietly.

Kol shifted his gaze back to her. "He did?"

She nodded. "He's never liked me and you know it. There's not one part of me that believes he sees the loss of anything important to me as a matter worth fixing."

Kol had pushed Annin well past the limits of his patience over the past several months, but the oraku had continued to work with him. Though Kol was uncertain where Annin's intentions lay now that Nessix was secure, he did know one thing. "Annin wants the other half of your soul back. Too much can go south if it slips into the wrong hands."

There hadn't been a warning in the statement, more of an observation than anything else, but Nessix shivered at the implications. As much as she hated the idea of Annin or Grell possessing her soul, the thought of having some unknown demon uninvested in her well-being claim ownership of it was a sobering thought.

Kol heaved a sigh and pushed himself to his feet. "I hadn't planned to let you know about any of this."

Nessix disregarded Kol's confession of dishonest intent, too busy trying to sort out means to remedy this problem. "Annin," she murmured, hating that she was forced to depend on the self-interested oraku. "He'll be able to locate it, right?"

"If anyone in the hells can come up with a way to do so, it will be him."

"And Grell will allow you to go out and find it?"

"Oh, I suspect he'll violently demand it once he's made aware of it."

Nessix nodded slowly. Maybe, between Kol and Annin, this wouldn't end poorly. She lowered her head and her voice, her actions drawing Kol closer. "What did... what did Berann know, Kol?"

The demon's hand shot out and grabbed Nessix's arm, fingers biting down into her flesh until she gasped in pain, and when she looked up at him, he wore an aggressive mask she hadn't expected to see him don in private after they'd made their truce. "You've already gotten our most dangerous opponent on that trail, and now you will forget everything you think you know about that traitor."

Despite being shackled, imprisoned, and under Kol's direct influence, Nessix was unwilling to accept that as an answer. "I need to—"

Before Nessix could blink, the back of Kol's hand had soundly silenced her. "Not the time, little one." He spoke the words through clenched teeth and in her mother tongue which few other demons were fluent in.

Her vow of obedience trumped Nessix's desire to demand answers; Kol was already under close watch by both peers and superiors and Nessix had learned well that Berann was not to be discussed. But Kol had said this wasn't the time, implying his explanation of this mysterious demon was, indeed, coming. And if Nessix wanted to keep them both alive until then, she'd be wise to let it drop. "Then how do I proceed in the meantime?"

Kol sighed, shoulders slumping as he marveled at the way Nessix was always ready to serve. "I will convey intelligence and orders to you as I am able, but until then, act as though nothing is wrong. Bear your punishment. Rally your troops. Do as I've told you."

It was Nessix's turn to lower her eyes. It wasn't that she doubted Kol's drive or desire, but that she doubted the feasibility of the task at hand. Without knowing the extent of the complications which might arise from having her soul in the wrong hands, she didn't know what to think. Perhaps if she could convince Kol to send a message to Mathias, he or the priestesses or that goddess of theirs could join the hunt for the missing vessel, as well. The paladin's parting words to Kol, that he'd kill him the first chance he had, came to mind, and Nessix's frown deepened.

"You don't take your vows lightly," Kol said, mistaking Nessix's grim expression for a different kind of concern. "And neither do I." He cupped the back of her head with one hand and pressed his lips into her hair. "I doubt I'll see you again before it's time for you to pay your dues to Grell, but I will get Annin on the case of your missing soul vessel as soon as he's coherent enough to do so."

Nessix hated damn near everything about what Kol just said, but had the sense to keep her mouth shut about it. She had landed them both in this mess. Her actions had deteriorated Kol's credibility, and she had to take whatever boons he was able to scrape up. Accepting his words with the obedience she'd promised him, Nessix watched Kol leave and hung her head as the bar of the door fell into place as she began building her walls.

THREE

Spurred by Ceredulus's crisp demands, Tristan spent near the entirety of his energy by the time he reached Zeal. Hair and clothes disheveled by the haste of his travel, he looked less like the nobleman he'd hoped to present to the guards, but found his story of having urgent matters to address in the Citadel more believable for it. Hungry and tired, it took consistent orders from his god to march past all of the easy means to replenish his strength which mingled about the streets, and at this rate, he wasn't sure he'd be able to generate the necessary speed to make it back to the gathering Ceredulus had orchestrated before the allotted day elapsed.

I have never left you wanting, Tristan, and I won't begin now.

Tristan had no reason to doubt Ceredulus, but that didn't stop his jaw from trembling as a pair of vibrant children chased each other past him, little hearts racing with the energy his body craved.

Later. Get in the Citadel before anyone grows suspicious of your loitering.

Tristan obeyed the order as he always did, though not without the fear of what would happen if he ran out of strength before this task was complete. Trusting Ceredulus, knowing no other way, Tristan followed the instructions his god harvested from Khin's wavering consciousness to the Citadel's infirmary. The halls were quieter in the upper level than they were on the main floors, occupied primarily by on-duty guards and a handful of young priestesses toting food and fresh bedding to the patients. Tristan kept his lagging senses as sharp as possible, scanning those armed with steel or Etha's wrath to gauge their strength and suspicions as he passed, but he met no opposition as he neared his destination.

The infirmary rooms, though private, had no doors, and even if Ceredulus hadn't guided Tristan directly to the one occupied by Talier, he'd have known he was in the right place after no more than a glance at the man's agitated pacing. Tristan stopped outside the room's entry, its gentle warding of divinity politely asking him to keep his distance, and watched Talier mumble frantic little worries to himself, one hand gripping at his hair while the fingers of the other rubbed a small silver object pressed in his palm. Tristan didn't know all of this man's story, but he didn't care to, either. Ready to be through with this, Tristan cleared his throat.

"Are you Talier Dalton?"

Talier yelped a humiliating jumble of half words and spun around, holding out the fist clutching that silver bauble as though it might repel this intruder. He backed away from Tristan, though the vampire had neither introduced himself nor made an attempt to enter the room.

"I haven't gone anywhere," Talier gasped. "I've stayed here, in my room, just like I was told."

Tristan cocked his head at the strange, defensive response. Mathias was certainly on a roll with upsetting helpless mortals these days. "You don't seem too content with that fact."

The hand pulling at Talier's hair flopped to his side. "What else am I supposed to do?" His voice climbed in pitch with each word, rattling pathetically with fear. "Mathias is going to kill me, and if he doesn't, then his sister will."

"And what about that demon?" Tristan asked in stride. "Will Kol kill you if she doesn't?"

Talier drew in a sharp gasp, eyes widening as his hands began to tremble. "Who are you?"

Tristan smirked and rolled his eyes. "Relax. I am a friend."

Talier shook his head fiercely, overgrown and unkempt auburn hair flopping about from the force. "I don't *have* friends.

Not ones tied to Kol—"

"I assure you, I am not tied to that detestable creature." Tristan crossed his arms. "Though I am tied to Nessix Teradhel."

Talier froze, color siphoning from his cheeks.

"Is she not your friend?" Tristan asked smoothly.

Talier's posture sagged and he shuffled over to his cot to slump down on it. "I—" Could he truly consider Nessix a friend after how he'd been convinced to lead her to harm? She *had* saved his life on multiple accounts, but he didn't know if it was safe to assume she'd continue to do so now that word had gotten out that he'd been working for the same demons she'd been running from. Tristan's eyes continued to bear down on him with a steady, commanding pressure, and Talier gulped. "She is," he murmured at last.

Tristan nodded once and dropped his arms to his sides before turning a shoulder to allow him the haste he needed to exit the Citadel. "Then come with me. She needs our help."

Talier jumped back to his feet but didn't get any closer to the door. Of course Nessix needed help; she'd been successfully reclaimed by the demons. Torn between wanting to help Nessix and trying to dissuade those trying to rescue her from Kol so he might yet keep his brother alive, Talier stood his ground. "I'm not allowed to leave my room."

Tristan's brows wrinkled in irritation and he turned his face back toward Talier. "There are neither bars nor wardings keeping you in there, only your fear of a muscle-headed buffoon and his whiny sister. Take your chances with them, if you'd like, but I've found a way to save Nessix which depends on your unique talents, and it would allow you to get far out of the Order's eyes."

The offer was enticing, but didn't work on Talier after how many other surefire solutions had blown up in his recent past. "I don't even know who you are."

"I am Lord Tristan Swift of Fallsmouth. Now you know who I am, and now you will come with me."

Tristan turned to leave once more and took one step before he realized Talier still hadn't budged. Hungry, irritable, and running out of time to fulfill Ceredulus's will, he huffed a brusque sigh and turned around. "You truly think you are safest here?" he asked. "Under the noses of the Sagewind siblings? Nessix *needs* you, Talier Dalton. *Come.*"

He hadn't wanted to use the force of such a command when his resources were already running so low, but Talier was weaker willed than most, and Tristan figured he'd have adequate strength to get them out of the city even after sparing the negligent amount of power required to sway such a simple mind. Talier was no more confident with his reaction to the vampire's influence than he had been with any part of this exchange, but he crammed the silver bauble in his pocket and didn't fight the impulse to step forward. The moment the timid human crossed the doorway, Tristan snagged him by the arm and briskly directed him down the hall.

"Stay quiet until we exit the Citadel," Tristan said through clenched teeth. "If we get stopped, we are both in for more trouble than you can imagine."

Talier whimpered, the noise easily caught by Tristan's ears as he kept his senses alert for any who might want to stop them. If they were confronted here in these halls, Tristan would have no choice but to feed on someone to buy himself the speed and strength to escape. He wouldn't be able to choose Talier—as haste would require him to go for the throat and he'd specifically been ordered not to leave obvious marks on this human—and neither would he be able to target anyone else without reducing this pathetic man into a screaming lump of noncompliance. Tristan's fingers clamped down on Talier's arm and the two of them slipped quietly from the Citadel.

My lord, I have secured—

As soon as they'd cleared the immediate vicinity of the Citadel's entrance and the guards posted about it, Talier scrambled up closer to Tristan than the vampire was comfortable allowing a man he didn't intend to eat to get. "What kind of help does Nessix need?" He did an admirable job keeping his voice hushed, given the frantic racing of his heart and the clamminess of his palms.

Too cranky with hunger to maintain his ruse of charm now that he had physical control of his target, Tristan peeled Talier's hand from his sleeve. "She needs us to deliver to her information which will allow her to combat the demons."

For the first time in this interaction and any other he'd been involved in all week, Talier's expression brightened. He'd seen Nessix do some amazing things with her sword… she might still be able to protect him and save Marcoux, after all. "So she's okay?"

"Last report I received she was."

"And you've got this information she needs?"

"I've got means to access it, yes."

Talier breathed out a great sigh, followed by a tittering chuckle, and he ran his hand through his hair. "This could actually work…"

Having found Talier's willing compliance at last, Tristan considered the tedious part of this mission through and allowed himself to agree with this human's assessment. *As I was saying, my lord, I have secured Talier and am—*

"How far away is she?" Talier asked, eyes directed thoughtfully ahead as his imagination dipped into fresh pools of hope.

Tristan, past annoyed with all of these pointless interruptions, declined answering. *I have him in tow and we are on our way out of Zeal now.*

Ceredulus's reply was lost beneath Talier's next question. "Did she escape from Kol and Annin? Or are we going to have to find a way past them to sneak this information to her?" The flush Talier had only recently recovered drained from his face as he contemplated that last option. He glanced at Tristan's refined cheekbones and fair complexion, frowning at the very average size of his arms and the lack of weapons on his belt. His speculations on whether or not Tristan would be able to stand against the beasts that were Kol and Annin, however, disappeared with the rigid clench of Tristan's jaw and the flash of irritation which darkened his hazel eyes. Tristan hastened his pace toward the city gates, Talier scuttling along beside him like an obedient puppy.

Nothing had made sense to the human since the evening Kol and Annin had attacked him and Marcoux on the road. He only barely understood how to rely on the innate senses of the wolf they'd bound him to, he didn't understand at all how the magic which let him view Marcoux's proof of life worked, and he'd yet to determine exactly *what* he thought of Nessix. She was, allegedly, the the reason he and his brother had been put in this peril, but she'd also gone out of her way to look out for him on their round about journey to Zeal. Talier had little doubt that if he could figure out where the demons held Marcoux, Nessix would fight to free him, and as Tristan so confidently led him toward freedom from Julianna's imprisonment, Talier was beginning to think that finding Nessix again might be the best outcome for everyone.

Yes. He would help Tristan however he could to deliver to Nessix this demon-defeating information she needed to finish her conquest and seek vengeance on Talier's timid behalf. There was just one uncertainty left…

"So are Kol and Annin dead?"

Talier watched Tristan obsessively, waiting for the reassurance he needed to hear. When Tristan's tight lips curled downward in a frown, brows stitching closer together, that annoying twitch of reservation squirmed back to life all over again.

"They have to be, right?" Talier tried, his words ticking with apprehension. "Because Nessix, as powerful as she is and all, wouldn't be able to get away from them both." Tristan continued his perturbed march forward, leading Talier to the inaccurate conclusion that he was brooding over the same impossible logistics. "…Could she?"

The longer these questions remained unanswered, the more frightened Talier became. He hadn't asked for any of this! He was just a simple messenger who had been thrust into sorting out Abaeloth's fate. Though he doubted Tristan's combative skills as much as he doubted his own, Talier did trust that the nobleman was more educated and intelligent than he was, and if he was reluctant to speak of the dismal odds before them, that meant this was not the sure bet Talier had convinced himself it would be. Pinching his lips together, Talier flicked his gaze back and forth between the city gates and Tristan's agitated expression. He couldn't stand this uncertainty any longer.

"Have you ever met those demons, Lord Swift?" Talier asked at last, a flimsy demand backing his question. "They are not to be disregarded. If they have not been dealt with, the two of us, no matter who or what you think either of us are capable of, won't be able to get close enough to Nessix to tell her anything."

Talier waited again for a response which didn't come, and suspicion clenched its maw around his neck at last. He knew nothing about this Lord Tristan Swift other than his name and that he knew who Nessix and Kol were. No more than a hundred yards from Zeal's western gate, Talier ground his feet into the street and cast a conflicted glance back at the Citadel's marble walls. Did safety exist for him anywhere anymore?

Tristan continued three more steps without Talier before slowing to a stop and snapping around to face his companion. He fit the human with a dark and dissatisfied scowl, already well in a deficit of patience for putting up with the difficulties this annoyance kept pitching. "Talier Dalton." Tristan's voice was devoid of the warmth which had coaxed the gullible human this far. "*Come.*"

The command, weakened by Tristan's exhaustion, worked only to drag Talier a single, stumbled step forward before he caught himself and shook his head fiercely. Tears rimmed his lower eyelids. "Not until you give me answers."

Tristan drew his shoulders back, raising his chin and narrowing his eyes. It was most inconvenient that Talier had found the nerve to defy him. Damn, he needed to feed… "I cannot give you the answers you seek," he replied sharply. "But if you want Nessix to live, you will come with me. Now."

Too weary to implement any more of his charm, there hadn't been one part of Tristan's orders which had come off as inviting or trustworthy and, defying what should have been an instant response to Tristan's authority, Talier scooted a step back. He'd already learned he couldn't trust Zeal's legendary hero or the High Priestess who was renowned across all of Gelthin for her lawful leniency, and he had no reason to trust this stranger. He didn't know where he could run to or what his odds of surviving past the end of the week would be if he tried, but Talier was through with just surviving. This was no way to live.

An apex predator older and more finely tuned than the wolf which had given Talier his enhanced instincts, Tristan recognized that quick flash of intent in Talier's eyes. The fool was going to try to run from him. Irritated and inconvenienced, insulted and starving, Tristan no longer cared that he was supposed to deliver Talier's hull as unblemished as possible. All he cared about was that his prey was being difficult, he was running out of time, and as far as he was concerned, he had no reason to ever set foot in Zeal again.

Even nearly drained of his stamina, Tristan's reactions were faster than Talier's, and he snapped his hand out to grasp Talier's wrist. The human yelped in surprise as Tristan jerked him forward, gaining the attention of a handful of passersby, and when Tristan's other fist connected with Talier's throat, those passersby screamed and shouted for the guards to come help. This was more the pace Tristan had been counting on.

Though he had to draw deep on what was left of his energy, Tristan was fueled by his god's orders and the thrill of his display of dominance. He was still faster than even the briskest mortal, and he wasn't keen on the idea of waiting around to see if the High Priestess or any of the city's knights would come out to assess the commotion he'd caused. Throwing Talier's limp body over his shoulder, Tristan looked forward to the fact that he'd have to do something to remedy the bruise that would soon be growing on the human's neck, and hastened out of the holy city for the last time.

FOUR

Chilled from blood loss and numb from pain, Sazrah succeeded in locating her scrying bowl just to have it slip out of her shaking grasp and tumble five yards away from where she lay on the ground. Still in her sights, it was well out of reach, and the beating she'd suffered at the hands of that inoga barred her from making any sort of rapid progress toward it. Yes, the filthy power of her own demon blood would see her through this ordeal, but it wouldn't pop her leg back into place or properly set her broken arm. And it wouldn't do a damn thing for her troops who had perished when the side of the mountain had given out.

Gritting her teeth against the pain of dragging her broken body across the ground, Sazrah clawed her functional hand forward and gave a feeble push with her working leg. A jolt of agony raced up her spine, forcibly seizing her strength and will to move toward her misplaced scrying bowl, and she cried out in pain and frustration. Curling her fingers into the coarse dirt, she bowed her head toward the cursed mountainside. She'd survived countless dismal situations in the past, but all of them had posed to impact her alone. Now Mathias, her troops, potentially all of Abaeloth, relied on her being able to force her body through these simple motions it refused to execute.

A heavy clomping of footsteps crunched her way across the

dirt and stones, and before dread or desperation had a chance to settle amid her swell of guilt and shame, Sazrah heard something beautiful.

"You still with the living, Shade?"

Sazrah closed her eyes and lowered her forehead to the ground, allowing a brief round of tears to be soaked up by the dirt. "I am, Karst."

The steps pounded at a faster rate and within moments, the dwarf, battered and bruised but far from defeated, crouched down before her. His rough hands cupped her chin and raised her weary face to his. "Bless the Mother. Tell me what you need."

"I need to hunt down the son of a bitch who buried my men and—"

Karst's weathered brows sagged in exhaustion. "What would you be needing *now?* Something that I can be doing for you?"

Sazrah bit back the defensive impulse to correct Karst for interrupting her and counted her blessings that he'd survived the attack at all. Her anger was not with him, and she did need his help. "I need to speak with Mathias, but I dropped my scrying bowl."

Karst stood before she had to voice a formal request for it, and located the device from nothing more than following her gaze.

"I thought I'd lost everyone," Sazrah admitted as the dwarf returned and knelt down to steady the bowl for her use.

"You should know a dwarf can handle a couple tumbling rocks." He assisted her in righting herself onto her sound elbow and plucked a knife from his belt. "Dragged thirteen more soldiers out of the rubble who were still breathing. It wasn't a complete loss."

Sazrah grimaced and nodded at the hand of her broken arm for Karst to do the honors of slicing her thumb open. "That still leaves thirty-five"—she barely felt the blade bite through her flesh from the pain of her greater injuries—"unaccounted for. And we failed our objective."

Karst dropped his knife to the ground and dutifully squeezed Sazrah's blood into the little silver bowl. "Yeah. Well. We had no way of knowing the demons planned to bury us. Mathias will have some ridiculous work around like he always does. Just you wait."

35

Often times, Mathias did have a ridiculous work around for when plans turned south, but this time, Sazrah wasn't so sure he would. This time, as it had been when the demons had captured her from a long-ago battlefield, matters were personal to him. She'd already witnessed the paladin preparing to make some terrible decisions in regards to relocating Nessix, and he'd told her himself he intended to make even more if he had to. He'd been counting on her and she'd been honor-bound to deliver on his faith, but she had failed in a tremendous fashion. The blood in the bowl rippled to reveal Mathias's face, and just a glance at him made the battle-hardened woman wish she would have found some other method to contact him.

His brows were knit together in a strict line, a fierce scowl curling his lips and carving wrinkles in the bridge of his nose. His eyes were cold with the sort of darkness he reserved for facing only the cruelest of opponents. He didn't even glance at Sazrah's reflection, focused instead on some point she couldn't view, when he addressed her.

"Tell me something good, Saz."

She gulped at Mathias's curt tone, ashamed of herself all over again, though she knew he had no way to fault her for what had happened. "I can't."

He flicked a glance her direction at her unusually timid tone and his expression faltered toward softness for just a moment before he returned his focus to his prior point of interest. "Then deliver the report you have."

Sazrah swallowed her disgust in her failure, salvaging the ability to persevere from her staunch adhesion to duty. "I led fifty soldiers to wait for Nessix and her captors. The demons were fronted by a winged inoga and an oraku who collapsed the ridge we stood on. Current count suggests we've taken thirty-five casualties from this single attack. I am wounded beyond my own repair, and the demons still have Nessix."

Mathias's lips pressed together briefly, nostrils flaring with a labored sigh, but Sazrah didn't detect the disappointment she'd felt due. That had to have meant that whatever stupid plan he'd been brewing had been a success, that Karst's suggestion of the paladin having a solution was accurate. While that should have comforted Sazrah, it didn't.

"Had Sulik been among the men you'd brought with you?" Mathias asked.

Sazrah closed her eyes against a brisk rush of tears. "No. He'd offered to come, but I convinced him one of us should man the temple and he agreed I was better qualified to fight demons." A rush of self-loathing flooded Sazrah's resolve. For all that faith Sulik had put in her, she'd fared no better than he would have, and may have even lost one of his sons in this tragedy. "Mathias—" Sazrah's voice cracked and Karst respectfully looked away from her surrender to unchecked emotions. "I need your help."

That frown pulled even lower on Mathias's face. "What injuries did you sustain?"

"Broken sword arm and dislocated leg, as far as I can tell. I won't be able to make it back to the temple as I am now."

"Of those alive and accounted for, are any of you mobile?"

Sazrah looked up at Karst and the dwarf shook his head. "Only Karst Boulderchoke, and he's already spent himself dragging our survivors from the rubble. Please, Mathias. I don't know what you're preoccupied with, but we're defenseless targets if the demons come out to see what's left of us."

Mathias closed his eyes, lips trembling as he drew in a ragged breath. "I can be there within a day."

"Within a—" Sazrah initially clamped her mouth shut around her argument, but as pain squeezed past her barriers and the muffled sobs and groans of her wounded petitioned for her advocacy, she couldn't hold it back. "I need you *now*."

Mathias ducked his head away from the firmness of Sazrah's plea. "Believe me, Saz, I would much rather be by your side, patching you up so you can go charging into the hells for vengeance, than where I am now. I'll be there as soon as I'm able. Has Karst set a bone before?"

Sazrah and the dwarf dodged each other's doubtful looks. "He has, but—"

"Then have him do it. I'm guessing he's even rolled one of his own legs back into place at some point, tough dwarf as he is. See if he can help you with that, too."

"No, Mathias." Sazrah, dizzy from pain and the adrenaline needed to talk back to her trusted mentor, balanced on the precarious cusp between panic and anger. "You owe me answers. You owe me the truth. What is going on?"

The image of Mathias's face rippled, as though he was preparing to fling the blood out of his bowl, but stabilized after he'd opened his eyes. "Nothing good," he said softly. "And I will give you more answers than you could possibly want after I'm sure nothing else goes wrong."

If nothing else goes wrong... Part of Mathias's frustrating charm came from his propensity to play games, but from his defeated tone, his refusal to look at her as she begged for his aid, Sazrah knew games were the farthest thing from his mind, just as she knew that now was not the time to ask what had gone wrong to land them in this current disaster. Sazrah had seen many battles over the past few decades, but this was the first time since she and Mathias had united to quell the undead that she had to accept the fact that they were facing the dawn of a war in which Mathias played a central role.

"I need more than that if you want me prepared to help you," Sazrah said.

Mathias's cheeks inflated and his eyes shifted from hers as he blew out little puffs of breath. The last bit was released in one, tired sigh, and he tilted his face back toward his bowl, though his eyes remained averted. "There may be a way to negate the demons' curse, a way to cure them of the corruption they'd sustained."

Sazrah stared at Mathias, eyes wide as she internally cursed him for his stubborn avoidance. A way to negate the demons' curse? To strip from them of the essence which made them the disgusting abominations they were? How had nobody discovered this sooner? She narrowed her eyes at Mathias's shiftiness, clearly reading his discomfort in what should have been a heartening discovery. "Is there a reason you chose not to implement this cure against those who took Nessix and killed my men?"

The grimace Mathias responded with was not the one of guilt which Sazrah had expected, but one of regret. "I don't know what it is."

"Then why even bother mentioning it?"

"Because I—" Mathias cut off his hasty response, lips turning down as though he was suffering a bad taste. "I've got a strong lead on it. But that is all I can tell you for now. Just… trust me. Please."

Karst grunted his rude opinion of Mathias's request. "Trusting him's what got us out here in the first place."

Sazrah chastised her captain with a firm glare, but didn't correct him otherwise. The dwarf spoke a sound truth. "Mathias. My troops were decimated. I have no way to aid the few survivors and no idea when the demons will return to finish what they started. I want nothing more than to trust you, but I need answers. I need help."

The corners of Mathias's eyes pinched lower with a deep sorrow he wouldn't let himself express any further. Sazrah seldomly asked for help. "I have given you all of the answers I currently have and will deliver the rest as soon as I can. I swear this to you, Sazrah."

She choked on her urge to continue arguing with Mathias, to demand he drop what he was doing and help her figure out what she was supposed to do to keep Elidae safe in the days to come, duty and discipline stifling the words to do so. Mathias wanted to be trapped in his circumstances no more than she wanted to be in hers.

"Yes, sir," she answered at last. "Please hurry."

"I will. You and Karst stay well. I'll do my best to not keep you waiting longer than you must."

Sazrah nodded to Karst to dump her blood from the bowl and she lowered her head to the ground once more. Whatever Mathias had planned, she would help him as much as she could, but the longer she thought over what it was he'd started, the less she believed she'd be able to.

"I know you look to that man as your father," Karst grumbled, "but your dad's a reckless idiot, thinking I'm some sort of field surgeon."

Sazrah grit her teeth, hearing more in Karst's criticism than his words conveyed. "Maybe so, but he wasn't wrong. My body's going to try to heal around these wounds and if he can't get here..." The concept still didn't add up to her, but she was out of influence on the matter. "I'd rather have my captain's best effort than a useless sword arm."

The dwarf pushed himself to his feet to trundle around in search of something long and sturdy enough to use as a splint. "Just don't demote me when it hurts or doesn't turn out right. This is a job for Etha-blessed paladins, not some battle-weary dwarf."

Sazrah couldn't have agreed more, but was too distracted to argue. Of all the frustrations Mathias had caused her in the past, he'd never left her in peril if he had any other option. *Whatever you're doing, Mathias... let it work...*

FIVE

Too disgusted and ashamed of himself to open a dialogue with Etha and beg for forgiveness for the reprehensible crimes he was participating in, Mathias busied himself doing the best he could to comfort Khin. A cold sweat now soaked through the young woman's bodice, her trembling coming in great waves which forced her to pinch her eyes shut, tight squeals of pain creaking like rusty door hinges from her throat. Between these tremors, she was able to peer her eyes open from beneath tightly furrowed brows, tears glistening over her brown eyes thick enough to reflect the sun. She accepted Mathias's soothing words and her balmy fingers limply held his hand, but she refused to meet his concerned gaze, confirming in no uncertain terms that even while suffering through the agony Tristan and his devious god had led her to, she continued to deny Mathias pardon for the slights he'd made against her.

As all of this guilt gnawed at Mathias, the lurking soul of an ancient demon hovered close by. Berann maintained his steady hold on Khin even as he orbited Mathias with a prying curiosity which made the paladin's skin crawl. Mathias had encountered more than his fair share of living ancients in his time and though he took all of them seriously, none before had been able to drag his heart so thoroughly into his throat. The paladin was no stranger to the taunts and torments of the fallen, but what remained of Berann,

41

this most powerful and evidently undying essence of the deceased magic user, didn't waste its effort on something as trivial as mockery. As aggressively as Mathias judged himself for the situation he'd landed in, Berann scathed him just as hard, forcibly stripping the paladin of his virtue until the added weight of the demon's disapproval threatened to crush him.

"He is quite displeased with your Order," Ceredulus said, as if he'd been sitting in to listen to all of Mathias's self-flagellating thoughts. For all the paladin knew, with his fragile state of mind, the evil god very possibly had been.

"Yeah?" Mathias muttered. "He can get in line."

"At least I can now rest assured Zeal has always rushed to judgement of those they don't understand."

"Shut up."

"Did I strike a nerve?"

Assuming Mathias had had any nerves left to strike, the answer would have been a resounding affirmative and the amused pressure of Ceredulus's steady gaze on his back suggested the god had asked his question already knowing the answer. "It is unwise of you to test me, Ceredulus."

"And why is that? Will you go back on your word, toss me into the Veil, and leave Khin to suffer a fate of possession by this demon and Nessix to never receive this vital information she's counting on to escape her captors? After all this time, are you truly tired of playing hero?"

Mathias *was* tired of being the hero, of shouldering all of Abaeloth's burdens for the ungrateful masses. The pains he had to endure, the decisions he had been forced to make, the suffering he caused those dear to him… His knees were buckling under this weight, but he couldn't quit. Not yet. Not until he found Nessix a path away from the demons—if that could even be done. So uncertain, so lost, Mathias wasn't even sure he believed Berann truly had the means or interest to help remedy any of this. All he knew was what he and Nessix had theorized about the dead oraku's long-ago intentions, what Mehalco had sputtered about a possible way to purge the curse from demons, and what Ceredulus told him about Berann's shoddy opinion of the Order.

Mathias's head snapped up from Khin, eyes hardening into sharp focus as he saw reality through his misery at last. Ceredulus had already found a way to communicate with this beast.

Turning to scour the vile god over his shoulder, Mathias tapped into his willful courage through all of this helpless self-loathing at last. "You ask Berann how to defeat the demons, and you ask him now."

Ceredulus puffed out a dry laugh and rolled his eyes. "Please, Mathias. You think I haven't already tried that? My idiot predecessors who catalyzed the Divine Battle did us the disservice of making him unwilling to trust the divine, and *your* idiot predecessors who once ran the Order made him unwilling to trust you. He's determined to carry out his mission himself, as he should have all along."

Mathias's glare narrowed on Ceredulus. It would not be unreasonable for him to assume the god was withholding some vital aspect of the truth, but the faint crease of agitation on his brow and subtle curl of his lips uncovered frustration on par with Mathias's own. At least the field between the paladin and his divine rival had been leveled. It was a pity it was a demon who held the cards.

"If he wants anything done, it will be with me accompanying him," Mathias muttered.

"Go ahead and tell—" Ceredulus cut himself off abruptly and spun as Tristan seemed to materialize just behind him, Talier's limp body, pale with little more than the final moments of life, draped over his shoulder. Ceredulus took half a look at the human's empty eyes and bared his teeth at Tristan, sweeping forward in a fit of unrestrained fury until Mathias's immobility forced him to stop. The vampire hastily retreated from his god's anger.

"You were ordered not to leave a mark on him!"

Tristan dropped to his knees in an instant display of complete submission Mathias had never expected to see, forehead bowing to the earth as he groveled before his god. Talier's body masked how the vampire trembled, but the wavering in Tristan's voice revealed his terror. "No marks to be seen by routine inspection, my lord. You have my soul." To prove his statement, still cowering beneath

Ceredulus's rage, Tristan reached across his chest to pull up the left leg of Talier's pants to reveal a single, careful puncture in the man's ankle. "There were complications leaving the city and time was running short. I *had* to feed, my lord." He lifted his head to look at Khin, careful to keep his eyes averted from Ceredulus. "I had no choice."

Color began to creep back into Khin's cheeks as Berann's interest shifted to the husk Tristan had returned with, and Mathias gaped in silent horror at Talier's lifeless body and the extinguished glisten in those eyes trapped in horror. Mathias wasn't particularly uncomfortable with dead bodies and he'd been the cause of a fair share of them in his time, but this was different. Though Talier had wronged Nessix in an unforgiveable manner, though Mathias himself would have contently pummeled his frustrations out on the pathetic man if Julianna wouldn't have stopped him from doing so, Talier hadn't deserved to be either a vampire's meal or a demon soul's host. And Mathias, Etha's great beacon of justice, had permitted this fate to befall him. Throwing another layer of stones on the wall he'd been constructing to keep his goddess's disappointment from reaching him quite yet, Mathias berated himself enough for the both of them.

Ceredulus had apparently finished chastising Tristan for his methods while Mathias tended to the ringing in his ears, because the vampire stood, walked closer to where Khin rolled to her side, groaning and rubbing at the pain behind her eyes, and deposited Talier's corpse on the ground. Even in death, Talier's helplessness persisted, eyes wild with doubts and begging for help, lips parted in a breathless gasp which anxiously insisted that he needed someone else to save him, that he didn't know what to do, that he was afraid. His soul had passed on and, judging by the smug pleasure now leveling Ceredulus's brow, a new one stood poised to replace it, but that hadn't been enough to erase that mortal desperation from the human's face. Disgusted and distraught, Mathias stood, spun from the budding production, and stalked away.

"Where are you—" Ceredulus never had the chance to finish his question before a choked gasp cut him off as the law which he'd bound himself to when negotiating his freedom with Mathias jerked him away from Talier to follow the paladin's immature retreat. "Mathias," he barked, lengthening his stride to pass the agitated human and stopping squarely in front of him. "Get back over there."

Even while actively avoiding Etha's guidance and disappointment, Mathias's fear of Ceredulus's dissatisfaction paled in comparison to his fear of facing the atrocity his actions had allowed. "I will be no part of this."

Ceredulus crossed his arms and shook his head, sending a brief glance toward the sky. "It is much too late for that."

"Yeah?" Mathias challenged. "Maybe it is, but I can refuse to take further action."

"I am not asking for any more of your involvement. You are of no use to the miracle to come, but I do require you to return to the body."

Mathias shook his head firmly. "I've nothing else to offer you in this regard and will not risk you manipulating me into one more vile act."

"You bound me to your side, you fool," Ceredulus snapped. "Sewing a soul into a corpse is a delicate matter, one which not even I can perform from a distance. You said we've got an oraku to sneak past to reach your girlfriend? That means I can't simply sling the threads together in a casual manner. This must be done with precision. We've got Berann's compliance, but not a great deal of his patience. Now, will you come back to the party with me, or do you insist on making all of these *vile acts* I've *manipulated* you into executing one great waste of my time and your honor?"

Oh, how Mathias hated Ceredulus and the sense he so often made. If what he said was true, if Berann lost his patience waiting for Ceredulus to carry out whatever disgusting procedure he had planned, the demon would return his interest to Khin and burrow inside of her, an act Mathias could only assume would come with great, prolonged pain to a living woman. It would mean more wasted time before Mathias could deliver on the promise he'd made to Nessix. It would mean Talier's purpose would be limited to nothing more than feeding a vampire. Clenching his teeth and gripping his fists tight, Mathias rigidly turned around, steeled

45

himself with a deep breath drawn in and let out through flaring nostrils, and marched up beside Tristan. Ceredulus followed, pleased with Mathias's sensibility.

"Alright," Mathias snapped. "Get this over with."

Ceredulus walked around his servant—who was helping Khin up to a seated position—and faced the contentious paladin, tisking his disapproval in Mathias's assumption and tone. "What part of this being a delicate matter does not convey to you?"

"The part where you implied we have no time to lose. Get necromancing."

There was not even a hint of respect in Mathias's words, but Ceredulus never expected much of it from Mathias. Berann hovered nearby, growing increasingly eager, and though Ceredulus would have loved to continue ruffling Mathias's feathers, he didn't trust the demon to be lenient of his pettiness. A god though he may be, Ceredulus took a moment to brace himself for the pain of his pending action. Meeting Tristan's eyes with the firm demand to make sure Mathias didn't attempt another tantrum, the god gripped his left forearm with his right hand, sucked down a sharp breath, and wrenched his hand against his arm, snapping the bones in half to jut free from his divine flesh.

"Blessed Mother!"

Tristan's hand shot out and gripped Mathias's arm to keep him from retreating in his shock as Khin choked on a gasp and scooted up against the vampire's leg. It had been centuries since Tristan had last beheld his god's miracles, and he watched on with a keen appreciation.

Ceredulus released the grip on his wrist, allowing the slack of his broken arm to dangle from his elbow. "Had you thought raising the dead was some romantic process, Mathias?" He pinched a sliver of protruding bone and winced as he snapped it free. "You, of all people, should understand that it takes sacrifice to create a blessing."

Chilled and dizzy with a creeping nausea, Mathias gawked as Ceredulus scrutinized the sliver of bone, and it wasn't until the god knelt down beside Talier's corpse that he was able to regain his breath. Ceredulus's broken arm set itself as Mathias watched, mending bone and flesh before his eyes.

"It is time, Berann," Ceredulus said, a reverence enriching his voice in a manner which Mathias had never heard from this particular god. "Come to me and allow me to bind you to this vessel so I may restore you to life on the mortal plane."

Mathias shifted uncomfortably in Tristan's grasp and sent a glance at the wide-eyed Khin clutching the vampire's calf. They'd already established that Berann spoke no modern, common tongues, and he couldn't help but assume Ceredulus's words had been composed simply to torment him. The dead were meant to go to Etha, to have their eternal repose.

"Quit with your fretting and morals," Ceredulus muttered to Mathias's silent protests, eyes now focused sharply at a position just above Talier's heart. "This young man is with your Etha, free of all his troubles just as you like, and Berann had never been welcomed into her glorious realm in the first place. We're tearing nothing from anyone. You're witnessing a benevolent deed and gift of salvation, if anything."

The thought occurred to Mathias to go ahead and ask Etha if Ceredulus was being honest about Talier finding peace in the divine realm, but the twist in his stomach continued to ward him against reaching out for her counsel. Instead, he continued to stand by in horrified shock as Ceredulus deftly ran his fingers across Talier's corpse, muttering words too soft to hear, brows pinched in deep concentration. Tristan placed his hand atop Khin's messy hair as she clung tighter to him. She gaped in confused awe at the developments around her, and if Mathias would have been able to move, he'd have pulled her away to answer the questions brewing in her fragile mind before Tristan or his god had a chance to brush off the blasphemous gravity of what was underway.

Mathias had known fear and heartache in his time. He'd known pain and anguish. But he'd never known this disgusting dread which flooded his stomach to the point he felt he'd burst. It was too late to stop the suffering which had already occurred, too late to shield Khin from the horrors of evil, too late to take back this decision and insist that Ceredulus find a better way to negotiate Khin's safety from Berann while Mathias sought more virtuous paths to the answers he and Nessix needed. He'd come this far out of desperation and fear, and it took until this very moment for him to realize that he'd been a fool to block out Etha's opinions on his irresponsible use of free will. Oh, she'd judge him fiercely. He'd cower beneath her disappointment today and for weeks to come, he was sure. But he needed her now, needed her comfort and reminder that she'd allowed him to maintain his free will for a beautiful reason. He needed to hear her confirm the pathetic cry in his heart which insisted there had been no other way. Mathias reached out to begin tearing that wall down...

And Talier's corpse sucked in a sharp, ragged breath.

Khin shrieked, nearly pulling Tristan off balance when she scuttled behind him as the demon-infused body thrashed out, succeeding in striking Ceredulus with enough force to knock the god over. As one, Mathias and Tristan drew a concerned step back while Ceredulus found his feet once again. Talier's limbs scrambled about in a frantic flurry, as though they had no recollection of how to function. He writhed on the ground, screaming with the agony of a man being burned alive. Just as Mathias was about to ask the older two of his stunned companions—who were far better versed in the raising of the dead that he was—if this was a normal part of the process, he made out a single word through the jumble of screamed phrases.

"Stop."

Compelled to help those who suffered, even if they were undead demons, Mathias's compassion drew him a step forward. Tristan attempted to hold him back, but Mathias easily pulled away from his halfhearted restraint. Talier's chest heaved, tears of pain squeezing out between pinched eyelids, and another word registered to Mathias.

"Hurts."

Ceredulus narrowed his eyes as he studied his creation's unusual behavior, and neither he nor Tristan moved to assist the screaming storm of limbs. They might not have had any idea what to make of this construct's suffering but, instinctively, the nausea Mathias had been contending with wrapped around his heart, squeezing tight until an aching pulse reminded him of what had given him his second life—and what had made Talier so valuable to the demons.

"Affliction." Mathias spoke firmly, stopping his approach just out of range of the flailing limbs.

Talier's eyes pried open at the name every divinely enhanced being knew, and met Mathias's with a deep intelligence which confirmed the timid human no longer had any part of coordinating this body. Swallowing the rush of malaise which came from this realization, Mathias thumped a fist to his chest then pointed at Talier's—or Berann's. If the weapon could slay gods, it couldn't be pleasant when lodged into the heart of one of the creatures perverted by their wrath.

"Affliction," Mathias repeated.

Berann closed his eyes again and sucked in a sharp breath. His body continued to spasm, but he managed tiny sweeps of his hands between convulsions, the flicks of his wrists becoming more graceful and controlled as each consecutive movement stretched and pulled his threads to wrap around the invasive artifact to buffer against its assault. Tense moments later, Berann was able to produce a groan rather than the twisted gasps and screams, and he rolled to his side, contracting into a fetal curl as one last roar of anguish pressed out of his lungs, draining every ounce of breath he'd held and dying out in a string of harsh coughs.

Nobody moved, even the god stared with wide eyes, wondering if perhaps he'd made a mistake, as Berann lay on the ground, heaving for breath.

"I take it this isn't normal," Mathias muttered to Ceredulus.

The god shook his head.

"Guess your brilliant methods still have their flaws."

Ceredulus would have snapped back at Mathias's bitter jab had he not just been tossed around by an ancient oraku like he was some feeble mortal. Instead, he was forced to focus his concentration on the one advantage he knew he had over Berann. It had been centuries since the demon had last commanded a physical body or mind. As powerful as he might be, at least in these next few moments, he had dreadfully few defenses against a god's prying ways. Ceredulus slipped into Berann's thoughts, actively seeking the information Mathias coveted, but was promptly lost in a deluge of Berann's own questions, spouted out in every language both he and Talier had ever known. Gritting his teeth in resistance to this chaotic flood of chatter, Ceredulus crossed his arms and waited for Mathias to make the first move. He hadn't expected it to be the one the paladin chose.

"You've got a body now," Mathias said. "Now tell us what you know about how to stop your kind."

Berann's breathing had slowed, his keen eyes narrowing as he tapped into Talier's intelligence to understand the words spoken by the voice which had guided him to the cause of his pain. Even before being able to translate the message, Berann heard the clear order in this man's tone, and that would be a problem if it persisted.

Still aching from, but no longer hindered by, Affliction's influence, Berann tested his new lungs a moment longer and stood. He tottered on his legs, dramatically shooting his arms out to his sides as he fought to manage his balance without the aid of his wings, but the disadvantage passed quickly. Whether from forgetting what it meant to keep a tidy appearance or simply a lack of caring, he didn't bother to dust himself off from the dirt and vegetation picked up while he'd thrashed on the ground, and he made a quick appraisal of the terrified young woman on the ground, grateful he hadn't been forced to possess her now that he bore witness to her naivety. He passed over the appraising gaze of the beautiful man Talier's memories associated with deception and terror, gaze lingering slightly longer on the god who scrutinized him with an equal intensity. Last, Berann's eyes locked on Mathias's breastplate, tracing over the emblem emblazoned on the alabaster steel. This must have been the man who had guided him to Affliction's interference. He had no way of knowing who this particular paladin was, as he'd been slain long before Mathias had generated any amount of distinction, but he recognized the lily-wreathed shield etched on his armor and had seen all he needed to.

Scowling, unmindful of the flimsy frame he inhabited, Berann rushed forward and punched Mathias square in the face.

Having expected all sorts of dangers from this risen oraku, the one attack Mathias hadn't anticipated was such a direct, cheap strike. The blow sent him reeling back two steps, tugging a chuckling god along with him, and he covered his nose, fingers instantly slick with blood as he glared at Berann in indignant dissatisfaction.

"That is for the stupidity of your forebearers," Berann said evenly, shaking the sting of the strike from his hand.

No further acts of aggression followed, and as Mathias gaped in shock at this demon's audacity—and his instant adoption of an even temperament now that he'd satisfied his urge for retribution—Ceredulus allowed himself a deep, hearty laugh. The god maintained a healthy distance from Berann, and shook his head in admiration.

"Welcome back, Berann," Ceredulus said. "You will find your justice at last."

SIX

Annin was in a particularly vile mood. He'd chased from his quarters the pair of alar who he'd woken to with nothing more than the threat of violence the moment they started blabbering about Kol's sure relief that he was well. The very fact that these underlings could confirm the alar lived provided Annin with an adequate reminder of the events he otherwise couldn't quite piece together. Kol had broken formation and Grell had ordered him to collapse the ridge supporting their opposition. He remembered the hateful look he'd branded Kol with, the regretful one the alar had returned to him. After that, Annin remembered nothing more, one more weakness to contend with. And he blamed it all on Nessix.

He lifted his left arm, holding his hand before his face, and sneered at the way his fingers trembled. He'd seldom felt powerless in his life, and the last time this sort of empty chill had filled his insides had been in those final mortal moments of the Divine Battle when his misguided determination to spite the will of the gods had urged him to protect his comrades.

The handle on his door rattled and he dropped his hand to hide its shaking. As the door swung open, Annin drew in a deep breath past his fatigue. "I told you to—"

Kol stepped into the room, meeting Annin's eyes just long enough to confirm that he was alive, before the oraku's bitter glower began to peel away at what little calm he'd found. Glancing down at the plate he'd brought with him, Kol cleared this throat.

"I brought you food and drink."

Annin scathed Kol's sheepish demeanor a moment longer before scoffing and looking pointedly at the wall opposite his bed. Of all the demons surviving to this day, Kol was the one who had seen him the weakest, and the only one he trusted to not make an issue about it. The fact that Kol was the reason for his current compromised state, however, and that he'd brought such a pitiful remedy to aid in his recovery, almost insulted Annin more.

"I'd given instructions to be left alone," the oraku muttered.

Kol figured that if Annin was planning—or able—to act against him with any sort of force, he'd have done so by now, and sighed away his uncertainty as he kicked the door shut and walked the rest of the way into the room. Shoving aside a small collection of glass jars on Annin's desk, Kol deposited the plate of fruit and freshly cooked meat he'd brought with him, and grasped the seat of the stool tucked beneath it.

"You are not welcome to stay."

"Am I ever welcome to stay?" Kol countered. Though he had no intention of obeying Annin's implication for him to leave, his friend's curt tone did succeed in keeping him from bringing the stool any closer to the bed.

"You realize what I did for you."

Kol lowered his gaze. "I've always known what—"

Annin pushed himself upright, fiercely shaking his head against the lag caused by the abrupt action, and wisely stopped himself from trying to leave the bed quite yet as the room rapidly spun around him. "You've put me in peril for the last time, Kol. There will not be another."

Kol looked up and stared deep into his old friend's pale eyes, seeing the blunt truth of his statement as clearly as he always did. Annin didn't have a use for lies, and there hadn't been a time in their long past together in which Kol had ever seen him express remorse upon settling on such a decision. He'd known he'd pushed Annin to the boundaries of his patience, but their entire lives together had been built on a deep understanding of and loyalty to one another. Annin had use of—but no love for—Nessix, and Kol's obsession with her had been a point of debate between the two of them for well over a year now, but Kol hadn't thought it would be enough to destroy centuries of camaraderie.

"We survived," Kol insisted firmly, "by working together."

"By—" Annin hissed sharply and shook his head. "You broke formation, Kol, one which you developed yourself."

"Me breaking formation is what kept us alive."

Annin sneered again, arm trembling with residual weakness as he flexed it at his side. "Anything in particular prompt you to come up with that tactic?"

"Nessix told me—"

Annin snorted. "*Nessix*. She's the one giving orders now?"

Kol had tolerated much of Annin's scrutiny over the past several months, and he'd done so without complaint, fully aware that he was deserving of it. But now that he had Nessix back in his hands, now that he'd had the chance to negotiate an alliance with her, he was no longer willing to accept Annin's grudges. "She told me those were archers' horns, which they were, and advised me to pull up out of their range. It was her tactical advice and me following it which prevented us from being shot."

"They wouldn't have taken more than two or three of us from the air before we could have managed a proper evasion, one which wouldn't have risked killing *me*."

"But you didn't die," Kol persisted. "And neither did those two or three sacrificial troops."

Annin's brows furrowed, eyes narrowing at Kol's untimely bout of sentimentality. "That is the entire purpose of *sacrificial* troops. Have you forgotten what we are?"

Kol stood and strode closer to Annin so he could lower his voice. "Have *you* forgotten what we'd been? We had wanted peace once, Annin. It wasn't always like this."

Annin struck his mattress, fingers sinking into its cushioning to keep him from falling forward in his desire to launch himself at Kol. "They wouldn't let us have it!"

"And that is why we created the akhuerai. To find it. Admit it, Annin. Nessix saved us back there."

Annin scoffed and looked away. "She saved herself and damn near got me killed doing it. Pardon me for not expressing what you feel is appropriate gratitude."

Kol shook his head, chuckling bitterly as he turned a shoulder to his fuming friend. "She said you'd told her to stay away from me."

Annin shifted his eyes to follow Kol's agitated pacing. "I did. And if what she nearly caused outside doesn't prove to you how dangerous her influence over you is, I don't know what will."

Kol quit pacing, but continued to shake his head, jaw fixed as he idly looked over the collection of jars stocked on the shelf near the door to keep from needing to look at Annin.

"Do you at least have her contained in a proper holding cell?" the oraku asked. "Or is she waiting for you in your bed?"

Kol's glare snapped to Annin, eyes flashing. "She is properly secured and awaiting her punishment. If you were strong enough, I'd take you to see her for yourself."

Annin pulled his shoulders back and cocked his head, shocked at Kol's uncharacteristic bluntness. Even before the alar had fallen under Nessix's spell, Kol had seldom taken such a tone with him. Annin had clearly struck a nerve, one which could prove dangerous if he continued to pluck at it. "If she *ever* puts my life in jeopardy again, I will kill you both."

Kol shook his head. "You'd kill me, but you couldn't properly end her. You gave half her soul to Lorrin to take to his grave."

That reminder rapidly diverted the course of Annin's anger. He may not like Nessix, but she was still a valuable asset in managing the akhuerai and the only hope any demon who wasn't Kol had of controlling her resided in that second, missing portion of her soul.

It wasn't often that Kol was able to put Annin in his place, but that one statement had succeeded in doing so, and the alar pounced on the advantage it gave him. "I'd told you giving him her soul vessel was a bad idea."

"Yes," Annin snapped, "but that was because you were too afraid to part with it, not because you thought Grell would show up and kill the idiot."

"It was because I knew the likelihood of something going wrong because, yes, Lorrin was an idiot." Annin rolled his eyes at Kol's reasoning and pointedly looked away. "If I'd have kept it, the worst thing that would have happened would be Mathias getting a hold of it—"

"And that would have—"

"And at least with him"—Kol raised his voice over Annin's temperamental objection—"we would have known it was *safe*."

The two demons glared at each other hard, spinning curses and threats between one another with a ferocity which life had never necessitated them to express before. As badly as Annin wanted to claim his dominance in this debate, he couldn't find the grounds to make his stand. Kol was responsible for most of the mistakes tied to their current circumstances—he'd chosen Nessix as the akhuerai's leader, he'd bonded with her, bound himself to her, became so infatuated with her that she could play him like a tin whistle, trusting her to the point that he'd let her escape for a dangerous world tour—but of all of the mistakes Kol had made, he'd not once misplaced the key to controlling and, should the need arise, ending her. That had been on Annin. The oraku was unaccustomed to accepting blame; even on the rare occasion when he did make mistakes, he could always find a way to bend matters back into his favor.

Annin had meant it when he'd said he was through with trusting Kol with his life, but he was smart enough to know that he'd always be able to trust the alar in matters of keeping Nessix close.

"Then we need to figure out how to get it back," Annin said at last.

"No shit."

Annin eyed Kol carefully, judging the simmering anger in his fiery glare. Kol's temperament often forbid him to openly blame Annin for anything and it was even rarer for Annin to feel like he deserved it. As agitated as Kol had become and as weakened as Annin was, the oraku didn't like his odds of pushing back against Kol right now, no matter how much he had it coming. Grudgingly, unaccustomed to being the one without answers and not about to admit that he was, Annin looked away.

"Do you have any thoughts on how to get back to Vesper to search for it?" Annin asked.

Kol puffed out a bitter laugh and shook his head, narrowing his eyes at Annin's unusual display of rattled confidence. "You are the one who always works out logistics. This time, it's not my mess that needs to be cleaned up."

Annin hissed his belligerence and snapped his glare to Kol. "After how many times I've fixed what you let go awry, you're honestly going to wipe your hands of my single error? An error made in *your* best interests, no less?"

Kol scoffed and turned to resume his pacing, ripping one of Annin's journals from the shelf beside the desk. He thumbed through the pages so he had an excuse to focus his ire elsewhere, still not certain of how easily Annin would be able to counter any bursts of aggression sent his way. "Parting with Nessix's soul vessel has *never* been among my interests, best or otherwise. Try again, Annin."

Annin sat up straighter, bolstered by the discovery that his head no longer spun from the effort. "I wouldn't have even set foot on Gelthin if not for trying to protect you from your terrible decisions."

Kol slapped a hand on the book, fingers curling back against the open pages. "Arguing over whose fault any of this was is getting us no closer to fixing this problem." He wasn't used to being the logical one when such problems arose, and he struggled with filling that role now. "Even if you intend to walk away from the akhuerai and me when this is through, you know we have to find that missing vessel as soon as possible."

"And I'm asking you how we are supposed to do that."

Kol was intelligent. He'd had to be to be heir to the chief of his long-extinct people. He'd had to be to claim authority among the demons when fate hadn't given him the strength of an inoga. He'd been among the group of ancients to first conceive the idea of gaining flight, among the first to receive wings. He'd designed a quarter of the siege machines utilized by the demons, developed the theory of the Undersea Pass and the tunnels used to link together the different regions of the hells. The akhuerai had been his brain child for the past hundred and fifty years. Kol may have been terrible at making decisions, but he was smart enough to know when an idea was a bad one, and he had no doubt in his mind that trying to sneak out of the hells so soon after Nessix had been recovered and while Grell was focused on his every move, was a terrible decision to even toy with.

"There is no way I will be permitted out of the hells right now," Kol said. "And we both know it."

"Since when have you cared about what you are and are not permitted to do?" Annin asked caustically.

Kol frowned at this cold judgement. "Since Grell has every viable reason to execute me and a firm grasp on something I very much want him to not have a hold of. If he's going to forget about any of this, it won't be anytime soon, and he needs to forget about it before I will have the leeway to do much of anything."

It was a point which Annin could not argue with, and he didn't favor any of the alternatives it presented. "Are you implying I'm the one who should be heading to the surface?"

Kol frowned. Annin was still the only demon he had any reason to trust, but even those reasons had fizzled out of him after Nessix's recap of what Annin had told her and the oraku's current aggressive stance against him. Though he did trust that Annin wanted to locate Nessix's missing soul vessel nearly as much as he did, he did not have even the slightest reason to believe that Annin would return it to him when—or if—he successfully retrieved it. Either way, Kol's options were limited and if he had to choose, he'd much prefer Nessix to be in Annin's hands than anyone else's.

"Who else would you suggest?" Kol asked.

"Someone else," Annin said. "*Anyone* else."

Kol furrowed his brows and cocked his head. "You don't want to take control of Nessix's vessel?"

"Oh, I am quite interested in doing that."

At least Annin's ire hadn't eroded his honesty. "Are you afraid to go up there on your own?"

The flash of Annin's pale eyes, coupled with his limited ability to genuinely do anything to correct Kol from his shrewd assessment, would have made Kol laugh if he, too, weren't so preoccupied with the crisis they currently faced.

"There's nothing I've ever feared in my life," Annin spat, a testament which Kol, even as doubtful and critical of Annin as he was, had no grounds to argue with. "But Grell said that Lorrin told him where to find us. Which means Grell asked for us by name. After we'd told Lorrin our plans. Assuming any of that clan still lives, you can bet that not one of Lorrin's men would so much as spit to offer us assistance after our use of their commander led to his death. Damn surface dwellers are soft, Kol. They *care* too much about the pointless things." Annin leveled his glare on the alar. "Sort of like you."

Kol grit his teeth and worked his jaw as he soaked in Annin's continued criticism. "We have nobody else reliable down here to send up. It's you or nobody."

Annin's eyes narrowed, a frigid challenge mocking Kol's attempt at authority. "Then I guess it's nobody, unless you can work out a deal with Grell."

A shiver tickled across Kol's shoulders at Annin's coldness and the notion of following his suggestion. He'd have to tiptoe carefully around Grell for weeks to avoid triggering his wrath as it was. Finding Nessix's soul vessel couldn't wait that long, and both he and Annin knew it. Kol shook his head, already knowing how trying to execute such an impossible feat would pan out. Nessix's entire purpose in the hells was to help him get rid of that damned inoga, and Grell still stood like an indomitable boulder in the way of everything he wanted to accomplish.

"I don't see how it can be done," Kol said at last, comfortable exposing his insecurity in light of Annin's mirroring doubts.

"And you hadn't been able to see how any of the other ideas you'd come up with in the past could be done until we started to curate them."

Kol studied Annin hard, catching the cunning in the oraku's eyes. They'd worked closely for all but eighteen years of Kol's life, and he had always thought that had helped him learn how to read his friend, but now he wasn't so sure. He'd seen Annin go up against countless opponents in the past, both with daunting intelligence and supernatural might, and Annin, even if there were ebbs and flows in his progress in doing so, always came out on top. He was playing Kol right now, of that the alar was certain, but it also dawned on him in this moment that he very well could have been playing him since the day they'd first met and Kol had been too blindly trusting to see it. All he knew was that he couldn't try to slip out of the hells. Not yet.

"We're both making a rather bold assumption," Kol said.

"What's that?" Annin asked. "Whether or not you'd be able to part yourself from your precious toy long enough to actually save her?"

This bitter goading of Annin's, far crueler now that he'd made so many alienating declarations, was getting old. "The only reason I'd be reluctant to leave her is because I don't trust Grell to not end her in a temper tantrum or you to do so out of spite."

Annin craned his head from side to side, brows raising in contemplation. "That is not an irrational concern," he admitted.

Kol swallowed his reaction to shuffle his worries behind a harsh reprimand of Annin's wasteful and careless nature. "Her welfare isn't the reason I'm reluctant to try."

"Your fear of Grell, then?"

This time, there was nothing mocking in Annin's tone. Harsh, but not cruel. Both of them had carried reservations about Grell's stability after the inoga first realized he could demand obedience through violence, but for once, Kol's nerves were not triggered by that fact alone.

"Lorrin had kept Nessix's vessel on his person," Kol said. "Or at least that's what he told us he'd do. Grell had looted him, evident by the fact that he had his eye patch. What if…" Kol grimaced at the thought of Grell having found that last influential piece of Nessix, of being able to demand her respect and obedience in the most powerful way possible. She would undoubtedly deny Grell those courtesies in a dramatic fashion, and there would be terrible prices to pay for it.

"Wouldn't he have made it known to you if he did?" Annin asked.

That had been Kol's theory from the start, but the longer he thought it over, the less sure he was. "He knew I carried it, knew it was means to control her. But unless you told him what it... what value I had placed in it, he'd have no reason to flaunt his possession of it and every reason to keep it for himself."

As much as Annin hated Nessix, as many terrible things as he fanaticized about doing to her, having Grell possess her soul vessel was not among them. It was too valuable—*she* was too valuable, flaws and all—for him to ever hope for that. There was an emptiness in Kol's eyes at the thought of what this would mean, a fear running deeper than simply losing control of his pet. If Grell had her soul vessel, he would be able to take the entire akhuerai force from them. He would steal their best shot at overthrowing the inoga and structuring the hells into the respectable society it should be. Annin and Kol had lived for this project for decades now, had devoted so much of their time and energy into perfecting their creations, and it could all be over from the loss of one tiny bauble which Annin had insisted they let go of. It was almost—but not quite—enough to make him overlook his decision to walk away from Kol.

"So that's it?" Annin asked. "You really think Grell has it?"

Kol shook his head, too lost for direction to speak further on his nagging fears. If Grell had Nessix's soul, at least it wouldn't be *lost*, but that didn't mean it was safe. He opened his mouth to reply just as Annin's door swung open, startling them both enough to jerk to attention.

"Really think I have what?" Grell leaned a shoulder against the door frame, crossing his arms over his broad chest.

Kol was out of excuses and didn't even let himself begin to fumble over trying to formulate any. One thing in all of this was certain; if Grell didn't have Nessix's vessel, if he didn't even know it was missing, everyone was safer with it continuing that way. Not trusting Kol to come up with any sort of answer Grell would believe and knowing well that the inoga expected one promptly, Annin wasted only one breath in concocting a solution.

"The means and authority to properly punish Nessix for her disobedience." Annin ignored the sharpness of the glare Kol shot him, a furious one which scolded him for opening the door to greater pain and torment for Nessix than was necessary. "Kol's worried that with the new development in his relationship with her that she'll find reason to excuse away anything he does to her."

Grell snorted and walked farther into the room, scrutinizing Kol's seething dissatisfaction with disgust. "I could make her wish she'd never even thought to engage our forces when we went after Elidae, but I beg to argue, Kol. I do think you are best equipped to deliver her punishment for thinking she could sneak off. It would do you both some good, if you ask me."

Kol ground his teeth together to keep from snapping at Annin and his cruel, seamless manipulation of the matter. If Kol protested Grell's observation, that would put him squarely at risk for gaining even more of the inoga's unwanted suspicions. "If you say so." The skeptical disregard Kol had hoped would bolster his words never quite made it there.

Grell didn't deem Kol's bitter response worthy of an answer, and stalked past the alar to approach Annin where he sat in his bed. "Came by to check on you," Grell said, any indication that he actually cared about Annin's well-being absent from his voice. He tilted his head in Kol's direction, but didn't look at him. "I thought you were supposed to be resting undisturbed."

Annin flicked his gaze to where Kol's lip curled and he crossed his arms. "Kol stopped by for my thoughts on punishing Nessix, considering I paid a higher price for her recovery than most."

A menacing decline of Kol's brows enhanced his scowl; he was fine with Annin going out of his way to make his life more uncomfortable, but in weighting Nessix's sentence, he was pushing too far. Ignorant to—or possibly acutely aware of—Kol's agitation, Grell nodded.

"And your thoughts on it?" Grell asked.

Annin settled his attention on Kol's fury-engulfed eyes once more, taunting him with how much worse he could make all of this, dangling his power and influence over Kol's head like that salvation he'd never reach, then blinked and looked back to Grell. "She will heal from anything we do to her, so her punishment needs to be slow and precise if we want the lesson to stick. Give her time to think about what she did and who she wronged. For that reason, I think Kol is the *only* viable option to conduct her torture, no matter how badly I'd like to tear into her for the trouble she's put me through."

Grell nodded again and turned a shoulder so he could look at Kol. "Go and tell my colleagues the good news," he instructed, a knowing smirk growing at the alar's sneer. "Tell them we'll have a show for them tomorrow morning over breakfast, once Annin's got himself patched up enough to join us for the fun."

Kol hated Grell, but he knew how to navigate him. Of the other three inoga in this region, he only tolerated Ehsmil, and he didn't get along with any of their elite troops or honor guard at all. He'd fully expected Grell to take out some degree of his frustrations on him, and he supposed this was the first step of doing so. Unable to secure solid purchase on his trust of Annin, Kol had to bank on their mutual fear of not knowing the location of Nessix's missing soul vessel to muster the confidence to drop his arms to his sides and accept the order he'd been given without objection. Considering neither his friend nor overlord worthy of a verbal response, Kol stalked out of the room.

Annin and Grell watched the alar leave in silence, and long moments after the door had closed, Annin heaved an irritated sigh and tested the stability of his legs. Satisfied he could hold himself upright, he retrieved the food Kol had brought him and returned to his bed to sit down.

"Why did you come here, Grell?" Annin asked, not bothering to glance at the imposing beast behind him. He'd already made a fair assessment that the focus of Grell's current agitation was invested solely on Kol.

"I told you, I came by to check on you, to see how you're feeling."

There was a fair degree of irony in Grell's tone which caused Annin to pause in his eating, and the words themselves contradicted anything the inoga had expressed over the past several centuries. "To see how I'm *feeling*?"

"Yes."

Annin scoffed and resumed eating. "I just babysat Kol on a

worldwide chase for his rebellious toy, composed a plan to take that toy from our longest-standing adversary, and very nearly lost my life to your reckless order to battle Abaeloth's own integrity. I feel *wonderful*, Grell. Thank you for asking."

Grell chuckled at Annin's sarcasm. On most days, the oraku's sharpness irritated him, only emphasizing the limitations of his own slow wit. It was a humiliating annoyance which had existed since the days when they were mortals, a sentiment shared by all but one member of that long-ago party, a man Grell refused to remember. But today, Annin's sarcasm and vitriol was refreshing and precisely what Grell had hoped to hear.

"You have identified the common threat in all of your troubles, haven't you?"

Annin sighed and flung the bone he'd picked clean back on his plate. "Kol has been the cause of my troubles since the day I first met him. You're bringing me no revelations."

Grell frowned at Annin's willingness to offer that aspect of the past. The one thing which had allowed Annin to remain in Vesper had been his devotion to Kol—Kol had saved Annin's life and, though Annin had never been one to make blatant displays of gratitude, he'd never forgotten that debt. It was what let Kol get away with half of the mad plans he concocted and have Annin follow behind to clean up his messes. And it was that debt which Grell had been searching for a way to sneak past for the better part of his existence, mortal and demonic alike. Grell had never been as sharp as he wanted to be, but Kol had opened a door which would make up for that. Echoing Annin's sigh with forced patience, Grell retrieved the stool Kol had been sitting on, plopped it down in front of Annin, and balanced his mass on it.

"You ever think it's time you put some more thought into those revelations?" Grell asked. "Whether or not Kol's *worth* all those troubles he's given you?"

Annin flicked a glance at Grell, not surprised by the simplicity of the inoga's objectives. "Kol is worth that trouble because he's still of use to me."

"How?" Grell pressed. "So he saved your life once—"

"He's saved it more than once," Annin admitted freely.

Grell growled at Annin's interruption but, as always, was mindful of correcting his calculating opponent more directly than was prudent. "Fine. But how many more times has he endangered it?"

Annin cast Grell a deprecating glare, arching one brow as he stood to leave his half-eaten plate of food to change out of his filthy clothes. "It is unusual for you to show concern for anyone. What happened while I was gone to make you go soft?"

Grell leapt to his feet, the little stool tipping over from his abrupt movement. Just before charging toward the indifferent oraku, he restrained himself by crossing his arms and throwing his weight back. "I don't care what sort of uses you think you have for Kol, you can't deny that he's becoming increasingly unstable, increasingly dangerous, for all of those around him."

Annin untied the harness which kept his shirt in place. "Nothing about the hells is either stable or safe, Grell." He looked up into the mirror and met the inoga's eyes. "*Nothing*. Kol is still manageable and because of that, it is still worth my while to tolerate him."

"Manageable," Grell grunted. "Need I remind you of—"

Annin spun around to face Grell, pale eyes spinning with wicked storms. "I am no fool. I have kept score long before you even knew we were playing a game."

Grell stood to full height, raising his wings from his back to increase his presence with the notion of masking his insecurity of what he was about to do. "I'd never thought you were a fool until today, Annin, and I hope you hear me well. As you have uses for Kol, I've uses for you, and I intend to ensure I get to cash in on them, understand?" Annin's eyes flashed at Grell's declaration, but he didn't protest. "Kol has already forfeit his life in the hells. You must know that, and you must know that there is nothing you can do to change it. I came to see how you were feeling, to see if you've finally faced the music, or if you plan to go down with him."

Annin stared hard at Grell, frowning at the ultimatum he'd just delivered. Kol had been dead, in the sense of the security he had in the hells, for years now, kept alive solely because of Annin's use for him. As long as the akhuerai existed, whether or not their forces continued to grow in strength or number, Kol was pivotal in managing them. Though Annin had begun to toy with the idea of abandoning Kol to his own fate once their objectives were complete, he'd fully intended, even now, to hold on to the alar until then. Grell, however, had lost that last wisp of patience and Annin wasn't sure he'd have the ability to talk Kol's way into another stolen chance.

"If you have use for me," Annin said calmly, evenly. "It is in your best interest to keep me content." Grell sneered at Annin's confidence but, just as Annin hadn't objected to his previous declaration, Grell held his tongue. "Now. You will leave me to finish recovering and you will trust that I will make whatever decision I deem in my best interest, just the same as any demon would."

Grell puffed out a dry laugh and shook his head. "Don't be a fool, Annin."

"I never have been." Annin turned back to his armoire to retrieve a clean shirt.

The pressure of Grell's glower remained on Annin's back as he shrugged the shirt's straps between his wings and pulled them around his waist, and after the inoga had either decided his point made or gotten too uncomfortable by his faltering confidence, he stomped out of Annin's room, slamming the door behind himself. It wasn't until then that Annin stepped away from his armoire and sat down, asking himself what it was that he truly wanted.

SEVEN

No less distraught over current events—though much better at hiding it—than Mathias was, Julianna had told the Council that she was reserving the remainder of the day for private prayer. After seeing the recovered priestesses to the infirmary and addressing the relevant staff in regards to the care they were to receive, Julianna issued orders to the temple that she was only to be interrupted if valid reports on demons, Talier, or Mathias's whereabouts after his latest disappearance were received. Part of the High Priestess had known that assuming her retreat and requests would be respected was nothing but wishful thinking, but that didn't stop the tight stitch of dread from twisting in her stomach when a timid knock sounded at her door.

Not rising from her chair, conserving her energy and patience as best she could for the trials that were bound to be waiting for her on the other side of the door, Julianna stared ahead in silence as she drew in a steady pair of breaths, feebly savoring the last couple moments before responsibility kidnapped her from her denial of reality and threw her back into the mess she was obligated to tend to. After her slow resignation, Julianna's weary voice welcomed the priestess to enter.

The door opened promptly and Delia, a high-strung, sandy-haired young woman, peeked her head around it, too timid to enter.

"High Priestess," she said, her voice climbing half an octave before she finished the simple address. "You asked to be notified if anything happened to the Afflicted man?"

Between the three concerns Julianna had asked to be kept informed of, Talier's status was the one which had worried her the least. Of course it would be the first to actually prove problematic. "I did. Do come in."

The priestess stared at Julianna with saucer eyes for a tense moment before obedience trumped her reservations, and she quickly squeezed through the door and let it fall closed behind her. Her fingers worked across her palms as she shuffled forward into the room, her gaze cast to the floor after an acknowledgement so soft Julianna had to assume it from nothing more than the subtle movement of the girl's lips. A chill of trepidation dragged its icy finger up the back of the High Priestess's neck, and she cleared her throat to be able to speak.

"Please, tell me what you know," Julianna prompted.

"Right." The priestess gave a single nod, still staring at the marble tiles at her feet, and a weak breath lifted her shoulders and carried out her rushed report. "He is missing from his room and, as far as the current search efforts suggest, the Citadel as a whole." She spoke even faster after Julianna sank back in her chair and raised a hand to drive a finger into her temple. "Reports came in that he was last seen in the streets, near the western gate, with a man who attacked and grabbed him before they both disappeared."

Logic urged Julianna to note the fact that the priestess hadn't named this assailant as Mathias, but it was hard to overlook her brother's current opinion of Talier, especially when paired with the claim of the two men disappearing. Few people in Zeal were capable of such feats, and Julianna's question came out on a groan; she really didn't want to hear the answer. "Was this man Mathias?"

"Oh, no, High Priestess." Delia shook her head, eyes wide as she clasped her hands tight. "It was some young nobleman."

Julianna's brows furrowed and she lifted her head from the press of her finger. "And you said he disappeared?"

Delia bit her lip as though ashamed of herself for not being able to deliver a more accurate explanation. There was simply too large a mess of information being flung about the Citadel between all of the calamities which had piled up around them. "Reports conflict a bit. Some say he flew. Some say he ran. The general consensus, though, is that this man struck Talier in the street and abducted him before any of the guards could act."

Julianna lowered her hand to tap her lip in consideration, but froze before her first touch. Mathias wasn't the only character capable of such power and movement to be causing trouble for her lately. "Has Khin reported back to the temple yet?"

"I—" Delia paused, brows furrowing at the apparent irrelevance of Julianna's concern. "No, High Priestess. None of us have seen her in two days."

Any illusion of denying that matters were rushing to a catastrophic head slipped from Julianna's grasp, and she couldn't help but think that Tristan Swift having a hold of Talier was far worse than anything Mathias would have done to the man. She looked up to the priestess's nervous eyes and her lips shrank into a tense pucker. This generation of both priestesses and Councilmembers had been spared any true toils of the dark side of Abaeloth. True, the Council thought themselves grand heroes in this time of peace and though Julianna had quietly resented their distance from such hardships, she'd have gladly carried the burden of such frustrations to spare Abaeloth—Zeal's Council included— from the times that were coming.

"And Mathias?" Julianna asked, discipline keeping her voice even and calm. "If he was not the disappearing man from the street, has anyone seen him about today?"

The priestess clutched her hands tighter, shoulders hunching forward. "Not that I've heard, High Priestess."

Of course, he's gone… Julianna waited several heartbeats for Etha to chime in with anything that might be helpful to guide her, but the goddess remained unusually silent. Which, given the rapid degradation of stability, pointed to the one thing Julianna had avoided thinking about. "Thank you for your report, Delia," Julianna said as gently as her own mounting dread allowed her. "You are dismissed to encourage your sisters to join in prayer for Etha to direct me in what this means and how to remedy it."

Blowing out a gust of brisk relief now that she'd been given something else to focus her attention on, Delia unclasped her hands to pluck at the skirt of her robes to issue the High Priestess a curtsey, and slipped free from Julianna's chamber to do as she was told. After a moment of contemplative silence, Julianna quietly stood and closed the door once again.

Her request for prayers would be spread quickly among those active within the temple, and while Etha may be able and willing to ignore a gentle question from her favored priestess, not even Mathias's propensity for rushing into activities which demanded the goddess's full attention would allow her to overlook the focused prayers of so many. It may not have been the most honest way to gain her goddess's attention, but it beat her brother's unconventional methods of doing the same.

Julianna gave the orders time to spread, casting a loathing look at the trunk which housed her travelling clothes. Demons and vampires and undead who fought for justice… Julianna had been a fool to think this crisis might sort out itself if she could manage to placate Mathias. She'd been a fool for allowing the Council to go about their usual operating procedures instead of invoking her divine right to push past protocol and expedite action regarding the reports they'd received. Mathias hadn't made the use of such force an easy path for a Sagewind to take, having abused that ability to the point that Julianna had no choice but to crutch on the law to counterbalance his disregard of the less convenient aspects of it, and Julianna hadn't taken matters into her own hands since that terrible day during the war with the undead when she'd marched into the hells to drag Mathias and Sazrah out of them. Though she didn't doubt her ability to successfully get her way now, Julianna didn't favor the price she'd pay for doing so.

Turning her back to the trunk, continuing to lie to herself that there must be some way around the inevitable, Julianna sank back into her chair. Enough prayers had been generated by now, she was sure. "Etha, you've been awful quiet about all of this."

I'm a little busy.

Julianna wasn't able to find relief in the shortness of the goddess's reply. "Busier with matters more important than those

I've been left to juggle?"

Busy with matters exactly as important as those you've been left to juggle.

Julianna frowned. Always honoring the concept of free will, Etha seldom dispensed direct information, but this was an even greater amount of avoidance than she typically invested in her attempts to cover for Mathias's hastiness. "Where is my dear brother right now?"

Oh… Etha's voice drew out with a ticking reluctance uncommon for her to show Julianna. *Please do not position me between the two of you.*

"Most revered Mother, I beg you not to give me a reason to," Julianna countered. She kept her voice polite, but her centuries of holding authority lay at the foundation of her words. "My duty, first and foremost, is to uphold your will and in doing so, I seek peace and balance and stability for my order. The priestesses are distraught. The people are distraught. The Council will be neither able nor willing to pull itself together to do anything about it if I cannot provide them with the answers they'll demand, and you know they're going to start with Mathias. I'm looking not to position you anywhere, Mother, but for your divine aid to remedy the turmoil infecting the Citadel's halls and the plague creeping closer to the surface of Abaeloth."

When Etha didn't offer a prompt reply to her carefully tailored argument, Julianna felt a brief, smug surge of victory in her chest. She'd been trained well in her youth on how to appease Etha, and though she seldom used that experience to fight as dirty as her brother did, she was, after all, still a Sagewind. She waited patiently for Etha to formulate the answer which wouldn't stomp on Mathias's free will, but would blow whatever cover he'd thought he had.

Mathias— Etha snipped the paladin's name with a tartness Julianna didn't quite recognize—*is on the trail of means to reverse what was done during the Divine Battle, and this is something which interests me more than peace within the Citadel.*

Julianna's eyes widened, not so much in the fact that one of the core tenets she'd always held true was being cast aside because of one of Mathias's crazy ideas, but because of that crazy idea, itself. "Means to reverse what was done during the Divine Battle?" She murmured those words as though unable to comprehend what they could possibly mean. "The demons can be cured of the Children's curse?"

That is what Mathias is trying to find out and I'm hoping to advise him through.

That last was spoken with an authority which stole all of the stubbornness from Julianna. She had always been the obedient one who didn't need the sort of firm reprimands and physical intervention Mathias often required to be guided away from pursuing matters best left alone, and as such, she understood and instantly accepted this as an indisputable order for her compliance. Wherever Mathias was, whatever mess he'd gotten himself tied to, Etha was with him and felt compelled to watch over him. Faith had never been a difficult concept for Julianna to grasp, but knowing that Mathias could be on the cusp of answers—genuine ones this time, as opposed to theories based on wishful thinking—pushed her toward a frustrated impatience.

Let Mathias throw himself at the physical dangers, Etha said to her daughter's unspoken unrest. *It is what he excels at. You are far better suited for navigating the intricacies of the political side of what is developing. If you wish to aid him in the mission he is on, that is where you must keep your focus and direct your energy for now.*

That was all one generous understatement. "Then am I to tell the Council about his discovery?"

I wouldn't until we have more specific information, unless you want *to deal with more of their tantrums.*

Julianna reflected on her vows of transparency and of the responsibility which came with her position of serving as Etha's indisputable voice before the Council. That indisputable voice of Etha, however, had just recommended she keep her mouth shut, and it wouldn't be the first time Julianna had opted to deliberately withhold information from Zeal's governing body as it related to the threat brewing beneath the surface. Sighing, she glanced at her office door and wondered how long she'd be able to avoid a proper summons to court. After the disaster which had been their last meeting, Henrik would soon be demanding to know Mathias's whereabouts and activities, and Julianna had no doubt he'd expect her to recite such answers for him.

"What about the vampire who breached the walls?"

He has been dealt with and will cause Zeal no more concerns.

The prompt delivery of that answer should have comforted Julianna, but there was a fine edge of guilt behind those words, suggesting that both Etha and Mathias had somehow gotten themselves tied up with that creature's treachery, but now was not the time to make a fuss about it. Julianna looked at her door again and frowned, shoulders sagging. She did owe it to the residents of Zeal to at least reassure them that the specific threat of Mathias's report of vampiric activity within the blessed city was of no concern. She sat there a moment longer as she gathered her will and fortitude, then rocked herself to her feet.

"And the Order?" she asked at last. "Are the knights and demon hunters to know what Mathias is up to?"

Etha chose for herself another prolonged silence which did everything but reassure Julianna that matters were as simple as she was letting on. *Have them secure Zeal's walls, but nothing more. No one is to approach Heiligate, as Mathias has an informant in that town who may yet prove beneficial, and I won't have an overzealous knight kill it by mistake. Send word to your deployed priestesses to stay put and send no others out. I will not tolerate one more of my daughters vulnerable on the road.*

Julianna frowned. "If the road is to be dangerous, all the more reason to deploy the demon hunters."

You were given my will, Julianna. You've been spending far too much time with your brother if you think it is up for negotiation.

Julianna flushed at the reprimand and bowed her head in shame for having thought to question Etha's demand. There was still much of this which wasn't quite adding up but, as she'd once believed Mathias was the only one able to stop the march of Ceredulus's undead forces, she had to believe he would be able to stop this threat, too. And this time, so she hoped, they were one step ahead of it instead of two behind.

"I will extend your will, Mother," Julianna said softly. "Please. Watch over Mattie. Don't let him do anything too stupid."

You expect an awful lot from a single goddess, Etha said, her voice grim. *But I will stay with him for as long as I can.*

Figuring that was as good as she was going to get, having known since the days Mathias had still been a rambunctious mortal that his was neither a safe nor comfortable life, Julianna accepted her Etha-given instructions. She stepped forward and placed her hand on the door's handle and, after a steadying breath, stepped out into the temple to deliver her goddess's will and buy Mathias time.

EIGHT

This is quite possibly the most irresponsible thing you've ever done with my blessing.

Mathias bowed his head, but kept his eyes raised enough to keep a wary watch on the small cluster of undead creatures around him, positioning himself between Khin and the potential threats sizing each other up. His nose had nearly quit bleeding and Etha's justifiable temper kept her from lending him the grace to combat the swelling and tenderness which accompanied the break. Mathias bore the punishment silently; if that was the worst thing to come from his actions, he'd consider himself lucky.

Oh, I'm not through with you yet, and I think it's safe to say that Berann *and* Ceredulus—Etha drew out their names pointedly, as though Mathias would have been able to forget them—*have only just begun.*

I'm sorry. Mathias's apology came out laughably small, timid and mournful, mindful of the fact that it would take very little effort for Etha to rip from his chest the shard of Affliction which sustained him and find herself a new champion, one smarter and more resistant to the goading of evil than he was. *I didn't know what else to do.*

Etha allowed Mathias to suffer in her silence for a long, tense moment. The punishments he'd been concocting for himself were all valid possibilities and would certainly serve their purpose, but the paladin's guilt, which he would carry with himself far after the cause of this immediate peril was remedied, had beaten him down enough. Besides, through disappointment and disgust, Etha genuinely loved Mathias. He'd made these choices out of desperation, but hadn't gone about them as recklessly as he would have in gentler circumstances. Ceredulus was bound to him in a strict time frame and with limited freedom. Berann, as humbling as his powers could be, had been deposited in a relatively weak body. Etha had chosen Mathias as her champion all those centuries ago because he didn't shy from the difficult decisions Abaeloth relied on someone making, and he was resilient to the weight which came from needing to make them. Mathias hadn't been the one to bring about this crisis, but he would continue to give of his sanity and peace to end it, and he would never cease trying to earn Etha's forgiveness for the terrible choices he'd had to make.

Well, your work here isn't through yet, Etha said shortly, not yet shedding the entirety of her disappointment from her voice in case Mathias was looking for permission to consider himself off any of the hooks he'd skewered himself on. *If you give Ceredulus much longer to think over means to negotiate with Berann, you'll risk losing what little control you have over them both. I'll let nothing happen to Khin, but Berann is your doing. Now deal with him.*

Had the circumstances not been so tense and dire, Mathias could have easily argued that little of the blame could solely be placed on him, but he was already in over his head and wouldn't press his luck against his goddess's stern stance. With one last, ginger dab at his nose, Mathias cleared his throat and gagged down the tinge of blood which had drained down his nasal cavity, and stepped forward.

"Ceredulus, you and your servant have fulfilled your purpose." The god slowly turned his darkening glare toward the paladin, though Tristan kept his strict gaze locked on the creature who was still experimenting with his balance before them. "I will see to Berann now."

Berann turned his face to Mathias at the mention of his name, eyes hard and sharp like an eagle's, his slight frown lending authority to features which had never embraced aggression in their life. "I am capable of seeing to myself, knight."

Mathias studied the inflexibility within Berann's decree, the demon's broad stance, and his unsteady equilibrium. It had been ages since Berann had needed to maintain his balance on solid ground, and the last time he had, he'd relied on a massive set of wings to negotiate the feat. He hadn't yet acclimated to this new body and though Mathias knew to be wary of the motions of this particular demon's hands—besides knowledge of Berann's status as an ancient, he'd proven his skill and strength with weaving threads by buffering himself from Affliction—the paladin was confident in his current advantages of speed and strength as it stacked against Berann's.

"It is paladin," Mathias said, "but I'll forgive you your ignorance, and you will hear out my demands."

Berann's expression neither faltered nor deepened from its established dissatisfaction. "And why do you presume I would be inclined to listen to you, paladin?"

Taking it as a good sign that Berann had accepted his blunt correction rather than reacting to it, Mathias continued his bid for control. "I am the reason you were tracked down and returned to this realm."

Now, Berann's brows ruffled in confusion and he flicked a glance to Ceredulus. "I'm quite sure it was this god's doing which returned me to this realm."

A delighted cackle rang from Ceredulus, but Mathias's firm step forward and raised voice, even unassisted by Etha, was enough to cut it off. "The only reason you were brought back was for the knowledge you carry."

"And what would any man of your Order do with this knowledge I carry?" Berann sneered, crossing his arms and raising his chin to look down at Mathias with a centuries-old grudge the paladin didn't feel particularly deserving of. "You petty mortals, so frightened of the world that you refuse to understand, hiding and wallowing in the illusion of bliss, have already proven to me that you do not want what I know."

"Petty mortals may not want it, but I am not mortal."

Mathias's statement succeeded in compounding Berann's confusion and, confident he was on the path to gaining ground, he continued. "Your prediction proved true, Berann. Your kind have only continued to grow more violent, and I plan to stop them."

"One man?" Berann asked.

Mathias shook his head. "You'd been one demon seeking to do the same. Your friends Kol and Annin have since generated an army they built from stolen and enslaved souls of mortals. The general of that army is deep in the hells, waiting for me to uncover the answers that will give her the edge she needs to overthrow her captors from the inside and hopefully bring about this peace you sought."

Berann tilted his head to the side, frown pulling deeper. "This general. Is she the Nessix this body remembers?"

Mathias gulped down the realization that Berann had so quickly found a way to navigate Talier's memories before they'd completely faded, and nodded. "She is."

"I will help her," Berann spoke his decision definitively. "She is a brave and noble woman, where you"—he looked Mathias up and down, lips twitching in disgust—"are a brute. You said she is in the hells?"

At Mathias's nod, Berann turned, briefly wobbling for stability at the abruptness of his movement. Arms lifted slightly from his sides, the demon began to march off, giving nobody in this gathering a second look. Both Ceredulus and Tristan snapped their accusing glares at Mathias, as though he'd intentionally driven away their key to uncovering what was going on with the akhuerai. It didn't matter whose fault Berann's dismissive nature was, Mathias had the strongest motive to do something about it, and he shouted his challenge at Berann's back.

"Does it not bother you that Kol and Annin had been your friends and that when next you see them, they will be your enemies?"

Berann clipped to a stop, refraining from turning back to the anxious group, and he hung his head. "It bothers me very much," he said, voice coarse with remorse. "But they chose their paths long ago, as I chose mine. If the memories this body carries are accurate, they've continued down that road to misery and destruction, only confirming that I must stay on mine." As though that justified all that had been and all that may come, Berann resumed his trudge away from the group.

Honor was an unusual concept to consider in a demon, and doing so now made Mathias just as uncomfortable as having been part of raising one from the dead in the first place. He'd invested too much in coordinating Berann's resurrection and refused to simply let him go. With a frustrated sigh, Mathias stalked after the demon's stubborn retreat. "This path you have chosen, will it lead you back into the hells?"

Mathias's prying did not slow Berann and as the paladin continued to chase the demon, Ceredulus hastily gestured for Tristan to help Khin stand so he could join the angsty procession before Mathias distanced himself too far and forced him back into his cage. Tristan, ever obedient, hauled Khin to her feet and practically dragged her along to catch up with his god.

"It will," Berann confirmed, indifferent to the anxious audience tracking after him, "after I retrieve my weapons."

"Then I have a warning for you."

This time, Berann did stop at Mathias's words and, after a moment's contemplation, he turned around to face the paladin. "Then speak it."

Mathias halted a stride away from Berann and stared into eyes so much calmer and more confident than Talier's had ever been, a gaze harboring a stoic intelligence even Mathias felt intimidated by. *Etha, punish me later, but please don't let this be a mistake…* "My Order may have slain you, but the demons have erased you from history and culled all who were willing to speak of you. Any allies you might have had down there have long ago been silenced."

Berann cocked his head, holding Mathias's eyes with a command which tempted the paladin to laugh off his concern and settle for wishing Berann luck on his merry way. "All allies but Nessix, correct?"

Mathias swallowed those doubts and fears, suppressing his growing concerns for the position he was inadvertently putting Nessix in. She'd already had one too many trials forced on her without getting tied up with an undead ancient, but if anyone was capable of handling one more complication, it would be her. When Mathias spoke, his voice threatened to fail him. "Correct."

"Then she will have to be enough."

For the first time in his life, Mathias finally caught a glimpse of how he must have made the Council feel when he refused to be controlled by them as Berann turned to continue his retreat. Gritting his teeth, well aware of the dangers even an outwardly civilized oraku could pose, Mathias reached out and grabbed Berann's arm to stop him. The demon halted, but did not turn back again.

"Are you attempting to stop me, paladin?"

Mathias clenched his teeth around the shivers Berann's hushed question let loose on him. "I have fought the most vile of your kind for centuries now, and I know their modern capabilities better than anyone living or dead."

"Better than they know themselves?"

Mathias bristled even more at Berann's question than he would have had it been intended as a malicious jab. "As far as I'm concerned, you were brought back to tell me how to defeat the demons' reign of terror so I can carry that information to Nessix. Nothing more."

Berann tipped a shoulder back to appraise Mathias once again. "You doubt she and I could carry out my objective, yet feel you would succeed in it without even knowing what it entails?"

When put so bluntly, the proposition did give Mathias pause. "I wouldn't be alone," he said, choosing to leave his connection to Etha ambiguous for now, given Berann's established and understandable distrust of the divine.

"And you think my kind would stand by while you led an army into their tunnels?" Berann jerked his arm free from Mathias's hold, displaying strength the paladin had never expected to discover in Talier's lean frame. "It has been *centuries* since I last dealt with men of your Order and you are *still* this dense?"

Mathias crossed his arms and prayed that Etha, as upset with him as she may be, had his back. "It *has* been centuries since the Order killed you for refusing to discuss matters of Abaeloth's security when questioned, and that is centuries of time your kin have had to become stronger and more devious than when you last saw them. I am offering to *help* you, Berann, but you have to let me."

Berann turned the rest of the way around and frowned as he looked over Mathias, balancing the paladin's limitations against his virtue. The judgmental curl of his lip gained a humored snort from Ceredulus. "Can you see or hear threads?" Berann asked.

"I—" Mathias silenced his debate before it could land him in even more trouble. "No."

"Then you cannot be of service to me."

"Wait," Mathias commanded before Berann resumed his departure. "At least tell me why my knowledge of thread manipulation would matter. Let me try to fix the damage done in the past. I believe we have the same goal."

This time, as Berann attempted to stare down Mathias, the paladin didn't flinch or fidget. The demon glanced over Mathias's shoulder to where Ceredulus and the nobleman who appeared to be missing a soul—the wide-eyed girl clinging to his side—stood and absorbed their interaction with eager attentiveness he had more than a passing notion to be suspicious of. "You want me to speak it now? With this audience here?"

The very reminder of Ceredulus's close proximity stoked Mathias's irritation, and he sighed away his desire to punch the god out of spite in an effort to maintain progress in gaining Berann's compliance. "I really don't."

"Mathias, you *wound* me…" Ceredulus said, though the laugh in his tone clearly conveyed the paladin's hatred didn't sting him in the slightest.

"But I don't see how I have much of a choice," Mathias finished, disregarding Ceredulus's interruption with little more than a snarl. "Help me right this broken world. Let me help you do the same."

Berann stared at Ceredulus a moment longer, weighing out how much he would allow himself to divulge to a god who had already expressed complete ignorance of such an important matter. Slowly, he looked back to Mathias. The paladin's tension suggested he was no more fond of Ceredulus than Berann was, but he'd made his decision, regardless. For the sake of obtaining assistance in the impossible task ahead of him, Berann spoke. "You know of Affliction."

Mathias swallowed the giddy lump which flew up his throat. Was this really happening? After all this time, was the answer he most coveted about to be uncovered? "Yes. The god spear which ended the Divine Battle."

Berann nodded. "It had been forged not only to slay gods, but to withstand the power of other divine weapons, those wielded by the first three children."

Mathias held his breath like a child being told a scary story at bedtime, so focused on Berann's insight of the war he'd served in and survived that he didn't even acknowledge when Tristan and Ceredulus drew closer from their own curiosity.

"Motag wielded the hammer which forged the people of the land. Eriv had his hook to bind the creatures of the seas. And Kalina…" A quick sigh vented out Berann's nose and a bitter remorse passed briskly through his eyes. "Her needles crafted the children of the skies. These three gods had all been given tools which they used to create such beauty until their ambitions pushed them to war.

"These tools, wielded by the divine and breathing with untold strength of their own, became weapons capable of destroying with the same ease which they'd once created. Most of the blame for Abaeloth's destruction and the demons' creation was given to the warring gods, but they could have done very little damage without those weapons. Tell me, paladin, what does your Order say about how the gods were stopped?"

Mathias cleared his throat, having been too intent on the wealth of information in Berann's story to be prepared to speak. "Etha created the fire god Muerick and armed him with Affliction to slay her disobedient children. He cut them down—Motag and Eriv each into four pieces, Kalina into five, and then Etha turned Affliction on him and cleaved him in two, destroying the shaft of the god spear so it could never again be used for such grievous destruction."

Berann nodded solemnly and hoarded the avalanche of memories which flashed in his eyes to himself for a long moment before speaking again. "And what then?"

Mathias shook his head, confused. "The mortals turned the ancient demons away, perpetuating their hatred for those left unscathed by the Divine Battle, and the god shards were eventually discovered by mortals to give rise to the new children."

Berann's brows rose and his attention snapped to Ceredulus before his concern settled. After all, compared to the gods he had known, this one was but a mere fraction of one. He looked back at Mathias. "What does your lore say happened to the god weapons?"

"Etha secured the spearhead of Affliction," Mathias replied, "but the shards of its shaft remain on the surface, still sought after today to be incorporated into various divine practices."

Berann briefly rubbed his chest where one of those shards had been lodged in this body, and nodded in understanding. "And what of the other three weapons?"

Mathias opened his mouth to reply before realizing he didn't have that answer. All of the Order's lore surrounding the Divine Battle revolved around Etha's creation of Zeal, of Affliction, and of the dawning of the demons. A significant percentage of those active within the Order couldn't even name the current pantheon, much less the first of Etha's children. Though Mathias was far more enlightened about matters of the divine than most, he flushed sheepishly, feeling as though this was something he should have investigated decades ago.

"Forgive yourself for your ignorance, paladin. My people had lived through that tragedy, some of us literally walked alongside the monsters who caused it, and it still took us a couple hundred years to wonder what had become of those weapons."

Berann quieted again, his eyes falling out of focus and expression sagging with the weight of memories he'd seemed much more content to deny himself from approaching. Too invested in this story now to risk losing the demon's willingness to talk, Mathias cleared his throat and Berann blinked, shook his head, and continued.

"It was Kol who first thought to seek out Kalina's needles

after we'd been driven into the hells." Berann ignored—or possibly hadn't noticed through the faraway haze still clouding his eyes—Mathias's sneer at the alar's name. "In our mortal years, he'd been our tribe's chiefson and was appointed as the leader of our squad by the air goddess, herself. He'd witnessed her use her needles to create and mend, and he theorized that perhaps if we found what had become of the needles, we might be able to mend the damages done to us during the war."

Mathias's frown deepened. That was a rather honorable and inconvenient report for his view of the vile alar. "And you expect me to believe that any of your kind supported investigating that theory?"

Berann shrugged. "More supported than objected to it. You must remember, it was the mortals and your goddess who turned us away long before we ever organized hostile intentions to declare war on your realm. We set out to locate the needles, secured them in the hells, and Annin and I invested the next few years studying them. It turned out Kol's theory was more right than wrong."

Had Mathias been flanked by anyone other than Ceredulus and Tristan, he'd have grabbed either of them for support against the weakness which crept into his knees. As it was, he broadened his stance and crossed his arms to try and generate stability for himself. "What does that mean?" His voice raked over the question with disbelief.

"The needles were incapable of mending us back into creatures the mortal world would accept. Divine though they were, they couldn't heal the scars dealt to us. But they could untangle the threads which held our souls in place, stripping us of the powers we'd fallen into and condemning us to age and die the way your Etha's parameters had designed creation to do."

Mathias did stagger now and pressed a hand to his head. All this time, there had been a way to neutralize demons? To remove the aspects which made them powerful enough to pursue their dark path? Possibly even to open the pathways to their redemption? *Etha... does Zenos have any record—*

Hush, her voice was no less subdued than Mathias's and no longer carried a scolding tone. *Zenos wasn't even alive yet. We had no record keeper then. Let Berann keep talking.*

"This discovery," Berann continued past Mathias's obvious distress, "caused a great deal of turmoil in the hells. Overnight, the curses we'd received from the Divine Battle became viewed as blessings, fear of how we'd survive in a world which continued to hate us without those unnatural strengths spurring the most powerful among us toward madness. There was a small faction who continued to want peace, who wanted to be cleansed, but there were so many more who wanted war, to bring suffering to those who had survived and abandoned us after we'd been so corrupted. That marked the rise of the inoga, and the point where I took Kalina's needles and ran. I wouldn't be able to face the hells on my own, but I'd believed if I could convey what I'd learned to those in Zeal, whose beacon had always shone for divine justice, I'd have help in doing so."

Mathias lowered his eyes, a surge of guilt on behalf of those who had come before him flooding him to his ears. "And we hadn't even let you speak."

"No," Berann said, his voice harsh. "You hadn't."

"And the other two god weapons?" Mathias asked. "What happened to them?"

"Last I knew, the demons came to the surface in force to hunt them down. I was slain before I knew if their search had been successful."

The demon war... Mathias thought bleakly. *It hadn't been about attacking mortals at all. They'd only been after securing what could be their downfall...*

"And," Berann said, his voice only breaking through Mathias's racing thoughts due to how hungry the paladin was for honest, unbiased answers after all these years of turmoil, "finding a way to use these weapons to cleanse my brothers and sisters from the sins forced upon them is what I'd sought to accomplish then and continue to seek now."

Mathias couldn't form words either out loud or in prayer. He could hardly form cohesive thoughts at all past his shock. The answer had been sitting right there on the surface, and the Order had killed the only one willing to share knowledge of it.

"Since you hadn't even known of the weapons' existence until now," Berann continued, "is it safe to assume you don't know if my kind were successful in finding them?"

Desperate to be of assistance now that hope had been unveiled, Mathias pushed through his disbelief to draw upon the reports Julianna had given him about how the demon war had concluded after his death, about how the bulk of the demons' forces simply disappeared from regions one at a time before sinking back into the hells. All of Zeal, Mathias included, had thought the beasts had lost interest after their years of terrorizing the mortals, certainly not thinking the demons had considered themselves beaten. But now, knowing what Berann did, Mathias and his tactical mind saw the truth at last. Demons didn't tire of asserting themselves; they'd withdrawn because they had accomplished their objective. Mathias moistened his lips and rubbed the back of his neck.

"I'd venture to guess they found the other two weapons, based on their marching patterns." Mathias frowned as he reconsidered every other divine attribute the first children had shed upon Abaeloth. "And as hungry as mortals are to claim power for themselves, if those weapons still existed on the surface, someone would have found them by now."

Berann's grim frown had sank deeper with the first half, but lightened with a humored ease as Mathias completed his statement. "I wouldn't be so sure of that."

"Oh?" Mathias crossed his arms. "Why not?"

"Because." Berann turned and resumed walking, his stride more buoyant than his earlier dutiful trudge. The others followed readily behind him. "After the initial reception mortals had shown my kind, I'd thought it best to hide the needles before marching on Zeal to protect them from hands that may not use them in the most appropriate manner. Given the way your Order greeted me, it seems as though doing so had been a wise decision."

"I'm sorry," Ceredulus interjected, his arrogance shining brightly through his previous concerns. "The moment word got out about the god shards and the power they held, there was not one stone on all of Abaeloth left untouched by mortal hands. And there are still enthusiastic brigades hunting down slivers of Affliction for use in the divine arts. You mean to tell me that you believe a pair of needles harboring the wrath of a primordial goddess had gone undetected for all this time?"

Mathias glanced from Berann's relaxed shoulders to Ceredulus's scowl and smiled. Perhaps they'd just stumbled upon one of the god's insecurities; Ceredulus often fancied himself a brilliant and observant scholar, yet the fact that he'd neither known the value of these weapons nor stumbled upon them himself in his initial quest to control the world couldn't be doing much to raise his self-esteem.

"Of course nobody found them," Berann replied. "I told you I'd hidden them."

Ceredulus snarled like an undisciplined puppy at Berann's dismissive tone. "You truly think *hiding* something is enough to escape treasure hunters?"

"If they were hidden by an average man? No. But they'd been hidden by an ancient oraku, and I know they are still above ground."

As much as Mathias would have loved to watch this scuffle between these two play out, he was still on a mission for information—information which would be exponentially more difficult to obtain if the opposing immortals sank any deeper into this debate—and he had to decide to be the mature one. "What makes you so certain?"

"I hear them."

All three men in pursuit of the demon shook their heads or narrowed their eyes in consideration of what Berann could possibly mean, but Ceredulus and Tristan allowed Mathias to be the one to voice his confusion.

"What do you mean?"

Berann shot a challenging look over his shoulder, designed solely to stoke Ceredulus's irritation. "Abaeloth has continued to refuse to evolve?" When the group glanced at each other, all silently asking what Berann could possibly be talking about, the demon sighed. "Most thread weavers operate off sight to locate threads in themselves and the subject of their manipulation. I've got that talent, but had always been able to hear them, as well. I'd tried to teach this skill to others in the past, but it seems to be a trait one must be born with. As it is, I'd attuned myself closely to the needles at the time I separated from them, and I know their song well. Even now, I can hear them—distant, but not out of this realm." He stopped again and turned to Mathias. "How far are we from Zeal?"

Mathias gazed around at the endless stretch of grassland around him. There were no curls of smoke from farmhouse chimneys, the haze of the horizon distorting what could have been mountains in the distance. It was quiet and peaceful, besides the company, but that didn't provide him any insight as to their location. "I'm not even sure where we are."

Tristan coughed and slowly shook his head to mock Mathias's ignorance. "By march on foot, we are a couple days northwest of the city."

Berann's frown tightened at Tristan's report, but he hadn't taken his attention off Mathias. "I would have you accompany me, paladin, in case there are any of your Order who seek to cause me trouble when I enter the region to retrieve my weapons. I've no desire to cause anyone harm, but I will not make the same mistake twice."

While Mathias trusted nobody but himself to escort the undead demon to his destination, it was simply an option he could not afford. "It would boot the soul out of your body—no matter who sewed it in place—if I tried to teleport you there and, besides, we need to get to Elidae."

"Elidae?" Berann asked.

"That's where the demons who have his girlfriend have gone to ground," Tristan answered.

Berann gave Mathias a curt nod, but no other consolation. "Unless there have been some extensive renovations since I was alive, there are only four locations in all the hells capable of completely shrouding the sort of power these weapons contain. One is here, beneath Gelthin, but the only song I can hear belongs to the needles. The next two are beneath the continent called Selian, and I doubt my old associates would have been foolish enough to store the weapons in such close proximity of each other.

The last—"

"Is beneath Elidae," Mathias concluded. It made perfect sense. Elidae was the oldest land mass, the one with the rawest divine connections. It was where Etha had decided to bury Affliction and the perfect tomb for any other artifact rumored to hold such power.

"Odds are good you and I will both find the treasures we seek under that island," Berann said.

"Then come with me," Mathias suggested, already trying to sort out how to convince Ceraphlaks to carry a demon. "Let us enter the hells there, together."

Berann crossed his arms. "As far as you know, is that still the region Annin resides in?"

"Yes, but—"

"He is too tenacious and formidable a foe to rush in on, even for me. I taught him much of what he knows, but that which I didn't teach him is what makes him frightening. First, I retrieve the needles and the second weapon to arm an ally. Then, I head to Elidae. I will not face Annin unprepared."

Mathias wanted to argue with Berann, to remind him that if not for his help, he'd still be a sad, lost soul floating about this field. He wanted to demand that Nessix was his first priority in all of this. But then, he thought of how disappointed and frustrated Nes would be if he showed up with information but no actual leads on any of these weapons. He thought of how Sazrah had begged him to come and how she and her defeated force were counting on him for their survival. Mathias *had* chosen to be part of bringing Berann back, a decision which still unsettled him, but one he'd executed without persisting regret. This demon, undead though he was, had been a traitor to his own people, and if Mathias truly wanted his help, he was going to have to try to trust him.

"I must reach Elidae as soon as possible," he said.

"And why is that?" Berann asked. "What could be more important to you than finding and implementing a cure to my people's curse?"

Mathias ignored the mocking glares from Tristan and Ceredulus, much more comfortable facing Berann's civility. He swallowed his reluctance to admit his weakness. "I've got troops there in desperate need of my aid, wounded when trying to keep Nessix from being dragged into the hells. They'd taken that position at my request, and thus I am responsible for their welfare and recovery. I must go to them."

Berann accepted Mathias's reply with a short nod, ignoring the other two men completely. "You are honorable, paladin. May I have your name?"

"I am Mathias Sagewind."

"Very well, Mathias," Berann said. "If you must reach Elidae within the day, I will release you to do so and trust that you have means to see it done. But I will not risk facing Annin without that which I know will give me the upper hand. I must locate the needles and that will take time you suggest not having. But if you wait for me on Elidae, I will find a way to send for you once I arrive. I will help you reach your Nessix, and we can finish what I'd tried to start long ago."

In the span of this single conversation, Mathias had gone from hating himself for the evils he'd participated in to hating himself for entertaining the idea of throwing his trust in this demon.

Hmm… I've never been able to pry all that deep into demons, and Ceredulus's hold on this one makes it that much harder, but I think he's telling the truth.

And if Mathias had thought he was frustrated before… *After all the grief you gave me, you're* liking *this undead demon now?*

Like's a bit of a relative word in this case, Etha said, *but he's at least speaking sense in regards to the potential of those weapons and where they'd mostly likely be found. Besides,* she added in stride, *he hasn't made even the slightest indication of trying to hurt any of you.*

Mathias frowned and cautiously touched the side of his nose.

Okay, but that was less directed at you and more payback to the Order as a whole.

I don't see how that makes any difference…

Berann stood by patiently as Mathias worked matters out with his goddess, and just as the demon was about to attempt another round of negotiations, Ceredulus beat him to speaking. "Mathias has all sorts of ways to flash himself to Elidae, and I've got an idea of how you can reach these weapons of yours faster than you could fly to them if you still had wings."

Berann, though he'd done a fine job expressing his distaste for and distrust of any resident of the divine realm, turned a curious eye to Ceredulus, and Mathias reactively gripped the hilt of his sword at the god's efforts to make headway in amending the demon's opinions. "Any assistance you can offer me will be appreciated," Berann said.

Mathias took a bold step between the demon and the god, holding a dismissive hand in front of himself to gain influence over Berann. "Now, hold on—"

Ceredulus grasped Mathias's wrist, freezing the paladin's movement and motives in one action as he slid him a sly glance. "The sooner we sort this out, the sooner you get to your troops, Mathias. The sooner Berann can find these treasures, the sooner you can find your Nessix, and the demons can be stopped just like you've always dreamed of. I'll throw in my voluntary return to my cage upon the completion of the current negotiations if you'll shut your mouth long enough for Berann to hear me out."

From behind Mathias, Tristan gasped at the god's ready surrender of his borrowed freedom, but Mathias was one step ahead of the vampire. Ceredulus was after one of these weapons; if Mathias's blessed blade could part the Veil, one of the original god weapons would be able to do the same and—Mathias suspected— much more to benefit the god.

Berann either missed or ignored all of these social cues just as he'd overlooked the previous ones, and crossed his arms. "Then speak, child god."

Ceredulus tilted his head to the side, brows twitching in muzzled outrage as he fought down the urge to correct his newest creation for his disrespect. "My servant, Tristan, is capable of fast travel and he is the one who carried the body you now inhabit here from Zeal."

"No—"

Berann raised a hand at Mathias to silence his objections, eyes locked firmly with Ceredulus's. "I've had a less than mutually beneficial history with the divine. What grounds do I have to trust either you or a servant of yours with my life's mission?"

Mathias followed Berann's focus, watching Ceredulus carefully for tells of the god's deceit. The only redeeming quality Ceredulus had was his lawfulness—it was a condition he had imposed on himself in order to take command over souls designed to thrive off free will. If the god gave his word, he would keep it, but that didn't mean he wouldn't search for ways to slip in terms he could later exploit.

"My domain is the undead," Ceredulus said. When Berann tilted his head, brows furrowing at the concept, the god elaborated. "Those returned to physical function after their mortal lives have ended. Those like you. For centuries, this miracle could only be achieved through worship of me or, in Mathias's case alone, the workings of the Mother Goddess. As you've so bluntly made clear, your kind have very little regard for mine, yet they've succeeded in finding a way to return sentience and function to the dead, bringing about these creatures Mathias called akhuerai. Creatures just like Nessix, who is waiting to help you overthrow your old friends. I intend to find out how they have managed this without my blessing and demand appropriate reparation for this practice, and I will do whatever I must to aid those who can guide me to this justice."

"You've got no interest in these weapons Berann spoke of?" Mathias asked.

"Oh, I've got great interest in them, but I'm smart enough to know that as long as you and Berann are up and running about and within Abaeloth that I don't stand a chance at possessing one. Rest assured, Mathias. Tristan will help Berann reach these artifacts, but he'll have no orders from me to make off with them." He flashed a cunning smile at Mathias, one which the paladin knew was hiding some sort of advantage he couldn't readily identify. "Now, how about you start delivering on some of that faith Etha's supposed to impart in those who walk her path and let us begin putting an end to the demons?"

Mathias's eyes narrowed as Ceredulus's plan began to take form before him. Etha had built Abaeloth to operate in balance, and ridding it of demons would leave a gaping void on the scales that someone else would have to fill. He had every reason to believe that Ceredulus's interests revolved around punishing the demons for overlooking him in the creation of akhuerai, but his ambitions were maturing rapidly now that he'd managed to suck Mathias into his plans.

At least you've got job security, Etha quipped.

I hadn't been looking for job security, Mathias muttered.

"Your fears are growing tedious," Berann told Mathias. "I thought paladins were courageous men of action."

Ceredulus's features sharpened into a smile and Tristan coughed on a laugh, leaving Mathias ruminating uselessly on the fact that all three of these creatures he'd convinced himself were untrustworthy monsters were right. The harder he dug in to resisting, the longer he took in compromising this final, easy step after he'd already compromised so much, the worse off everyone would be. It should have said something that not one of them had given any indication of shady behavior, but Mathias missed the trusty advice of his morals. None of this was going how he'd planned.

And just how had *you planned to extract the secrets of a centuries-deceased demon?* Etha asked.

A quiet groan of displeasure creaked in Mathias's throat. This mess he'd made was bound to get messier the more time he wasted trying to justify his actions. "Fine," he said, meeting Berann's steady gaze with what hardly passed for authority. "Gather what you must to give us the upper hand and meet me on Elidae to find Nessix. If I have even the slightest whim that you mean to betray any of the intentions you've let on so far, I will personally march into the hells and warn every last demon I encounter where you are and what you're aiming to accomplish."

"Now, Sir Sagewind," Tristan scoffed, "blackmail is hardly a noble virtue—"

"That is fair to demand," Berann interrupted, earning Tristan's shock and Mathias's gruff approval. "His mission relies on the success of mine and he has no inherent reason to trust me on my word alone." He met Mathias's eyes and gave him a nod of solidarity. "I continue to want peace between your people and mine. That can only exist through obtaining these weapons, and I have no desire to imperil my chances of success. Take my word for what you will."

Mathias nodded and turned next to Tristan. "And if *you* do anything to hinder his pace or objective—"

Tristan rolled his eyes and flung a hand Mathias's direction as if to swat away the paladin's concerns. "Please. What do you think you could possibly do to me?"

"Your god has already agreed to return to the Veil once the current negotiations are through. If you do anything at all to thwart Berann, I will fling you in there after him and neither of you will set foot outside its confines again."

Fury, as refined as everything else about Tristan, set in across the vampire's brow, and Khin instantly launched into a tirade of objections in his defense, but Ceredulus interjected smoothly before Mathias's demand of expedited pace was needlessly imperiled. "Tristan will serve Berann as he would serve me and escort him to each location he must reach as briskly as possible." Tristan's lip twitched as he swallowed the urge to complain about his god's order, and he clapped a hand over Khin's mouth to silence her. Ceredulus accepted the vampire's grudging compliance with a slight incline of his head and returned his gaze to Mathias. "You have my most sincere word."

Mathias still couldn't settle the twisting ball of discomfort that came from Ceredulus's willingness to return to his prison, but no matter what scheme the wicked god was concocting, it would simply have to be dealt with later. There was just one more arrangement to be made. Mathias turned to Khin.

The girl met his eyes with an indignant pout and pulled Tristan's hand from her mouth. "I'm going with him." She nodded her head toward Ceredulus before Mathias could begin addressing her.

Mathias stared at the girl mutely, ignoring Tristan's sharp smirk and actively pushing back against Ceredulus's steady glow of satisfaction. "Khin," the paladin spoke firmly, "you don't know what—"

"Quit talking down to me," she snapped, her eyes darting away from him and an anxious flush brightening her cheeks.

Though she was ready to stand her ground, she was still afraid to do so. "I know exactly what I'm doing."

Mathias shook his head. "Three weeks ago, you barely knew who Etha was. This"—he flung a hand toward Ceredulus, neglecting to give the god any more recognition or respect than that—"is—"

"Ceredulus," Khin snipped. "God of the undead. Tristan's been teaching me. He's been answering my questions."

Mathias gaped at Khin in disbelief, each beat of Ceredulus's gentle laughter from behind him digging another finger into the wounds in his discipline. "Trusting in Ceredulus nearly got you killed."

Khin swallowed the lump in her throat which begged her to let this all drop and gush apologies she wouldn't mean. She'd been meek for too long. "But it didn't. He got here when it counted."

Mathias groaned and threw his head back. How could he explain to this misguided child the danger she was in? "If you go with Ceredulus, he will have no choice but to take you into the Veil."

"So?"

"Those who enter the Veil, Khin, are not able to leave it."

A momentary pulse of concern passed through the girl's eyes at Mathias's cold warning, lingering a moment longer as her timid glances between Tristan and Ceredulus revealed that Mathias was telling the truth. Committed, Khin crossed her arms and imagined that she had the confidence to raise her chin. "I've seen enough of life on your side of the Veil and choose to believe the other side can't be any worse."

Ceredulus rewarded her determination with a smile before sliding his eyes to the perturbed paladin. "She will be treated well in my care, Mathias. The chivalrous thing to do is to respect her decision."

"Respect it?" Mathias's argument rapidly shriveled away as one last, bitter swell stormed in Khin's dark eyes. All she'd ever been looking for was his respect and, due to the volatile circumstances of Abaeloth's impending doom, he'd never given it to her beyond common courtesy. He wouldn't keep it from her now, but that didn't make him any less displeased with the circumstances. "You could have had so much more."

Khin's frown rolled deeper as she recollected all of Mathias's laments over Nessix, how he'd spoken so highly of her skills and worth, the fondness behind the looks and touches he'd given her. He'd invested all of his thoughts and energy into that woman who had led the demons here, overlooking everything Khin had to offer and everything she had needed, and she would not allow him to pretend to care now. "No," she said. "I couldn't have. I know what I'm doing, Mathias. I've made enough mistakes in my life to know when I'm walking into one, and this isn't it. Thank you for rescuing me. Thank you for leading me to where I was destined to go. But now, you have to let me walk my own path."

The determination set across the young woman's face dared Mathias to try to challenge her again and he realized he'd have to use physical force against her if he wanted to stop her. As far as he'd already fallen, that was a step he simply refused to take. Ideals singing their final song as they rolled over to die in the harshness of a reality Mathias had sacrificed so much to keep from dawning, the paladin lowered his head in submission at last.

"I wish you well, Khin," he said softly. "If you believe in nothing else I've ever said, believe that. If I could have prevented any of—"

"Stop," Khin said. "I know your feelings on it, but this is my choice to make, my responsibility to claim. Go fight for Nessix and Etha and those worthy of your attention, and let me build a place for myself."

There was nothing Mathias could say to her declaration and so he stayed silent as Ceredulus walked past him, hand extended. Khin shot Mathias one final, resolute glance and, with a deep breath, took the god's hand.

"Tristan?" Ceredulus said, not taking his eyes from the emboldened young woman. "You have your orders. Do not disappoint me."

"Never, my lord."

Ceredulus didn't look back at Mathias or throw him any last antagonizing remarks as he smoothly closed the distance between himself and Khin. He released her hand to slide his arm across her shoulders like the protective wing of some great carrion bird and, after a quick moment of regret that his bout of freedom was nearly and prematurely through, he snuggled Khin closer against his side, fingers closing down on her arm, and stepped away from Mathias until the terms of their agreement had been breached. Both god and his charge disappeared in a flash.

A hand slapped down on Mathias's shoulder and the paladin bristled at the touch.

"Well, that's that, Sir Sagewind." Tristan, comfortable that Mathias wouldn't do anything that would risk Berann's success, didn't flinch at Mathias's biting glare. "I'll make sure Berann stays on track. You've got your urgent matters on Elidae to tend to. We will see you there." Tristan held Mathias's vicious sneer easily, mocking the paladin's helplessness with how much more control he had over the current circumstances, and with a soft laugh, he turned to face Berann. "To protect us both, I suggest we waste no more time exchanging ugly looks."

Berann, too, kept his eyes on Mathias, but his focus was less on the fact that the paladin was barely clinging onto control and tied up more with why that was. He hadn't been lying when he said he had no desire to cause any unnecessary harm, and though the Order had wronged him in the past, besides a little inconvenient fussing, Mathias had not yet done so and Berann wished him no ill will. As Berann had vowed to protect Abaeloth from the retribution of demonkind, Mathias had made the same pledge, and Berann was witnessing firsthand the sacrifices this man was making to uphold it. The fastest way both to satisfy himself and this unlikely ally was to get moving.

"I will find you on Elidae," Berann said. "And we will finish this together." He turned from Mathias to face Tristan. "If you have a way to get me close to Zeal, I request you do so now."

Berann may have taken the high road, but Tristan couldn't be bothered to search for it. "We're there."

Before Mathias could offer even another glare, the vampire took a step back to hook a shoulder beneath Berann's arm and with a burst of air from the hastiness of his departure, left Mathias standing quiet and alone in this field somewhere in the west of Gelthin. Closer to answers than ever before, on the brink of healing the greatest wound Abaeloth had ever received, why did he still feel like he was failing? For better or worse, Etha didn't aid him in settling on that answer and, determined to do *something* right, having only one logical destination, anyway, Mathias departed for Elidae.

NINE

Sleep came to Nessix in brief glimpses, letting her exhaustion from the hasty flight sink her into its embrace only to catch horrifying visions of the grotesque tortures awaiting her. Her stomach churned for food now that her dream stop had been fully digested, and though the pain of hunger bore into her, she was grateful she wouldn't have to contend with substantial nausea when trying to block out Grell's amusement. She'd just let her eyes close once again when the bar lifted from her door and by the time it opened, she'd pushed herself upright.

As Kol had predicted, it was two underlings who had come to fetch her, and before she could stand, the faster of the two rushed up and smashed his fist into her face. Nessix cried out at the sudden impact and crouched over to try bringing her fingers to her nose and assess for damage, but two pairs of rough hands gripped her shoulders and pulled her to her feet. They didn't wait for her to find balance through her daze before dragging her out of the barren room, and it took Nessix a few minutes to gather her cramped and tingling legs to coordinate so she could walk alongside them.

"Where's your fight, bitch?" the one on her left asked. "We were told you'd bring one."

For a moment, Nessix entertained the idea of coaxing these

two demons into killing her and postponing Grell's fun, banking on the notion that he'd vent his displeasure on them, but she wanted fewer complications, not more. If Grell was already at his wit's end with Kol, they may not have much time to put whatever plan he'd concocted into motion. Nessix hung her head from her escorts.

"What's there left for me to fight for?" she asked. "Haven't you already won?"

The demons cackled in predictable acceptance of her bluff. "Think Grell will let us hang around to watch?" the one on the right asked.

"He never does," griped the other. "He reserves all the good stuff for those with real rank and station."

"How good you think good's going to get this time?"

"For *this* rotten wench?" The demon gave Nessix a rough shake which she accepted in the dejected nature expected of her. "I'd be surprised if he's done with her before dinner."

As the two demons continued to speculate on how Grell would punish her—and speculate was all they could do since neither of them had ever witnessed one of his torture sessions—Nessix concentrated on walking, one foot in front of the other, like the brave soldier she was. She wasn't familiar with the halls they were taking her down, and the fog of fatigue did nothing to help her recollection of the hells' layout. All she could determine for sure was that they were travelling up a mild incline, decidedly away from the chasm which she sorely prayed still housed her functional army. Several more minutes passed of her guards' increasingly violent wishes for her before the lag of exhaustion and the final numbing wisps from the dream stop filtered away enough for Nessix's memory to ignite at last.

They were heading for the conference chamber, the same room where the inoga gathered to pitch their fits and engage in their inane bragging.

Bound, starving, and still dazed from a combination of physical and mental strains, the only resistance Nessix managed to deliver against her guards was a slowing of her gait before the demon on her left slapped her on the back to propel her forward again.

The days of Nessix having the luxury of wants were once again behind her, and her hopes of even Mathias being able to fix her problems dashed from sight the moment Grell's voice boomed out the open door. Unable to fight, not seeing what good it would do her now anyway, Nessix let the guards shove her through the doorway and in front of the panel of inoga lords and their respective subordinates. The rich aroma of seasoned meats wafted to her and her stomach twisted tighter at its influence. Buffering the sensation as much as she could with a hearty gulp, Nessix quickly surrendered to the fact that her torture would be their meal time entertainment.

She kept her eyes lowered in an effort to hold her courage intact as over a dozen malicious demons perked up at her arrival. Their conversations cut off, though the smacking of chewing suggested they weren't quite interested enough to abandon their meals, and Grell's mocking voice punctuated the sounds of their eating.

"Have you got anything to say for yourself, little one?" The inoga continued to use Kol's term of endearment for Nessix in some grand effort to further degrade them both, his voice slightly muffled by food he'd yet to swallow. "Any pleas you feel like throwing to us or your master?"

There was a dull thump and sharp choke as Grell slapped Kol on the back, but Nessix still couldn't raise her eyes. She was here to receive her punishment, wanted it through with as quickly as possible, and would do what she could to protect Kol from getting further caught up in it. Everything about Grell's questions—from his patronizing tone to his word choice and his physical indication toward Kol—had been formulated to antagonize her, but Nessix had already faced too much in her life to give in to such simple goading so easily. Inwardly smirking at how offended Grell would be at her defiance, Nessix stayed silent and deepened her focus on a loose stone on the floor to keep from betraying Kol with a hasty glance his way.

Gradually, the slurps and chewing came to a stop as every demon in the room waited for the excuses and begging that always came with these sorts of meetings. When Nessix continued to hold

101

her tongue, Grell slammed his hands on the tabletop and sprang to his feet.

"I said explain yourself, whore!"

Nessix clenched her teeth around the urge to flinch from Grell's anger, but continued to stand her ground as the beast fumed before her. The angrier he got, the more careless he'd become, and the faster this would be over.

"If that's how you want it," Grell growled. "Bear her soul for us and string her up."

The guard on her left departed and the one on her right stepped in front of her to tear her blouse down the middle to expose the ring in her chest. The ominous clank of a chain passing over gears groaned from overhead. Nessix's only fear in this ordeal was something irreparable happening to what little she had left of her soul, and her heart leapt to her throat at the sudden instinct to swing her shackled wrists around to clock the nearby guard in the face. So outnumbered and so incredibly vulnerable, she curled her fingers into fists and prayed that Kol still had enough influence to keep her safe at least in this regard. The chain's clacking stopped and Nessix allowed the demon beside her to grab her bound wrists to secure them over the hook dangling above her, and the clanking came again as she was lifted from the ground.

Her slow ascension stopped mere seconds after her feet left the floor, tormenting her aching shoulders with how close stability was, and she fought against the screaming of her muscles to twist around in search of relief which wouldn't be there. From this elevated position, she was able to sneak a glance across the panel before her as they casually went about their dining. The entire chamber could have been packed shoulder to shoulder with demons and Nessix would have still gotten hung up on Kol. Her alar sat to Grell's right, teeth clenched and eyes hardened with a discipline Nessix hadn't seen in him before. He met her gaze firmly as she swept hers by, refusing to react to the brief spark of hope she felt briefly flicker to life, and a nauseating emptiness bloomed in her gut until Grell's voice intercepted her fretting.

"I told you we'd bring her back," the inoga declared, prompting Nessix to hang her head once more. "And, as promised, punishment is due. The two of you are dismissed." The pair of demons who had brought Nessix here grumbled obscenities and scuffed out of the room, slamming the door behind them, and Grell continued. "Finish your dining, and we can all savor her screams for dessert."

Nessix shuddered at Grell's words and the mixed commentary which followed. It wasn't that she feared the methods he would employ to find those screams—though she couldn't claim she looked forward to them—but the humiliation she faced hanging before these monsters like a side of beef. Pride urged her to fight to free herself, but her greater desire to deny Grell the satisfaction of seeing how well his chosen tactics worked overruled it. Nessix grit her teeth against the provocative discussion Grell drummed up of how he planned to use her army and tried to disregard Inek's steady insistence that he deserved at least a few swings at her after how many of his troops had died because of her. She kept her eyes focused on the ground below her and bit back her snarl as a bare bone was flung at her, pelting her bare chest before falling to the ground. She couldn't look up as the sounds of the demons' feasting tapered off into the scraping of dishes being shoved aside, satisfied groans announcing the end of their meals.

"We've all been patient for this day," Grell said as two heavy clunks of metal objects being placed on the tabletop sounded. "Though this maggot has proven a benefit to the function of our akhuerai, it hasn't been without cost to us." Another clunk followed. "As Inek's been crying about, she's killed our subordinates." There was a new sound, a metallic rattle and snap which repeated like a lazy metronome. "As Annin's reported, she's left her army in disarray." Nessix lifted her head just enough to catch the glint of the metal device Grell twirled in his right hand before slapping it into his left. "And as we all know, her stay in Zeal has put our realm in grave danger. It is time she learns her place." The twirling stopped as Grell held the device out to his right, aggressively maintaining eye contact with Nessix. "Kol, the honors?"

Nessix had taken beatings from Kol in the past, but they'd always been quick reprimands expressed in the most effective way he knew how to deliver them. This, however, was meant to be different and they'd both known it going in. This was supposed to be Grell's grand display of dominance as he took out his frustration on Nessix for all of the trouble she'd made for him. She and Kol both knew that the inoga wanted to see them both suffer and this decision he'd made, the smug smirk and narrowed eyes he cast on Nessix, adequately conveyed that he wasn't completely ignorant to her sense of loyalty to Kol. Nessix's shudder as Kol tore the device from Grell was blocked by the strain of her hyperextended shoulders, and she bit down on the insides of her cheeks to keep from objecting to what was unfolding before her. It wasn't supposed to be like this.

Kol's eyes had steeled over with a cruel resolve Nessix had seen him throw at lesser ranked demons, but never at her, the clench of his jaw sharpening the angles of his face as he gracefully leapt over the table and approached her. He'd hidden every underlying sign of his affection for her so thoroughly that Nessix, in her vulnerable position, had to wonder which version of him was the act. That shudder forced itself on Nessix now, pinching so sharply through her taxed muscles that her eyes watered as Kol stalked up to her. Each step closer deepened the resolve in his eyes, but also revealed to Nessix the rapid tremor of his upper lip which he disguised as a snarl.

"Cut her down," Kol commanded, his voice foreign to Nessix with the chill of orders.

Nessix dropped to the floor in an instant, battered by the chain which had held her as it raced free from its pulley. Exhausted, dazed, and rapidly succumbing to the fear Grell had meant to impose on her, Nessix squirmed beneath the chain's weight until Kol's hand closed over hers. She froze at the gentleness of his touch, breath catching as she looked up to see the quiet plea for obedience buried deep in his burning eyes. Half a heartbeat later, his fingers bit down into her flesh and he dragged her to her feet and pulled her close, invading her space like he'd done so many times before.

"I do not wish to hurt you, little one," he murmured in Nessix's mother tongue.

The reassurance touched the most frightened parts of Nessix, but she could have gone without hearing his regret. Unable to respond without the risk of falling apart, Nessix swallowed her nausea and tried to tune out how hard her arms trembled on the other end of Kol's steady grasp. She'd known her punishment was coming and though it was being delivered in a manner she hadn't expected, she would face it.

"Do be thorough, Kol." Grell's voice boomed through the still chamber. "You do remember how much she likes to grab weapons she's not supposed to have, don't you?"

Nessix glanced for the first time at the wicked pair of pliers in Kol's hand, paling at the wolf-like teeth clenched along its crushing surface. Hot waves of panic swept over her as she internalized the anticipated pain of what was to come, and Nessix silently pleaded to Kol to free her from her bindings and arm her properly. They were close enough to the door, they could flee before any of the inoga could organize their wits or their bulky bodies to react. If he were to pull her out of the hells again, if he could fly her to the temple where Sulik and his troops were hiding, she'd find a way to convince them to spare them both. She truly believed Kol's gentle vow of not wanting to hurt her, and that was why her blood froze as he wedged the fingers of his left hand into her clenched fist to work her fingers free. She tried to recoil, but his grip held fast, and he smoothly fit the pliers over the first knuckle of her right pinky. Nessix had prepared herself for a lashing, for the bite of clean lacerations, rhythmic punishments she'd be able to desensitize herself to, not the agony that waited on the closing of Kol's fist. Her stomach lurched.

"N—" Nessix tensed her muscles to try to pull away, but Kol grimaced and crushed his grip down on the lever before she had the chance to misalign his efforts. Having clung to the ridiculous hope that she'd had a chance at talking Kol out of this barbaric torture, Nessix hadn't fully braced herself for the pain, and she screamed in agony as her joint fractured, knees buckling.

Kol frowned, eyes growing colder as he methodically denied his feelings for Nessix. This was the only way to keep them both alive.

Nessix reactively pulled away, casting tear-rimmed eyes up at Kol's darkening ones, as he snatched her arms back and jerked them forward again. The device slid over her next knuckle and crushed down, and then the next. When trying to escape Kol didn't work, Nessix attempted to curl her functioning fingers closer against her palms, but the tugging of her tendons against the existing injuries prevented her from being able to do so with the necessary strength to fight Kol's grip. By the fourth finger, desperation beat out any notion of obedience, and Nessix made an attempt to twist her arms around to knock the pliers from Kol's hands. The audience which Nessix had nearly forgotten about gasped in anticipation of the fight she now offered and burst into a chorus of laughter as Kol drew back his hand and bludgeoned her with the wicked device. The blow stunned Nessix even through her existing agony, and she was saved from collapsing only by Kol hefting her back into balance.

"Do not. Fight me."

Nessix could hardly register his words through the ringing in her ears, much less identify the concern woven deep within them. The next joint burst and she could no longer differentiate that pain from the constant throb coursing through her hand and up her arm. The voice which frantically told her that Kol was doing all of this to ensure their safety became increasingly difficult to hear.

This continued until Nessix's screams had tapered into sharp groans through chattering teeth. Her knees threatened to give out, but pride and fear of what Kol would do to keep her standing refused to let her fall. Fingers effectively crushed and useless, there was little Nessix could do against her captors, and that was when Grell made himself known again.

"That was some effective work," the inoga commended amid Nessix's strained gasping. From the haze in her field of vision, she was only minutely aware of the massive beast's hand closing around the handle of a great wooden mallet.

Kol, nostrils flaring from his effort to restrain himself, turned from Nessix's anguish to face Grell, eyeing the mallet in his hand. "She will not be fighting us any time soon," he agreed.

Grell lumbered his way around the table of his peers and their subordinates, idly twirling the hammer in his hand. "And what of this matter of her disobedience? Do you think that lesson has been thoroughly understood?"

Kol turned back to face Nessix. The arm he held shook uncontrollably in his grasp as she held her chin tucked close against her right shoulder, pressing it there to keep her jaw from trembling. She'd pinched her eyes shut, her brows stitched close in agony, her beautiful face flawed with the pain and torment which Kol had once adored seeing in those he deemed beneath him. And through her raw display of anguish, Kol knew beyond a doubt that Nessix would continue to disobey until she had successfully carried out both his mission and her own, or until someone decided to end her. There was no amount of torture that would break Nessix in the way Grell hoped to achieve, and Kol briefly thought about tearing her soul vessel from her chest here and now to spare her from his efforts to do so.

"The lesson has been understood," Kol said at last, for it wasn't a complete lie. "Though I cannot say how long it will stick."

Grell grunted his opinion of Kol's assessment and continued his casual stroll forward. "Yeah, I figured as much. She does have a bit of a soft spot for you, doesn't she?"

Nessix shrank herself even smaller at Grell's words and Kol turned an ear toward the inoga. "She understands her role beneath me."

"I'll bet she does." Grell now stood beside Kol and reached out his free hand to grab a fistful of Nessix's hair to pull her face from where she'd hidden it. She gasped in pain and anticipation, keeping her eyes tightly closed as Grell leaned closer to her. "Look at me when I address you, little one," he growled.

Mustering strength generated from her hatred of this repulsive monster, Nessix peered her eyes open, unable to control her expression reliably enough to craft the sneer she wanted to give him.

"Kol here says you know your place beneath him," Grell said. "While I'm not entirely sure how much I believe that, I do have to ask if you know your place beneath *me*."

Nessix's only place beneath Grell was with a knife plunged

into his femoral artery, but she suspected finding any way to convey as much would do nothing to benefit either her or Kol. Resigned to the fact that this beating would continue until she perished—and possibly resume after she recovered—Nessix closed her eyes again and shifted her face away from Grell as much as his hold on her allowed. That response spoke enough.

"You will *kneel* before me!" Grell roared.

A fresh storm of pain as Nessix had never felt before erupted past the dulling aches in her hands as the enraged inoga smashed his mallet into the outside of her right kneecap, snapping her leg in half at the joint. Her scream filled the entire chamber, causing the viewing demons to cringe and curse her for what they gladly labeled weakness. Agony consumed her senses, stinging along her nerves and chilling her extremities as she fought Kol's hold to crumble to the ground. Playing his part as Nessix no longer had a choice but to play hers, he held her fast as she gasped and convulsed until Grell gave his next order.

"Let her fall. Let her writhe in the dirt at our feet as she should."

Kol did as he was commanded and released his hold. Nessix screamed again as she hit the ground, the shattered fragments of her kneecap digging into the surrounding soft tissue. Unable to control herself, she stretched her shackled and maimed hands toward Kol's foot, longing for some sort of physical contact, some amount of reassurance that she still had his support. He allowed her hands to brush him for the briefest moment, then kicked them away, drawing another sharp yelp from her.

Through the ringing in her ears, Nessix barely made out Grell calling Kol back to the assembly, something about leaving her to recover, though that option left Nessix far more distraught than if the demons had just continued to steadily push her toward death. The chill of numbness eased over her like death's blanket, but not enough to smother her, and she laid on the floor for what seemed like ages before the suggestion of feeling began to leak back into her extremities. This creeping effort of her body trying to restore such grievous wounds was far more jarring than waking from death, as the worst she had to wade through then was the terror of nightmares and possibly some residual aches and tightness when she woke. Now, the hot throb of each of her broken joints returned, lashing her senses in the most antagonizing manner until the accumulation of all of her injuries forced a strangled sob out of her and she hunched her upper body toward her broken leg as though she'd be able to escape the demons' notice.

That was when the indecipherable hum of her captors' voices stopped. That was when she once again heard Grell give Kol—and this time, Annin, along with him—the next round of orders.

"Annin, get that thing upright. Kol"—the metallic chime of a blade sweeping across a whetstone sang along with the alar's name as rough hands dug beneath Nessix's arms to hoist her to a seated position—"Start bleeding her out."

Nessix closed her eyes for just a moment to hide her gratitude, opening them again as Kol's steps returned to her.

"And make it slow."

Kol's lip twitched at the amendment, assuring Nessix that he'd hoped to end her suffering, but he didn't object. He looked down as he crouched before Nessix, focusing on his task as he gripped her shackles and pulled them forward to expose the soft undersides of her arms and passed the blade across the insides of her elbows. The pain was dulled by everything else screaming for Nessix's attention and, against all means of judgement she commanded, Nessix slumped back against Annin's unwilling support as her blood drained out of her. Kol rocked back on his heels and turned an ear to Grell to see if he was supposed to continue or let his chosen injuries run their course.

"Go ahead and condemn her," Grell said. "Sink it in her gut."

That was exactly the order Kol had hoped to hear and, meeting Annin's eyes as means to avoid watching the light fade from Nessix's tormented ones, he plunged the knife to its hilt into her abdomen. The influx of blood which wanted to leap to her throat was hindered by her weakness and Annin's firm support, and Kol jerked the knife free and stood.

"Very good," Grell commended. "Next."

Kol swept his eyes over Nessix's now, very briefly conveying that she'd almost survived, that she only had to bear this a few minutes longer. He stood, and strode back to Grell. The inoga took the knife from Kol and replaced it with a fine razor which Nessix sorely prayed was meant for her throat.

"Now dirty up that pretty face of hers."

Kol hesitated amid the handful of lewd objections voiced from some of the other demons as Grell picked up and admired a pair of gauntlets affixed with bladed claws twice the length of his fingers.

"Go on," Grell urged, as though Kol was a nervous child too afraid to speak to strangers in the market. "Take your time and have some fun. She'll heal up just as pretty as she is now by the next time you want to play with her."

Kol couldn't hesitate any longer, not without causing complications neither he nor Nessix cared to deal with and, after a quick, grounding breath, he stepped forward. Time distorted in Nessix's close proximity to death, making Kol's approach seem much more of a predatory prowl than she wanted to believe it was. The strength to fight her need to rely on Annin's support was gone and she felt the humiliation of tears stream down her cheeks at last as Kol gripped her chin and forced her to face him as she successfully sputtered up the first mouthful of blood. He studied her features with a clinical intensity, tilting her chin to catch the different ways the light accentuated the angles of her face and the tears flowed faster as Nessix realized this was something he'd done before, an act he'd hoped he'd walked away from.

Before her tears had a chance to dent Kol's resolve or blow his cover, he drew a slow breath, deadened his emotions, and pressed the razor into Nessix's cheek. She released a strangled whimper as the blade passed through her flesh and feebly tried to jerk her chin away. Kol withdrew the blade and slid the thumb of his restraining hand up to dab at the fresh flow of blood.

"You shouldn't have run, little one."

Nessix couldn't determine for whose benefit those words had been spoken, but as Kol cocked his head to contemplate the opposite side of her face, her eyes were drawn up to the movement of Grell leaping over the table. Those clawed gauntlets were equipped on his hands as he silently charged ahead, and by the time

110

Nessix realized the inoga's beady eyes were fixed on Kol, not her, it was too late for her to rally her dying and tormented body to even give him a warning.

Grell, unintimidated by the tiny razor he'd armed Kol with, raised his arms high overhead and sank those claws into the peaks of Kol's wings, throwing his arms toward the ground to shred the leathery membrane of the fragile appendages. Kol screamed in agony, knees buckling under pain and shock, and before he lost his balance completely, he spun around to face Grell. The inoga had never fought honorably in his life, always aiming for cheap shots, and as Kol flashed his eyes to the table of weapons, calculating his chances of reaching it to arm himself with something more substantial than this blade Grell had given him, Grell smashed his fist into the alar's face.

Kol was launched to the side, spectating demons scampering out of the way as he crashed against the far end of the table. He shook his head fiercely to scatter his confusion, and began to pull himself to his feet as Grell closed in on him once more.

Nessix's will was to rush to Kol's defense as she had in the past but, at Grell's insistence, he'd methodically robbed her body of its ability to do so. Hopeless and despairing, it was all Nessix could do to lean against Annin's hold on her. "No…" she squeezed her lament past the bubbles of blood. Her attempt to murmur Kol's name failed her completely.

"I'd warned you," Annin growled quietly in her ear. "I'd *warned* you."

Nessix gaped in helpless horror as Kol took one hit after another, wings shredded, face bloodied, his cries filling the chamber as none of the demons around them lifted a finger—or even showed an interest—to assist. She wanted to scream at Annin to do something—anything—to help Kol; she was certain the alar would be killed if nobody intervened and, as Annin had been so polite to point out, it would be her fault. Refusing to accept this fate, Nessix tried to coordinate her limbs through the growing weakness of lingering death. She needed Kol.

Blood splattered across the far end of the chamber as Kol tried desperately to use his tattered wings to gain distance from

Grell's rampage. His efforts failed miserably and Grell grabbed him by an arm to fling him back into a wall. Kol, a third of Grell's size and now stripped of his agility, had no means to escape this attack, and when his screams became too much for Nessix, when she simply could not stomach this carefully coordinated torture against them both any longer, she inhaled the next spurt of blood in her mouth and escaped the pain.

TEN

Tristan hadn't been particularly thrilled with the idea of venturing close to Zeal so soon after his recent expedition, but the intrigue which came with Berann's promise of uncovering one of these artifacts which not even Ceredulus could gauge the power of easily trounced the inconvenience of his reservations. Though Ceredulus had not given him any instructions to claim the weapons—rather, the god had promised Mathias that Tristan would not even attempt to do so—the vampire was eager to lay his eyes on some of Abaeloth's oldest relics. Fortunately, this current version of Berann was just as leery of the Order as he had been in the past, and he instructed Tristan to stop more than half a day's casual march from the blasted holy city, its fields of lilies not even a halo on the horizon.

After the brisk race across the countryside, Berann once again took his time finding his stability in this foreign body he now possessed as Tristan slid out from under his arm. The landscape had changed little from what he'd remembered—two farm houses had sprouted up in the distance, and the footpath he and his few allies had followed had been reclaimed by nature over the past centuries, replaced by a wider, straighter route. Far from natural water sources, the sprawl of civilization hadn't yet reached the quiet field. Berann focused on the song of the weapons he'd been attuned to so long ago, their melody wailing and sad in the cold, lonely prison he'd left them in. He set off toward their call.

Tristan parked his hands on his hips and glared about the bright field as Berann mechanically went about his objective. "Out of all of the options available to you, you, a demon, decided to stow your weapons out in the driest patch of boredom Etha herself has forgotten when marching on Zeal? What was it you *thought* would happen to you?"

Berann was unmoved by his companion's scrutiny and continued to walk away, raising his voice accordingly. "I'd figured my chances of death were high as it was, even greater if I arrived armed, and didn't want such artifacts to fall into the hands of the holy city."

Tristan cocked his head as he processed that last bit of reasoning and, realizing that Berann had no intention of stopping, grumbled and jogged to catch up to the demon. "You didn't think those righteous dandies would have put them to good use doing the exact same thing you had planned?"

"Give a mortal too much power and he will gleefully topple toward corruption." Berann continued ahead, indifferent to the gentle fluctuations of the wild field's footing. "Look at what it did to you."

Tristan couldn't decide if that was meant to be an insult or a simple observation, and as such let it slide in favor of curling his lip at the filthiness of their location. Berann, every bit the uncivilized beast Tristan had expected a demon to be, gave no consideration to his refined tastes, and the vampire tugged his sleeves toward his elbows as if that would help keep the dirt from soiling his clothes as he picked his way through nature. "All I'm saying is you could have chosen someplace... cleaner to hide this priceless artifact." He frowned at how deep his feet sank in a pocket of dirt freshly loosened by some burrowing varmint.

Berann didn't look back. "Could have, but didn't."

"Don't know what other conclusion I expected from a demon's simple mind..." Tristan muttered.

Berann slowed his gait enough to tilt his head toward a shoulder. "I beg your pardon?"

Unaccustomed to people being able to hear his hushed musings, Tristan flushed under the inconvenient reminder that Talier's body had been fused with a wolf's and that Berann—beyond the powers he'd crawled away from the Divine Battle with—now commanded the same enhancements which his human host had enjoyed. There was no use for Tristan to lie about what he'd said but, in light of keeping his peace with the companion he'd been assigned to, he delivered a more appropriate answer with what he hoped was a passable illusion of respect. "It seems less secure than would be ideal for something so valuable."

Berann accepted Tristan's hasty backpedaling with grace. After all, he had, at one point, dealt with far more vile tempers than a fussy and inconvenienced nobleman. "They are quite secure where I left them."

Tristan retained his bitter response to Berann's correction and, as if to mock him further, the demon pointed toward a great boulder lodged in the earth. Berann lengthened his stride as he trudged ahead and Tristan rolled his eyes as he navigated the least inconvenient route to their apparent destination. The two stopped before the great stone and Tristan crossed his arms, waiting for his blunt companion to give his dry assessment of what would happen next.

The boulder stuck out of the ground to just past waist height, the top of its surface large enough to bask on for those who favored sunny days. Dozens of scrapes marred its surface from where picks had been taken to it over the years and scars from the hooks of plow attachments remained from at least one attempt to pull it from the ground. Otherwise, it seemed no less extraordinary than any other rock Tristan had seen. He slid his gaze to Berann and felt his smugness sink at the twinkle in the demon's eyes.

Berann glanced at Tristan's humbled balk and smirked. "Right where I left them."

The demon took one more step so his toes touched the base of the boulder, and pressed a hand against its surface. His eyes closed and a faint smile raised his lips as the needles' song brightened. After centuries of restless purgatory spent cycling through his failures, alone and unable to fulfill his duties, there was nothing sweeter than this melody.

Tristan, though he could only access threads as Ceredulus saw fit for him to do so, understood the basics of magic better than the average man. It had been made plainly clear to him from the start of this ordeal that Berann was well versed in the ways of handling these strands of divinity, possibly even more skilled at doing so than the current pantheon. He just hadn't expected someone as wary and smart as Berann to leave a relic of this sort of world-altering magnitude in such a mundane and exposed location.

"You buried one of Abaeloth's most precious artifacts, one arguably capable of reconfiguring the very essence of *life*, beneath a rock?" Tristan scoffed.

Berann didn't merit Tristan's judgement with a look, too focused on locating the proper threads which would unravel his spell when plucked, but he did offer an answer. "Not beneath." His focus on the boulder prevented him from witnessing the refined tantrum of indignation Tristan let flash across his fair features at the manner which he spoke down to him. "Inside."

Tristan would never doubt Ceredulus, neither to the god's face nor in his own mind, but he was having an increasingly difficult time finding any sense in this old demon's rationale. "Inside."

Berann, deep in far more important concentration, gave a single grunt in reply and wrapped a finger around the first relevant thread he found. What Tristan didn't know and had no way of understanding was that his power, even centuries after his death, had knit such an impenetrable shield around the needles that it would have taken an average practitioner of thread manipulation two lifetimes to untangle the knots he'd formed, and one familiar with his patterns weeks still of frustration.

Offended and outraged that Berann was not giving him more attention after the generous gift Ceredulus had given him, Tristan stalked past the demon and leaned a hip against the boulder. He traced a finger along one of the pick marks gouged into the stone, throwing a challenging glare at Berann before raising a hand to inspect his nails. "I will do you the courtesy of not doubting your might, but it seems the prison you made for your great solution is rather sturdy. If centuries of mortals grinding away at this rock couldn't free these needles, what makes you think you can get to them again?"

Berann did look up at Tristan now, glowering a refined dissatisfaction which Tristan suspected he'd find great fun playing with when they reached a time where matters weren't quite so urgent. "I know I can reach them because I am the one who put them there." He shifted his focus to the boulder once more. "You're going to want to move."

Tristan disregarded the instruction as readily as Berann had disregarded each of his own demands, smirking at how he seemed to have struck the demon's nerves. After a moment of patience— more than Berann truly considered Tristan worthy of—Berann sighed, shrugged, and gave a stout tug to the threads he'd wound around his fingers. Suddenly, Tristan's base of support caved out from under his hip, the mighty boulder chunking off into dozens of smaller stones like marbles rushing from the bottom of a slit pouch. Vampires were agile and quick, but Tristan did lose a moment of dignity as he flailed his arms to catch his balance, throwing his weight to the side to avoid falling into the which he found so repulsive. Startled by the rapid result of Berann's magic, accustomed to the lagging response of devices and the show which went along with Ceredulus's feats of splendor, Tristan took two steps back from where he'd been casually provoking the demon and gaped at the complete destruction of the boulder—and the smooth, curved scabbards of twin sabers which poked out from the rubble.

A fine line of sweat glistened across Berann's brow, but after a single satisfied breath, he wiped it away and stepped forward to pull the blades from where he'd left them stowed so long ago. Their bone colored hilts still snuggled against his fingers as if they'd been crafted just for him, the balance of the blades perfect and weight negligible even to these scrawny arms. Berann drew one from its sheath, eyes shining with awe and he let Tristan stare stupidly at the blade's flawless perfection without commenting on his stricken state. He'd been seized by awe of their power and beauty enough times in the past to understand the vampire's reaction. Once the initial bliss of this reunion had passed, Berann kicked aside a couple of the stones until he identified the leather strap of his sword belt. Spinning the right blade, he lodged it beneath his left arm to retrieve the belt, slid the sheaths onto it, and secured it around the waist which was a bit too narrow to hold it securely. He turned to Tristan at last.

"What was it you were saying about this not being an appropriate hiding place?"

Tristan shook his head and, with notable effort, raised his eyes from the blades to Berann. "I suppose I'd underestimated you," he admitted slowly. "You must understand, the nature of mortals has conditioned me quite well to dismiss such boasting as you seemed to deliver."

Berann sheathed the blade he'd drawn. "I am not a mortal, but I do hope you took note of what you witnessed."

Tristan crossed his arms, already past the embarrassment of his recent loss of balance and in pursuit of establishing some sense of dominance over this companion he now saw increasing power in. "You need me, Berann, do you not? Threats should be the furthest thing from your mind."

"Threats are only applicable to those you feel threatened by." Already, Berann had turned from Tristan, moving in a slow circle as he hunted for even the faintest whispers of the other two weapons. "I simply wanted you to acknowledge that you're a fool to doubt my abilities, much as I'd been one to doubt yours."

Everything about Berann's mannerisms—from his steady defiance of authority to his humble certainty in his self-sufficiency—pricked at Tristan's calm, even when receiving a compliment. It wasn't often he had to contend with a being older than he was; Ceredulus himself was less than a decade his senior. And perhaps that was why the god had been so willing to compromise with Berann. A creature this old, this wise, this powerful, would make a formidable enemy. Or an unparalleled ally. Surrendering to what he must do to ensure he established the latter for his god, Tristan prepared an equally flattering acceptance to Berann's words but never managed to speak it before the demon interrupted his effort.

"I've found our heading. Let's go."

Even this bout of tolerance Tristan had just found for his god's benefit didn't keep him from needing to suck back a snarl at Berann's casual disregard for matters beyond his objective. This lack of influence was something Tristan had thought he'd left behind in his mortal life. Drained of patience and stamina, his needs repeatedly overlooked by this disrespectful creature who so openly looked down on the one who had given him life, Tristan planted his feet and squared his shoulders.

When the vampire didn't move, Berann half-turned to face him and shook his head. "Well? What are you waiting for?"

It had been so long since Ceredulus had commanded awe and fear on Abaeloth, so long since the general masses even had to contemplate what a vampire was, that most mortals thought the god and all of his creations were myths. Tristan had embraced this ignorance while finding his way into Zeal and infiltrating the Citadel, but bearing the same from Berann—this great and powerful ancient magic-using demon—had grown stale before they'd even parted company with Mathias. And they still had two more weapons to find and allegedly half the world to cover in search of them.

Oh, if only Tristan hadn't vowed to Ceredulus that he'd serve Berann as he'd serve his lord... "Tell me a bit about how your magic works, Berann."

The demon frowned. "Mathias expects our haste."

Tristan sucked his teeth and looked away. Leave it to that blasted paladin to find a demon's obedience. "And Mathias doesn't have to know that we took a moment to discuss the nature of how the world works."

Berann surveyed their quiet surroundings, gathered his bearings despite his help's unhelpfulness, and began walking south to keep his word to Mathias that he would not relent or rest on his search for the weapons. Tristan's request had been a fair one, though, and it had been too long since Berann had had a reason to explain how threads worked to those curious of their power. "Threads of divinity compose the entirety of the living world. People, animals, trees, the land itself are all held together by this force. Most thread weavers work by sight to manipulate them to

119

their will. As far as I know, I am among the few who hears them, as well."

Tristan rolled his eyes at Berann's persistence to stick to his word—as though Mathias had a way of knowing what they were up to—and followed after him, catching up in a few long strides. He had a working knowledge of thread manipulation, including the flaw in that system which limited a mortal practitioner's use of the art. "You may be able to hear these threads, but does that grant you the ability to manipulate them indefinitely, without a chance to recover?"

"No." Berann cocked his head in consideration. "Perhaps I could now that my soul has been sewn into this body, but I am in no hurry to test it. A thread weaver must fray or snap their own threads to access others, so we must pace ourselves to keep enough of our own threads intact to hold our souls in place."

Tristan nodded. Every divinely enhanced being he'd encountered, save the gods themselves, operated within an established set of boundaries, and Berann's acknowledgement of such would only validate his own loathed weakness. "I… am governed by similar restrictions. As much as I'd love to think otherwise, I do not function on an endless font of energy."

Berann stopped walking and turned to Tristan, his expression softer and stoic eyes now more thoughtful. "If it's rest you need, then you should have said so. Sleep, so we can resume our quest."

Tristan grit his teeth, wondering for the first time if this was the sort of frustration Mathias had to deal with when trying to negotiate with those who didn't understand or accept his laws. "I respect," Tristan's words popped out caustically, "that you've been dead for some time and have thus forgotten the nourishment requirements of those residing in physical bodies."

Berann crossed his arms, contemplations of this inconvenience working clearly across his face as he studied the unusual lay of Tristan's threads and the lack of an obvious juncture for his soul. "I thought you were more closely bound to the spirit realm than mortals are?"

Tristan bore a finger into his temple, trying with the rest of his remaining might to find his patience. The fact that Berann was simply seeking a better understanding of this new version of Abaeloth and not intending to irritate him made that effort all the more difficult. "I still have to eat to maintain my stamina, and so do you."

Berann thought over Tristan's terse declaration for a moment before drawing back his shoulders and nodding. "You are right. A mortal shell is rather feeble. It would be wise to pick up some provisions before we head to Selian."

Tristan hissed at this greater concern than his urge to feed, and looked away. "About that..."

"Your god ordered you to obey me." Berann didn't hesitate to wield this reminder against him, and Tristan bristled at his callousness.

"Yes..." Tristan drew the word out like a mother two seconds from paddling her unruly children. "But I—" He shook his head fiercely, refusing to claim this disadvantage solely as his own. "Due to the unnatural nature of how the lands had been split during the Divine Battle, my kind cannot cross the oceans." He spat this confession with Ceredulus's own bitterness; it had been this roadblock which had kept the god of the undead's practices from spreading beyond Gelthin before the Order stopped his progress.

"That is an unfortunate disability," Berann said, overlooking the feral gnashing of Tristan's teeth. "Can you travel beneath them?"

Tristan's resentment fell away into confusion. Travelling beneath the oceans was such a ridiculous concept that he'd never thought to question it before. *Ceredulus?*

This wall exists at the shoreline. The god's voice wore a keen eagerness, already contemplating ways to use whatever method Berann had at his disposal to his advantage. *But depending on how deep these tunnels he's alluding to go and how far from the barrier they start, there is a chance you'd survive.*

Tristan had never doubted Ceredulus, never defied him, never even thought of telling him no. But he did hesitate at his god's willingness to dispose of him in the name of scholarship.

This could be revolutionary, Ceredulus answered his servant's justifiable concerns. *And, in my name, it is worth investigating.*

121

Tristan unclenched his jaw before he cracked his teeth from the pressure. "I've never tried," he muttered.

Berann accepted the answer as a far more ready compliance than it was, and turned, squinting toward the horizon as he listened for the shrillest buzzing of threads which would guide them toward the nearest city. "Then let us go and gather our provisions. The less time we waste, the better."

As with everything else so far, Berann didn't wait for Tristan to agree to his decision before purposefully marching off in the direction he wanted to go. Tristan tightened his fists and swallowed his ire before trudging after the demon, doing his best to remind himself that this had to be better than being chained to Mathias.

ELEVEN

Taking to heart Sazrah's claim of the mountainside's collapse, Mathias had teleported farther down the rise than he suspected she'd be camped at to avoid dropping himself into the crater which had claimed so many of her troops. He'd done well in assuming she'd maintained her position near the entry point to the hells, neither her diligence nor limited mobility allowing her to leave it unguarded. Following the smell of campfire smoke, Mathias hastened his climb, driven by anger and the need to feel like he could run away from the horrors lurking around him. Sazrah had said she needed his help, and he would use what aid he could offer her as means to seek his own redemption.

Given Sazrah's report on the handful of survivors Karst had pulled from the sinkhole, Mathias had expected at least a dull stream of chatter to greet him as he neared, but it was still as he clomped his way toward the campsite, the crunching of his boots on the rugged ground the loudest source of sound in the immediate area. It wasn't at all common for any who marched with Sazrah to lose their enthusiasm through the normal tides of battle, and Mathias's glimmer of hope was squashed by the guilt he hadn't managed to escape. Heart heavy, he called out ahead of himself as he neared what remained of the ridge as not to frighten the reactive soldiers awaiting him.

"Saz, you awake? I'm here."

"About damn time." Karst Boulderchoke's voice carried his bitter remark far better than was necessary, but Mathias let the biting criticism in his tone slide. If put in the dwarf's position, he'd have been no more cheerful with his savior's tardiness.

"And I'll have all of you patched up in no time," Mathias vowed. He surveyed the survivors quickly, approving of the triage measures they'd pulled off with their limited supplies and in the absence of a specialized medic.

Karst snorted and turned his back to Mathias so he could poke about at the pot of stew hanging over their campfire. Before Mathias had crossed the site's perimeter, Sazrah, who had been propped into a seated position against a boulder, left arm snuggly secured against her chest, immediately began to pursue her only interest.

"This demon cure, Mathias," she insisted, holding him with a demanding gaze he had few remaining defenses against. "What is it?"

Mathias had hoped he'd get to concentrate on healing these soldiers—the benevolent task he was most equipped for and preferred over the alternative Sazrah was after—rather than immediately digging into this particularly fresh wound. There was still much about this entire arrangement he'd yet to come to terms with, certain aspects he hadn't figured out for himself, much less enough to explain to the woman whose spite for demons and the undead were practically all that kept her alive the past couple hundred years. Sazrah bound him tighter with humorless green eyes as he neared, and Mathias stifled his groan. There would be no pretending he hadn't heard her question and even less use in changing the subject, but that wouldn't stop him from trying to buy time to sort out the best way to disappoint her.

"What makes you so sure I know it?" He knelt down before Sazrah and reached toward her arm.

With her good hand, she shoved his away. "Because we'd still be waiting on you if you didn't have it. And there are others worse off than me. Start with them, and talk while you work."

There had been a time when Sazrah hadn't dared defy

Mathias, days when he'd so badly wanted her to find the confidence to speak her mind freely to him so they could communicate properly. This was one of the few instances he regretted helping her find that nerve. Hoping Sazrah wouldn't take his compliance to her instruction as his inclination to accept such blunt and disrespectful demands, agreeing that Etha's grace would be better spent reviving the injured mortals in this group, Mathias took advantage of the excuse to put distance between himself and Sazrah's agitation. As he approached the nearest, a fleman man sporting compound fractures to both legs, he grit his teeth as the prolonged scraping of a body fighting to rise followed him. Sazrah's stifled grunt came next as she successfully navigated the lingering pain of her relocated leg to stand and stagger after him.

"If you're so eager to talk," Mathias said to her as he knelt down beside the man, "you can start by telling me what happened here."

Sazrah snorted and leaned against the boulder closest to where Mathias appraised the soldier's injuries. "I told you before. The demons showed, the oraku dropped the ridge, and that orange-eyed alar pulled Nessix into the hells. What more do you want from me?"

Mathias's brows furrowed and he turned to chastise Sazrah with a firm glare. How would her tone have changed if she knew what he'd just gone through? "A *solid* report, Saz."

She huffed an irritated sigh and attempted to look away from his scolding, but respect didn't let her make it far. "Nessix appeared unresponsive, and the oraku dropped from the sky as the ridge fell. I'm hoping he's found his grave in Havoc's maw, but you never know with them."

Mathias sucked in a sharp breath. Annin was dead? That seemed like too great a boon, given the avalanche of recent events, but he wouldn't question it quite yet. He turned his attention back to assessing his patient as he asked Sazrah the next question. "What about you? How did you end up in such a rough shape?"

Sazrah scoffed and flushed, succeeding in pulling her gaze away from Mathias as she shook her head, angry tears welling in her eyes. "Inoga."

It was the only word she could choke out between shame and the residual fear which came from facing one of those behemoths. Sazrah was a courageous woman, but the last time she'd been tossed around by an inoga had left her with far more permanent scars than these physical injuries Grell had given her. No stranger to the emotions muddling Sazrah's confidence, having survived the scenes which flashed through her eyes alongside her, Mathias clenched his teeth and nodded, reminding himself to keep his touch gentle as he worked on the fleman's lesser injuries.

"He refused to kill me," Sazrah continued after a rough clearing of her throat. "He said something about the demons having other plans for me."

The curse of Sazrah's heritage meant that they'd always had plans for her, and Mathias would do everything he could—even through the current raging crisis—to keep them from succeeding in enacting any of those fates. "All the more reason to get you healed up and back to the tem—"

"Back to the temple?" The sharp outrage in Sazrah's voice, completely shrouding the broken helplessness of her recent traipse toward repressed memories, berated Mathias for his assumptions. "No, Mathias. I'm marching down there to stop this bastard myself."

"Saz…" Mathias ceased his work to close his eyes. Keeping a hold of any semblance of calm, even for the sake of the ailing soldiers, was becoming increasingly difficult. "The demons have been hunting you all your life and you're not of clear mind right—"

"Of course I'm not of clear mind right now! Thirty-five good men died because of this trouble you found and dragged us into, and you won't even tell me what made that price worth paying!" Her voice trembled with a very mortal fear, baring the fragility of the tortured soul she'd learned to keep so well hidden, and Mathias hung his head.

"Saz," he petitioned softly, unable to look up at her, too afraid to see this stoic woman crumble before him one more time. Etha knew he was on the brink of falling apart as it was, and every soul in this camp was depending on his strength. "I will tell you everything I know after I tend to the wounded, but for now, you

126

need to rest."

"I've been resting all damn day," she snapped, voice strained against the firings of pain in her hip. "This great secret you were after is half the reason we came up here and you *will* tell me what it is so I can be sure those I lost didn't die in vain."

Mathias had reached his limit of being talked down to and ordered about as though his emotions meant nothing. He was tired of being disregarded as nothing more than the tool to seek answers, the one to fix everyone's problems, the great scapegoat to all which plagued Abaeloth. How could Sazrah not see that he was suffering? That he needed help and guidance? That he was every bit as frightened as she was? He hadn't been badgered this aggressively since his early days of trying to win over Nes's trust, and back then, he'd still understood the concept of hope. His eyes burned with the effort to repress these foul emotions until a calming breath was forced into his lungs.

She doesn't want to fight you, Mathias. Surely, you know that. But she needs these answers. She deserves them. Even if you still want to hide from them.

I'm not— Another surge of heat battered the backs of Mathias's eyes, forcing him to pinch them closed despite his concerns of weariness waiting for the opportunity to overtake him. Etha was right. He did want to hide from the truth of his reality, more than he'd ever wanted to hide from anything before in his life. But hiding wouldn't heal these men or help Sazrah avenge those she'd lost. Hiding wouldn't pull Nessix out of the hells or stop the demons or eviscerate Kol. "Find me a piece of leather," he muttered to Sazrah, still refusing to raise his head to face her.

"Karst!" she barked. "Bring us something for the men to bite down on." She waited for the dwarf's grumbled reply before prodding Mathias again. "Give me hope. Please."

Mathias returned his attention to the wounded soldier, hoping that finding purpose in his work would distract him from his tension. "You promise to accept the answer I have to give you?"

"I'll accept it easier than I can accept you keeping it from me."

Mathias clenched his teeth for a moment to swallow his frustration and build walls against those to come. "There are blessed weapons capable of righting the knots in demon souls."

Karst thrust a thick strap of cut-off belt in Mathias's face. "These weapons can be forged?"

Mathias accepted the dwarf's offer and held it out to his current patient to bite down on. "No," he corrected, effectively dulling the faint flicker of appreciation the dwarf had shown him. "They must be found."

"Do you know where they are?" Sazrah asked.

Mathias met the fleman's eyes until he grimaced and nodded, then gently laid his fingers on the first exposed bone. Waiting for the tail end of an exhale, Mathias realigned the break in one smooth motion, quick to move his left hand to the man's chest to keep him immobile from the spasms of pain as his right channeled Etha's grace into the broken leg. Though Mathias had vague insight on these weapons' general whereabouts, he wasn't quite prepared to tell his agitated student that they were supposed to be in the hells. "I don't."

Sazrah didn't have the presence of mind to censor her scoff. "Then what good is knowing about them at all?"

Mathias hadn't slept, hadn't eaten, and had just come rushing over here after being dragged about by Ceredulus's manipulation. He'd failed Nessix, failed his sense of justice, and was acutely aware of how he was failing Sazrah. Though he couldn't deny he deserved it, he no longer had it in him to tolerate such criticism. He speared Sazrah with a firm glare which dulled some of her righteous fury with uncertainty. "Because I've been in touch with those who *do* know where they are and how to find them. Contrary to what you seem so eager to believe, I was busy making arrangements to secure these weapons when you sent your scry. I hadn't wanted to leave any of you suffering. I would have been standing beside you to face these demons if I'd have been able to. Now. Would you like me to resume healing your troops or do you have more to fuss about?"

Sazrah flushed under the strict angle of Mathias's brows and the sharp tone he'd taken with her. She couldn't recall the last time she'd lost her discipline enough to show him such disrespect, but though she would have given her sword arm to alleviate Mathias's disappointment in her, she couldn't look past the devastation her troops had faced due to this quest of his which still hadn't bore fruit.

"Did these insiders of yours suggest when we will have access to these weapons?"

Mathias flexed his jaw at Sazrah's persisting stubbornness, frustration seeping from him in the form of a tight smile. "Tell me, Sazrah. Is it safe for me to risk healing you once I'm through with your troops?"

She blinked in confusion and shook her head. "What sort of question is that? It will take days before I'm in fighting shape if I'm left to heal on my own."

Mathias turned the rest of the way to face her as his patient's breathing regulated once again. "And you're usually smart enough to not go hunting for trouble even when you *are* in fighting shape."

Sazrah grabbed her left shoulder with her functional hand, fingers curling into the linen of her shirt. "Mathias, I'm going down there, with or without—"

"You need to recover!" Mathias cried, exasperated. "I've fought alongside you longer than I've backed anyone else, and I've never seen you this eager to blindly throw yourself at death before. You're smarter than this, Saz, smarter than I am. I understand that you want to destroy the demon who wronged you, believe me, I know that better than you can imagine, but in order for either of us to succeed in finding our vengeance, in order for us to actually secure the opportunity to end the demon scourge, we need to bide our time and wait to mobilize."

His plea had nearly won Sazrah over before that last part drew her suspicion out once again. "On whose orders?"

"Mine," Mathias said definitively.

"No," Sazrah countered. "Who is instructing *you* when to move?" It had better be Etha herself or no one at all.

Mathias contemplated his options as carefully as his aching and worn mind allowed. He'd already kept so much from Sazrah and was exhausted from the deceit, but he couldn't fathom that she'd accept the truth of who he'd fallen in line with even a quarter of the grace she'd shown him so far. Given her childhood spent on the run and tumultuous past, she'd sworn a justifiable oath to destroy every demon she could get her hands on and had been the only military leader, a society-scorned mercenary, attempting to hold back the undead hordes before Mathias had been resurrected. As much as Mathias hated himself for the actions he'd undertaken over the past few days, Sazrah would hate him even more once she found out he'd been working with Ceredulus and a vampire to bring a demon back from the dead. If he wanted to ensure the rest of these injured soldiers were tended to, those specifics would have to wait, in the inevitable case that Sazrah forgot her place upon his confession and decided to act against him.

"I'm following no one's orders," Mathias said at last, "but have chosen to take the sound advice of an ally I've found."

More shady answers. Sazrah narrowed her eyes. "This ally have a name?"

Mathias weighed this question carefully before deciding that, if Berann had been removed from demon history before the demon war had concluded and well before Sazrah had been born, she would have no way to know who he was. Providing such a specific detail would give her less to continue arguing about and, hopefully, add validity to Mathias's report. "His name is Berann."

She accepted his answer and discarded it as irrelevant in the same instant. "And he's the one who knows more about these demon-cleansing weapons than you do?"

Though Sazrah's eyes still burned and her posture hadn't eased from her rigid hunch, Mathias could hear sensibility sneak into her voice at last. He turned back to the fleman man and waited for the next tense nod to set and heal the other bone. "At some point, he picked up the language of the ancients"—it wasn't a complete lie—"and he's dedicated years of his life to researching these weapons. He knows of our current predicament—of how the demons control of the field, their practices of necromancy, he even encouraged me to hurry here once he was made aware that you and your men were injured. His goal is to be part of righting all of these wrongs."

Sazrah had served under and beside Mathias long enough to know that he wasn't being wholly forthright with her, but that experience also assured her that no amount of digging, begging for, or demanding a more thorough answer would do anything other than rile them both up. Mathias made all choices consciously and for what he interpreted as the greater good, and Sazrah finally had to make herself concede to letting him continue to guard these final morsels of the truth for himself. No matter how many problems Mathias had caused or how badly Sazrah wanted to take matters into her own hands, he wanted to see an end to Abaeloth's horror worse than anyone, and Sazrah, exhausted from how hard she'd worn this shell of strength while waiting on Mathias to arrive, settled back against the boulder to take the pressure off her wounded leg.

"So we're sitting around and waiting for this friend of yours to find these weapons?" she asked.

Mathias frowned at her choice to label Berann his friend, but in the interest of avoiding another burst of outrage, wouldn't correct her for her assumption. "We are, and with as much as he's researched them, it shouldn't take him long to locate them." At least, with Tristan's assistance, that was what Mathias hoped. The fleman man nodded his gratitude, and Mathias stood to move to the next wounded soldier.

Sazrah didn't follow him this time around. "And what happens then?"

"Then"— Mathias crouched down to investigate the human's crushed collar bone—"he'll be coming here, hopefully arming me with one of these weapons, and he and I will return to the hells to find Nessix."

Sazrah didn't respond to Mathias's explanation, so quiet that, after he'd located the point of his patient's break, he turned his head to make sure she hadn't limped off. He grimaced at her sharp expression, promptly opening the door for her to take her next stance. "How many of these weapons are there?"

"Saz—"

She cut him off before Mathias could even begin shaking his head. "I have spent my entire life dedicated to ending demonkind and now that we found means to do so, you'll have to do a lot more than chastise me with your disappointment to keep me from being part of it."

Mathias sighed and spent the remainder of his time healing this patient thinking over Sazrah's words. Truth be told, there were few warriors he'd trust charging into the hells with him more than he trusted Sazrah, but though she wore a tough façade and even now pushed herself past pain just to prove her point, the hells had come close to destroying her once before, and Mathias couldn't stand the thought of opening her up to that potential ever again. But just as she was cursed with the blood of those she hated most, she also carried the curse of a Sagewind's determination, and Mathias knew she'd find a way to get her hands on one of these weapons and use it, no matter the cost. The smartest and easiest path for them both would be to accept it.

"There's three of them," he conceded.

"Perfect." Sazrah was looking away from Mathias, toward the darkness of the hells' entry point, when he glanced up at her. "How long did you say it would take your friend to reach us?"

Mathias wrapped up his work on his current patient and heaved a sigh as he stood to move to the next. "Sazrah, I really think you ought to—"

She snapped her attention back to him, pushing straight past the weathered concern in his tired eyes. "When will we be entering the hells?"

Enough was enough. Sazrah may not want Mathias to protect her, but he wouldn't allow her to endanger herself with the same recklessness he threw about. While she was resilient and unaging, she wasn't immortal. "We will enter the hells," he said sternly, "after you've calmed down enough for me to believe that I'm the only fool between us."

Mathias hated raising his voice with Sazrah, reserving such strictness for only the most important addresses. She'd grown up idolizing him for his heroic acts against the demons, had been subservient to him from the moment they first met, and always aimed to follow his guidance. Fired up in her own right, Sazrah met Mathias's eyes and recognized instantly the pain he slogged through. He'd searched for months for his lost lover, found her and lost her again, and his best lead on how to liberate her was tied to a third party operating on theories he had no way to prove. As always, he'd shoveled the blame for all of this—Nessix's death and subsequent fate all the way to the catastrophe Sazrah had endured—onto his own shoulders, and the last thing he needed right now was Sazrah, one of the few, reliable constants in his life, to try him even harder. Ashamed of herself for letting her discipline slip, for allowing that chaotic greed of her heritage that she prided herself on overcoming take over her, Sazrah lowered her head and her shoulders relaxed in submission.

"What do we do in the meantime?" she asked.

Mathias looked down the line of wounded soldiers, doing his best to make a quick appraisal of the obvious injuries and balancing them against his growing fatigue. "If you plan to accompany me for my fight in the hells, I suggest you rest up. I'll stabilizable those who need it then go tell Sulik to send relief up here to get these men home. I need to recover, myself, and have a couple last matters to tend to in Zeal before I can be ready for this final assault."

Sazrah snorted. "If you return to Zeal with the ammunition you're carrying, the Council won't let you leave for months."

Mathias tried to find a chuckle, but it got stuck in the tightness of his chest. "If I have my way, nobody from the Council will know I was there until well after I'm gone. I'll be as fast as I can."

Karst grunted and spat to the side. "That's what you said last time."

Mathias spared the dwarf a spent glance, wondering when this bitterness would wear off. "Believe me when I say their excuse for bureaucracy is one of the last things I'm in the mood to contend with right now."

"Bah. Shade's right, you know."

"About what?"

"You're a blasted idiot." Karst turned his shrewd eyes to Sazrah. Her temper had mellowed back into respect for and obedience to her father figure, and the dwarf shook his head and trundled off to resume distributing his stew to the troops.

Mathias watched him leave, seeing past the rough exterior to the concern lurking deeper inside. "I am through making promises," he told Sazrah softly as Karst cursed when he slopped a steaming scoop of stew on his hand in his distress. "Etha knows I have been unable to keep even the most basic of them of late. But I will not stop trying to right the wrongs of this world."

Sazrah blinked the strain from her eyes and bowed her head. "I know you won't," she replied. "And that is why you will always have my sword."

Content that the current bout of tension had dissipated as much as it ever would, Mathias returned to his task of patching up the soldiers as Sazrah settled back against her boulder to get the rest she so badly needed. Waiting was not one of her greatest talents, but loyalty was. Closing her eyes as the sun beat down on the mountainside, Sazrah let herself get lost in the tides of vengeance she'd wanted to wade in for so long as Mathias finished his rounds.

TWELVE

Nessix didn't dream of those horrifying final moments of the Divine Battle, but of clear blue skies, the energizing freshness of a nipping breeze rolling off snow-covered peaks, and the quiet serenity of a herd of some sort of long-haired goats chomping their way through the wilted brush. She was surrounded by comfort and peace, friendly smiles of strangers she knew on a level deeper than she could address cast her way with admiration and respect. And then she met a pair of chilly pale eyes just as cruel in this blissful setting as they were in the hells where she'd gotten to know them, laced with the same malice they'd scolded her with in those final moments before she'd died amidst Kol's screams.

She jerked into consciousness, fingers stiff and a dull ache throbbing in her gut as she rolled over in the pile of tattered blankets meant to serve as a mattress. Kol's screams rang in her ears, and her skin prickled with warmth as she saw the spray of his blood each time she blinked. Choking on the shock she hadn't escaped, but now able to fight it, Nessix sat upright in a hurry, hands patting the ground around her for something to arm herself with as she frantically searched her surroundings for signs of her safety, for signs of *his* safety, and was disappointed to be greeted by the familiarity of the chasm's sleeping chamber.

"Go tell Garrett and Pierson," an urgent woman's voice from

135

nearby instructed. "The general has recovered."

Nessix groaned and sank back down onto the pile of blankets as her heart raced with the need to take impossible action against an unreachable force, flexing her fingers to work mobility back into them. The worried face of a middle-aged woman peered over her and Nessix managed a weary smile as she fought to repress the inner turmoil she could never hope to make any of the other akhuerai understand. She had survived her punishment—at least the physical portion of it—but what had become of Kol? Grell had torn into the alar, not with the slow, methodical means expected of one distributing torture or a lesson to be learned, but with a violent aggression meant to break. Meant to destroy. Annin's words came back to her.

I'd warned you.

Kol's fate, whatever it was, was Nessix's fault, and she couldn't even lament about it to those around her.

The woman urged a stone cup filled with water into Nes's hands, and she drank it readily to wash down the aftertaste of rancid blood and the hot lump of remorse climbing her throat. Now wasn't the time to fret. Now was the time to gain insight. "How did I get down here?" she asked.

The woman took the emptied cup from Nes's hands to shove it at a younger man beside her, and shooed him along to go refill it. "There was a procession of those huge demons who showed up at the chasm lip. The one with wings told us to look sharp, that we'd better make sure you were alright, and tossed you down, shattered and torn like we've never seen. That was two days ago."

Nessix pressed her fingers to her forehead. Two days ago? Kol had inflicted significant injury to her, but besides her crushed joints, he'd been careful and clean. Grell must have done more than simply toss her down here for it to have taken so long for her injuries to heal. "What's happened in those two days? Have Kol or Annin come by?"

"No, ma'am. No demons have been down here besides the normal guards."

It had been a feeble hope, but if Kol had come to check on his creations while Nessix was out of commission, that would have meant that he was alive and functional. It would mean he hadn't had this army and his connection to her stripped from him. It would mean that the plan of overthrowing the inoga, of righting the hells for Kol and the akhuerai both, was still achievable. Nessix needed Kol to be alright, needed him to come tell her what their next move was. She needed to see that he was alive.

Nessix's vision began to spin, a sweltering flush working over her skin, and she shoved the blanket off herself and snatched the next cup of water to drain it. If Kol was gone, who would she be expected to answer to? How would she be able to coordinate a resistance without him serving as a shield against those who wanted to see her suffer?

"He's got to be…" It was easy to stop her breathy murmur before her thoughts betrayed her, but not before they were heard by her anxious audience.

"Who's got to be what?" the woman asked.

Nessix frantically waved a hand to dismiss the woman's concerns, pressing a palm to her spinning head as she closed her eyes and tried to come up with a way to explain to anyone in her army how she worried about the alar who had caused them all so much grief, the one who she'd assured them all she'd been manipulating and using. Her thoughts were interrupted by a pair of hasty footsteps entering the barracks chamber, rescuing her from the need to make up an answer as the woman excused herself from the official business about to unfold.

"General, please tell us you reached Zeal."

Nessix lowered her hand to look up at the characteristic nervousness of Pierson's eyes and to the equally predictable skepticism of Garrett's guarded glower. Neither of the two captains had gained the adequate confidence to effectively command an army, especially one as broken and terrified as the akhuerai now were, not the way Auden had developed under her guidance. Already susceptible to such dismal thoughts, a rapid flood of guilt struck Nessix all over again for the role she'd played in Auden's pathetic demise. Her gambit in leaving the hells hadn't even paid off in the end. Not for the akhuerai. Not for Kol. Not for herself or Mathias. And now, separated from Mathias and banking on the hope that he'd be able to reach them, rapidly succumbing to the most logical fate Kol had met, Nessix couldn't see how the pieces to victory fit anymore. Trained from childhood to find the right thing to say to rally the disheartened though she was, Nessix couldn't hold her captains' eyes for long, and she drew a ragged breath she was content to attribute to her recent recovery.

"The Order knows of our plight," she said, delivering all of the truth she could. "And the demons exchanged the priestesses they'd used to create our kind for me, so we may have put a stop to the practice of harvesting mortals to add to our numbers." If only she could convince herself to concentrate on the good that meant.

Half of the worry lines eased from Pierson's face, but his eyes continued to glisten with his deeply embedded anxiety. "So, you were successful?"

Nessix swallowed the hot lump of regret which returned to her throat. Her job as a general was to bring hope to those who needed it, but there was so little hope to be had and so few places left to hunt for it. The akhuerai had risked and sacrificed everything they had in supporting her escape, yet she'd barely convinced even a handful of those in Zeal that her army needed and was worthy of their help. It had taken her days of tedious, asinine pleading to crack the surface of their suspicions and to begin pressing toward finding answers that might aid them. And she'd failed in obtaining those answers before Kol had finally caught up with her to bring her back here. She shook her head to try chasing the alar from her mind. So much suffering, so much fear, so much invested faith, and Nessix had no way to assure any of those who had counted on her that it had paid off. She lowered her head, lashes hooding the shame in her eyes.

"I did all I could," she said. "It's up to the White Paladin to organize our rescue from the surface." She'd used Mathias's renowned title in hopes that would rouse something akin to relief in her nervous officers, but she was just as disappointed by that effort as she was with all the rest of them.

Garrett crossed his arms and shook his head to cast his gaze toward the rest of the army as they puttered about the chasm in their best imitation of living. "Nobody's coming for us. Are they?"

Nessix curled her lips between her teeth and shook her head into a shrug. "I know Mathias will come—"

"How?"

Garrett's belligerence succeeded in stoking just enough of Nes's irritation for her to snap past her fear and self-pity and glare up at him. "Because I *know* he will." He had to. There was no other way any of this would have been worth the price. "And he'll come alone if he must." And he likely would, because of her inability to rally anyone else to her cause. "Matters between this realm and the surface are not quite as straightforward as I'd first thought, but aid *is* coming and we *will* find our way out of here. I made a promise to you—" She swallowed a choke as the other person she'd promised to help came to mind yet again. "I made a promise to my people. I will not rest until I see it done."

Garrett made one of those dry puffs of laughter and flung his gaze aside, as though looking for Nessix to start a fight with him but too daunted by her skill and authority to accept one, and Pierson's face warped with uncertainty as he attempted to stitch together remnants of the quiet charisma which had made Auden such an effective officer for this timid force. "What do we do until he gets here?" Pierson asked.

"We show—" Nessix coughed as her agreement to Kol's request tried to reach her lips, her mind dumping a bombardment of every possible fate he could have met on her. He hadn't given her many more instructions beyond honoring her vow of loyalty, had told her they'd discuss future tactics—possibly even Berann's relevance to the hells—after matters regarding her punishment and her missing soul were settled. Right now, well under the watchful eyes of Annin and Grell, without Kol to direct her toward the right turns to avoid them, Nessix couldn't even begin to worry about her missing soul. Pierson hadn't yet drawn a breath as he waited for her reply, and Garrett watched her with an offer of respect if she could provide him a valid response. Nessix dug her fingers into the meat of her thighs and searched for the first hint of resilience she could find. She *had* to keep moving forward, with or without Mathias or Kol or her own damn security.

"We keep the demons happy," she said, too shortly to buy her own feigned confidence. "We show them obedience and prove we are not threats to them." Discomfort at how naturally she wore this shoddy imitation of confidence to deliver her order thrashed about inside Nessix, flailing her harshly with the dismal truths she hid from her troops because of her greater desire to deny them. She couldn't stay idle any longer. Regardless of whether or not Kol had lived or died, she'd given him her word. And if he'd fallen victim to Grell's temper in the permanent manner which Nessix loathed to consider, after Annin had sat back and watched with indifference as his comrade was torn into, Nessix was the only one able to carry out the dream they shared. Riding this bout of determination before fear had a chance to throw her to the ground again, Nessix sprang to her feet. Now, more than ever, was the time for action. "And we resume our training."

Pierson shook his head, the haze of remembered torment swiping across his eyes at Nessix's suggestion that they surrender to the demons, even if it was just to placate them. After everything those beasts had done and all the vile things they'd coerced the akhuerai into doing… If the Order of the White Circle—even if it was only the legendary Mathias Sagewind—was coming for them as Nessix said they would, they should be able to abandon everything about this horrific act. Summoning up his courage, Pierson faced his general and voiced his doubts for the first time. "Training for what?"

Vulnerable without her sword and armor, without Kol's diligent eyes keeping watch over her, all Nessix had left to demand respect and claim authority with was her presence. Though her own confidence was shaken and weeping for someone to help her stay on her feet, she had worn this mask enough times in the past to know how to find it now. She threw back her shoulders and raised her chin, leveling her brows as she looked over her two doubtful officers. "We are training," she said, "for the day when we turn this around."

Pierson blanched and lowered his eyes, having spent all of the day's courage in that one attempt at defiance, but Garrett still had a little bit of bluster left. "That's supposed to be the Order's job. And you just told us they were coming."

Kol's screams still hadn't died from Nes's ears. The mist of Mathias's tears when he'd kissed her farewell still warmed her cheeks. Her homeland, stripped of its leader, was still in turmoil. Nessix had survived far more painful fates than anything Garrett would ever think to do to her, and she stalked up to him, eyes dark and demanding his compliance. He withdrew a step from her advance, having never witnessed her lose her temper at any of the akhuerai before, and gulped down any other cocky remarks he might have wanted to throw her way.

"Mathias is coming," she assured again. "But until he gets here, we still must survive. Our captors are more wary of us than ever, and when our reinforcements do arrive, we will have to be ready—to run, to fight, to help each other. That cannot be accomplished by idly sitting around, hoping none of the demons get bored and come mess with us. They expect us to be an army, and we need to be one. We've all sacrificed too much to give up now. We will resume our training."

It wasn't the answer Nessix had hoped to give when she'd first slipped free on Elidae and as Pierson grimaced through forcing himself to accept it, she hated it even more. But there was even less stability in their circumstances now, and Nessix had to keep them alive until she was able to change that. Lowering her head, she placed a hand on each of her captains' shoulders.

"I will not rest until all of those I've sworn to serve find their salvation," she vowed. "But I cannot stand against the hells on my own. Please. Stand beside me a little longer. Help me see this through. Help me change the hells."

If Nessix would have had to attempt this same rallying speech certain of Kol's safety as he waited for her to drum up motivation in her army, she never would have struck the same chords she had now. But she wasn't certain of Kol's safety. Without his insight to the state of affairs outside the chasm, she had no idea how to position her army for the most efficient strike. And all she wanted, what she needed, was to hear somebody else agree to help her accomplish Kol's mission, even if she had to mislead them in doing so. She couldn't do this alone.

"The army is afraid," Garrett said.

Nessix closed her eyes against the rapid rush of tears. "So am I."

It had been such an honest vulnerability from the woman they'd only seen courage from, that neither captain could find another argument to her suggested course of action.

"I am afraid," Nessix repeated, admitting this weakness freeing part of the tension which tried so hard to pull her into despair. "But together, and only together, we can persevere."

Her words were consumed readily but processed slowly through hearts which still ached with fear of what the demons were capable of. But this was a fear which united them, a fear they could withstand together, and Nessix, who had returned to them as she promised she would, was prepared to stand at their head. Garrett muttered a brief curse and pulled away from Nessix's touch, turning to exit the barracks to spread the news. Pierson stayed behind a moment longer.

"What will happen, General, if the White Paladin doesn't come?"

When Nessix had still known Kol's fate and had assumed the greatest complication to their plans would come from him being monitored a bit more closely, Nessix could have come up with an answer to that question. The two of them would have led the akhuerai down a similar road as Mathias would, though their path to freedom would be wrought with far more hazards. As it was, with this uncertainty, Nessix didn't have an answer for Pierson, not one which would give him heart. "Mathias will come," she vowed. "And if something holds him up, that makes it even more imperative that we continue training so we can make a difference ourselves."

Pierson heaved a dissatisfied sigh which Nessix couldn't blame him for, and glumly followed Garrett out into the body of the chasm.

Nessix had drummed up her captains' obedience, had found the proper means to motivate her troops into action, but she was a far cry from restoring their enthusiasm. A sob offered itself to her, willing to carry out that fear she'd just admitted to, or her regret for the evils she'd done on her way to this grand failure, or her torment of having lost Mathias and Kol and very nearly her sanity. She stifled this surge of emotion, denying it from taking the flimsy grip she had on these hardships which drove her. If she wanted to kill Annin and Grell, she couldn't let go of a single wrong they'd made against her.

"I made a promise," she whispered to all of those who counted on her. "I will see this through."

Nessix flexed her fingers one last time and strode out into the chasm to rebuild her broken army.

* * * * *

Kol wasn't sure what woke him first, the piercing throb which ricocheted through his skull or the stomach-turning stench of decomposing flesh and liquified organs. Having spent the majority of Abaeloth's history as both a hunter and warrior, the ripe odor of death didn't typically offend the alar, but this current smell had saturated all of the viable air, so integrated and thick that it was as if Kol was breathing in rotting organs and the soup of entrails. He gagged, empty stomach heaving as he spun to the side and retched, regretting the action all the more as he tasted lingering death when he panted for breath. Once the sensation stabilized, he pried his eyes open to see…

Nothing.

His heart stopped for just a moment before racing at double speed to catch up to where it should have been. He blinked several times and when that failed to clear his vision, he rubbed them vigorously, confirming that they hadn't been plucked from their sockets. Still, nothing but darkness. The rancid aroma of death was no longer his greatest concern, and he held his open palms to his face to feel for the batting of his lashes as he blinked some more.

No, his eyes were functioning just fine; it was his surroundings which had something wrong with them. And it was reaching that conclusion which made Kol realize there was something gravely wrong with him, after all.

There were only a few locations in this region of the hells which weren't lit by orbs. And there was only one which had any reason to reek of death.

Kol froze in the darkness as he made a valiant attempt to weave through the pounding of his headache to sort out how he'd ended up in solitary. Ultimately, it didn't matter how he'd gotten here, because nobody sentenced to this chamber ever left it, alive or otherwise.

Memories of the events which passed prior to his waking flooded back to him, and all he could envision for the longest time were Nessix's tormented eyes begging him to find some way to stop torturing her, silently swearing she'd play along with whatever else he would throw at her if he would only spare her one more crushed knuckle. Her screams had tapered to whimpers as agony sapped the strength from her, and Kol felt them build up in his own throat the longer he held these memories in his mind. Had she ended up back with her troops? Were Grell and Inek at war with each other over which one of them would claim her as a plaything? Had Annin been able to keep her from being ended? Kol hunched forward against a flood of nausea, cold chills exacerbating the tremors running deep through his bones.

A sharp throbbing in his wings and right hip jerked him upright moments later and pulled him away from his regrets to dump him back to the more immediate concern of his mangled state and how he would escape the certain death he'd been locked in. He'd known Grell would find some barbaric method to torment and humiliate him for his fondness of Nessix from the very first time she had shown an inclination to disobey. He'd even accepted the fact that, by this point, he'd very possibly earned his death due to his inability to put a stop to her rebellious nature. But he'd assumed his end would have been drawn out at the hands of the inoga, savored over days of blood and dismembered body parts. The death he'd been sentenced to here in solitary would be no faster than Grell's murderous intent, but it would be much worse. It would be long and painful, filled with fears and contemplations Kol wasn't ready to face. And he'd be alone.

It was that last aspect which bothered Kol the most as he sat amid the decaying carcasses and mummified remains of the dozens of demons who had earned this sentence before him. Kol had never before had to face this world or any part of it by himself. Born a leader, integral in the raising of the demon forces, even when on this wild search for Nessix, he'd always had someone by his side. But now, he had no one to scheme with. No one to find comfort in.

Kol opened his mouth to try to speak, his voice hanging up on the dryness of his throat. He tried to dampen it by swallowing, but the rancid air around him made the effort too difficult to stomach. A faint drip sounded from somewhere several paces behind him, and he unsuccessfully tried to get to his feet, a fracture in the old injury to his right hip screaming at his effort to load the leg.

Crying out in frustration and fear, Kol grit his teeth and tried again. He'd dragged himself on this injury in the past, and this time, the socket still held his leg in place. It should mend itself within a few days, provided he lived that long. His second try to stand saw him upright, and though pain demanded he still favor the damaged limb, he successfully hobbled over the uneven footing of dead bodies toward the sound of the dripping. Navigation over these hazards became more difficult the closer he got, teasing him with the ironic notion of hope that this was a genuine water source which the others had hovered near in their efforts to survive, and his suspicions were confirmed as his steps yielded into soggy footing and the cool splash of moisture tickled his nose and cheeks.

Slowing, he reached his hands out in front of himself to avoid hitting the wall face first, his fingers brushing up against wet stones. Heart racing, he brought his fingers back to his nose, unable to smell anything past the ambient rotting of corpses, and tentatively stuck his fingers in his mouth. The taste of blood and earth danced across his tongue, but he was willing to assume that filth had come from his hands and not the water source. Eagerly, Kol cupped his hand beneath the trickle and brought the water to his lips to drink. Dry throat and dehydration remedied, he stumbled his way across the bodies until his feet no longer splashed in the moisture, and eased himself back to the ground to take the pressure off his wounded leg.

Calming his mind as much as he could past his pain and shock, Kol drew on what he knew of these cells. Three of the walls were composed of Abaeloth's core, the fourth made of stone raised by an oraku. This barrier was thick and too magically reinforced for an attempt to break it down to be either wise or worthwhile, but along the top of this front wall would be a couple of holes to allow enough airflow to prolong the captive's suffering. As slim as it was, that would be Kol's best chance to beg for information on what had happened to Nessix.

"Annin?" he called, coughing as he breathed in another breath of putrid air. He hadn't expected the oraku to be trapped in here with him, but should anybody be waiting within earshot, calling for him first was a far smarter idea than calling for Nessix, who stood a far greater chance of being similarly imprisoned. "Annin, I need your help."

His voice didn't even bounce off the stone walls, devoured by the insulation of the dead. Nothing besides the dripping of the water and his own breathing answered him at all. Loneliness and fear already playing tricks on him, Kol went as far as to hold his breath just to confirm that he was alone. No other sounds followed his effort, but that didn't stop him from voicing one last attempt.

"…Nessix?"

Of course, she didn't answer. If she had been sentenced to solitary, she'd have been thrown into her own cell; that was the point of this particular type of torture, and Kol was certain Annin would have had quite specific instructions against letting the two of them have any chance of trying to concoct an escape together.

That was it.

Nessix had never wasted a single moment of her days, always planning routes on how to get ahead of her circumstances. She wouldn't have sat around wondering where everyone was or how she'd gotten here. She'd be coordinating some sort of tactic to sneak out of her confinement as a final insult to those who thought she could be so easily dominated. She'd proven to have more luck on her side than Kol had ever enjoyed in his life, but he'd been around long enough to be able to find his own answers.

Following the same path as every other demon who had been thrown in this condemning chamber, Kol began to plot the possibility of an escape. A feeble stretch of his wings suggested the damage they'd taken would prevent him from flying up to the ventilation sources, so there was no use in entertaining the idea of trying to muscle those holes bigger to squeeze through them. Even if anyone bothered to stop by to check on him, bargaining for freedom wouldn't work and any attempts to do so would only give Grell more of a thrill. Kol didn't need means to visually assess himself to know that he'd been thrown him in here in condemned shape, and he decided he'd take advantage of that fact. In a day or two, someone would be down here to shout for him to see if he was still alive. Provided he was, he'd keep quiet. If he was lucky, they'd open the chamber to witness proof of his demise. And that would be his one chance to escape. It wasn't much, but it was something.

"Keep your focus, little one..." he bid Nessix, wherever she was. "You know what to do."

Surrounded by corpses in a sealed chamber, there was nothing but the darkness hindering Kol from looting bodies and arming himself with a repurposed femur for when this cell opened. Kol had always been the clever one, the schemer. He'd been the architect of half the hells. And he would not sit by and let Grell take that from him.

THIRTEEN

There wasn't much which made Tristan uncomfortable these days, but the ocean was at the top of that short list. One of the few weaknesses of the undead, capable of shriveling a vampire to nothing more than a memory as easily as it could disintegrate spun sugar, the danger posed by these waters was one of the most closely guarded secrets of his kind. And Ceredulus had told Tristan that he would attempt to journey beneath the ocean for the sake of appeasing this demon Mathias had demanded to bring back to life. Tristan had died once for his god and had always claimed he'd be glad to do so again, but he'd never imagined in all of his undying existence that it would be asked of him. Least of all in such a horrifying way.

If my understanding is correct, you will not once have to touch the sea nor its shores, Ceredulus said. *Consider this a scholarly pursuit and yourself a pioneer toward what could be a revolution for your kind.*

That was such an easy stance for a god locked safely in the heart of Gelthin to take.

Do not make me wake Waldek Septes to take your place, Tristan.

Tristan bit back his urge to growl at the notion of that old boot licker surpassing him and wrestled with his doubts and fears, swallowing his juvenile petitions that he'd served Ceredulus unflinchingly and more loyally than any of his brothers or sisters had. He deserved far more consideration than he was receiving, but he couldn't even begin to express as much to his god. Such tantrums would gain him no leverage at all. Ceredulus possessed Tristan's soul and that was enough to force his compliance—or erase him from Abaeloth completely—whether or not he agreed to this death sentence. And so, Tristan continued to press toward the coast.

After Berann had hunted down supplies and Tristan had covertly fed, they spent a full day moving south from Zeal, and when Berann requested Tristan to stop, the vampire was only too happy to oblige. Both the smell of the sea and the roar of its waves were evident to Tristan's superior senses, though he wasn't yet able to see his doom, and that was enough to bleed him dry of what little calm he'd pretended to have.

"The entry to the pass is nearby," Berann said, surveying their surroundings with his trademark intensity. Closer to a shoreline made by divine hatred, the landscape was largely bland, infertile earth, left uninhabited. It was the perfect place for the demons to craft a doorway to the surface.

Tristan rubbed his palm on the leg of his pants and followed Berann's distant gaze as he tried to conjure up some distraction from what he was about to undertake. "That's great."

The demon turned to observe Tristan's agitation, stoking more of the emotion with the glint of curiosity in his eyes. "You gave your god your word that you would assist my mission to obtain each of the weapons. Have you reached the point where his requests have led you to doubt your choice to serve him?"

The question hadn't been meant to antagonize the way it did, but it served as a blunt and untimely reminder to Tristan that everything he had and wanted could be taken from him in an instant if he continued to fight this. Fear was such a troublesome emotion.

"I doubt nothing I do in Ceredulus's name," Tristan said through a tight scowl.

Berann let Tristan hold on to that sentiment a moment longer before giving a short nod. "Then let us get moving."

He marched forward, his relaxed confidence mocking

Tristan's growing anxiety.

That demon is wise beyond his years, Ceredulus said.

Tristan clenched his teeth and rigidly strode after Berann until they reached a crater in the packed earth. The demon descended the steep decline which sank beneath Abaeloth's surface without hesitation, disappearing into the darkness without so much as a glance back at Tristan, confident—or perhaps simply expecting—the vampire to follow. After grumbling over Berann's lack of reservations but before Ceredulus had the need to remind him yet again of why he was going to do this, Tristan winced and stepped into the tunnel.

Berann had stopped just a few yards inside the passage, giving Tristan a brief flicker of hope that he'd changed his mind about this journey.

"This body sees well in the dark, but not with the complete absence of light," Berann said in place of what Tristan would have preferred to hear. "Can you?"

He should have known better. "I am a creature of the night," Tristan answered sharply. "I can see just fine."

Berann nodded in satisfaction. "Then please escort me as briskly as you can."

Tristan briefly wondered what would become of Berann and this quest if he did disintegrate out from under him while trying to race down this sunken highway. The demon had just admitted to being unable to see well, leaving him vulnerable to the darkness. Perhaps that would be a worthy consequence of these demands placed on him. Unaccustomed to fear at this point in his existence, Tristan couldn't quite control the tremors in his arms and legs, but pride ordered him to ignore it as he silently ducked a shoulder under Berann's arm, grabbed a firm hold on the demon's wrist, and dashed forward.

He moved brisker than usual, pushing himself to the extent of his limits in his haste to leave this dreadful fear—or expedite his inevitable demise—as fast as possible.

The journey passed with a constant stream of Tristan repeating to himself that he would make it out of this dismal death trap and was made all the more tense by Ceredulus's silence as they descended deeper into the hells. No calm guidance or even curt goading to assure Tristan he was there. There were rumors that the reach of the divine couldn't penetrate the deeper expanses of the demons' realm, and though Tristan favored this excuse over the notion of Ceredulus willingly casting him aside, it did not ease his compounding anxiety. Tristan pushed himself harder, burning through the energy he'd recouped in the last town they'd passed through far faster than was wise, and by the time fist-sized orbs began to offer a dim glow to the passage and Berann instructed him to slow his approach, Tristan was trembling with fatigue on top of his residual fear.

If Mathias had been informed as well as he let on, Berann's old clan was now stationed beneath Elidae, making the odds of him knowing the demons guarding the weapon hidden in these halls beneath Selian less likely. While this may have been a cause for concern to the average man, Berann considered it a benefit to his objective. He may be ignorant to the powers which might be protecting the artifact, but that meant they'd be just as likely to underestimate him. Berann wasn't arrogant enough to assume that he was the most powerful oraku to have his fate tied to these weapons, but he had the element of surprise in his favor and ample means to deter any mundane demons who might try to keep him from achieving his goal.

The relic's song grew louder by the second as Tristan sped along like some sort of divine hare and the gentle hum of sea life had hushed.

"Stop," Berann instructed.

Tristan followed the order and deposited the demon on the ground, turning to stare in awe at the walls of the sunken highway. Somehow, he'd survived, and he straightened the wrinkles from his clothes in an effort to distract himself from the shame of how frightened he'd been. Ceredulus would be pleased with the information he'd gathered. "Where did you bury this one?" he asked, drawing his attention forward once more as he strolled up to the wall of the tunnel to poke a light orb which cast a dull orange glow through the passage.

"I buried it nowhere. I've never even seen it before."

Tristan's hand dropped to his side. That was simply fantastic. "And you think you'll be able to find it without knowing anything about it?"

Berann twisted the pack he'd acquired in town around to his side and rummaged through it. "I know everything I must about what I seek. It will be either a hammer or a hook, and though I am unfamiliar with the halls beneath Selian, I can hear the weapon's song clearly. We will continue on foot and exercise caution in tracking it."

Tristan eyed the piece of jerky Berann drew from his pouch and growled. He'd fed well when he'd snuck off while Berann had secured the usual provisions, but with the distance they'd travelled and his haste to escape the perceived danger hanging over this accursed tunnel, Tristan had depleted nearly all of the energy he'd obtained. As Berann continued down the hall, Tristan pinched his lips together and hissed out his frustration as he scraped up his enthusiasm to follow. He'd have to find a way to teach this demon some better manners. Berann, not even glancing Tristan's way, clamped his piece of meat between his teeth, fished out a second piece, and held it out. Tristan puffed out a bitter laugh and shook his head.

"You've been carrying me for over a day at an enviable pace." Berann shoved the declined piece of meat back into his pouch. "After that tantrum you threw outside of Zeal, you haven't stopped to eat once. Aren't you hungry?"

"Of course I'm hungry," Tristan muttered.

"Then you should eat."

Tristan appraised Berann's neck, wondering if the demon's soul would impart any of a demon's strength into that lanky body he wore. The vampire took a step closer to the pulse of life but only had to imagine Ceredulus's stern disapproval before abandoning the notion of snacking on Berann. With a quick sigh, Tristan turned his gaze away from the demon's flesh to combat temptation. "I've got a restricted diet."

Berann slowed so he could turn his attention to the vampire, an inquisitive glint in his eyes. "Does that have something to do with your lack of a soul?"

Grouchiness surpassed by a wary curiosity, Tristan looked back at the demon. "Up until you were risen, you didn't even know my lord's name. How do you know the status of my soul?"

Berann turned his eyes forward and let his stride lengthen once more as he scanned their uniform surroundings for tells of the next artifact's location. "Your threads all hum with evidence of an exhausted life, but instead of anchoring to a soul, they are tied to each other where it ought to be. Any thread weaver could see it, and this configuration makes your song… shriller, composed more meticulously than a normal life's. It is an unnatural phenomenon, but then again, so am I."

Tristan much preferred Berann's placid intelligence to Khin's timid simplicity and Mathias's judgmental brooding, and for the first time since witnessing Mathias's pathetic objections to this arrangement, Tristan was pleased Ceredulus had put him on this path. "You are correct. The god who stitched your soul into that human body possesses and guards mine far from this shell."

A frown tugged at Berann's lips, the inquisitive light in his eyes darkening. "I'd pledged my soul to the divine in the past, and it was too great a price to pay."

Tristan smirked, glowing with a momentary burst of superiority over the ancient. "It was a negligent price to pay when it purchased me immortal life."

That frown tugged deeper and Berann bowed his head, contemplating what all had been torn from him and his comrades to achieve their undying status. Tristan was constructed differently than any creature Berann had ever laid eyes on, though, and he couldn't dismiss the possibility that their circumstances may not be all that similar, despite Mathias's marked prejudice against them both. It had been so terribly long since Berann had been able to keep up on current events that he'd be woefully remiss to draw any hasty conclusions based on a disagreement of how differently they valued their own souls.

"So, what does that have to do with your diet?" Berann asked.

"My soul cannot power my body from where Ceredulus keeps it, so I must tap the essence of the living to function."

Berann jerked his shoulders back, but kept walking. Though

necessity had coerced him into bringing harm to others in the past, he'd never done so with the pleasure of the average demon. "Which means what, exactly?"

"I feed off their blood."

"That is repulsive."

"It is efficient."

"And is blood what you hunger for now?"

Tristan's smirk broadened to a toothy smile at the scathing disgust in Berann's voice. "It is all I hunger for. And"—he added before the conservative demon had the chance to further debate the facts which governed Tristan's life—"I will require nourishment before the next time you expect me to be able to act as your stagecoach."

Berann set his jaw, brows settling low over brooding eyes. Who'd have thought a demon would have a harder time accepting the more violent aspects of Tristan's nature than a mistreated young woman did? Berann could disapprove of every last aspect of how vampires functioned, but as long as he had to rely on Tristan to complete his objective, as long as the vampire and his disgusting needs didn't risk complicating his success, he would overlook such barbaric practices. And perhaps keeping in good graces with one who embraced such selfish aggression would allow Berann to dirty his hands less in the process of obtaining the last two weapons.

"Are you a noisy predator?" he asked.

"Seldom," Tristan answered, smugly inspecting his cuticles at Berann's grudging acceptance. "Unless, of course, my prey puts up a fight." He slid a glance at his companion. "Are you making dinner arrangements for me, Berann?"

Berann remained silent for some time as he thought over what would have to be done to secure this next weapon. Whether or not he was prepared to kill his kin to reach it, he would still need Tristan able to carry him out of this region and to Elidae to reach the last relic. This would require speed Berann didn't have and ferocity he didn't want to implement with his own hands. Of course, he understood war; he'd been among Abaeloth's first generation of warriors. His entire purpose of hunting down the god weapons revolved around knowing that they would be used, whether to purify or purge, and that violence would follow him for the rest of his life. But this knowledge didn't mean Berann liked the idea of perpetuating what it meant to be a demon. If Tristan could aid him through the acts he dreaded to carry out himself, Berann was willing to accept it.

"Once we reach the main cavern network, there should be plenty of demons guarding the weapon, if they will provide you with appropriate nourishment."

Tristan swallowed his anticipatory salivation. "I've not yet fed off a demon, but with your innate abilities and superior power, I look forward to trying one."

Berann's lip twitched with his desire to scold Tristan for his inhumane levity, but preferred this compromise to losing the vampire's compliance. "We will need to be quiet and brisk. You've proven your feats of speed to me already."

"And you need me to stealthily clear the paths we must travel to find your weapon," Tristan concluded.

"Is that within your capabilities?"

Tristan chuckled. "Oh, it's not an ability of mine, Berann. It's a pleasure. Direct me to where we need to go and I'll make sure the halls are cleared for you."

Berann still didn't favor the idea of the amount of violence this arrangement pointed toward, but it beat him needing to employ the sadistic talents Annin thrived on. As competent and powerful as he was, Berann was not guaranteed an easy mission in stealing these weapons from those who desperately wanted the world ignorant of their existence and, burdened with the same responsibility which had killed him before, he bowed his head and trudged onward.

Berann's talent for hearing threads allowed the pair, much to Tristan's famished displeasure, to avoid many of the populated halls as they wound down narrow corridors leading away from the core compound of this branch of the hells. They progressed at an agonizing pace, with Berann demanding silence as he concentrated on the artifact's call, and the more time that passed, the harder it was for Tristan to remember that Ceredulus distinctly counted on him to not eat the undead demon. After what felt like days later to the starving vampire, Berann finally stopped his forward progress with a tired, disappointed sigh. He turned back and closed in on Tristan to keep his voice low.

"I believe we are as close as we can get without entering populated halls."

Tristan's expression brightened immediately, but Berann grabbed his arm before he had the chance to charge ahead to the promised feast.

"There are a dozen souls gathered around this weapon. Can you get to all of them?"

Starving as he was, Tristan wanted to claim that a dozen demons wasn't even a threat worth mentioning just so he could get to nourishment faster, but then he remembered demons were not fragile mortals, and his own powers were less than bolstered right now. "If you'd have let me fill up on something on the way down here instead of hiding from everyone we passed, I'd have them taken out in three seconds. As I am now? I could handle a dozen, but it won't be as quiet as you'd like."

Berann grimaced at Tristan's assessment and peered down the hallway. His threads were all mended and accessible so he'd be able to assist if Tristan needed him, but that was assuming their opposition remained at a manageable number. He didn't know these tunnels and had no idea where to raise walls to prevent reinforcements from rushing to the sound of Tristan's pending assault. The needles hummed at Berann's sides, calling to their long-lost compatriot as they reminded him of the power they held, and the demon sighed.

"How do those your god raises perish?"

Tristan smirked at the flutter of Berann's insecurity. "We don't. Not in combat, at least."

Berann wasn't as confident as Tristan seemed to be that the divine weapon awaiting them wouldn't be able to undo Ceredulus's handiwork, but he had no other choice. "If anything happens to me, you grab the weapon we find and the needles and flee to the surface, pray to your god to find Mathias, and the two of you finish this."

"Nonsense." Tristan pulled his arm from Berann's grasp and

smoothed out the lace at his wrists. "You and I work together much better than Mathias and I ever will. You'll live. Now. May I dine?"

Berann briefly mourned the deaths of those demons who would never find salvation, then nodded his permission for Tristan to disappear down the hall.

Even in his depleted state, Tristan moved at a speed defiant of mortal efforts, and he struck his first victim in a flash. Biting down on the throat rather than the neck, he silenced this first target of anything more than a gasp interrupted by a gurgle and swallowed two mouthfuls of blood as the body sagged. Wasteful though it was, Tristan discarded this unfinished meal, systems warming from the quick bite he had consumed, and dashed farther down the hall. The second guard fell identical to the first, but the third had witnessed the attack and raised his voice to alert his comrades just before Tristan could silence him.

At least Tristan had gained a head start.

Two faces poked around the corner of a doorway a few strides in front of Tristan and flung a string of hasty, foreign curses at him. They charged out of the room, weapons in hand, and were soon joined by two other guards from deeper down the hall. Fueled enough by those previous guzzles of blood, Tristan met this challenge briskly, disarming the first to come from the room with a quick strike square in the chest. Bones cracked from the force of the blow, and the guard choked on his attempt to cry out, staggering backwards and colliding with his companion. By now, the other two hall guards had arrived, and Tristan ducked beneath the swing of the first's sword and sprang up before the second had prepared an attack. Pulling that demon close, Tristan stole another rushed mouthful of blood and used the surge of energy to wield his victim as a club against the other hall guard. The pair crashed to the ground and Tristan tore the daggers from their belts, ending their lives with clean punctures to their throats.

A creaking rumble sounded from down the hall, but Tristan didn't spare the time to wonder what had caused it before the remaining room guard succeeded in shoving his incapacitated companion off himself to withdraw into the room. The door slammed behind him and the heavy clunk of a bar dropping came from the opposite side. Shrugging, Tristan stepped over the two dead demons at his feet and bent down to drag the one clinging most valiantly to life upright. Increasingly sharp eyes locked on the door for signs of movement, Tristan nicked the beast's jugular and drank deeply as Berann reluctantly passed by the three bodies between them.

"You said you were a quiet predator," the demon said.

Tristan didn't rush his response, waiting for his victim's weakening pulse to give him the opportunity to pull away. "I said this one was going to get loud." He caught the next spurt, humored by the disgusted curl of Berann's lip as he tried not to look at what Tristan was doing, and continued after he swallowed. "What's the plan now?"

"Are you through with your meal?"

Tristan rolled his eyes, using Berann's question as permission to take one final drag off the demon and released his hold to let the beast slump to the ground. Lifting his hands wide from his sides as he stood, Tristan took a step away from his victims. "Waiting on your instructions."

Berann wasted a moment staring at Tristan, working through his doubts about the sort of people he was relying on to seek justice and salvation. His attempt to stop the one hall guard who had run away from combat by closing off the tunnel had failed, which meant he was free to seek reinforcements, limiting Berann's ability to concentrate any longer on Tristan's repulsive nature. Unable to force himself to commend his companion for his effectiveness and blocking out the thought of the bloody massacre he was about to witness, Berann stepped past Tristan to face the closed door. At least they were on the same side.

"There are four left," Berann said quietly.

Tristan's eyes focused on the door like a cat prepared to pounce on an unsuspecting rabbit. "Child's play."

Berann steadied himself with a deep breath, widened his stance, and nodded. "Then we're going in."

The demon reached his right arm across his chest and clenched his fist before slicing his arm back to his side. The sound of the door's bar exploding and splintering came from inside the room, followed by a rapid string of surprised cursing. Tristan didn't wait for any other instructions and slammed the door open. It connected hard with the face of the demon attempting to hold it shut and Tristan snapped the neck of a second demon who instantly rushed to try stopping him. He spun to face the last two, his actions jerking with involuntary spasms as a constricting pressure tightened around his neck. Devoid of the biological need to breathe, the sensation was little more than an annoyance to Tristan, and his eyes darkened as he zeroed in on the magic user parked in a back corner of the room. He stepped toward the defiant beast and snarled as blood began to trickle from his eyes and nose, draining him of the strength he'd just recouped, and his attempt to demand Berann's assistance failed as he was unable to push air past the invisible hold on his throat.

A sharp pain pierced above his left hip, and again near his navel, and Tristan looked down in shock to see the barbed end of a massive bronze-toned hook sticking out of his gut. Blood drained from this wound rapidly, sapping his strength at a dangerous rate, and his nostrils flared in his attempt to growl at the desperate actions taken against him. These had been nice clothes.

The oraku in the corner sputtered and wheezed for breath and the hold on Tristan's neck eased up as the demon clutched at his own throat and sank to his knees. Tristan hadn't questioned Berann's aid until one of those sabers flashed to swipe across the throat of the demon grasping the opposite end of the hook. Tristan snagged this demon's collar as his legs gave out and pulled him forward to begin negating the damage done in this attack. With his free hand, Tristan swatted Berann's away as the ancient reached toward the blessed weapon. The demon respectfully waited on Tristan to finish what he was doing and once the vampire was certain he'd be able to heal from the damage dealt to him, he dropped his victim and backed up to sit on the table in the middle of the room.

"Is this"—a tense grunt accompanied the quick jerk Tristan made to the end sticking out of his abdomen as he pulled the weapon free—"your damn hook?"

Berann rushed to Tristan's side, catching the weapon in reverent hands as the vampire let it fall from his grasp so he could lay down and groan on the tabletop. "It is. Are you well?"

"My eyes are bleeding and I was quite literally gutted like a fish. What do you think?"

"I meant will you live?"

Tristan groaned again and slammed a fist against the table as he used his other hand to prod shredded organs back into his body cavity so they would be in the proper place when he began to mend. "Define live."

Through worrying about his companion, Berann turned to search the room for the hook's holster. "Well, do whatever it is you do quickly. We won't have long before reinforcements arrive after that show you put on."

Tristan's brows ruffled in irritation and he propped himself up on an elbow, swallowing a squeal of pain as he twisted to glare at Berann. "Oh, I'm sorry. I was a little too preoccupied killing those you refused to so we could reach this treasure of yours."

Berann located the holster where it had been knocked to the floor and secured the hook to his belt, staring at the walls to keep from being drawn into Tristan's goading. "You are right," he said. "I would prefer to minimize casualties in this quest which demands thousands of them. It is a flaw and you are not wrong to hold it against me. What do you need to expedite your recovery?"

Tristan poked at the exit wound, not quite deeming it ready for him to sit upright. "Find me the least dead of this lot and bring him here. If you want haste, I need more blood."

Berann was far from the first member of this unlikely crew to compromise his morals and, in the interest of making everyone's sacrifices worthwhile, he scanned the bodies in the room for those closest to life. The one Tristan had hit with the door skated along the line between unconsciousness and death, and Berann dragged the body over to the table.

Carefully, Tristan rolled to his side and helped situate his next meal into the most convenient position on the table. "Do demons ever wear anything nice?"

"You've got to be kidding me."

Tristan huffed a sigh and jerked the dying demon's collar from his neck. "Fine. I'll make do with these tattered garments, but you owe me new clothes when this is through."

Berann glanced at the doorway and frowned. "Hurry up. We need to get moving."

Tristan could have played with Berann the rest of the day, if not for his desire to heal and escape this dismal hole. Caving to the maturity expected of one his age, Tristan drained the last of their living opponents to ensure they could be on their way to the final weapon beneath Elidae.

FOURTEEN

Nessix hadn't gained even a fraction of what she'd hoped for while on the surface, but her brief stint of freedom had given her valuable insight. She didn't require dream stop to make it through the night, and she'd discovered that she knew how to work with her chaos in a productive manner. Now, facing the reminder that it was Kol's mind she tapped into while asleep, she clung to those dreams as desperate proof that the alar still lived, and embraced her ability to focus on conditioning her army without the dream stop's hindrance.

Despite the benefits Nessix had found, the majority of her troops declined her suggestion of going without the drug. The hauntings of Auden's demise, recounted to Nessix in vivid detail she was grateful to have missed firsthand, were made worse from withdrawal. Though Nessix accepted their reasoning, it was the first time this army—or any other—had chosen to ignore her instructions. She did her best to accept their fears, but her own anxiety over why Kol hadn't come to check on her since her recovery and whether or not Mathias had succeeded in finding what it was that Berann had been erased for stood poised to rob her of what little grace she pretended to have left.

Pierson and Garrett carried out her orders of putting the troops through their paces, but each exercise seemed to drain more and more from the akhuerai, pressing them closer to their fears of what would happen when the demons saw them all as a threat. Nessix had rallied demoralized troops often enough in the past that stoking those fires she'd lit once before should have been easy, but with all of the factors stacking up against her, she found her charisma flagging. And as the enthusiasm sputtered out from the drill she oversaw, halfhearted shouts of duty-bound obedience reduced to dejected murmurs, she had to step in.

"If you have any intention to stand against our opposition, this is not enough." She snatched the bladeless polearm from Garrett's hands and stalked toward the group of soldiers who hastily fumbled with their own sticks at her advance. "We need to survive!" She swung the staff at the first soldier, grimacing as his defeated stance nearly prevented him from raising his weapon in time to block. "And we can't do that by feeling sorry for ourselves. Now stand up. Act like you care. Act like you want to see the sun again. Act like you want to *live*."

It hadn't been the sort of bright rallying speech the akhuerai had grown accustomed to hearing from their general, but they dragged themselves to a slightly sharper form of attention, sneaking cautious glances at her. Nessix had heard the whispered murmurs passed between her troops these past couple of days, the weight of their doubts and concern over what had happened to take the warmth from the woman who had taught them the meaning of hope in this prison. Each of those whispered worries and muttered speculations had cut deeper into the wounds Nessix's sacrifices had opened on her heart on the path so far, but she couldn't let herself snap, not fully. The akhuerai had already rediscovered their fear of the demons and were well on their way to developing a fear of her, as well, and that had not been the sort of leader her father had raised.

"Lead them through the sequence again," she told Garrett as she tossed the polearm back to him.

He caught it and watched her in silence as she stopped beside him and turned to face the unit. "This isn't the way you told us this would be."

The criticism bit into Nessix on the level she'd only shown to a few, and she wondered if perhaps she should allow herself a taste of dream stop for her army's sake. Garrett was right and nobody in this chasm could argue it. They were supposed to be rescued by now, walking on the surface as free men and women. Their current circumstances weren't those Nessix had been promised, either, but they were in this together. She looked out over the timid troops, their emotional fatigue pounding against her like hailstones. She'd wanted so much more for them, to deliver them from this nightmare the demons had forced on them. She wanted the plans she'd coordinated to work out. She wanted Mathias's damn Council to pull their heads from their asses and rise to this threat almost as bad as she wanted Kol to glide down here, laugh at her for how much she'd worried about him, and direct her on how and where her army would strike. Nessix crossed her arms tightly across her chest.

"I vowed to give you better," she agreed. "And all of you *deserve* better. But it's where we are now, and we must keep going. Run the sequence again."

Garrett stared at Nessix hard, eyes fluctuating rapidly between obstinance, fear, and a sinking despair Nessix had come to know well. The captain wanted to shout at her to fix this, to demand that the one akhuerai who they'd all idolized as a hero live up to that title, but even if he found the courage to do that, it wouldn't make any difference. Whether or not he wanted to believe or accept that Nessix had arranged for someone to come rescue them, she was now back in the hells, just as helpless to reach those on the surface as he was. But although she'd failed to lead an army of knights in the akhuerai's defense, she hadn't quit trying to save them. Garrett gave Nessix a nod, took up a firmer grip on his staff, and turned back to the unit.

"You heard her." The command didn't carry half the authority that it would have if delivered by someone who truly meant it, but it did motivate the troops to pull into loose formation. "Let's start again."

The akhuerai, just as tired—but nowhere near as disheartened—as Nessix, slowly worked through their sequence of footwork, alternating between defensive and offensive shifts of their polearms to Garrett's count. Their spirits were dying as every day that beautiful hope and drive to fight which had been cultivated in them dwindled away to seem little more than naïve fantasies, and Nessix saw how easy it would be to let herself slip into that void with them.

She cast a pleading glance up at the chasm's lip to search for signs of Kol as she had a hundred times over the past few days, as if her wish to see him up there would make it so. She needed him to tell her if there were reports of Mathias's movement from the surface. She needed him to tell her that Annin had come up with a way to find the other half of her soul. She needed to see that he was alive so she could concentrate on her duties instead of fretting over his fate.

"Was that better?"

Nessix jerked back to attention at Garrett's question and flushed. "I'm sorry," she said. "I... thought I saw something up there. Try again."

A couple groans answered her, but most of the akhuerai heaved their weight off of their weapons as they resumed their combative stances. The air of dissent hadn't yet departed and was made tangible when one of the makeshift soldiers spoke.

"Why are we doing this, General?"

Nes's eyes snapped to Jakob, a dark-skinned human farmer who had trampled his plow horse over one of the demons who had come for him before they managed to kill him. He'd been one of Nessix's earliest supporters, one of the crew who harvested dream stop from the agricultural plots, and one of the few able to look most of their captors in the eyes. Not once had Nessix heard him complain, and his question struck her in her masked vulnerability, pulling out the fear and anger she'd kept bottled up from those who needed to see her strong and collected even as she felt herself crumbling away.

"We're doing this because I swore"—Nessix caught her defensive outburst before her vow to support Kol had the chance to lower her troops' opinions of her even more than her task driving already had—"that I would see us avenged, see us freed from the demons' rule."

"You swore you would bring us knights of the Order," Jakob contested. He didn't balk when back talking the demon guards, but he did cross his arms in a defensive shrug when voicing his grievances to Nessix.

Nessix winced at the cruel truth of his words, but a lifetime of diplomacy and juggling politics prevented her from responding to his implied criticism in a hasty manner. "I've arranged for someone much better than an army of knights to come for us."

The bulk of the squad looked away now, some burrowing holes in the ground with the toes of their worn boots, others drumming their fingers against their training weapons, all of them wishing Nessix would dismiss them so they could avoid the awkward weight of this long-overdue conversation. Nessix *had* given them purpose and hope, but most of them had come to accept that they only had one place, beneath the demons. Their lives in the hells had been drudgery before Nessix had been thrown down here, but it had been consistent and tolerable. She'd brought them promises of a brighter future and given them the will to fight. But with those virtues, that tolerable drudgery was lost to pain and paranoia none of them had bargained for. They weren't soldiers or heroes, but Nessix was. She wasn't afraid to face the demons, and the general consensus had quickly become to stand back and let her handle those monsters while the pathetic common folk resumed trying to find their crumbs of peace.

"General," Jakob said, his voice soft and harsh with regret none of them wanted to express. "We don't want—"

The shrill shouts of lost confidence from the akhuerai on break announced the arrival of a noteworthy demon, and Nessix's heart leapt to her throat when the flash of a shadow swept over the chasm. Barring her relief from her face, she turned her eyes upward to follow Kol's descent, and promptly choked on that welcomed influx of hope as she identified Annin, instead, spiraling down toward them. It was unusual for the oraku to come to the chasm without Kol having dragged him there, and Nessix didn't care for any of the reasons which might have motivated Annin to stop by for a personal visit after his cold warnings to her and the beating Kol had endured.

As he circled the chasm, Annin casually surveyed the fidgeting ranks with that disinterested regard he showed the majority of what he encountered. Without Kol to influence the oraku, Nessix was anxious to know what Annin's intentions were, and the akhuerai were rapidly fighting to abandon their current positions here in the open. Caught between duty, her worry over Kol, and trying to piece together what she could of her limited knowledge of Berann, Nessix barely had the sense of mind to safeguard her army from the threat Annin posed.

"Fall back," she ordered her troops.

They obeyed instantly, released by her words and driven by their ingrained respect of the oraku who had played a part in Auden's demise. Garrett hastily ushered the unit away from their general and those who were off duty disappeared behind boulders and into the barracks as Annin slowed his flight for descent. The oraku paid the scurrying ants little mind—he hadn't come here to deal with them—and turned his sharp focus to Nessix as she picked up a dropped polearm and stood prepared to face him. His feet hit the ground, hands loose at his sides as he stalked ahead, refusing to balk at her waiting aggression. He'd set his demands on his face, but Nessix had her own bones to pick with this particular son of a bitch, and had already survived some of the worst demons had to offer. It would take more than the cold glint in Annin's pale eyes for her to back down.

"Where is Kol?" she demanded before Annin could act on any of those thoughts he'd carried down here.

The oraku crossed his arms, keeping the fingers of his right hand free and relaxed as they rested on his opposite arm. "You seem quite concerned about him, considering all the terrible things he's done to you." Annin spoke the statement loudly enough to carry to the closest of the akhuerai, daring Nessix to speak in Kol's defense with those who expected her to loathe and fear him so near.

Nessix, however, refused to give Annin that kind of power over her. He'd already confirmed his knowledge of her willing alignment with Kol, and she was prepared to wield that in her favor. "I answer to him."

"And in his absence, you answer to me."

Nessix gnashed her teeth in a temperamental snarl which succeeded in making Annin's fingers twitch closer to one another. "Where is Kol?" she repeated.

Annin raised his chin and narrowed his eyes, observing with great dissatisfaction that Nessix held her ground through his disapproving scrutiny. She couldn't have been stupid enough to think that Kol had been forgiven for her behavior, and he didn't entirely trust that she wouldn't attempt—and, most likely, succeed in—some sort of rescue mission if she figured out just how much trouble the alar was in. The truth of Kol's predicament could prove too dangerous to disclose to Nessix, but letting her conclude for herself how imperiled he was could be even worse.

"He is alive," Annin said at last. "For now. That is all you need to know."

Nessix gulped down the uncertainties which came with Annin's choice of words. Kol wasn't safe and he wouldn't be able to come discuss tactics with her until he was. She'd have to take the next best route to proceed toward their goal. "What about my studies?"

Annin scoffed. He'd been against that plan of Kol's from the start; nothing good ever came from teaching an enemy general one's most guarded secrets. "Those studies are irrelevant to my purposes for you and I have chosen to discontinue them."

It was not lost on Nessix how Annin had chosen to emphasize his personal role in her future. "*You* have chosen it? What does Kol think of that decision?"

"The only decisions Kol is in the position to make is when to sleep or piss. It is a waste of your energy and productivity to dwell over what he thinks of how you are managed."

Nessix's fingers tightened around the polearm at Annin's reply, teeth gritting at the cold acceptance in his eyes. The oraku had never deserved Kol's loyalty or respect, and Nessix's hatred for him bordered on shoving her to impulsively attacking him. Catching herself before she gave Annin the excuse to cripple her, Nessix slammed the butt of her polearm into the ground and attempted to enter negotiations like the respectable officer she'd been harvested for being. "I could serve you better if I was able to continue my studies. There is still more I need to learn to be most effective."

Annin cocked his head and leaned his shoulders back. "About what, Nessix?"

Was that an invitation or a warning? Nessix cursed the fact that she'd never found a way to penetrate the demented shell Annin wore to access his deeper thoughts. "About demon society. About your history."

"About Berann?"

Nessix's gasp hit her before she had a chance to stifle it, her heart stalling in the bluntness of Annin's question. He hadn't expressed the same panicked rage which Kol had at the mention of that demon's name, but the cool tone of his voice frightened her just as much. Berann and whatever news he'd tried to carry to Zeal had become her best bet to save her army and Kol. She continued to have faith that Mathias was trying to learn all he could about the dead demon, believing they'd be able to combine their gathered knowledge for some grand final attack, but if Annin knew that was her plan… If he'd shared it with any of his peers…

The helplessness must have translated clearly on her face, because Annin produced what passed for a laugh and shook his head in pity of Nessix's last hope. "You thought Kol was the only one who knew you'd been trying to figure out who that peon was? You think we were stupid enough to leave clues to his identity in any of our literature or spoken lore?"

Nessix had to take the gamble. "If I knew why he was so feared—"

"He is not feared," Annin snapped, dropping his arms to his sides as he took a step forward. Nessix sucked in a sharp breath and straightened. "He is dead. And so is every last person who wouldn't listen when they were told to quit asking about him."

It was a valiant attempt to gain control over the situation, one which would have worked on any of the akhuerai and likely most demons, but Nessix wasn't ready to bend quite yet. The fact that Annin hadn't yet taken physical measures against her assured her that, despite his personal detestation for her, he still found worth in her remaining functional. Annin's flaw, at least the only one Nessix had ever been able to identify, was that he plowed his way through life thinking he was the only one smart enough to win the fights he picked. It was time to remind him that she wouldn't roll over for him the way Kol always did.

"You won't tell me who he is? That's fine." Annin's eyes narrowed as Nessix extended this invitation. "I'll ask the chasm guards who he is and motivate my troops to do the same."

Annin chuckled and shook his head. "I told you. He's been erased from history. Your guards are far too young to have any idea what you were talking about."

"Do you think that matters?" Nessix asked, undeterred by Annin's misguided logic. "How long do you think it will take for them to grow curious about what we keeping asking and start talking amongst themselves and their superiors? How long do you think it will take for their questions to reach Grell and his disgusting cohorts?"

Annin's hand snapped forward and grasped a fistful of Nessix's hair. Though a chorus of gasps rose from the surrounding akhuerai, some nervously shuffling a retreat while others fidgeted with their training arms as memories of how they once might have rushed to her defense encouraged them to stand their ground, Nessix allowed Annin to pull her closer, having intended to draw such a reaction from him all along.

"Do you *want* Kol dead, Nessix?" There hadn't been an appropriate amount of remorse in the question for one inquiring about the fate of a friend, but Nessix had long ago come to terms with the fact that Kol and Annin shared a rather one-sided relationship.

"Less than you do, I'm sure." When Annin's expression didn't change, chiseled with that coldness with which he viewed the world, Nessix tried one more hushed request. "Take me to him, Annin."

The oraku's eyes flashed at the command in Nessix's voice and her use of his name, and he jerked her closer still so he could growl in her ear as he had when they'd watched Kol be beaten half to death by Grell. "I told you to stay away from him."

"I have," Nessix said. "It's a little hard to be near him when you won't even tell me where he is."

"And you will not find out where he is as long as Grell and I allow you to keep breath in your lungs." Annin held her fuming eyes with strict promises which dared her to take the chance of continuing to defy him, her loathing radiating from the flare of her nostrils and rigid clench of her jaw. This time, Annin's threat had been conveyed effectively, and he shoved Nessix away to relay the message he'd been told to deliver in the first place. "Fix this mess that's become of your army before we decide the lot of you are better off gone."

Nessix grabbed Annin's arm as he turned to leave and he snapped his face toward hers. Annin, as much as she hated him, might be her only chance at pulling Kol out of whatever doom she'd landed him in. Sacrificing a fistful of pride for the greater good, Nessix blinked back her tears of outrage. "We do not have to work in opposition," she said in hushed tones.

Annin tore his arm away and slapped her, making no effort to lower his voice as he replied. "I work in opposition to everything which stands against my interests."

"To Kol?"

"He's served his purpose."

Nessix had long ago identified Annin's sociopathic tendencies and the manner which his descent into the demons' corruption had only enhanced them. Even before she'd embraced her connection with Kol, she hadn't thought Annin worthy of the alar's loyalty or affection, but it wasn't until hearing the oraku's intention to abandon Kol to whatever dismal outcome her disobedience had landed him in that she understood just how soulless Annin truly was. It was no wonder Kol had been shocked by her display of loyalty.

"So, you're content to simply discard him?" she asked.

"After his sensibilities have been sullied by the likes of you? Gladly." Annin calmly noted the ripple of horrified disbelief which drained the color from Nessix's cheeks. "Now. Bottle up that anger you're brewing and distribute it amongst your pathetic troops. If you want to preserve any part of Kol, do everything you can to prove he wasn't wrong about you. Make this army into something halfway functional."

Nessix trembled in restrained fury as Annin backed away from her and took to the air. What all had Kol told his peers and lords about her that she now had to prove? That she was a competent leader? A fierce warrior? Had he mentioned to them her loyalty and righteousness? She suspected her use of any of these virtues in the manner which she most wanted to express them was neither what Annin hoped to see from her nor means to secure Kol's safety or redemption, but Nessix would use them to drive herself closer to the goal of ensuring the demons were humbled and held accountable for their crimes.

Sneering at Annin's back until he'd disappeared over the lip of the chasm, Nessix spun back to the akhuerai who hadn't quite shaken themselves free from the tension of this encounter. "Well. If that son of a bitch wants to see us as an army, that's what we'll be. Let's get back to work."

Dubious glances were passed around before Jakob stepped forward. "But, General—"

"But nothing," Nessix snapped. "The demons want us proficient. They want us deadly. And that is what we need to be for our own sakes. Fall in line. We've got a long road to travel."

Nessix's determination was still a hard sell on most of the akhuerai, but it was an alarming strength which they could all cling to. They were more afraid of their captors than ever before, but that also meant the stakes were higher. They could continue to cringe in fear, to sink into their fears and insufficiency. Or they could run one last act of defiance against those who had taken so much from them, led by their general who had come back for them, who continued to shield and lead them, who, despite her own evident turmoil, still pressed toward her goal of defeating their circumstances.

Their general hadn't lost her fight, and her resolve to keep trudging forward, to continue to deny the demons' control over her spirit, was something they could all admire. Every last akhuerai in this chamber may end up a blubbering fool before Mathias and his hypothetical reinforcements reached them, but if they could take the demons down with them, it would be vengeance enough.

Nessix's soldiers stitched together their fragile nerves and broken spirits, and did as they were told.

FIFTEEN

Julianna had exhausted every excuse to avoid the numerous requests for her to speak with the Council over the past week. She'd put together enough of what was going on from Etha's vague recounts of Mathias's activities to know this was exactly the sort of situation Zeal's governing body ought to be made aware of, but their knowledge of it would do nothing to either fix this madness nor aid her brother. She'd managed to escape the Council's earliest interrogations by claiming the recovered priestesses needed her attention, but it had become too difficult to continue with that lie, which was how Julianna found herself facing Henrik and his disgruntled peers today.

It was debatable when any of the officials had last slept, indicated by the bags under their eyes, their disheveled hair, and demeanors which were more crass and irritable than normal. The entire Council had been running just as thin as Julianna was, and it served them right. Of the three dozen members of Zeal's governing body, eleven routinely supported Mathias, and of those, the Regent of Noble Affairs, Second District, the Chancellor of City Defense, and the Minister of Petitions were missing from this meeting, hopefully looking into the logistics of mobilizing the forces they kept on reserve. The High Priestess tried to tell herself all of this was a good sign, an indication that the Council was finally taking

Abaeloth's looming crisis seriously. But that optimism didn't carry her far into the pending conversation.

"So generous of you to grace us with your presence, High Priestess," Henrik snapped as she ascended to her seat on the right-hand side of the room. It was unusual for him to utilize such shortness with her, and Julianna would allow him few more displays of disrespect before retaliating with her own venting of stress. "We have been trying to reach you for some time now."

"Yes," Julianna agreed with conditioned grace. "As I asked to be conveyed, matters regarding the priestesses' welfare demanded my attention. I'm sure you understand."

"I trust they are well?"

"They are recovering."

"We do expect reports of what they witnessed while in the hells. The sooner, the better."

Julianna grit her teeth against a retort meant to scrutinize Henrik's lapse of humanity. "Once they are well enough to deliver reports, I will arrange for you to receive them."

"You are the High Priestess," Henrik scoffed. "Your powers supersede mere mortal efforts. Get them well enough. If you can't, order that fool brother of yours to do it."

Julianna settled herself—barely—with a brisk breath and scanned the assembly for a less obnoxious face than Henrik's. Finding several more approachable but none boasting adequate patience, she braced herself to stand on her own. "Master Caldwell, esteemed sirs and madams of the Council, there are some wounds much deeper than those of the flesh, ones which take the touch of time rather than that of those who wield Etha's blessing to heal."

"While we're on the subject of your dear brother"—Julianna raised a hand to massage her forehead as Henrik spoke—"where has he happened to run off to in Zeal's time of need?"

"I don't know," Julianna muttered.

"You. Don't. Know."

Julianna huffed out her disapproval of Henrik's arrogance, channeling some of what Mathias must have always felt toward the pompous man. "No," she snipped, a forced civility in her voice which challenged Henrik to continue pressing her. "I do not. He's a grown man, and I am not his mother."

"Ah, but can your mother even vouch for his whereabouts?"

Etha's sharp gasp passed through Julianna's cloud of frustration. *You ought to chastise that man for assuming he is in a position to make such demands of me.*

That was a course of action the Head of Court was well overdue, but his inquiry was one which Julianna couldn't ignore. *He does have a point. You* do *know where Mattie is, don't you?*

As the Council waited on Julianna's answer with borrowed patience, accustomed to the High Priestess venturing to the distractions provided by her goddess, Etha squirmed over her answer. *He's been so busy these past few days, it's hard to say just where he is...*

Julianna held up a strict finger as Henrik crossed his arms and drew in a breath to pursue the matter. *Or maybe,* she pressed, *it's hard because he's been employing vampires to abduct key witnesses? How do you propose I explain that to the Council?*

I propose you opt to forget that he has.

Julianna flicked her gaze across the waiting officials, beads of sweat taking form on the back of her neck. Etha had just confirmed for her a fear she had repeatedly tried to dismiss. *How am I supposed to forget that?*

Because I told you to.

There hadn't been a time in Julianna's educated life where she'd had even the slightest inclination to disobey Etha—Mathias did enough of that for both of them—but the need to pursue what her brother was up to drove her thoughts to the brink of such disrespect. She clenched a fistful of her gown, flushing in shame as she came so close to unraveling before this room of hawks, hating Mathias just a little bit for putting her in such an impossible predicament.

You can't get too mad at him over his current course of action, Etha soothed.

That sounded like a rather useless request to Julianna. *And why not?*

Because I was the one who encouraged him to go speak with Ceredulus in the first place.

Julianna gasped at Etha's confession, feeling draining from her extremities. Ceredulus had been the most defiant of the new children, certainly the most dangerous of them. He'd been the cause of the blasphemy of soul manipulation, the precursor to the same horrific problem the demons had brought upon the world and which Mathias was currently destroying the last bits of his good name battling. And Etha had encouraged him to make a deal with that monster? At what cost? Julianna leaned back in her seat, eyes wide and lips parted.

"Are you ready to give us an answer, High Priestess?" Henrik's voice only barely made it through the rushing in her ears.

"In a moment, Master Caldwell." Julianna assumed those words had come out coherently and dabbed at the sweat on her forehead. *Making deals with Ceredulus doesn't explain where Mathias is.*

Tell them he is on Elidae.

Is that a lie?

It wasn't a few minutes ago and it won't be in a few more. That answer works. It will keep them satisfied.

It might keep the Council satisfied, but it didn't suit Julianna. She had spent nearly her entire life learning to interpret Etha's will and had learned how to read the unspoken aspects of the goddess's words, which let her hear the truth clearly now. *He's not* here*, is he?*

Etha sighed. Where Mathias was so fond of making his own interpretations of her words, Julianna had always been adept at the far more sinister feat of hearing what she left unsaid. *He's only grabbing a couple of things before heading out. He has no time for Council business.*

Mathias never had time for Council business... *What sort of things is he gathering?*

Julianna, Etha's voice took on a stricter tone, though maintained enough of her gentle warmth to not frighten her justifiably distraught daughter. *If Mathias had wanted you aware of his actions, he'd have told you about them himself.*

Right now, that doesn't matter, Julianna said. *Right now, I've got a room full of spoiled and cranky aristocrats demanding to know where he is, when he'll be back, and what he plans to do about solving their problems. They are looking to* me *for these answers and I must be able to provide ones they will be inclined to accept. I have let Mathias cause me enough grief with the Council in times of relative peace and stability, but I think we can agree that these times are neither peaceful nor stable. They are looking to me, Mother, and because of that, I must look to you. I am begging you, please, help me.*

Julianna had always been better with words than her brother, and Etha, finely attuned to her children's suffering as she was, caved. *He's gathering Nessix's belongings.*

Julianna had thought she was juggling a grim reality two minutes ago when she and Etha had been discussing Ceredulus and vampires, but this revelation compounded the situation gravely. *He's going down there after her, isn't he?*

I… never said that.

Julianna lifted her head, chin raised. *But neither did you deny it.* There was no reply, and Julianna's heart sank. Mathias had clearly set his path, appeared to have entwined himself with some distasteful characters to get there, and Etha had allowed it.

Drawing upon the surge of adrenaline which rose from her desire to protect her brother from the recklessness his station demanded of him—and that which he provided in abundance all on his own—Julianna stood to address the Council. "Mathias is occupied with matters on Elidae," she said, bending the truth as not to deliver a blatant lie. "But for now, you will excuse me."

Oh, Julianna, that is not a good idea…

"We've still got more questions that need answers," Henrik added to Etha's objection. "Questions regarding—"

Julianna threw her arms to her sides, hands trembling with the closest thing to genuine rage she'd experienced in decades. "And I don't care!" she yelled to both man and goddess. All of the voices around her shrank into silence; Mathias was the one prone to losing his temper, not their fair High Priestess. "Now"—her voice had not yet found its normal, pleasant tone—"if you'll *excuse* me."

Nobody, not even Etha, attempted to reach out to discourage Julianna from flouncing out of her seat and storm toward the courtroom's exit. The guards hastily pulled the doors open, ushering her through with timid murmurs of respectful farewells she didn't react to and an air of fierce dignity carried her out of the Citadel and into Zeal's streets. Julianna had paid Mathias's favored smith well to pass along what he knew of Mathias's exploits, and she had no doubt that her brother had tasked the man with ensuring his beloved's sword and armor were in immaculate repair before the war that was to come.

The dirt and dust of the streets clung to Julianna's fine gown and each and every pebble she stepped on ground through the soft soles of her slippers, but she did not let that deter her. When she made it to the smith's shop, she found Mathias right where she'd expected him to be, pieces of dark armor far too small to fit his sturdy frame being collected on the counter before him. Julianna ducked her chin and clenched her fists, marching toward the men with a determined stride. The smith caught the storm of her arrival before Mathias did, and a nervous chuckle beat out of him as he hastily shoved a bracer into Mathias's hands, and ducked behind his forge as Julianna clipped to a stop beside her brother.

"The Council needs answers," she snipped. "Answers I cannot provide them."

Mathias frowned and gulped down his initial reaction to start spouting excuses Julianna would see straight through. At least he'd given himself time to rest in the temple on Elidae before making his trip to Zeal.

Julianna waited for his explanation longer than she was accustomed to wait for anything, but when it became evident Mathias had no intention to frustrate her with the half-truths he often used to distract her, she tried a dirtier route to get through to him. She laid a hand on his forearm and sighed away her anger. "You need to talk to me." He turned his face from her gentle plea. "Something. Anything. You gave me a demon's name. Etha mumbled something about Ceredulus. Whatever you're involved with is racing toward us all now, Mattie, and I need your help figuring out what it is before it arrives."

Mathias chewed on his options quietly as he buffed some accumulated dust from the street off Nes's breastplate. This wasn't the first time Julianna had manipulated him in this manner, and she was more skilled at doing so than he wanted to admit. He blamed that formal education she'd received while he was off learning how to kill demons. "Tell the Council," he said slowly, "that they'll have their answers—from me—within a week, two at the most."

Julianna shook her head. "That's not enough. You've failed to deliver on that exact same promise too many times."

"You said Etha told you something about Ceredulus? You remember me talking about the vampire who found access to the Citadel? I'm caught up in something bad right now, Jules, and the Council already hates me for it. Don't get drawn into it and get them hating you, too."

Julianna's shoulders fell at the weight of Mathias's words. For the first time, he didn't sound annoyed with the Council or like he wanted to return to them the frustrations they saddled him with. He sounded tired, guilty, as though he was genuinely worthy of the suspicions they often viewed him with. Julianna had developed the habit of writing off Mathias's behavior when dealing with Zeal's governing body as a byproduct of his boredom, but today she was forced to realize that he'd walked this path of alienating them and risking their wrath as an extension of his vow to protect others.

"They're already starting to hate me, Mathias."

He frowned. "Because of me?"

"Because of my defense of you."

"Then quit defending me."

"And let them kick you out of the Order? Ban you from Zeal?"

Mathias chuckled, despite the gravity of their subject. "Why not? It's not like they can take Etha from me, and she is who I need to do the little good I manage. Not those fussy aristocrats. Not an arrogant city."

Julianna dropped her hand from his arm to wrap her fingers around themselves. "But the city needs you. The people need to know their hero is with them, protecting them."

"I am protecting them better away from Zeal than I could ever manage by sitting in the courtroom, waiting for the Council to shut up."

"Protecting them like you protected Talier Dalton?"

Mathias winced at the mention of the Afflicted man's name and cleared his throat to shout above the roar of the forge. "Remus, I'm still missing a couple pieces."

Julianna turned to lean against the counter, crossing her arms. "Where is he, Mathias?"

"Right now?" He cleared his throat again to chase off the crack in his voice and fixed his anxious focus on the smith's workstation. "I don't know."

Julianna tilted her head, ever aware of how actively Mathias was avoiding her eyes and even more suspicious of how Etha was ignoring the subtle questions she sent her way. "I was told a disappearing man removed him from Zeal. A man who wasn't you, but one I suspect you know."

Remus returned to the counter with the last three pieces of Nes's armor and her fully equipped sword belt, dumping them all on the counter. "Today, it's on the house," he muttered. "The two of you play nice. Someplace else, if I may make such a request."

The smith retreated to his workstation once again, the clanging of hammer on steel rising a moment later, and Julianna continued to bore into Mathias with that strict expectation which often worked on her targets. Mathias went about bundling up the armor, doing his best to withstand his sister's steady, silent prying. She allowed him to work in silence, his guilt steeping under her pressure, and after he'd secured all of the pieces in the cradle of Nes's breastplate, he sighed and closed his eyes, pressing his fingers into the sturdiness of the dark metal to remind himself what strength felt like.

"Let me protect you from this, Jules," he said quietly. "Do not make me get you involved. We'll both be much happier for it."

She'd expected an argument or more blatant evasions, but Mathias's heart had been in his voice, reflecting that same concern for her safety which he'd developed in their mortal youth. How she hated what duty and station had done to them both. "I'm already involved."

Mathias bowed his head and shook it. "No, you're not. Not like I am. And I will do everything I can, including frustrate you, to keep you from doing so. I am involved in something bad that is likely to get worse before it can start getting better. Let me carry this burden and you stay as far away from it as you can."

One of Mathias's favorite evasions had always been claiming

Julianna was better off not knowing what sort of trouble he was getting into, and while she never liked being drawn into his shenanigans, this was the first time she truly believed his warning. *Mother, watch over him...*

"I need something to tell the Council," she repeated quietly.

Mathias kept his eyes on his hands as he rubbed the steel of Nes's armor. "Tell them... tell them I'm going into the hells to put a stop to the demons' plans and that the next time I need to even cross their minds is when you are preparing my memorial or I'm able to report to them that the demons have been permanently dealt with."

Julianna heaved a sigh and flicked a pleading glance toward the heavens at Mathias's overly dramatic response.

It's not as dramatic as you'd think, Etha warned her gently.

A heavy lump gummed up the back of Julianna's throat. She'd gotten used to worrying about Mathias's fate—how much pain he'd have to suffer through, the terrible decisions he had to make when every second mattered—but it wasn't often that Etha expressed such grim concerns herself, and that was enough to bring tears to the High Priestess's eyes.

"Mattie," she whispered. "Don't do this. Not however you're planning it. Not alone."

His fingers quit rubbing the armor, wrapping around the smoothed edges of it instead. "I'm not doing it alone. Sazrah's geared up to accompany me and I've got help on the inside—"

"You *hope* you've got help on the inside," Julianna corrected, sliding a hand over his. "Demons don't forgive those who—"

"No." The tendons of Mathias's neck twitched and he bowed his head in a manner which assured Julianna he was still hiding vital information from her that she'd have to use physical force to dig out of him. "I've got help on the inside."

Julianna shook her head, tears slipping out to line her lower lids. "I don't like this."

Mathias looked at Julianna at last, soaked in her exhaustion and fear to add to his own, and turned to take her in his arms. He tucked his chin into her hair, part of him wishing he'd listened to his parents and taken over the family farm instead of chasing his childhood dream of becoming a knight. "I don't like it, either."

The two stood there in Zeal's busy street, heroic paladin and revered High Priestess, both wondering how their lives had ended up at this point, longing for the same balance and simplicity their goddess craved. And in the bustle of Zeal's market, just for a moment, they were nothing more than brother and sister, leaning on each other to hold up the weight of their troubles as they braced for the trials and sacrifices they'd continue to make for the world which had no idea how badly it needed them.

"I'll find a way to make this up to you, Jules," Mathias said, "when it's all over."

"Will it ever be over?" she mumbled into his chest.

That was the same question Mathias had been toiling over, the biggest fear he'd carried with himself since he'd sliced Ceredulus free from the Veil. Holding Julianna a little tighter, he answered to comfort them both. "It will be. And when I am successful, Abaeloth will be changed for the better."

"And if you fail?"

Mathias swallowed the sting of that question and answered a moment later. "I won't fail, because if I do, that means Sazrah and Nessix failed, too. And if the three of us are gone, Abaeloth will have lost her fiercest guardians, the demons will know it, and the world will enter an age of agony we only thought it had known in the past. Etha guide me as she has thus far, I will not fail."

Julianna pushed against Mathias's chest to draw back and look at him. Outwardly, he'd found that confident expression he wore to soothe those of ailing mind, the relaxed brows and warm smile, but he hadn't quite flushed the final traces of doubt from his eyes. In less tense times, Julianna would have smacked his chest and told him to quit lying to her, but she wanted so badly to believe his words as she had when they were children, when they both thought heroes lived glamorous and exciting lives.

"Then don't fail, Mattie," she said softly. "Protect me from the demons hiding under the bed just one more time."

That confident smile briefly faltered into a broken frown. "Just one more time." He kissed the top of her head and repelled from her quickly to gather his bundle of Nes's belongings. After a steadying breath, he turned back to his sister once more. "I'll see you when this is over, Jules."

She couldn't pry her lips apart to answer, and so she settled for a feeble nod. Before either of them had the chance to break there in public, Mathias flashed away to return to Elidae.

Etha—

I've not left him before and I won't start now.

Julianna accepted Etha's answer just as obediently as ever, though it wasn't enough to completely alleviate the uncertainty which even the goddess's hushed tone had conveyed. Mathias had left to carry out his duty, and Julianna had to do the same. Wiping her palms on the skirt of her gown, looking around as if she'd forgotten where she'd been standing, Julianna turned and made her way back to the Citadel to deliver what she most sincerely hoped was not the last of her brother's lies.

SIXTEEN

Comfortable in the Undersea Pass now that he'd survived his first trip down its tunnels, Tristan found himself looking forward to heading out on the next leg of their journey. The hells were far easier to navigate than the surface, demon blood bordered on intoxicating in all of the best ways, and the sooner he helped Berann accomplish his objectives, the sooner Tristan could report to Ceredulus about how they had discovered means to spread his word and influence farther than mere rumors had carried them. Tristan had no doubt his god had a plan in place to wriggle free from the Veil now that he'd successfully found means to manipulate Mathias's sensibilities, and it was an honor to be the servant to facilitate this grand revival.

So pleased with this revelation and increasingly wild fantasies of the glory to come, Tristan nearly missed Berann's request to stop and thought to ignore it completely until he considered how Berann was his guide in this realm he'd had no firsthand knowledge of until just a few days ago. Jarring to a stop, Tristan allowed Berann to slide to the ground and awaited what they would do next.

"How is your hunger?" Berann asked.

Tristan couldn't decide if the demon was genuinely concerned for his welfare or simply sarcastic with the question. "I wouldn't turn down a meal, but I'm not starving yet."

"Good. We will continue from here on foot." And Berann moved on to do just that.

When Tristan stilled his thoughts from his irritated reflections of his companion, he could still hear the muted drone of the ocean over top of them, implying they hadn't quite reached Elidae. Frowning at Berann's reasoning—or lack thereof—Tristan lengthened his stride to catch up to him. "I could keep going for another few hours with no problem," he insisted, insulted that Berann had interpreted his last bout of feeding as some sort of animalistic flaw against his dignity.

"Then you can make it twice as far spending less energy at this pace."

Tristan dug his feet into the ground and parked his fists on his hips, glaring at Berann's back until the demon dragged himself to a grumbling stop. "And this pace is a pathetic fraction of the speed. We are in a hurry to find this sacred hammer, are we not?"

Berann bowed his head, internalizing his regrets and doubts which were tied to his desire to restore the demons to what they'd once been. He'd never been a good demon, less proud than he was honorable, and shown respect solely out of fear of the power he could call upon and Kol's loyal vouching. Despite these traits which his kin viewed as weaknesses, Berann was reluctant to volunteer a confession of the bitter confusion he continued to battle now as he had before his death. What he had set course to carry out was a single step away from genocide, an irrevocable action which would grant him and whoever he deemed worthy godly might over those he'd served beside in Abaeloth's most trying time. He'd not once considered Tristan trustworthy to command such power, and he hoped Mathias had distanced his obedience to the Order enough to be able to wield one of the sacred weapons without being shaped by the institution's influence. He'd yet to meet this Nessix who the paladin so desperately wanted to reach, but the residue of Talier's memories of the woman, of her effectiveness and an honor which mirrored Berann's own, suggested she might be a suitable recipient. He'd known this time was coming, knew he had to be the one to initiate it, but that didn't make him any more eager to complete this task.

"Well?" Tristan asked, indifferent to Berann's emotional struggle. "Are you wanting to reach Elidae or aren't you?"

Berann gnashed his teeth and resumed stalking ahead. "I'm really not."

Tristan straightened and shook his head at the sudden personality shift in the driven demon, and he caught up to his companion in a heartbeat, keeping a close eye on his expression. "You've been dragging me around at your will for this entire journey, insisting we not keep Mathias waiting. Now is not the time to have a change of heart."

Berann appreciated Tristan's prying no more than he appreciated his own self-loathing. "This is not a change of heart, but a feeling I've carried with me since I first stepped out of the hells in search of aid."

Tristan, in touch with the divine realm as few other men were, understood Elidae's significance in Abaeloth's balance and could easily accept that a demon wouldn't be thrilled to set foot on Etha's homeland, but there hadn't even been a moment of hesitation in Berann when he'd first charted their course. What could have changed between then and now?

"If it's any consolation," Tristan said, "I'm more likely to be unwelcome on the blessed homeland than you, and your kind has already proven to be able to flourish there. I doubt there's any reason for you to be afraid."

"This is not fear."

The answer had come quickly, fast enough to have seemed like a defense if not for the creaking in Berann's fragile tone. This was becoming more and more interesting by the moment, and Tristan hovered closer to the demon as he hunted out more information. "Then what suddenly killed the drive which had pushed you to your death once before yet failed to dissuade you from trying again?"

Berann didn't seek physical distance from Tristan, but settled for retreating into himself. Perhaps it was his persisting good nature or maybe how much time he'd spent in the purgatory of ancients, but memories of a past time, a better time, a simple time which knew love and loyalty and sacrifice, were still fresh in Berann's mind. He remembered Kol's nobility, the way he'd contended with Kalina herself in defense of the mortal lives he'd been put in charge of. He remembered Annin, so lost and broken and in need of guidance he'd been the only one to come close to delivering. He remembered Grellandier's simplicity and selfless devotion to carry the weight his friends had stumbled under. Theirs were the faces he knew and loved, those he'd stood by, prepared to throw down his life to defend.

And in the end, he'd thrown down his life to see them dead.

It was a weight Berann had never expected to carry, least of all alongside the beastly man who had quite literally carried him this far, and it was a burden he doubted he'd ever fully shed. Talier's memories should have helped make this easier—Kol had deteriorated into a possessive tyrant and Annin, left unchecked, had fallen into the sociopathic tendencies Berann had so carefully tried to cultivate him away from. The human had no knowledge of Grellandier, barely anything more than a terrified impression of inoga at all, which Berann figured was for the best. Even through their disagreements on what the future ought to hold for demons, Kol had been sensible and patient. If life had driven him to the point of indifference to the cruelty he'd subjected Talier to, there couldn't be much hope of saving any of his old friends, and Berann had to stop them from falling any further. It couldn't be helped. He'd tried to sway them in the past and they'd made their choice against him.

That justification didn't make it any easier to swallow.

Tristan's haughty sigh interrupted Berann's introspection, his words cutting through to the demon's motivation. "I will not allow your cold feet to jeopardize either myself or my lord. You swore to Mathias—"

"I'm still moving forward," Berann snapped.

Tristan silenced himself immediately. That was the first time Berann had interrupted him, the first remote sign of danger or aggression the demon had shown after being put into a body. Though Berann's mannerisms and temperament painted him a pacifist and the demons back on Selian had offered Tristan relatively few challenges, the harshness in Berann's voice was something every last instinct in the vampire wanted to avoid encouraging. Swallowing this untimely bout of caution, Tristan inched away from the demon and carefully tried a less direct approach.

"Is there anything I can do to encourage you to move faster?"

Berann maintained his silence a moment longer while he sorted out a response. "Do your kind form clans?"

Tristan's attention snapped to Berann now, but he was still too wary of the previous flare of anger to outright laugh at the question. "Our loyalties lie only with Ceredulus. If he orders our cooperation, we comply, but with the exception of a few servants and the occasional thrall, we prefer solitude."

"That must be nice."

"It is."

Berann sighed. "Is Mathias an honest man?"

Tristan snorted and looked away to hide his smirk. "He is transparent."

"That means my old clan currently resides beneath Elidae, and I will be required to face them."

Tristan kept his face turned away so he could roll his eyes without the risk of angering the demon. "Then let's just sneak in and out through the boring back halls like we did to get the hook. Problem solved. No clan to face. No need to worry."

A deep frown settled across Berann's face. If only it would be that easy. "The purpose of finding these weapons is to end demonkind as Abaeloth has come to know it. These men were my friends, and I intend to ensure they truly cannot be saved before I sentence them to death."

Tristan shook his head in disbelief. "Mighty Ceredulus, a demon with a conscience… I truly have seen all Abaeloth has to offer."

Berann snarled at Tristan, quickly redirecting the vampire's humor back into a more appropriate caution. "I wasn't always a demon, and neither were they."

There hadn't been the same warning in Berann's tone as before, more a hasty excuse, and so Tristan was comfortable meeting his eyes. "And I wasn't always a vampire. Men change, especially those of us who find immortality. Even our dear Sir Sagewind has changed over the centuries. I commend you, I suppose, for your concern for your friends, but know they are not the same men you'd once worked with."

That was precisely the kind of logic Berann needed to hear and believe, though the latter came with considerable difficulty. "Same men or changed, there will be no avoiding them."

"And why not?"

"Elidae is where Nessix is being kept, a prisoner to these same friends of mine you propose I somehow avoid." Berann waited for Tristan to offer some unhelpful advice here, but the vampire remained quiet. "We can target Motag's hammer, but at the cost of recovering her, a feat we'd promised Mathias we'd accomplish. Is that something you are willing to do?"

Tristan had promised Mathias nothing, but the same couldn't be said about his vows to Ceredulus. Had Nessix's value been limited to the paladin's lust, Tristan would have invested little more than a passing pity in leaving her in the hells, but Ceredulus wanted access to her, as well. "No," Tristan answered grumpily. "It's not."

"Then I must face my old clan, whether or not it's smart to do so."

"And you seem to think walking there will make it any easier?" Tristan asked. "As set as you are with trying to keep Mathias happy, you are delaying his reunion with his lover more than you have to. I say you let me tear this bandage off for you; the longer you take, the worse it will feel."

Perhaps if Berann had been alive through any part of the Age of the Undead, he'd have known the dangers of trusting a vampire with any sort of emotional rationale, but as he'd been blissfully unaware monsters more barbaric than his own kind had existed until just a few days ago, Tristan's words resonated with the parts of Berann which needed to hear them. To this day, he was committed to this path, and the ugly sides of his old crew had only had time to fester. The actions he was destined to take against them were every bit a mercy to them as they were for Abaeloth. Prolonging the inevitable only made it harder to bear. Heart heavy,

Berann stopped and waited for Tristan to do the same.

"Very well," the demon said. "Take me to Elidae and let me end this."

* * * * *

The final leg of their approach on Elidae hadn't given Berann adequate time to find comfort in the terrible decision he'd settled on, but he made the best of it. Tristan leaned a shoulder against the wall and watched the demon's agitation wind up to an unstable peak as he paced the width of the hall, the emotion settling after a few more passes before rising again. After so much racing about, hunger clawed at Tristan now, and he suspected if he planned to wait on Berann to get a hold of himself, he'd snap and end up draining his companion before they ever entered the main halls.

"What's the plan, Berann?"

The demon continued pacing for another half dozen breaths, eyes narrowed in consideration. When he stopped, he approached his conclusion with care. "This body is known and assumed to be owned by two rather influential demons," he said. "I plan to use this to my advantage and see how easily I can simply walk into their den."

Tristan grinned. As careful as Berann had been so far, this was exactly the kind of reckless gamble the vampire thrived on. "What's your plan for if it's not easy?"

"At least at one point, I'd been among the most powerful oraku. I'll come up with something."

Tristan shoved himself away from the wall and moved a hand to dust off his shoulder before stopping the action. His clothes were already filthy and torn; what did a bit of dust matter to him? Swallowing the bitterness of his grumbles, Tristan forced himself to brighten. "They would recognize and accept you, but what about me?"

Berann squared his stance and crossed his arms, blocking Tristan's direct path to the expanse of the hells beneath Elidae. "It is wisest for us to not be seen together. I've only got a vague idea of how they will accept me, but every oraku we come across would see what was wrong with you." Berann continued speaking past Tristan's exaggerated gasp of offense. "If we were seen together, my ploy would be over."

Tristan frowned at the suggestion of separating. Combative fancies aside, his primary purpose had been to keep track of Berann for Ceredulus and the damn demon wanted to run off on his own? That wasn't even to mention that Tristan had no idea how to get himself out of this cursed hole if Berann went missing or found his demise while they were apart. "You would leave me by myself in this dismal realm?"

Berann looked Tristan over and gave him a brief nod. "If I had to. I've seen enough of your abilities to believe you'd survive— hunted like mad once you made those abilities known, but you'd survive. I'm not planning to leave you alone, only unseen."

"Ah." Tristan's worry fluttered away with a keen smirk at Berann's praise and the clarification of his plan. "Staying unseen is something I am quite capable of doing."

"That means no eating anyone."

A perturbed frown wiped away Tristan's smirk. "How long do you suspect I'll have to stay hiding? Because I will have to feed eventually, assuming you want me productive."

"I'll be as fast as I can." As if that settled the matter, Berann turned and lifted his foot to continue forward before freezing in place. He rested his hands on the hook and sabers secured to his belt.

Even if Talier had been the type to carry arms, both Kol and Annin—and any other ancients lurking about this region of the hells—would recognize these weapons in an instant. Tristan had proven both useful and reliable so far, but that didn't mean he'd earned the trust needed to be given these most powerful relics, least of all when Berann knew how grateful Ceredulus would be if his servant brought them to him. Yet they were too coveted to simply be left unprotected so close to the same hands he was trying to keep them from. Mathias had said Ceredulus was trapped behind divine bars on Gelthin, and Tristan had said he was incapable of travelling by sea. The vampire had expressed several uncanny abilities but none of them confirming any notable divine gifts unique to him, and after Berann had carefully bound the weapons into their respective holders, he sealed off the tunnel ten feet behind the vampire.

Tristan jumped at the passage's closure, spinning around to watch the stones draw in on one another, and hastily turned back to watch this even-tempered, undead demon with a wary eye. His spike of adrenaline was stopped by confusion as Berann unfastened his belt.

"Until I can locate Nessix, you are all I have that can pass as an ally down here." Berann gathered the belt in his hands, lips creasing in a grim frown as he gazed down at the relics he'd sacrificed so much to obtain. "We cannot risk any demon other than myself getting their hands on these weapons. I need you to keep them just as hidden as yourself."

Tristan glanced back at the sealed tunnel and chuckled at Berann's safety measure. He wouldn't fault the demon for distrusting him with items as valuable as these; Tristan, himself, wouldn't trust another vampire with his favorite chalice, much less weapons of Abaeloth's salvation or demise. He did his best to withhold his eagerness as Berann held the equipped belt forward and succeeded in keeping a leash on the greedy impulse to simply snatch it from the demon's grasp. Accepting it like a gentleman, Tristan slung the belt around his waist, not regretting taking such firm possession of it until Berann stepped forward and grasped the tightened buckle. The demon's thumb brushed twice over the metal.

"There." Berann allowed the offended vampire to retreat once he'd snuggly locked the belt in place. "You will be unable to part with it until I remove it from you, nor will you be able to draw any weapon from it unless you make a deal with an oraku who can decipher my work. And do know that any demon who sees what you carry will attempt to dismember you to take them, and that I need these weapons to see you out of the hells and back to your god when this is through. Any plans you may have concocted to try to claim them for yourself or your god are best left here. Do you understand?"

Tristan was unaccustomed to not being the sharpest man in

the room, and though he'd lost to a creature who had been around nearly since the dawn of time, he didn't care for how insignificant it made him feel. Despite Berann's weighty warning, Tristan attempted to loosen the belt, unable to find enough slack in the leather to work his fingers under. He'd yet to see what sort of dangers Berann could pose to him, but the instincts thriving inside of him knew better than to go provoking the demon to find out. Submission tasted vile, but Berann had carefully secured every upper hand that had been available to Tristan.

"I understand," Tristan said at last, the gleeful warmth absent from his voice.

The sudden chill of the vampire's demeanor meant nothing to Berann, and his willingness to turn and resume walking down the hall only confirmed that Tristan's speculations of his might couldn't be that far off.

"Stay silent," Berann ordered over his shoulder. "Stay hidden. And wait for my call to next make yourself known."

Tristan sighed and shook his head, wondering if he'd met his match at last. "If you say so…"

Berann didn't have a particularly good reason to invest much faith in Tristan doing as he was told, but was moderately comfortable the vampire wouldn't blow his cover after how many opportunities he'd had to turn on him and the promises he'd made to his god. As content with the arrangements as he'd ever be, Berann dashed toward the populated halls, trying to draw on the remaining memories of Talier's terror as he waited to be found.

Trusting he'd find some way to make this all worthwhile to Ceredulus in the end, Tristan sank into the shadows as he was so good at doing, and followed Berann into Elidae's heart.

SEVENTEEN

The stench of solitary had quit being quite so overwhelming once Kol was forced to consider his only option of a food source as his hunger pangs intensified. He'd attempted to sate his stomach's cries with water, but it neither flowed fast enough nor offered a satisfying amount of substance to soothe his belly. He'd spent the past hours or days or however long had passed blindly groping his way through the rotting corpses, feeling for anything sharp or heavy which would serve him better than the scavenged leg bone to try dislodging stones from the wall but, of course, none his silent companions had been sentenced with anything able to shorten their time spent suffering.

Weak from fatigue and slowly being eaten by the infection blazing through his wings, Kol slumped amongst his grisly company for a break in his worthless search and wondered what had become of Nessix, how she'd fare in an identical circumstance. He couldn't spare the energy or effort to laugh at the absurd question. If Nessix would have been in this situation, she'd have been halfway through some impossible tactic to sneak out of her prison before hunger had even become a distraction. He pressed a fist to his aching stomach and thought he closed his eyes. Would starvation even kill an akhuerai? Of all the tests and trials he'd put them through, Kol had never bothered to see what would happen if one of them starved to their next death. If they died from lack of nutrition, what energy would they tap into for their recovery? It was a fine question, one which Annin would have taken at least a passing pleasure in investigating.

Kol slid a hand into his hair to pull at it for sanity, and the lonely chamber mocked him for being unable to escape the oraku.

"Where are you, you fiend…"

Kol's feeble murmur was devoured by the dead, and they answered with the silent promise that such questions wouldn't mean a thing once he joined them. Too tired to stay awake but too frightened he wouldn't wake if he fell asleep, Kol hunched over himself against the chill of the chamber and the pain radiating through his wings and tried his best to not think about the future.

* * * * *

It was too quiet with Kol gone. Annin had thought he'd enjoy the peace when he'd first been informed of Kol's sentence, but he'd come to rely on the annoyance of the alar's steady stream of theories to break up the monotony of his miserable existence. Now, without those unplanned shoves to investigate the improbable, Annin found himself zoning out at his studies as he waited on a fresh viewpoint, no longer driven by the inconvenience of interruptions to hasten through one task before the next was asked of him. Though he'd had quite enough to complain about Kol over the past several months, he now had to acknowledge that there were certain traits about the alar which he had taken for granted.

Just as the first inklings of nostalgia were about to pry at the door of regret bolted shut in Annin's heart, the physical door of his chamber slammed open. Annin was on his feet in the same instant, fingers brought together to act against the sudden threat, but he shook his hand loose as he recognized Grell's frown. Already sick of looking at that scarred face, Annin turned and sat down once again at his desk.

"You look agitated, my lord."

Grell had never been completely comfortable when dealing

with Annin and had crutched on Kol to help him manage the touchy oraku without risking a broken knee or ruptured eardrum. Without Kol to navigate that treacherous slope, Grell barreled down it face first.

"When did you say was the last time you went and checked on that damned army of yours?"

Would Annin ever escape the akhuerai's curse? He flipped the page of the day's reading selection. "I hadn't mentioned it."

A throaty expulsion of air puffed from Grell, but based on the observation that none of Annin's belongings had begun to break or be thrown across the room, the inoga hadn't yet decided a loss of temper was worth causing a scene. "Then mention it now."

Annin dropped his hand on his open book and bore his perturbed glare into the wall in front of him to keep from needing to look at Grell. "Two days ago."

Grell grunted. "And did you know they've all quit eating that sedative?"

"I don't suppose I cared enough to ask."

"Well." Grell spat the word with the same force which had always made Kol take a moment to appraise his stability, though if Annin was moved by it, he gave no tells. "You should have. The last time they went off their drug, it resulted in that attempt they made at a revolt."

Annin looked longingly at his book, regretting that Grell's paranoia would keep him from concentrating on it. If he couldn't be happy, then neither of them would be. "That revolt had been easy enough to control."

"That revolt," Grell snapped, "had been organized when that upstart general of theirs was away from them, getting cozy with Kol. They've got her with them now."

Annin felt the ability to smirk inside of him, but couldn't motivate himself to show it past his irritation. "Certainly, you are not afraid of them, my lord?"

Grell grit his teeth at the slight elevation of his heart rate which came from Annin's provocation. He much preferred giving orders to Kol; the alar had been just as guardedly respectful of Grell's power as Grell was of Annin's, and had been infinitely easier to manipulate because of it. "No," he insisted peevishly. "But their champion's there to rally them, and that's the sort of thing she's good at. Look at what she did to Kol."

"Kol is a soft, pliable fool, effortlessly swayed by anyone he takes an interest in." Annin turned in his seat and leaned an elbow on his desktop. "And from my observation, the akhuerai aren't terribly thrilled that Nessix has put them back to work. After that tantrum you threw against their commander, they've lost most of their will to fight. *If* they find the nerve to try another rebellion, it's just as likely to be against Nessix as it is to be against us."

Grell blinked his small eyes as his equally limited mental capacity tried to sort out the truth of Annin's statement. Resenting the oraku's smug confidence, but too cautious to mention as much, Grell crossed his arms. "What makes you so sure they'd turn on their only line of defense?"

Annin truly wasn't sure they would, he simply wanted this conversation over so Grell would leave him alone. The only way to achieve that goal, however, was to give the inoga the answer he wanted to hear. "Because," he sighed, turning back to his book. "It is her fault that they continue to suffer."

"It's her fault they know anything at all about fighting," Grell countered stubbornly.

Annin frowned. "No, I believe *that* is our fault." A rapid flush of rage flooded Grell's cheeks at Annin's blame, but the oraku continued without regard to the inoga's quiet seething. "We decided to build this army specifically to achieve a combative edge. Any leader we would have found for them with the skill and charisma to lead them would have yielded the same results. We built an *army*, Grell. Fighting is their purpose. We knew about their chaos going in and you have no need to worry about it now if you hadn't worried before."

"That chaos was meant to remain contained until *we* chose to let it out."

Annin heaved an inconvenienced sigh and spun around on his stool. Grell's face was twisted about like that of a spoiled child trying his hardest to act as though he was in charge, but Annin hadn't expected much different. "Is this you asking me to go deliver a new set of ultimatums?"

That was precisely what Grell wanted, but Annin's bored tone, often the prerequisite to firm and ruthless power grabs, frightened away his ability to speak it so plainly. "With Kol stripped of his station and influence, you are supposed to be Nessix's lord."

Annin's typical frown pinched deeper in response to Grell's ignorance, and he turned back to his desk. "Supposed to be, but she's adamant that she will only listen to Kol."

"Then we will force her to obey you."

Annin lifted his eyes from the same page he'd been trying to read since Grell arrived, already detesting what he knew was coming.

"Punishment wasn't enough to tame her," Grell said, "nor was torturing her lover. Come with me, and we will force the little bitch to submit."

With Kol sentenced to a slow death, Annin had accepted the fact that he now had to find a new angle to approach his quest for dominance. Faced with this challenge, he'd been content to let the akhuerai sort out their problems amongst themselves, but he'd only get to stay content if he satisfied Grell's demands before they steeped much longer. He pushed his stool back and stood to face Grell.

"I'll see what I can do."

"You'd better do more than that."

There was no part of Grell's aggression which worked on Annin and the twitching strain in the inoga's posture as he internalized his frustration over that was a small consolation for the inconvenience he caused. With Kol removed from the equation, Grell *needed* to keep the oraku's compliance at any cost, and they both knew Annin's impatience was fickle and thin. Either way, if only for the sake of being left alone, Annin stalked past Grell to leave his room and go address this army—again—for whatever good it was supposed to do. Grell followed, much as Annin had expected him to, and the oraku's attempt to forget he was there was thwarted by the inoga's steady ranting.

"You should have ended her up there on the surface the moment you got your hands on her."

"That would have been a waste of resources and a dangerous move."

Grell harrumphed his disagreement. "Everything about her was a waste of resources, and there's nothing dangerous about ending one of these miserable louts, just annoying."

Annin slowly flexed his neck from left to right, stretching out the tension his irritation with Grell's simplicity brought him. "Need I remind you that Nessix is very dear to someone none of us want to cross?"

Grell spat to the side, a deep chuckle rumbling in his throat as he found a swell of confidence in his physical distance from that particular threat. "Speak for yourself. I'd love the chance to cross Mathias Sagewind."

"He soundly defeated four of your peers not even a month ago." Behind him, Grell sucked in a sharp breath to fuel a growl and lifted an arm to grab Annin to drag him to a stop. The oraku beat him to the assault. "Touch me and I'll burst your kneecap."

Grell's fingers recoiled into a trembling fist before he pulled it back to his side. "All I'm saying is—"

Annin stopped abruptly, raising a hand to direct Grell to do the same. The inoga was quick to respond in light of the recent reminder of what a tiny flick of Annin's wrist was capable of doing. Rapid footsteps marched toward them, accompanied by a feeble voice of protest which Annin had thought he'd never hear again. After a moment spent analyzing the current facts, curiosity drew the oraku forward, and Grell followed reluctantly.

Turning from the hall which led to Annin's chamber, the pair was soon met by two demons dragging a timidly protesting human male their direction. The escorts halted as Annin neared, averting their eyes as was appropriate for their stations.

"Sir," one of them spoke quickly, "this man claims to know you, asked to be—"

"Silence," Annin ordered, and the demon obeyed.

Annin had wanted to get his hands on Talier again, almost more than he'd wanted to get them on Nessix, and had thought this experiment of his lost to Kol's obsession. Though he was pleased his toy had found his way to him, he was equally wary; Talier, as he'd last seen him, would have given anything but the life of his brother—something Annin didn't have a current status on—to escape him. Annin resumed walking forward, Grell trailing behind, until he was half a step from Talier.

The human stood squarely and with shoulders erect, but kept his head bowed and gaze driving so hard into the ground he must have been relying on his other enhanced senses to keep apprised of his surroundings. His threads beat with a different pattern of wariness than the last time Annin had assessed them, and those connected directly to the bundle of his soul glowed dense and brighter than before. Annin reached out a hand and raised Talier's chin with one finger, narrowing his eyes at the lack of trembling on the other side of his touch.

"How did you get here, Talier?" Annin asked.

Talier looked past Annin to stare at Grell with a blank expression Annin couldn't quite attribute to shock. "By running." A heavy moment of silence passed before Talier swept his eyes across Annin's suspicious glare and hastily looked away. "Um, sir."

Annin drew a step back and crossed his arms, cocking his head as he contemplated the changes in his creation. "And how did you locate the Undersea Pass all on your own?"

"It wasn't on my own." That answer had come out much too quickly and without the anticipated reluctance which had always accompanied everything Talier said and did. "I asked for help from some of the demons in Heiligate."

"What is this—"

Annin turned his head sharply and hissed Grell into silence before slowly bringing his focus back to Talier. Where had he found the courage to start working with demons and, more importantly, to face him without cowering? "You'd found sanctuary in Zeal. What made you want to leave her safety?"

This answer came rapidly, too, but Annin couldn't quite question it. "That Mathias Sagewind is insane. He tried to kill me for having wasted Nessix's time, and I didn't want to wait around and see if he'd succeed his next attempt on my life."

Annin flicked his attention back to Grell. It seemed Mathias was out for more than just demon blood right now. Accepting this answer better than the previous ones, deciding it could explain the abnormalities about the condition of Talier's threads and be a valid reason the Afflicted decided to return to the unreliable protection of his master, Annin raised his chin. "I suppose I'm part to blame for that."

"I suppose you are," Talier agreed.

This unusual bout of bluntness both irritated and intrigued Annin, but with Grell breathing down his neck, he didn't have the freedom to investigate deeper at the moment. Dropping his arms to his sides, Annin gestured vaguely at the two demons restraining Talier. "Take him to my chamber, and stay with him. If any one of you touches a thing, you're all three dead. I will be back shortly."

The demons gulped down the weight which always came with Annin's threats and squeaked out affirmatives before shuffling their charge past their two lords.

"*Now* may I ask who that was?" Grell asked.

Annin continued walking, more eager to carry out this mission Grell had demanded of him so he could get to work studying Talier as he'd wanted to since losing him on the surface. "He's the Afflicted I made to hunt Nessix. I thought he'd been lost to me, but it seems a wolf's pack instincts run stronger than I'd expected."

"You and Kol with your fascination of mortals…" Grell sneered.

"Mine is a fascination of progress," Annin corrected. "I will not expect you to understand."

Grell grumbled his censored criticism at Annin's back, but in favor of seeking silence, Annin didn't offer a response, and the pair continued their trek to the chasm without another word. Annin would facilitate whatever it was Grell hoped to accomplish with Nessix, sign her over to the inoga if he had to, and begin the pursuit of something worthwhile. Attainable plans falling into place for the first time in months, Annin found something to look forward to at last.

* * * * *

Nessix had only just excused herself from her training troops when the alarm was raised. As the akhuerai pulled themselves into sloppy formation, confidence not yet where it needed to be to stand against the caliber of demons coming their way, Nessix returned to their head, frowning up at Grell who plummeted toward the ground. Annin glided behind him, eyes cold and chin raised in a manner which assured Nessix that there were problems to be dealt with. Grell landed and growled as he stalked toward Nessix, chest puffed out and shoulders aggressively squared.

"Stand down," Nessix ordered her troops before striding ahead to intercept Grell in an effort to establish a buffer zone between this monster and the soldiers she was struggling to bolster. Her bold approach—and the akhuerai's wary obedience to her instruction—struck a nerve with the inoga. When she spat her next question, holding his temperamental eyes with a fearlessness he resented, Grell clipped to an abrupt stop. "What do you want?"

Beside him, Annin halted as well, and Grell crossed his arms to mask the uncertainty brought about by Nessix's courage. "That how you talk to Kol?"

After the last visit from Annin, Nessix internalized her relief in how Grell still spoke of Kol in the present tense and used the inoga's question as a foothold to pursue what she'd been after since waking from her most recent death. "No. I respect him more than that. Where is he?"

Grell sneered and disregarded Nessix's question, as though withholding such information would assert dominance over her. "You *respect* him?" he asked. "After all those horrible, violent things he's done to you?"

Nessix held her tongue. Each day which passed without confirmation of Kol's welfare and safety had increased her expectations of Grell coming to make his own play for her obedience; Annin had neither the patience nor interest to deal with her more than was deemed absolutely necessary. Nessix had held onto the hope that she'd be able to glean some sort of instruction from Kol next time she saw him, because she absolutely intended to fight Grell over anything he sought to do against those who she held dear. But Kol hadn't come to speak with her, Annin had given her little indication of his whereabouts or state of mind, and Nessix had no choice but to risk complicating the alar's plans if it meant pursuing the safety of her army.

Grell stepped forward at Nessix's silence, incorrectly reading it as her fear of him rather than her more accurate fear of betraying Kol's trust. "Or maybe it's that you respect him *because* of those horrible things he's done to you. Do you like to be touched, little one? Do you like to be owned?"

Nessix snarled at Grell's use of Kol's term of endearment for her and silenced the anxious grumbling of her army by swatting the inoga's hand away as he reached out to grab her chin.

Grell straightened and tried to stare Nessix down, remembering the days when he'd been able to do so with little effort. Forget her army, where had *she* found this surge of confidence? Grell would not stand for this disrespect. He doubted there would be much he could do to milk any more compliance out of Kol, and since Nessix had decided she was fond of the alar, it was time, at last, to tend to that fool for good.

"Dismiss me all you want," Grell spat, his voice hushed and harsh. "Because you won't be respecting Kol much longer."

From her peripheral vision, Nessix caught an uncharacteristic flinch in Annin's expression, a fleeting and subtle tell of disappointment and regret which divulged all of the insight to Grell's plans that Nessix needed. The inoga had no intention of assuring she developed this respect of him by assigning Kol to break her again. This punishment would be taken out on Kol alone. The chaos Nessix had managed to control so well these past couple of weeks bloomed in her core, snaking through her limbs and whispering all about the furious strength it could lend her. She hadn't yet shared the truce she'd made with Kol to her troops, having considered that information too sensitive upon her initial return, but as his fate hung so precariously in the balance in which she served as the fulcrum, she didn't care who knew that she would fight for him.

Nessix shook her head and spoke through clenched teeth. "If you lay one more hand on him—"

"You'll what?" Grell bent toward her, fists planted on his hips. "Kill me? You failed before and you'll fail every other time you're dumb enough to try. But you have my word. I won't lay one more finger on that cock sucker. Ever."

Annin's jaw clenched and he narrowed a scathing glare at Nessix, accusing her of bringing about Kol's demise just as clearly as he'd addressed it when she'd demanded to know where he was. And now, fueled by chaos, backed by her army, Nessix was determined to get her answer and stop whatever it was Grell was threatening to do to Kol.

"Take me to him," she demanded.

Grell chuckled, the hint of concern he'd carried at Nessix's swollen confidence easing into humor at last. "Looking to give him one last ride before—"

"Take me to him, you bloated cow, or I will gut you alive the next time I get my hands on means to puncture your flabby hide."

Grell's chuckle matured to a booming laugh and he leaned back to display the entirety of his body, mocking how Nessix had no means to carry out her impassioned threats. "Oh, you don't want to go where he is. Trust me."

"I don't care," Nessix said for, as far as she knew, she truly didn't. "He is my lord and I will receive his orders in person before I command my army to do one more thing to benefit your kind."

Grell lowered his shoulders to a menacing hunch and stepped forward until he was close enough to grab Nessix by the throat, yet she still didn't move. He leaned lower to growl in her face. "He is your lord no longer, and you will forget that he ever was."

For the first time since Grell had arrived, Nessix balked at him. There were no more games in his words, no doubt or uncertainty or desire to see what he could instigate out of her. Kol would be removed from his station above her, from her life. And that could only mean one thing.

"Where. Is he?" she asked again, her voice fluttering with seething anger and crippling fear and her inability to force her heart to slow down.

Objective complete in the second most gratifying manner Grell could think of, the inoga flashed Nessix a toothy grin and straightened, backing the first two steps away from her before turning toward Annin. "Close up the bastard's cell and snuff him out," he said. With a great grunt, he launched himself into the air and awkwardly climbed the stagnant air out of the chasm.

Annin stayed behind a moment longer as Nessix's breathing turned to shallow heaves she couldn't control and the color trickled out of her face, and he met her forlorn, pleading eyes. He had never had a problem killing people, not even in his mortal youth, and though Kol had dodged death more times than anyone should have been able to, Annin hadn't expected to be the means to the alar's demise. And it was all because of Nessix. She was still regarded as untouchable, but it did seem as though they had finally found the appropriate punishment for her.

"You had to have known this was coming," Annin said at last.

Tears sprang to Nessix's eyes as she felt herself begin to crumble before the demon she hated most. "Tell me where he is, Annin," she begged, hands timidly reaching for his as though he'd ever dream of offering her support. "Please."

Annin yanked his hands back and scoffed at Nessix's weakness. If anyone could find a way to get Kol out of his death sentence, it would be her. But if Kol did escape his doom, Annin knew he would be the one to replace him. "It doesn't matter where he is. He is dead."

Nessix gaped at the cold declaration, the warmth filtering from her extremities and stomach chilling as she realized that she was helpless to save Kol, that she'd pressed the last of the demons' limits, and that she'd have to carry out Kol's legacy—somehow—without his guidance.

Satisfied that Nessix understood her place at last, taking comfort in the storm of defeat which was rapidly devouring her, Annin launched himself into the air to put an end to his oldest friend.

EIGHTEEN

Berann stood quietly between the two demon guards, idly familiarizing himself with the lay of their threads as they griped about Annin's strictness. They'd stationed themselves outside of Annin's open chamber door, but made no indication of wanting to enter the room, unwilling to gamble with the oraku's demand that none of his possessions were to be touched. The few glances Berann had snuck inside showed meticulously kept quarters with jars and books lining most of the walls, a plain wooden desk, and a plush bed luxurious enough to make up for the hardships of Annin's past.

If it wouldn't have been an obvious blow to his cover, Berann would have dropped the two guards so he could go inside and scour the collections of journals before Annin returned, but he'd already gained the fiend's suspicions and wouldn't give himself up so easily. After he'd taken in all of the information he could about his surroundings, Berann diverted his attention to studying the gentle play of the shadows, speculating on whether the movement he saw within them was due to the light orbs' flickering or Tristan's lurking.

His quiet observations were interrupted by the agitated buzz of Annin's threads as he rapidly approached the chamber, and Berann slinked away from his guards, doing his best to assume a timid posture. He'd known by the shrill tone that Annin was irritated, but he hadn't quite expected the malevolence which sharpened the oraku's face when he turned the corner and stalked their way.

"The two of you are dismissed," Annin snapped at the guards before he'd reached the small group.

More than eager to put distance between themselves and the most nefarious demon they knew, the two guards mumbled what might have been respectful responses and scurried away before Annin changed his mind about his expectations of them. Talier's residual fear of Annin's ruthlessness urged Berann to keep his eyes lowered, and he accepted the instinctual suggestion as Annin's hand snapped out and grabbed the back of his collar. Noosing Berann with the ferocity in his pale eyes, Annin yanked him away from the wall.

"You're coming with me."

Annin was a cruel creature of finesse, often above the use of physical force, and so Berann made a careful note of how roughly he was shoved into the hall and prodded to begin walking. Berann had hoped, before the Divine Battle had so distorted what it meant to be sensible, to find a way to guide Annin away from the darkness in his soul. After they'd been forged into demons, he'd had to amend such hopes that, at the very least, Annin wouldn't get any worse. When Berann had beheld for himself where Annin had ended up, he'd met a cunning but calm demon, and had allowed himself to entertain the idea that he may be able to reason with his old friend or possibly pluck careful bits of information from him. The beast who had come to gather him, however, fuming with agitation and short on patience even with himself, assured Berann that Annin had only matured into that unpredictable edge of his youth. On guard and rightfully wary to allow the sociopathic demon to remain behind him, Berann tapped into Talier's ingrained fears and cautiously approached the reason behind Annin's current bout of instability.

"Where are we going?" Berann didn't look over his shoulder when he asked the question, keeping his chin tucked and eyes forward as the buzz of Annin's threads grew quicker still.

"To find Kol."

Berann's head snapped up and he was grateful that Annin was behind him and thus unable to see his shock. "Find him?" Kol and Annin had been nearly inseparable in the time when Berann had known them both, more due to Kol's efforts than Annin's, and Talier had distinctly remembered the two of them working together. "Is he lost?" *Or perhaps,* the persistent nudge from hope suggested, *had he run away?*

"He's right where we left him," Annin muttered, grabbing the back of Berann's shirt to fling him down an adjoining hall. "But I wasn't the one to leave him there, and I need you to guide me to him."

Berann staggered to catch himself from Annin's interpretation of guidance and swallowed his initial impulse to ask what that request meant. Talier was Afflicted, bound to a wolf, and though Berann had only begun to understand the basics behind the annoying skill of tracking things by scent, that must have been what Annin expected him to do now. Talier's memory bank came with a scent assigned to the alar, but there was one major problem with using this method to track Kol. "The only signs of his scent I've had since coming down here were in your room and down the other end of the hall."

"You'll pick up on his trail once we get closer to where he's at."

Annin's tone—shorter than was usual, even for him—warned Berann to shut up and accept this order, and he spent the next hurried strides trying to piece together how—or why—Kol could have ever gotten himself lost from Annin, and what had put Annin in such a foul mood about it. "I..." Berann hesitated, his gut suggesting he didn't want the answer to his question. "I thought the two of you were friends?"

"We had been," Annin replied, just as cold and distant as ever. "But those times are to be forgotten. Turn here."

Berann did as he was told, keeping his stride long enough that Annin wouldn't be able to catch a glimpse at what he was thinking. There were few places in the hells where demons went to be forgotten or misplaced, none of them providing a positive outcome

209

for those sentenced to them. Kol was supposed to be the mastermind behind Mathias's Nessix, and he'd been one of the few war-bound demons to show Berann any respect through their conflicting approaches to integrating with the rest of Abaeloth. It may have been centuries since Berann had last seen Kol, but from how little Annin and Grellandier had changed from the demons he'd left behind when seeking the Order's help, Berann had hoped to find a source of security—or at least information—in his old leader.

Not much caring for what Annin's demeanor pointed toward, Berann followed the directions he was given without further complaint or question until they reached a hall lit by just a handful of orbs and humming with a few pathetic, dying threads. Residual sorrow hung through the hall like drowsy cobwebs, the tormented souls of those who had passed unable to escape their sentence even in death. The mournful air clogged Berann's lungs and barreled into his stomach, and a balmy sweat dampened his flesh.

Berann jarred to a halt, unable to enter this cursed hallway, even with the power he commanded. What had Kol done to end up here?

Annin casually strode past Berann as though on a morning stroll to the market, and stopped to turn back and face him after a few strides. "Is something wrong?"

"I—" Berann scanned both sides of the hall, listening for the bright, melodic hum he'd known as Kol. "No. Nothing's wrong. Just surveying the surroundings."

"Do it while moving."

Berann choked down the sharp correction he would have barked at Annin's lack of compassion in the past, and stepped ahead, creeping by Annin slowly as he hunted desperately for Kol's signature among the weak epitaphs fluttering from this prison. Five cells deep, the faintest hum of familiarity reached out to Berann, signifying life—though it was weak—from behind the sealed stone wall. He stopped there and walked up to the wall, pressing a hand against it to feel the state of its resonance.

Annin was the only thing stopping Berann from grasping a hold of Abaeloth's threads and tearing down this barrier to drag

210

Kol from the fate he'd been thrown to, but that was all that was needed to keep him from doing so. The faintness of Kol's song confirmed the alar's current physical condition would not allow him to fight, and Berann would have to expend too much of his own strength in too short a time frame to both tear this wall down and stand a chance of facing Annin's wrath for doing so. Berann swallowed a sob at the inevitable.

"This is where Kol is," he murmured to Annin, grateful the expectation of Talier's timid nature masked his sorrow. "Now what?"

Annin strode up to Berann and jerked him away from the wall, shoving the human-turned-demon back to the middle of the passage. "That is none of your concern."

It was very much a concern of Berann's, not that Talier could make as much known. He and Kol might have had their differences, but Kol had been honest, he'd been rational. He'd been the one demon Berann had thought he could possibly save rather than slay, a thought now validated by the circumstances he was viewing. Berann couldn't fathom what sort of chaos now existed in the hells as he only had Mathias's incredibly biased reports and Talier's terrified memories of recent events to go off of, but the sorts of crimes which earned demons—especially those with skills their superiors could to put to use—an end through solitary were few and far between. Kol had to have been guilty of treason just as bad as Berann had committed to be given this sentence, and Berann had yet to figure out what that meant. Desperately craving information which might help his odds of success, Berann stayed obediently quiet.

"Kol?" Annin called toward the wall. Long moments passed in silence and Annin speared Berann with a harsh glare which clearly demanded his silence now and after they left this hall before trying again. "Kol, do you live?"

"…Annin?" The barrier of stone which Kol was trapped behind muffled his voice, but the tremor of frailty made it through just fine. "You… you need to get me out of here."

Annin frowned and took a step back from the wall, as if doing so would help distance him from the inconvenience of regret. "I

211

cannot do that."

"There's nothing you can't do."

Kol's voice, as weak as it was, rang with a faith Annin to this day hadn't felt worthy of but would have continued to exploit had Kol had more days left of his life. "Then let me phrase it more bluntly," he corrected. "I will not do that."

Annin had expected a debate from Kol, some sort of attempt at negotiating against the inevitable as he'd always been so good at doing, a sentimental rally cry of the life they'd shared and the future they might have lived together. But Kol, whether through pride or defeat, didn't offer such arguments, and silence persisted for long moments, plucking at Annin's own confidence until he was about ready to call out again. But Kol spoke first.

"Is Nessix—"

Annin would have preferred Kol hadn't spoken at all. As much as he loathed the cursed woman, perhaps this was all Kol needed to hear to pass in some semblance of peace. After all the alar had done for him, Annin supposed that was the least he could do. "She is with her army and doing well."

"And her objectives?"

Annin shook his head in disbelief. Beaten and condemned, Kol *still* clung to this story he'd once convinced him to believe in. It was as pathetic as everything else the alar had fallen to over these past few months, and Annin's brief glimpse of sympathy puffed away like dandelion fluff. "Her objectives... *our* objectives are dead. You must know that."

"Not until you let them be," Kol answered, voice gaining strength as he found some sort of hope to grasp onto. "Tell her what happened to me, Annin. She needs to know. She'll rally her troops for our cause with or without me. She will change the hells. I *know* she will."

Annin sneered. "She is the reason you are trapped with the rotting remains of two dozen other traitors, condemned to death, and you still believe she cares about your fate? All because she told you she'd be obedient after how she chose to betray you?"

Kol fell into another spell of silence and Annin regretted bringing up memories that were tied too closely to emotions Kol had never figured out how to manage in an appropriate manner. The alar had become too damned delusional. Perhaps his death was more of a mercy than a punishment. Finally, Kol spoke, and when he did, it was with the serenity of a man who had surrendered to his circumstances.

"Do not let her fail, Annin. Abandon me if you'd like, but don't abandon our objective. Not after we made it this far."

Annin stared at the wall, disbelieving that Kol honestly thought there was any logical way to restructure the hells after the disaster which had been assigning the akhuerai army to Nessix's command. Annin and Kol had been quietly searching for means to accomplish the task of humbling the inoga's rule for the greater part of their existence, and Annin finally had to admit that there was no way to see it done, not like they'd dreamed. As it was, Annin commanded Grell's fear and respect, and that granted him more than enough comforts in this realm. He was ready to accept that this was the future he'd have to live. It was just a shame he'd have to do so without Kol by his side.

"Goodbye, Kol," Annin murmured, trusting neither his words nor their intention would reach the pathetic alar, as he studied the upper edges of the cell's boundaries. Grasping the threads surrounding the ventilation holes, he twisted them together, pulling the stones closed to cut off the cell's air supply. If starvation and dehydration didn't kill Kol first, he would suffocate within a few days. Through with his task, Annin waited for the tingling of his snapped threads to numb, and turned from the cell as Kol began to call his name.

"Come, Talier," he bid to Berann. "Let us leave this dismal place."

* * * * *

It took Berann half the tense walk back to Annin's chamber to process what he had witnessed down in the solitary wing, and it took him the remainder of the journey to connect what it meant to the memories Talier harbored of the kind of woman Nessix was. Kol had a vested interest in her, had counted on her for some objective Annin was content to kill his lifelong companion over—just as he'd contently stood by while Berann's own legacy was erased from history.

Demons were a violent bunch, needing few excuses to do away with one another, but the slow, creeping death provided by the cells Kol had been sentenced to was only used to serve as a statement to the masses. Nessix stood for justice and Kol had backed her openly enough for Annin to have a strong opinion about it. Berann was meant to be a timid mortal in the hells, terrified of Annin, but he couldn't keep his questions to himself any longer. He'd taught Annin half of what he knew about safely manipulating threads and had been the more disciplined, stronger magic user from the start. Though wariness was wise, he would not allow himself to fear this demon. The moment Annin shoved him into his chamber and closed the door, Berann turned to face him.

"You never told me. What had been Kol's objective?"

Annin paused from walking over to his desk, pulled his shoulders back, and studied Berann with that inquisitive intensity which could have been interest just as easily as outrage before sighing and continuing forward. "He had hoped to use the akhuerai to overthrow the inoga and build a more sensible society for the hells."

That sounded much like the Kol Berann remembered, but wasn't enough on its own to reassure him. "Sensible in what way?"

Annin's brows angled steeply and he hooked a foot around the leg of his desk stool to pull it back. "In the way that would have put him in the position of influence."

Berann caught himself gaping at that revelation Annin had just uncovered for him. Of course Annin would have been content with this arrangement; Kol was one of the few demons who had understood structured leadership before their fall, and would have allowed him to get away with anything in this new realm he created. "Could they have done it?"

"In time?" Annin frowned again as he was forced to acknowledge the positive influence Nessix had made on the akhuerai army and how thoroughly she had bent Kol to her will. "I believe so. But such fancies are dead and I am sick of dwelling on them." He flung a hand toward an empty nook formed between a freestanding bookshelf and a locked trunk across the room. "That is where you will wait for me to have time for you."

Berann stood there until Annin's jaw clenched and, with the slightest turn of his head, the oraku glowered in dissatisfaction of his insubordination. Shaking off his shock before Annin's suspicions could further mature, Berann coordinated his tingling legs to carry him to his assigned corner. The plan Kol had come up with to address the demon plague wasn't quite what Berann had been after, but it was close enough. And the alar was now paying for his desire to fix what had gone awry in the hells by slowly suffocating in the bowels of Elidae. "Can Nessix not lead this army without Kol's guidance?"

Annin's lip curled at Berann's persistent prying as he retrieved a journal from the shelf mounted above his desk and sat. "Oh, she's more than capable of leading any army she wants, but rest assured, the inoga will not allow her to remain at this one's head. I suspect we'll end her soon. Once she comes to terms with Kol being dead, she is bound to rebel. Grell is already wary of her, and that is not a safe place for anyone to be."

Grellandier had always been excitable but not easily daunted, and the fact that Nessix had managed to demand his concern was a positive sign for Berann's intention of recruiting her, if not a terrible one for Nessix's well-being. "Had she been relying on Kol's protection?" It warmed the tired part of Berann's soul to think back on the charismatic leader Kol had once been.

"Here in the hells, she needs him, but not the same way he'd needed her. The two of them are—were—a destructive force, far more dangerous than any inoga I've met when they worked in tandem." He leveled a glare on Berann. "Now *sit.*"

Annin had never had any reason or motivation to lie, and the fact that he definitely stated that Nessix and Kol could have reformed the hells was all Berann needed to know to settle on what he had to do next. Suddenly missing the weight of weapons at his hip, Berann flicked his gaze toward the door as he inched closer to the nook Annin had assigned him. The mischievous plinking of Tristan's threads assured he was honoring his word of keeping close. "And what about you?" he asked, narrowly keeping the remorse from his voice. Annin could have become something beautiful under the correct guidance, and Berann regretted that he now showed every sign of being irredeemable. "Do you still want to see the hells reformed?"

Annin pushed back from the desk and spoke down to Berann like he was an ignorant child. "What I want and what will be are two different things. I am a survivor and I will not throw my life away on a lost cause. I've waited centuries to humble the inoga, I can stand to wait a few more."

"But next time, Kol won't be with you."

Annin turned his head to look at Berann and frowned. That had sounded more like a warning than another annoying question, and Annin shook his head, brows furrowing. He must have been getting tired. "No. He won't be. Get in your corner and shut up."

Berann held Annin's perturbed glare a bit longer, making absolutely certain that this damaged creature truly disregarded the history he'd shared with Kol. There had been a time the two would have died for each other and though Berann had very limited firsthand knowledge of what had happened since then, he wouldn't try to convince Annin to change his mind. His choice to abandon Kol for his own purposes had been one thoroughly thought out, reached after the same ample consideration he put into all of his decisions, and there would be no swaying him. Annin's brows arched in irritation and Berann quickly bowed his head, wedged himself in his place, and sank to the floor.

Based on the insight he'd scavenged from Talier's memories and Mathias's shrewd opinion of the demon who had claimed his lover, Berann had been skeptical as to whether or not there was redemption available for Kol. But after hearing the longing ache in his old friend's voice as he pled for Annin to stay their course, after hearing Annin's testament that Nessix was the key to Kol's humanity and strength, matching that report to Talier's frightened and awed impression of her and Mathias's demands that she be saved at all costs, Berann was content, at last, with what he had to do. Nessix had been captured by the demons, but she hadn't yet been broken by them. Kol had found something in himself worth saving. And, if the two of them needed each other to see the end of the demons' reign, then Berann needed them together, too.

Careful not to disturb Annin's studies, Berann drew deeper into his corner and closed his eyes to concentrate on the hum of Annin's threads.

NINETEEN

He is dead.

No matter how hard Nessix tried to concentrate on the task of commanding her troops, those words interrupted every thought, every instruction she tried to deliver. She should have asked for some dream stop.

He is dead.

And there was nothing she could do about it. Annin never wasted time and, though Kol had been unashamedly fond of him, the oraku had never displayed a genuine concern for or care of Kol outside of what he could gain from him. Twice now, Nessix had thought about trying to scale the stairs leading out of the chasm, but both times, the looming threat of the guards stopped her. They watched her like starving hounds, undoubtedly ordered to do so in light of the astute assumption that she'd want to go causing the demons trouble, and they'd take her out in moments from their number alone, leaving her army vulnerable and sending an ill-timed confirmation to the demons who called the shots that the akhuerai were not worth the risk of taking any more chances on. Besides, even if she did succeed in climbing out of the chasm, Nessix didn't know where to begin her search for Kol.

"Nessix!"

She shook her head at the pointed demand, flushing in shame

218

for having let herself get so drawn into her runaway fretting to forget what she was doing. This wasn't the time to lose her focus or discipline. She needed to keep her mind if she had any hope of avenging Kol.

Avenging Kol.

Because he was dead.

Running a trembling hand through her hair, trying to ignore the balminess of her forehead as the heel of her palm pressed against it, she turned to face her soldiers.

"I'm sorry," she murmured, voice barely carrying enough strength to deliver the apology. "What's the matter?"

The troops passed reluctant looks between each other, each of them looking for someone else to explain the nature of their growing concerns. None of them volunteered an answer and as Nessix waited for any of them to speak their grievances, her constitution rapidly failed her. She'd locked her knees to secure her stance enough to keep her feet beneath her, and each wave of the truth that washed over her brought with it a hot flush across her flesh.

There has to be something I can do…

Her troops stood before her, anxious to alleviate her concerns and theirs. Nessix glanced at the chasm's staircase, her head swimming from the action. With the numbers they had, overwhelming the guards wouldn't be impossible, and if she could consult with Kol, hear what plans he'd concocted, the akhuerai wouldn't have to fight with blind luck. It was time to confess to them that she'd befriended the demon who had started this all.

"We need…" Her words came out breathy and weak, the chasm spinning faster the harder she tried to focus on keeping it still. "I know it won't make sense—"

Nessix didn't hear the cumulative gasp from her troops nor the thumps of dropped weapons hitting the ground as the three nearest her rushed forward to catch her as she collapsed. She was aware, however, of the two men easing her to the ground while the woman darted off, calling for Garrett and Pierson. Nessix leaned into the support of the men for a moment before trying to sit upright. She successfully curled her feet back to the floor, knees raised in front of her, but the effort of standing seemed beyond her reach. Head reeling and ears ringing with the precursory taunts of fainting, Nessix pressed her forehead to her knees, her weakness efficiently hiding the distress she could no longer control.

"You need rest, General," said the man on her left.

She needed no such thing. What she needed was to figure out where Kol was so she could drag him out of whatever deathtrap Annin had secured for him. What she needed was for Mathias to hurry up and bring his knights down here so her army could be freed. Nessix didn't need rest, she needed more action than one broken woman could coordinate on her own.

"Your quest on the surface must have been trying, and you've been working nonstop since you returned to us. Rest, General. We can resume training later. You *need* to rest."

Face still crammed between her knees, Nessix shook her head. "Not until we're through." Her words were muffled by her position, but carried to the hushed crowd gathered around her.

An awkward silence persisted while the soldier gained his nerve to speak the doubts all of them suffered from but had been too reluctant to bring up to their overzealous leader. "Will we ever be through?" he asked timidly. "Or is it always going to be more of the same?"

Show me obedience. Show me loyalty. And we will change the hells.

We *will change the hells...*

Nessix's fingers curled around her shins, her clammy palms burning through the leather of her breeches, and she raised her head just enough to allow herself a silent growl at the injustices of this world she'd destroyed her life to protect. Kol needed her and he would continue to do so even after death. She'd given him her word, and she would see it through at any cost.

"It *will* end," Nessix vowed. The strength hadn't yet restored itself to her voice, but there wasn't one man or woman in the chasm who could question her determination. "And I will not rest until it does."

A timid debate was hastily thrown together by the men flanking her as Nessix pushed herself to her feet, and they scrambled up just in time to catch her again as her abrupt movement, coupled with her physiological instability, stole consciousness from her completely.

* * * * *

As relieved as Annin had been that Grell had calmed his reactive self down after confirming Kol had been tended to, he'd much preferred the convenience of having the alar be the one Grell went to vent at. So far, the interruptions of filling that vacant hole had been a great waste of time, comprising mostly of the inoga griping over his fear of how to manage the akhuerai, his musings over whether or not Kol had paid a hefty enough price for his crimes, or when Annin thought their army would be ready to deploy to the surface—this time to Elidae, to punish Nessix for her insubordination. All trivial and tedious problems Annin hadn't let himself care about. Until today.

The door of his chamber flung open, slamming against the wall so powerfully the glass vials stored on the adjacent shelf rattled. Annin, threads from closing Kol's vents mending but still frayed, believed he had ample defenses against Grell's temper, and looked up to glare at the inoga's unwanted arrival. The snark of his usual greeting never made it to his tongue. Grell's eyes were alight with a deadly frenzy, irrational with a rage Annin had thought had been alleviated through torturing and condemning Kol, and the oraku cautiously stood, subtly freeing his hands for defensive actions.

"I just got word from Selian, Annin." Grell's words were breathy and far too even to balance his external signals of instability, and Annin silently latched onto the thread of the brute's consciousness, grimacing at the impact severing it would have on his own health. "The hook," he continued, "is gone."

Annin's concentration snapped away from protecting himself from Grell, not out of the reasoning that the inoga had come to him for some sort of guidance, but out of the same numbing disbelief which had launched Grell into his current fit. Annin's first instinct was to ask if Grell was certain, if he'd not somehow misunderstood whatever report he'd received, but the oraku intended to stay alive. Discarding his shock as thoroughly as his choke of nausea allowed him, Annin sorted through the same slew of questions Grell must have been grappling with, primary among them how anyone would have even known the hook existed.

Unlike Grell, however, Annin had a probable answer, he just didn't want to advertise it. Turning sharply, he strode to his armoire and pulled out his old leather bracers and a belt equipped with knives and spots to slide vials of vitality potions. "Do we have recent reports on Mathias Sagewind's whereabouts?"

"Who gives a fuck where Mathias Sagewind is right now!" Grell roared. "The hook is—"

Annin threw an arm toward the ground so sharply and with such authority that the harmless action alone silenced Grell's raging. "Nessix knows about the weapons!" he shouted, breath pummeling him in an unexpected and humiliating bout of hyperventilation.

"She *what*?"

Grell's voice had been soft and sharp, and Annin shuffled a step back to lean an arm against his desk for support. "She had to have told him. It had to have been why he gave her up so easily. Nessix knows about the weapons, and now Mathias is seeking them."

The inoga's cheeks burned with flush, random patches of white from the suppressed terror of what this might mean poking through. "And did..." An ironic laugh beat out of Grell's chest. "Did *Kol* tell her about them? Is he the cause of this, Annin?

"He hadn't needed to tell her," Annin answered, enough function returning to his fingers for him to begin fitting the first of his bracers to his arms. "She'd learned how to access his memories. She uncovered the traitor herself."

Grell erupted into a monumental fury, barking an enraged howl as he spun and slammed his fist into the shelf of components on Annin's wall. His chest heaved as his sanity strained at its limits, and Annin, eyes wide, held his breath as he waited to see if he'd be held accountable for these revelations as Grell swung around to face him once more. The inoga tilted his head temperamentally, furious glare targeted on Annin, and he drew in a deep breath.

And promptly collapsed in a limp heap to Annin's floor.

The oraku stood frozen in place, staring at Grell's body and the wildly frayed threads of his snapped consciousness, unsure if he should be concerned or relieved by the beast's sudden collapse. Mortals were fragile and prone to succumbing to death tied to poorly coping with such extreme emotions, but he'd never known a demon to meet such a pathetic and useless end. Inoga's threads were woven tighter than any other living being's Annin had ever encountered, granting them a stout resistance against even the most skilled and precise thread manipulation. But there Grell lay, his web of consciousness cleanly snapped. A faint breath expanded the inoga's torso. Brilliant mind simply unable to figure out what had happened, Annin blinked back his confusion as the sound of panting cut through his confusion.

Turning his head, Annin saw Talier standing in his corner, feet firmly braced between the trunk and bookshelf, and knees bent for stability. This couldn't be right. Annin couldn't be seeing this. Talier hadn't harbored even the slightest inkling of magical abilities.

Except now, it seemed, he did.

The scrawny human's right arm was extended to his side, a trickle of blood running out of his nose, and he focused on Annin with a feral intensity the oraku would have been delighted to have seen expressed at any other time. Between his timid experiment's confidence and Grell's unconscious body at his feet, no part of this scene made an ounce of sense to Annin, and he scoured his mind for answers, excuses, *anything* which might shed light on what was going on. He met that sharp focus in Talier's stern eyes, shocked that the human had the nerve to hold his gaze this long or so firmly or with such disgust and keen disapproval, and he followed the graceful sweep of Talier's arm, the precise arching of his fingers…

Nobody had dared to scold Annin with such a look since…

"I'm sorry, Annin."

Annin didn't have the chance to even twitch his arm in defense before Berann swept his hand across his chest and back again, swatting the threads of consciousness from Annin's grasp. Annin collapsed beside Grell and Berann gripped the side of the bookshelf until his head quit spinning from the exertion he'd expended to drop an inoga and a seasoned oraku. As soon as he believed himself steady enough, he staggered to where Annin had dropped his equipment, downed one of the vitality potions, and slung the belt around his waist. He looted the remaining four potions he could find and, after checking to make sure Annin still had a pulse, sparing only a regretful, withering glance at the disgusting mass of muscle Grellandier had become, Berann exited the room to follow the trail of Annin's scent toward the akhuerai's chasm. Kol was not well, and Nessix could just as easily be in danger, herself. He had to use haste.

"You know," Tristan said, arriving at Berann's side from the shadows. "I could—"

"You won't kill either of them," Berann said.

Tristan frowned. "They're going to come after you the second they wake."

Oh, Berann was well aware of that, but something as trivial as fear wasn't enough to impact his morals. There had been a time when they'd been his friends, and he had a slim hope that he'd at least be able to bargain for a truce once he commanded the last of the god weapons. "If you're hungry," Berann muttered, "I've got a better place for you to find your next meal."

Tristan's frown lifted in anticipation. "Now that's more like it. It's been absolute misery watching so many cattle mill about without being able to touch any of them. I do have to say—"

Tristan choked on his words as Berann spun on him, but only managed to lift a foot in preparation to retreat before the demon's fingers wrapped around the weapon belt's buckle. Two quick swipes from Berann's thumb cut the binds which had kept it secured around Tristan's waist, and the vampire eased his weight back into a square stance as Berann unbuckled it. The demon lifted the belt to look over the weapons, pleased to note there were no signs that Tristan had attempted to tamper with any of them, then slung it around his waist.

"Hook and sabers, safe and returned to you just like you asked," Tristan boasted. "You can pay me for my service—"

"I'm paying you for your service by not closing you up in a hole," Berann said as he tucked the tail of the belt in its keeper.

Tristan fingered the tear in the front of his jacket and poked at the stiffness of blood-stained velvet, eyes darkening. "You'd have not even made it down here if not for me, demon."

"Nor would your god have ever made it out of his prison if not for me. We've enough enemies down here, let's not make more out of each other."

It was a fair request which Tristan believed Berann, with his bizarre sense of honor, would do his best to respect. Figuring that was all he could ask for, Tristan sighed and followed as Berann set off again, eager for this feast he'd been promised.

* * * * *

For the past several nights, Nessix had dreamt only of darkness. No pain, no horrible screams, no bolts of lightning to tear at the fiber of her being. Initially, she'd embraced this change, able to sleep deeply and with ease in the few hours of it she caught. Then, her eyes adjusted to the dark.

She hadn't imagined nightmares could get much worse than those Kol shared with her of the Divine Battle, but they'd found a way. At first, she could make out shapes in the darkness, just enough to pique her curiosity. When she peered closer, the forms of those vague shapes sharpened, contorting into skeletal faces with eyeless grimaces which screamed at her for help. Her fear of the long-dead aside, these corpses were no less real to Nessix than Grell's gaping wound and the crushed hip she suffered in her usual nightmare, and they'd chased her back to the waking world two nights in a row. Burdened even more with guilt over Kol's demise, she broke her fast by trying to chase the images away with a heavy dose of dream stop. When the bitter root's calming properties failed to aid her, Nessix resorted to sleeping near the barracks' entrance to ensure the severity of her developing fears didn't affect the army she'd been working so desperately to bolster.

On that third night, Nessix sat with her back pressed against the reliability of stone, staring at the dark wall across from her as fatigue from her deficient sleeping schedule and the amount of physical exertion she'd undergone in training stalked her.

Exhaustion quietly wrapped its hands around her neck, telling her delicious lies of how comfortable and revitalizing sleep was. Sighing into this malicious embrace, Nessix succumbed to its influence, too weary to fight it any longer. She hadn't had her eyes closed long enough for any sort of dream to find her before a quick yelp echoed from the empty chasm, and her eyes flew open once more. She must have been hearing things in her delusional state and, grumbling, she shifted her shoulders against the hard wall to relieve some nagging pressure points, and eased her eyes closed again.

This time, there was the noisy clang of a polearm clattering against stone as it fell to the ground, followed promptly by the first syllable of a demon's shout which cut off before she could even guess what his order would be. Adrenaline shoved Nes's exhaustion aside, warning her that something was amiss in the chasm and poised to come after her slumbering army. Pushing herself to her feet, she cast a glance back at the cavern filled with sleeping men and women, only briefly contemplating if she should wake her officers before shooting down the notion. The demons had demanded a curfew for the akhuerai after Nessix's return, and the army's fear had made them all agreeable to obey. Whoever was causing trouble out in the chasm was not one of her own and was likely looking for her. Fed up with her captors' torment, Nessix would continue to shield her army from the demons' boredom and tempers as long as she could.

Cautiously, she peeked out from around the corner of the barracks' entry, brows furrowing at the two guard-sized lumps lying near the foot of the chasm's rickety staircase. The bodies were still intact and not obviously broken, suggesting Grell wasn't the one who had taken them out, and she doubted the stairs would hold the weight of the inoga who were incapable of flight. It was too soon, by Nessix's estimation, for Annin to have returned, but a shiver worked across her skin at the thought. A flurry of movement to the left caught Nessix's eye, but in the time it took her to snap her attention toward it, she caught only the vague impression of a humanoid form blur out of sight. A muffled gasp sounded a moment later and Nessix began to doubt the sensibility of investigating this situation alone.

"Mathias Sagewind sends his—"

Nessix spun to the right at Talier's calm address and before she was able to make sense of how or why he'd ended up in her chasm in the hells, half a world away from where she'd last seen him, Mathias's words came back to her. Talier had been working with the demons all along. He had been the reason she hadn't had time to dig deeper to uncover the information which would have forced Zeal to listen to her pleas. And now, here he stood, facing her with his head held high, shoulders erect with a confidence he'd never even suggested having command of as he met her eyes without an ounce of reluctance. Where had this Talier been when she'd needed a lookout? His ruse of spinelessness had been so thorough, so convincing, had played into Nessix's ingrained need to protect those who couldn't protect themselves, that she'd simply *let* him misdirect her. And for that, Nessix hated Talier even more.

"Talier, you lying, rotten son of a whore."

Forgetting the shadow zipping about the chasm and the guards mysteriously dropped by it, Nessix darted forward. Even unarmed as she was, she still had her hands and she aimed the heel of her palm at Talier's throat as he stood, staring at her in bewilderment. Her strike didn't land, stopped by a hand roughly grasping her wrist.

"Nessix, Talier is—"

Nessix had run out of any inclination to listen to this traitor's excuses a week ago, and she briskly drove a knee into his groin. With a humiliating gasp, Talier's hand loosened enough for Nessix to slip free and as he staggered a step away from her, she sprang for the belt he wore. She'd practically had to threaten Talier with death to get him to hold a dagger while under attack by assassins, but now he carried not one, but two sabers, a trio of knives, and what looked like an oversized fishing hook with greater ease than Nessix handled her own heirloom sword. That was six more weapons than she had known him to own and six more than she currently had, herself, and she was determined to get her hands on at least one of them. It wouldn't level the field, but it would at least grant her better odds.

She'd cleared half the distance spanning herself and her target when the muscle of her supporting calf seized, pulling into a knot so tight it dropped her to the ground. Talier had straightened after her cheap shot, though he gingerly kept his off-hand near the site of impact, and he shook his head, an expression of mortified wonder on his face as Nessix gripped her spasming leg and glared at him with a ferocity befitting of Kalina herself.

Just as Nessix was about to throw her weight onto her aching leg and force herself to stand, a brisk gust shot past her from behind, her loose hair stirred up toward her face. Her brain didn't work quite as quickly as her eyes did when Lord Tristan Swift casually turned to face her, dabbing a thumb at the corner of his mouth.

"I told you we'd see each other again." He licked his thumb and sucked his teeth before flashing her a charming smile.

Nessix hadn't managed a solid night's sleep since returning to the hells. She was overtaxed and distraught, bogged down by too many impossible duties and crippling emotions, and her tactical mind was too weary to sort out any of this by itself. Favoring the knot in her calf, she stood and positioned herself to keep both of these men in her sights.

"What is going on?" Her voice rattled with exhaustion, but she didn't have the energy to care about that right now. "Are *you* who Mathias sent to aid us?" It seemed improbable that the paladin would resort to two of the most unsavory characters he'd dealt with of late to fulfill the promise he'd made to her, but if they were who he chose, she would do her best to honor his decision.

Tristan laughed at her question, eyes glittering. "As a matter of fact, he was quite adamant that we reach you."

She shook her head as comprehension continued to evade her. "But… why *you*?"

"Dear sister!" Tristan stepped forward and held his hands wide to his sides. "Don't you recognize a miracle when you see one? This is Ber—"

The man who Nessix had recognized as Talier quickly clapped a hand over Tristan's mouth, his deep growl of, "Do not speak my name in these halls," menacing enough to wipe the spring of outrage from the vampire's eyes.

But Nessix, in her desperation for answers and hope, hadn't needed the entirety of that name to be spoken to fill in the rest. Despite all of the impossibilities Nessix had witnessed between Mathias's initial arrival on Elidae and now, this one seemed just a little too far-fetched to take at the word of a traitor and a man she'd been warned to distrust. "But you… you're dead."

Tristan pulled the hand from his mouth and raised a finger. "He *was* dead."

Nessix studied Tristan's face, unable to settle on if the gleam in his eyes was arrogance or mischief, then shifted her gaze to the other man.

Berann lowered his head in a humility Nessix appreciated far more than Tristan's cockiness. "And I have come seeking your help."

Nessix stared a moment longer, hardly believing that after so much had gone wrong in her quest to stop the demons and free the akhuerai, the most pivotal factor she'd been counting on had not only been discovered but now stood before her, humble and willing to take up arms alongside her. A frantic slew of questions bombarded her: How, exactly, had Berann been put into Talier's body? Had Mathias been the one to coordinate this? What was it this demon knew that had made him so feared among his peers? The simplest of her questions was the one to sneak out of her lips. "You need *my* help?"

"I have been led to understand your value and virtues to resisting my kind," Berann said. "And I believe you are imperative to accomplishing my objectives."

So many objectives she was meant to be tied to! "And what would you have me do for you?"

Berann didn't miss the weary skepticism of a woman stretched too thin by the demands of others, and held Nessix's eyes with an understanding care. "The same tasks Kol had requested of you."

Nessix bit down on the insides of her cheeks, fingers curling against the sharp aching in her heart. She gulped down her remorse, but still couldn't get words to form on her tongue, and Berann raised his chin in approval of her leaked fondness for the alar.

"What does he mean to you?" Berann asked her quietly.

The tears Nessix had held back for her troops' benefit rose rapidly. She wanted to answer Berann, to comply with his requests so she might actually be able to succeed in reshaping the hells in Kol's name, but there was only one thought in her mind, one fear she was able to express. "Is he alive?"

"Do you want him to be?"

"I *need* him to be."

Berann nodded, jaw setting in resolution. "Good. Then you will come with me." He turned toward the staircase, but Tristan pulled him to a stop to drag him back around when Nessix only made it a step forward before turning to send a worried look toward the cavern which held the entirety of her sleeping army.

"What about my troops?" She located the lumps of dead guards across the chasm floor, wondering how close they were to shift change. The moment any part of this hastily coordinated plan Berann had brewed for them leaked out of the chasm, there wouldn't be one akhuerai she'd consider safe. "I can't just leave them—"

Tristan released his hold on Berann to walk forward and lay a hand on Nessix's shoulder. She sneered at his touch, but didn't pull away, and when she turned her warning glare to him, he held it with a placid confidence which massaged compliance from her sensibilities. "I assure you, sister, there is not one living demon— besides the one you're making deals with, of course—anywhere near this pit. Your troops will be well in the few minutes you must be away from them."

His words slipped right past Nessix's doubts and concerns, gently stroking the parts of her mind susceptible to suggestion until it gave her chills. She shifted her shoulder back to pull away from his touch. "And why am I trusting you?"

"Because"—Berann took a step toward her—"if you want to remedy the demons' curse, we need Kol, and to save him, I need your help. I know where he is, and we haven't much time if we want him to live."

When Nessix had been a mortal, she'd had no problem making such hasty decisions, but that was before she knew anything about the world outside the bubble which revered her. It was before she'd known about demons, about the true value of sacrifice, about the real cost of the duty she'd sworn herself to. Her troops counted on her, but so did Kol. And, oh, how she counted on him... Nessix sent a lingering gaze back to her sleeping army, choked down the whispers of regret, and raised her eyes to Berann's.

"Take me to him."

TWENTY

Pathetic as it was, Kol had called for Annin until his parched throat failed to carry the oraku's name any longer, at which point, he sank to the ground, staring blankly into the depths of the darkness surrounding him. The rasp of his breathing had become louder, though he couldn't decide if that was from his growing weariness and rapidly fleeing sense of control or the cessation of his dripping water source. Either way, the silence mocked him openly, whispering all about the uncertainties which death held for demons, and he was left in this screaming void, wondering how everything had gone so wrong, wondering what Annin planned to do with his legacy, wondering if Nessix would seek vengeance for his demise.

He was too dehydrated for tears to form, and that only made the dismal wracking of sobs hurt that much more. Longing for comfort of any kind, his trembling fingers sank into the decayed flesh of a nearby arm, grasping it to feel less alone as time led him steadily toward death.

The dull groan of rocks shifting creaked from the wall to his right, just as it had when Annin sealed his air supply. Unlike that time, however, the sound didn't originate from a point overhead, but from a more central location on the wall. Had Annin or some other oraku come to crush him between the stones? Was this how

232

he'd die? The limited supply of oxygen kept Kol from sinking into the sort of panic such a possibility was due as he toiled over how excruciating such an end would be. Before he could dwell on that thought past horrified speculations, a chunk of stone tumbled down the side of the creaking wall, and then another, and another.

Too weak to stand, Kol released his hold on his mute companion and pushed himself around to face this concerning development to his sentence, a new—and not much less frightening—thought springing to mind. Perhaps Grell had come to finish him off himself. As he was, Kol was too malnourished and his muscles too atrophied to offer much of a fight, and it would align perfectly with Grell's demented plans to offer Kol one last breath of fresh air, the briefest acknowledgement that freedom was so close but so incredibly unattainable, before permanently removing that chance from him. Kol groped around for the femur he'd repurposed as a club and gripped it as tightly as he could with the vague notion that maybe he'd be able to use it in self-defense against a robust and enthusiastic inoga.

A rapid cascade of stones tumbled down now, followed by a faint glow which seared the vision from Kol's dark-adapted eyes. Raising a feeble arm to block the assault, Kol tried to pull his legs beneath himself, only able to shift his left foot beneath his knee, and sucked in a deep breath of clean air which rushed in behind the light.

"Go," a strained voice—one Kol recognized but couldn't quite place—said. "Now."

"Kol?"

That generous flood of fresh air was promptly driven from the alar's lungs as Nessix called for him, his defeated mind unable to process how any of this could possibly be happening. The urge to cry scratched at his eyes as he tried to answer her, and the last drops of adrenaline remaining in his system motivated him to drop his makeshift club and press up to his knees. His strength didn't hold long, the weight of his limp wings pitching his balance forward.

"Kol!"

Nessix cleared the small chamber in an instant, ignoring the rotting corpses underfoot as she grasped Kol's wasted shoulders and pushed him upright. Enough tears for both of them streamed down her cheeks as she smoothed filthy strands of hair from his vacant orange eyes.

"Lih…" He pinched his eyes closed and tipped his face from Nessix's before trying again. "Lih… How…"

"Stop trying to talk," Nessix said, sliding her hands down his arms in a precursory assessment of his soundness. Alar had to keep themselves lean and light to maintain their agility in the air, but Kol's bones jutted through withered muscles at his shoulders and elbows, cheeks and eyes sunken in from days of dehydration and starvation. Swallowing her discomfort and the whispered suggestion that Kol may not be able to overcome the injuries and malnourishment he suffered from, Nessix hauled him to his feet and tried to ignore the weight he had lost. "Let's get you out of here."

Kol sagged against Nessix's support and, delirious and overwhelmed by the fact that she had somehow come for him, reached an unsteady arm out to embrace her. He didn't know how she'd found him or how she'd broken through the oraku-sealed wall, and he couldn't bear to think about the agony she'd suffer when Annin discovered what she'd done, but Nessix had come for him. She hadn't sat around and let him die. Too parched to thank her properly, Kol let her catch the arm meant to hold her and leaned his forehead onto her shoulder.

"Dear sister," came a haughty voice from the direction of Kol's freedom. "When this is behind us, you really do need to explain your standards to me."

Kol opened his eyes but hadn't quite regained the energy to raise his head, to find a blond man with chiseled features standing a stride away, arms crossed and upper lip curled in disgust as he judged Kol like a rancid side of beef. Nessix sneered at this man for his mocking tone, but she didn't act against him, and so Kol relaxed when this stranger walked closer.

"What a waste, what a waste." The man shook his head as though disappointed as he picked his way through the corpses with a casual ease uncharacteristic to humans of his apparent breeding.

Reaching the defeated demon, the man shouldered Kol's free arm and looked to Nessix for instructions.

Together, Nessix and the blond man made a path across the decayed company which Kol had looked at as his peers. His legs had forgotten how to carry him, and his efforts to aid their progress to the freedom waiting on the other side of this wall hindered them more than if he'd simply let them drag him along.

They emerged from the solitary cell, part of Kol convinced this was some grand hallucination, a benevolent trick of his dying brain to ease his transition out of life, but the dim light of the orbs in the hallway drove searing pikes into his brain, assuring him in no uncertain terms that he was still alive and quite susceptible to pain. And leaning against the wall across from the cell's opening, sweat running down his temples and a winded grimace contorting his face, Talier pulled a glass vial filled with blue liquid from his belt, rubbed off the wax seal, and downed it.

All of Kol's awkward efforts to move came to an abrupt halt. He had to be delusional at this point. Talier pulled a second vial from his belt and held it out to Nessix before nodding Kol's direction.

Nessix looked over Kol's hanging head to spear her able-bodied companion with a fierce, commanding glare. "You keep him standing, Swift."

The blond man gave her a little shake of his head and blinked at the accusations implied in Nessix's tone. "Yes, ma'am."

Nessix waited a moment longer while convincing herself that Kol was thoroughly supported before slipping out from under his arm to retrieve the vial. She opened it on her return and held it to Kol's lips, gently assisting him in raising his head. Confused by the wicked tricks paranoia continued to play on him, sensibility urged Kol to inquire about what he was being fed. Unfortunately for sensibility, however, his instinct to drink and his trust in Nessix prompted him to accept the offer without debate.

The liquid was cool and kicked him in the back of the throat, searing up through his nasal cavities so his next breath burned from the chill. He coughed at the fluid's bite, keeping his lips clamped shut as much as his limited strength allowed to avoid spitting any of it out. He swallowed the sip of potent liquid and by the time a rush of alertness let him lift his face from Nessix's support to survey his surroundings for other needed resources, Talier had peeled himself from the wall, holding a flask out to him. A prickling warmth tingled beneath Kol's flesh and he was able to extend his arm to take the offering, though he appreciated Nessix's assistance in holding it steady at his lips.

He drank ravenously, flooding his mouth faster than his weakened muscles allowed him to swallow. The sudden surge of water clenched his stomach up in knots and his knees, feeling restored to them at last, threatened to buckle. Nessix and the man on his left lowered him to the ground as his weight sagged between them, and he panted in recovery. A dull ache invited itself into his head courtesy of the rapid abundance of fresh air and cold water, but for now, it was a joyous reminder that he was alive. And as that thought settled in Kol's mind, Talier crossed his arms and looked down at him.

"I'd always told you trusting Annin would be your end, Chiefson."

Kol's senses were returning to him too rapidly for those words to be a trick of his mind, and he gaped up at the man standing over him, chilled and elated by the same statement which had scolded him from the back of his mind for centuries. "No…" His voice was raspy against his recovering throat, but at least it served him now. "This isn't possible…"

"And neither is raising young women from the dead, but you found a way," Berann said.

Kol looked from Berann to Nessix in persistent disbelief. He'd known his blunt correction to her asking who Berann was hadn't been enough to quell her curiosity on the matter, and while he'd fully expected her to continue her pursuit for answers about the demon's identity, he hadn't imagined she'd have found means to not only locate his friend's soul but insert it into Talier's body. And that didn't even begin to touch how impossible that feat would be now that Nessix was being monitored by Annin and Grell. The akhuerai had been created after thousands of trials executed in a controlled environment and through the use of caged souls, not in the wilds of Abaeloth with a missing target by a woman who had no previous understanding of raising the dead. Kol couldn't fathom Berann's revival being possible, least of all by someone as out of touch with the use of magic as Nessix was.

"But… how?" Kol asked.

Nessix, still wanting this answer for herself, looked to Berann expectantly, gritting her teeth as her blond companion was the one to speak.

"You can thank my lord Ceredulus—"

"We will discuss the specifics later." Berann ignored the blond man's annoyed scowl and handed Kol a smashed roll which he produced from a small pouch at his hip. "We need to get moving. It won't be long before Grellandier and Annin figure out who I am and what I've done."

Kol tore a bite off the roll and looked between Nessix and Berann, waking mind sorting through this at last. Nessix hadn't done a thing to raise Berann besides cluing Mathias in on him. The rest had been coordinated after she'd been brought back into the hells. And Berann was right. As soon as Annin and Grell figured out what was going on, it would be the end of all of them, if they couldn't find an escape first.

After Nessix's interactions with the two demons in question, the very notion of how they'd react to the disruptions she'd gotten involved with recently was not one she was pleased to entertain. Berann had proven honest and honorable so far, and she would trust him now. Sliding under Kol's shoulder once again, Nessix prepared to resume helping him as much as he needed until he tensed against her, as though ready to put up a fight on the matter. She sent a worried glance at Berann, wondering, not for the first time, what Kol knew about him that she didn't.

"Where are we heading?" Kol asked.

"Back to where your akhuerai live," Berann said.

Nessix winced and gripped down harder on Kol's arm. "That… may not be the best idea," she said.

Berann was unmoved by her reluctance. "Do either of you have a better idea of where we can hide while Kol finishes recovering?"

"I don't know," Nessix scoffed. "Maybe… somewhere *out* of the hells?"

Berann shook his head, frown sinking deeper into his face. "Not until I've secured the hammer."

Kol's arm reflexively tensed around Nessix's shoulders, his sharp gasp drawing him upright so fast he threw off his balance, and it took the casual press of the stranger's hand against his back to keep him standing. It was now that he looked at the weapons on Berann's belt, recognizing the hook from ancient lore and the bone hilts of the twin sabers from much more intimate memories. Berann had not forgotten the mission he'd died pursuing, and he'd built himself a team much more skilled than the handful of rebels he'd brought with him the first time. He wasn't looking to reform the hells the way Kol had aimed to, but to bring about their end. Conflicted as much now as he'd been back then, it took Nessix squeezing Kol's hand and her soft question to remind him that the hells may very well need their end.

"What hammer?"

"We talk while we move," Berann ordered.

Tristan, accustomed to Berann's mannerisms by now, heaved a weary sigh as the demon spun and began a hasty press down the hall. Shouldering the side of Kol opposite Nessix, the vampire followed with the same limited appreciation he'd had all along, Nessix hurrying to stay with him so Kol wasn't dropped.

Satisfied that he'd been obeyed, Berann gave his next order. "Tristan? I believe Kol's recovered enough for Nessix to keep him supported. It is time for you to fetch Mathias."

Nessix gasped, her heart leaping to her throat and then promptly plummeting to her feet at mention of Mathias's name. That both Tristan and Berann were familiar with the paladin meant he'd somehow tied himself to them, and while that assured Nessix that he'd stayed true to his vow to do all he could to assist her, it also meant he'd had to travel some shady roads of his own to get there. And that didn't even scrape the surface of her fear regarding what Mathias would try—and likely succeed at—doing to Kol once he was down here. Nessix hadn't managed to coordinate her thoughts well enough to express these concerns before Tristan slipped from under Kol's shoulder and disappeared into the darkness like the light from a snuffed candle.

Nessix hoisted Kol a bit more securely on her shoulder, a sharp ache developing in her side as she and her alar hustled after their guide. "Berann, I'm not sure bringing Mathias down here is the best decision."

He didn't turn back to face her. "He is a competent fighter and your lover, is he not?"

That was a loaded question these days if Nessix ever heard one and she flushed, looking away from Kol's curious glance. "He is," she answered at last. "But he's not had the most pleasant history with your kind."

"Few humans who have encountered us have."

Nessix closed her hand tighter around Kol's and gushed the next words on one rapid breath. "Kol is the demon who killed me." When Berann didn't offer another one of his generic excuses, she explained the matter further. "I am bound to him and that's not something Mathias is ready to let go of."

"Mathias strikes me as a sensible man," Berann said. "I'm sure he can be reasoned with."

Nessix glared at Berann's back. Mathias *was* a sensible man... when he was in the mindset to access such sensibilities. But Nessix had witnessed his fatigue upon finding her in Fairmont, his insecurity over the connection she and Kol had built with one another. She'd watched the Order's own Council carelessly burn through his patience and soaked in his anxiety as she tried to to dig answers out of those ancient texts. Mathias had apparently come undone enough to be part of a demon being brought back from the dead and whatever fate had befallen Talier in the process. And Berann hadn't heard Mathias's vow to kill Kol when next they met.

"I'll be fine, little one," Kol said. "Let's deal with placating the akhuerai first."

And the akhuerai... she still hadn't told them that Kol was no longer the enemy.

"Keep steady," Kol said to Nessix's new wave of faltering. "I'm still counting on your support."

"Then it is done," Berann said, as if Nessix's valid and

superiorly insightful concerns had all been alleviated by Kol's words.

Outvoted and far too involved to escape the inevitable conflicts they were rushing headlong towards, Nessix took a deep breath and bit down on her rebuttal. With so many factors well out of her hands, she had to focus on the few matters she could control. The more air she saved for marching, the faster she'd be able to get Kol out of these halls.

* * * * *

"Would you please sit down?" Mathias had lost count of how many times he'd had to make this request of Sazrah. Though he'd succeeded in convincing the rest of the surviving troops—Kast included—to return to the temple once they were healed, Sazrah had heatedly refused to accompany them.

"I've got to put this energy somewhere," she muttered, continuing her restless pacing across the trail leading to the demons' cave. "And Etha knows you won't let me throw it anywhere productive."

Mathias blew out a frustrated breath. This was the exact reason he'd wanted Sazrah to leave with her troops. "If you're serious about contending with an inoga, you've got to save your strength to use more carefully, not waste it all before you even find the beast. Besides, your movement's distracting me from my surveillance."

Sazrah exaggerated a sigh and threw herself on the same boulder she'd attempted to make her grounding point these past few days. "I've got perks mortals don't."

"And so do I, but that's not enough to make me careless when planning a one-man crusade into the hells."

In an unusual bout of childishness, likely drawn out by anxiety and exhaustion, Sazrah crossed her arms, and set her focus on the cave to wait for this ally Mathias had been so tight-lipped about. "There's two of us. This will be a one-man nothing."

Under almost any other circumstances, Mathias would have been grateful to have Sazrah's sword against such daunting odds, but as each day passed without a sign from Berann and with Sazrah growing increasingly agitated, he began to doubt if the undead demon he'd set free on Abaeloth with nothing but a vampire to keep him honest had ever planned to carry out his end of this bargain. Time had helped settle Mathias's reactivity and remove the driving urgency which had prompted him to trust Ceredulus and the creatures brought back to life by his hands. He'd logged enough sleep to clear his mind from the hastiness which had led him to make so many terrible decisions. But no matter how clear his mind was or how calm he felt, he couldn't suppress his greatest gnawing fear.

Is Nessix alright?

He'd already asked this of Etha at least twice as many times as he'd told Sazrah to quit pacing, and was able to answer it for himself. Etha had no way of seeing that deeply into the hells. All they could do was hope.

"I still think it's stupid for us to just sit around and wait," Sazrah said.

Mathias stretched a leg out in front of himself and leaned back on arms braced against the ground behind him. Hearing Sazrah voice as much didn't make it any easier for him to disregard his own rendition of that same thought. "My offer stands for you to go back to the temple. But if you insist on coming with me, we're waiting."

Sazrah turned to face Mathias and pegged him with a challenging glare. "You don't even sound like you agree with that."

"I don't have to agree with it to know it must be done."

"In the name of all things divine…" Sazrah muttered. "What if something's happened to your friend—"

"Ally," Mathias corrected.

Sazrah flung a hand in the air and let it slap down to her thigh. "Whatever. What if he's dead or incapacitated or otherwise unable to come get us? Would you sit here until the rest of this mountain crumbles waiting for him? Or are you going to charge in there and find Nessix yourself?"

It was so incredibly difficult for Mathias to accept that Nessix wasn't the only important variable in Berann's mission in the hells, and Sazrah's criticism did a fine job of emphasizing that fact. Etha had been able to confirm that Berann had recovered his sabers and that he and Tristan had soon after struck out down the Undersea Pass closest to Selian. Mathias could only assume they'd succeeded in locating and claiming the next weapon. But what if they hadn't? What if somewhere along these roads, the demons had stopped them? It seemed an unlikely feat between an ancient oraku and a vampire, but Mathias would have no way of knowing until he had eyes on their bodies in one form or another.

Oh, Mathias… This might be a good time to be a bit more open with Sazrah.

Mathias shook his head, struggling to make sense of Etha's suggestion, but would do just about anything to brighten the circumstances. "Alright," he admitted. "I am afraid—"

Not about that.

Then about what?

Etha didn't manage to squeeze in her answer before it unveiled itself.

"Sir Sagewind," sang Tristan as he strode from the cave both Sazrah and the paladin had foolishly taken their attention from while tending to their petty debate. "I've—*Oh.*"

Tristan's words hastily snapped to silence and he ceased his confident stroll out of the hells as he saw, not just the paladin he had such fun playing with, but the formidable woman who leapt to her feet to face him. He hesitated. Though Sazrah couldn't kill him, she'd tried to a few times in the past and was of a much more volatile temperament than her mentor, but Tristan found a mote of relaxation as her knee-jerk loathing twisted into disgust as she peeled her attention from him to glare at Mathias.

"Mathias…" Sazrah drew his name out with a refined temper, reminding him of all of the sacrifices she'd already made on his behalf, of all of the answers he kept asking her to wait on, insisting she'd hear them when she needed to. "Why is Tristan Swift this friend of yours in the hells?"

Tristan pressed a hand to his chest and gave Mathias a patronizing smile. "Your *friend*, Sir Sagewind? I'm touched."

Mathias choked down the retort Tristan deserved and inched

away from the weight of Sazrah's glare. "He's not." Mathias slid a scathing look at the grinning vampire. "He was the tool which helped me talk to Berann."

Tristan let go of Mathias's degrading correction, his smooth laughter ruffling both of his companions. "You told her my lord helped you *talk* to Berann?"

Sazrah bared her teeth at that remark. "His *lord*, Mathias? You said *nothing* about that monster!"

Mathias could have skinned Tristan for the fun he was having, and he'd have found pleasure in every moment of it. "You were much happier not knowing," he mumbled.

"You call that happy?" Sazrah demanded. "I'd asked for your honesty!"

Tristan batted a hand at Sazrah's seething but rethought his approach as she snapped her focus to him. "The past couple weeks have been quite trying on your dear, glorious savior, Shade. You can't fault him too severely for forgetting to mention such a… *minor* player as myself."

Mathias glared at Tristan. There was not one part of the past few weeks which Mathias was pleased about and he was still in denial of nearly everything he'd taken part in and witnessed during that time. He didn't need Tristan's help remembering any of it or giving Sazrah more time than necessary to process what he was going to have to ask her to tolerate in the name of the vengeance and justice they both sought. Mathias had learned to find good in the fallen and had convinced himself to believe the lies that he could at least depend on the risen. Sazrah, however, was less forgiving and far harder to sway, and Mathias cringed as she spoke again.

"Mathias forgets nothing."

The paladin raised his eyes to the heavens, wondering—though not demanding—why Etha couldn't have told him *this* was what she'd been alluding to when she'd suggested he open up to Sazrah.

You keeping your secrets isn't my fault, she scolded. *You'd had days to figure out how to break this news to her.*

Of course, Etha was right, and she was determined to make

him sort this out for himself. "Fine. Here's the truth. All of it. Tristan helped me negotiate terms with Ceredulus so I could access what Berann knew."

Sazrah crossed her arms. "And the reason you had to turn to the god of the undead to speak to this scholar friend of yours?"

Tristan cleared his throat, and Etha firmly chided, *You may want to expound on that part, too.*

Mathias looked between Sazrah and Tristan. He'd already asked her to trust him so much and was rapidly losing her willingness to overlook his reticence as new truths were coming out. Might as well finish ripping this bandage off to give her the greatest chance at mental recovery before her inevitable confrontation with Grell and introduction to Berann. Mathias pushed himself to his feet and retrieved Nes's bundle of weapons and armor. Stopping in front of Sazrah and ignoring Tristan's amused smirk, he sighed.

"Berann was..." He looked away, doing a mediocre job at ignoring Sazrah's fuming and how capable she was in a fight. "I mean, he *is* the ancient who may have started the demon war."

Mathias flinched as Sazrah burst into action, but instead of charging him, she spun to stalk away, pressing a hand to her head. Composure contained, she turned back to Mathias but refrained from approaching him. "Run that by me one more time?"

Swallowing his reluctance, Mathias looked away. "Berann is an ancient oraku who had been seeking the demon-purging weapons at the time when the Order killed him, and he's been brought back to life to help me find them."

"An *ancient*," Sazrah said, just to be sure. "You were part of an *ancient* being brought back to life."

"Now, Sazrah dear, it's not like—"

"Shut up," she snapped at Tristan before turning back to Mathias. "An undead demon is the ally you're counting on?"

Mathias swallowed the excuses he wished he could make. "He is."

"The one *I* am supposed to be counting on?" she asked for good measure.

Guilty, Mathias bowed his head. "If you're adamant about

coming with me, yes."

"And"—Tristan hastily held up a hand to petition against Sazrah's furious glare—"this partnership has paid off well. Berann has already found two of the weapons *and* your sweet girlfriend."

Relief slammed Mathias in the chest so hard he momentarily lost his breath and saw past Sazrah's boiling temper. "I have your word on that, Tristan?"

The vampire flashed a smile, holding his open hands wide before himself. "Just as Ceredulus has my soul."

That was as close to a solemn vow as Mathias would ever hope to receive from a vampire, and so he accepted it, ready to move out more than ever. Renewed, if not confident, Mathias looked up at Sazrah. "They are not ideal and not once did I pretend they were, but these are the conditions we have to work with, Saz. I may have been wrong both to make them and to hide them from you, but now you know. Do you still want to come with me?"

Sazrah spit out a gruff snort of a laugh. "I've even more of a reason to go with you now to make sure you don't do anything else this stupid."

"That's fair," Mathias granted, counting his newly accumulating blessings that a well-deserved insult was the current limit of Sazrah's residual irritation with him. Wanting to keep it that way, Mathias strode between her and Tristan and toward the entry point of the hells.

Sazrah shifted to follow him but was stopped by Tristan's long fingers gently wrapping around her wrist, the chill of his flesh brushing against her flushed skin. She spun back to face him, prepared either to fend him off or accept whatever cryptic warning he was prepared to give her about Mathias and froze when she met his warm eyes.

"You know, Sazrah, the hells are a dangerous place, and I—"

Disgusted, Sazrah sneered and snatched her hand away before shoving Tristan a step back from her. "Don't waste your time, vampire. It will take more than your dead flesh to entice me."

Tristan chuckled and shrugged off his failure at charming the woman rumored to boast the blood a succubus before lengthening his stride to catch up with his two new charges as they approached the cave which delved into the mountainside.

Sazrah was determined to personally rid Abaeloth of Grell, even if it would cost her life. It was a consuming desire which had dominated her waking hours and brought her the most fulfilling dreams. Her need to see it done was on par with her need to breathe and eat. But her feet slowed as she followed Mathias and Tristan toward the hells' opening, and upon reaching it, they failed to carry her forward any farther.

Unlike Mathias, who had entered the demons' realm a fair handful of times—all of them on his own accord—Sazrah had only been in their depths once before, and it hadn't been willingly. So much time had passed since her imprisonment that she'd heaped enough anger atop her trauma to allow her to forget about it in her day to day life, but as she stared down the darkening shaft, those vile memories of helplessness and humiliation called to her from the depths, reminding her that she could kill every last demon on Abaeloth but still never be able to escape her past. She shrank back, catching her breath as her determination wavered under a sudden assault of nausea.

Mathias stopped after a few paces without her following and turned back. It wasn't with an order on his brow or disappointment in his frown, but with a heartfelt reluctance in his eyes. His quest to rescue Sazrah from the demons had been his first voyage into their realm, and though he'd better maintained his resilience than she had while trapped and tortured, he'd witnessed the infliction of many of the scars Sazrah's soul carried and would not ask her to pick them open if she'd had a change of heart.

"Saz," he said gently, taking a step closer. "If you need to—"

She blinked back the stinging in her eyes and swallowed the faint bite of bile in her throat as she strode ahead, cheeks pale but eyes hard enough to make up for it. "What I need is to kill that inoga," she muttered. "Let's get on with it."

Mathias watched her with a skepticism she scoffed at until she passed him. They'd both grown in skill and reputation since the time they'd shared a cell in Abaeloth's bowels, but Mathias was more certain than ever before that the demons had adapted and evolved as well. *Etha,* he prayed before the curse of the hells slammed the door on his ability to communicate with his goddess. *Please let us be enough to see this done…*

Oh, Mathias, that is my most sincere dream. Be quick. Be safe. Be victorious.

The goddess's unspoken doubt daunted Mathias, but her orders overrode his fear. Etha had told him before that she'd been able to hear his prayers on his previous ventures into the hells, even if he could not hear her replies. He had her blessing. He had her expectations. And he would not let her down.

TWENTY-ONE

A steady pressure bore down on Annin's temples, crushing his head with such force he felt as though his eyes would pop out of his skull. Careful and proactive, he'd only lost consciousness a few times before, and never had this sort of seizing ache accompanied his recovery. He groaned and rolled from his side to his stomach, connecting with a nearby body. His first attempt to open his eyes failed him and he drove the heel of his palm against the side of his head to counteract the pain then tried again.

The light momentarily blinded him, driving its sharp claws deep into his brain, and he turned his face into the body at his side to avoid their direct glare. As the pain pulsed into dissipation, Annin was better able to gather his wits, and the moment he recognized that it was Grell who he was lying beside, he choked on a humiliating gasp. The last time he'd woken up beside another demon under these physiological conditions had been in the bleak aftermath of the Divine Battle. Logic—his most trusted guide—frantically grabbed at explanations of how he was reliving an alternate take on the most devastating day of his life.

Adrenaline spiked as the unwelcome sensation of panic took a hold of him, and Annin scrambled up to his knees, groping at his waist for weapons that weren't there as he threw his spinning gaze across his surroundings. Once that initial burst of fear settled and the world began to hold still once again, he was able to ground himself with the familiarity of a plain wooden desk supporting a collection of well-loved books, the softness of satin sheets on a nearby bed. He saw a shelf lined with jars of nettles and diamond dust and fine metal shavings, components he knew fifty ways to use for or against the events in his life. His gaze flashed past an open armoire—*his* open armoire—and the dropped bracer to match the one strapped to his arm, then to the empty nook where he'd assigned Talier to wait for his orders. A single drop of blood had splattered on the floor.

The truth flooded back to Annin now, catching him in a riptide which dragged him straight toward a terror he'd long ago thought he'd left behind. Briefly assessing Grell's condition, not so much to ensure the inoga still lived but rather to make sure he didn't witness Annin's inevitable loss of composure, the oraku hastily staggered the rest of the way to his feet. He pulled at his short hair as though that would help stop his mind from reeling with what it begged him to deny, but as he played back the last memories before it went dark, he couldn't find an excuse or explanation beyond one.

He'd been in the process of preparing to go to battle in response to Grell's report of Eriv's hook going missing when Berann—*Berann!*—had taken him out, and his belt and entire supply of vitality potions were gone along with the traitorous creature who had somehow possessed Talier. That bastard had coordinated the theft of Eriv's hook, and he was now after Motag's hammer.

The demon who had proposed the movement to strip the advantages from their kind was alive and hunting the means to finish what he'd started before the Order had slain him. And Annin had done nothing to stop him.

Roaring with fury, refusing to admit how stupid he'd been to overlook the anomalies he'd so easily identified in that man's threads, Annin grabbed his stool and launched it across the room. It shattered when it struck the wall, but the inanimate object's destruction did nothing to alleviate his rage. How had he not seen this coming? He'd been suspicious of Talier—of Berann—but for the sake of scholarship had chosen to trust that the puny man would be as easily controlled in the hells as he'd been on the surface. Annin had been so distracted with managing Grell's frustration with Nessix and the duty of executing Kol that he hadn't bothered to raise questions against Berann's own—and the deceitful cur had asked far too many of them.

Annin didn't make mistakes; every action he'd made in his life had been calculated, outcomes and their alternatives determined before he'd act. It was how he'd survived so long, what made him so feared. But he'd screwed up worse than Kol had in any of his misadventures this time. Berann was more powerful than Annin, but his compassion had always made him slower to react in manners appropriate for a demon. Annin could—and should— have killed Berann the moment he'd identified that Talier's body had been tampered with. But he hadn't. He'd wanted to study Talier, to determine whether or not using one of his shards of Affliction on the scrawny human had been worthwhile, a more salvageable experiment than Kol's akhuerai. He'd been too greedy, and it had finally caught up to him.

Rushing out of his chamber, chest heaving and heart thumping in his ears as an aggressive bout of insecurity chased after him, Annin looked both ways down the hall. With only a single, nearly dried drop of blood, he couldn't track Berann with magic, and the hells were expansive. He had no way of knowing how long he'd been unconscious, but he did remember how fixated Berann had been on Kol and Nessix and what they could accomplish together. That cursed woman had taken so much from Annin, and he would not allow her to seize one more advantage over him.

Annin had never had a need to develop healthy coping mechanisms, always relying on Kol's rendition of optimism—and how easy it was to pass all blame into his willing hands—to deal with the few setbacks he did encounter, but he now found himself at panic's mercy as he ran down the hall toward the akhuerai's chasm. Murmurs of confusion and concern from startled underlings flit past him as he charged ahead, and as he neared his destination, the rumble of even more discontent reached toward him as he came increasingly unhinged. Flying through the hells' corridors was no easy feat, but flying was faster than running, and Annin lifted himself from the ground for the final leg of the journey, spurred on by the disorder he knew—and feared—Berann had caused in the chasm.

He glided off the chasm's ledge, immediately prompting the akhuerai scattered below to churn in a frantic chaos, pointing up at him in horror and crying out warnings of his presence. The disorganized groups dispersed rapidly, uncovering the entire population of their demon guards crumbled on the ground. Had they been rallied into another revolt? And how had not one of the guards succeeded in calling for reinforcements? Annin's stomach clenched in a manner he could no longer disregard as annoying at how few options were left to answer his concerns. He'd never known Berann to conduct himself in a violent manner, but it wouldn't have taken much more than a promise to lead Nessix to Kol—something Berann could now do, thanks to Annin's foolishness—to get her to execute his dirty work. With too many variables thrown at him too quickly, and without a faithful sidekick to dump the inconvenience on, Annin dropped to the ground to investigate the nearest body and determine the nature of the guards' defeat.

Annin expected to find their threads of consciousness snapped or some sort of thorough death delivered by a vengeful Nessix. But he hadn't been remotely prepared for what had actually taken out the guards.

If Berann would have killed anyone, he'd do it quick and mercifully, and Nessix had a preference for defeating her targets with decisive slashes and punctures aimed low on the body. The dead demons on the chasm floor, however, had met their ends from brutal wounds to their necks, throats torn open as if mauled by some apex predator. Annin straightened after investigating the third body bearing the same marks and looked through the crowds of akhuerai scuttling away from him and trying to avoid his notice. This couldn't have been the work of that old pacifist or Kol's pet, but neither could Annin fathom any of the akhuerai would have been able—or, in their current state of disarray, willing—to pull off such a gruesome feat. The hook had been taken, demons were

251

having their throats ripped out, and all Annin could think about was how none of this could possibly be happening.

Annin wheeled on the nearest group of akhuerai and when they gasped and scattered, he shoved off against the ground to glide and catch one of them by the arm. The man dropped to the floor in submission the moment Annin's grasp closed around him, but the oraku jerked him back to his feet.

"Who killed these demons?" Annin asked.

The akhuerai cringed, tucking his chin to protect his neck and curling his free arm around his chest where his ring was as he turned his face into a shoulder. "We don't know."

An animalistic snarl came from Annin's throat and he jerked the man closer. "You do not want to try me, worm. Who killed these demons?"

Tears spattered across Annin's wrist. "I don't know!" the man wailed, ducking his head beneath that curled arm as though it would protect him from an oraku. "We... we'd all been in the barracks because of the curfew. The morning bells never came and... and..."

Infuriated by this man's inability to deliver what he wanted, Annin flung him to the side. The akhuerai landed with a yelp rooted more in fear than pain, and frantically scurried away on all fours. Seething at the incompetence of those around him—and his own which he still refused to own—Annin raised his hand to snap away the function of this man's legs. It wouldn't have been considered any sort of loss to end this akhuerai here and now, but discipline caught his impulse and shackled it tight. He needed answers, and he could only get those from compliant voices which hadn't been silenced by death or terror. Once panic engulfed much more of the masses, he'd lose that opportunity. Writing off any chance of this man's cooperation, Annin hissed and turned his sights on a trio of men staring at him in shock. At least they hadn't run.

He marched toward these men, bristling as—though they shifted like horses debating the depth of a stream—they held their ground. Clenching his fists at his sides, Annin stopped just out of their flight zone.

"Where is your general?" he demanded.

One man slid half a step back, the second opening his mouth to produce nothing more than a weak wheeze. The third managed to speak. "We don't know."

Through with that answer and patience flying from his grasp, Annin roared in fury, frantically snapping this man's threads one by one, numb to the screams of the agony he was causing until his head swam, warning him of how stress had already compromised his stability. The rest of the akhuerai froze, staring in horror at the oraku's sudden bout of violent insanity as their peer fell to the ground and into a puddle of blood which rapidly grew from his draining orifices. Annin didn't have the sense of mind to care about pride. The very security of all of demonkind hung so delicately in the balance and he, the demon most capable of doing something about it, remained clueless to what could be done. This hadn't been the way he'd agreed to restructure the hells.

"Reveal yourself, Nessix!" he shouted, his voice bouncing off the stone walls. "Do not make your people answer for you!"

Gasps and a couple of strangled cries answered Annin's call, but none of them belonging to Nessix. He waited for half a dozen heaved breaths for a reply not one part of him genuinely expected, no matter how pleading that pathetic notion of hope begged for it. Nothing but the whimpers of the akhuerai reached him, the weight of dread rapidly crushing down on his shoulders and strangling him. Annin bared his teeth and shook his head against his weakness and the barricade of his disbelief when a voice from his right raised in haste to try placating his swelling anger.

"She's gone! We woke this morning, she was gone, and the guards were dead. We haven't seen or heard from her all day. I'm begging you to believe me!"

The bulk of the akhuerai were too aware of their position beneath the demons to consciously aim at catching their attention with bad news, and though the doubts which Kol's behavior had conditioned Annin to resort to insisted this was some act to protect Nessix, he was at least certain that she would never have stood by to watch harm come to those she felt responsible for. Just as she'd protected Talier. And Berann had protected her.

Annin spun his gaze back to the nearest dead demon. He still hadn't figured out who had killed them—or how—but what he did know was that their deaths were tied to Nessix and whatever Berann had planned for her. Already regretting his loss of temper and how he'd so carelessly snapped threads he may have to call on in the near future, Annin launched himself into the air and climbed out of the chasm as rapidly as his shortness of breath and aching limbs allowed. There were only two places Nessix and Berann would have gone, and only one of them which relied on their haste.

* * * * *

The vitality potion had bolstered Kol's physical strength so he could stand again, hydration and fresh air waking his senses, but none of these factors had been enough to completely counteract his exhaustion. Nessix clutched him close to her side, determination set across her brow. Though Kol had lost considerable weight, she breathed heavily, but she didn't give up, never once considered the option of discarding him as a lost cause, even though Kol was sure she and Berann didn't need him—least of all in his current condition—to reach Motag's hammer. Gritting his teeth, resenting his weakness and the burden he posed to those of able body and more resilient spirit, Kol looked for a way to be useful. He clenched a fist, his strength just barely coming back to him, but physical might wasn't the only advantage he had access to.

"There are back ways to the chasm," he said between puffs of breath. "I don't know how you managed to get this far, but if we stay in the main halls, we will be seen."

Berann stopped and turned back to Kol and Nessix, the two of them leaning against each other to catch their breath. "Which route is faster?"

Kol shook his head. "The main halls, but they are too populated to miss a human, the most hated akhuerai, and a dead alar racing down them." He eyed the weapons on Berann's belt and swallowed the sob of fear which tried to accompany his shivering at the power they possessed. "Armed as you are, I've no doubt that you and Nessix could handle your own for quite some time—"

"Me and Berann?" Nessix asked. "What about you?"

Kol closed his eyes and sagged deeper against her. "I am the weakest link here, little one. Berann's only got weapons for two."

"That's nonsense," Nessix snorted. "He's an oraku, at least as powerful as Annin, from what I've seen. You and I could be armed and—"

"And then we'd lose one of the relics this entire mission depends on when I'm unable to keep up and am overcome by our enemies." The sharpness of Kol's tone silenced Nessix's objections, and he cast his weary eyes at Berann, silently asking his old friend—his true friend—if he was still the same virtuous man he'd once known. "If your goal is speed, leave me behind and take the main halls—"

"No."

The answer had come firmly and from either side of Kol, and he was suddenly struck by a blow of emotion he'd forgotten the name of. He'd turned his back on Berann centuries ago and had destroyed Nessix's life, but here they were, refusing to leave him to the fate assigned to him. How had he made it here? Why hadn't Annin ever been this devoted to him?

"Direct me to those back routes and we will take them," Berann said, sparing Kol from the path his questions tried to drag him down.

Kol didn't deserve either Nessix or Berann after the life he'd lived, but neither of them were bound to leave him now that they'd dragged him away from death. Nor did he want them to. Kol had sworn to Annin that he would change the hells, and the horrifying actions he was about to take part in would do that in a spectacular way neither of them had planned. There was no turning back and there hadn't been for decades.

"Keep moving," Kol said at last. "I'll tell you where to go."

Accepting the instruction with the same quiet resolve he'd used when a mortal, Berann nodded, turned, and resumed his position on point as the three of them left Kol's condemnation behind.

* * * * *

The average demon approached the solitary cells with the same withering reluctance Berann had displayed before entering the hall. Such weak foreboding had never been an issue for Annin until today, and if he'd resented Kol before, he was absolutely through with him now. He hesitated for the briefest moment before stepping into the dim corridor, temporarily immobilized by the nagging assurance that he'd discover Berann and Nessix had beat him here and that his future would be imperiled because of it. Never in this life or the one before had Annin been afraid to engage in conflict, always confident he had all of the tools necessary to handle whatever was thrown at him, but now, he wasn't so sure.

Cursing this humiliating limitation of dread, Annin strode into the hall, rigid strides propelled by the most irritating of motivations. That same pathetic concept of hope which he'd criticized Kol countless times for hanging onto frantically whispered over and over again that he couldn't be too late, but common sense, his faithful guide through life, shook its head in grim disappointment of what he was sure to find. Driven faster than he had been when Berann led him to Kol's cell, Annin wasn't completely sure how close he was to his destination until, all of a sudden, he had no doubt that he'd arrived.

Rocks scattered into the hallway beside a hole in the wall twice as broad and half again as tall as Annin was. It was a clean doorway with smooth edges, clearly not hacked open by physical means, reiterating the terrible truth that Berann was, in fact, alive and armed with the gods' weapons, loose in the hells, and gathering dangerously effective troops to aid him. Without any additional light sources besides the few orbs embedded in the hallway, Annin couldn't see too deep into the cell piled with corpses to confirm whether or not Berann had been too late to rescue Kol. He stepped back from the hole to search the dirt for signs of the alar's escape and discovered two discarded vials and a damp spot where some sort of liquid had soaked into the ground among a modest stampede of footprints.

Kol was not only alive, but he had been rescued by the

demons' greatest threat and bolstered by Annin's own handiwork.

Chest heaving as he failed to secure a muzzle over the maw of his panic, Annin spun away from the open hole in the wall, raising both of his hands to grasp whatever threads were in reach to throw a monumental tantrum, determined to prove to himself that he was still powerful, still worth being feared. As he wrapped Abaeloth's threads around his numbing fingers and felt their resistance tug back against the pulse of his anger, he froze.

This was not the time to give in to recklessness like some sort of mundane underling.

Berann had already claimed the hook. Odds were good he'd previously gathered the needles from wherever he'd hidden them before he died. He'd found Nessix, freed Kol, and the three of them were together. The hammer would be their next target and if Annin wanted to capitalize on even a slim chance of preventing them from gaining the last of these holy relics, he could not succumb to this madness, he could not snap one more of his threads without care.

"I should have killed you the night we met..." Annin muttered to the memory of Kol.

Fury didn't have an opening to sneak through amid the avalanche of fear which dragged Annin closer to despair and for the first time in his life, the oraku didn't know what to do. Berann, Kol, and Nessix, could be anywhere in the hells right now. Kol, even after consuming vitality potions, couldn't be in optimal fighting condition, but he wouldn't have to be if armed with one of those divine relics. Neither would Nessix let him fall, and Annin would be even more of a fool to think that she wouldn't sacrifice her own safety to distract him long enough for Berann to seize the advantage. And seize the advantage he'd do, as he already had and had always done.

Annin was, for the first time in centuries, outclassed.

Ill-equipped to accept such a revelation, he threw himself into action, thinking only that he had to get to the hammer's vault ahead of Berann. But what would he do once he got there?

Berann might be a pacifist, but Annin was relatively certain that softness wouldn't spare him a second time. Berann had the advantage of hearing threads on top of seeing them, and though Annin didn't have firsthand experience with this phenomenon, it was his understanding that Berann would know—and thus prepare himself and his party for—when he was getting close. Annin was being force-fed a rotten banquet of inconvenient truths today, and as much as he hated to admit it, this was an emergency he wouldn't be able to remedy himself.

With few options left available to him and only one of them bound to yield success, Annin drew in a deep breath, clenched his teeth around the protests he wanted to scream against himself, and ran toward the main halls.

He could hate Grell all he wanted, but inoga were the only demons capable of withstanding such dangerous weapons long enough to do something about those who wielded them, and Annin had no choice but to depend on those simple monstrosities now. Win or lose, it looked as though Kol had succeeded in changing the hells, after all.

TWENTY-TWO

Nessix had become rather guarded with her distribution of hope as of late, the virtue stolen from her by the steady flow of insecurity she'd been subjected to, but it was all she had left to cling to as Berann hastened her closer to the destiny she'd been assigned. Kol's directions brought them into a tight network of tunnels which ended in a narrow crack at the bend in a wall, and the three of them squeezed through it. Several minutes later, they came upon the fringes of a plot of dream stop. Relief that they'd made it out of the immediate peril of public passageways and to the chasm lasted for one fleeting moment before Nessix was left with a more dismal thought; they may have escaped the danger of the demons in the upper halls, but she still had to explain to her army why they were sheltering Kol instead of killing him while he was so vulnerable.

"The two of you should wait here," she said as Berann resumed his dutiful march through the haphazardly cultivated crops. "Give me five minutes to inform the akhuerai of what's going on before we ask them to accept Kol."

Berann shook his head and kept going. "We've already lost time in those tunnels. We'll just have to trust between your charisma and my powers that we'll be able to placate them."

Nessix hesitated at the simplicity of Berann's plan. He may be brilliant and mighty, but he'd been dead for the majority of

Abaeloth's history and apparently had an outdated understanding of how people reacted to the things they hated. "We *just* rescued Kol," she debated stubbornly, "and now you're suggesting we—"

A firm hand clasped Nessix's shoulder and Kol looked down at her with a strained smile. "It will be fine, little one. Even if they do engage, I'll offer no fight. You may not have built a fierce army out of them, but you've trained them well in both justice and compassion. Do not doubt yourself now." Still moving stiffly, his balance compromised by the limp weight of his crippled wings, Kol stepped away from Nessix to follow Berann across the field of dream stop.

She watched the two of them stride toward the chasm, so full of confidence and knit so closely to their duty, and was struck with a great remorse that Kol had chosen to stand beside Annin instead of Berann. How might history have been different if they'd made that initial approach to Zeal together? Nessix clenched a fist at her side and jogged to catch up to them. It was time to find out.

The dull hum of voices patched together as they neared the agricultural plot's exit, and Nessix lengthened her stride so she would be seen before either Berann or Kol. Freshly on guard, the troops spotted her easily, and the volume of their voices doubled as they rushed her way, inquiring about what was going on and why she'd left them, about if she knew how their guards had died and with grim warnings that Annin had been asking them of her whereabouts.

Before she could answer any of these questions, the mass of soldiers jammed to a stop, their multitude of questions cut off in an instant as Berann and Kol—an unfamiliar human and the demon they most resented—entered the cavern behind her. It was just as she'd expected.

Confusion and a sudden air of insecurity worked across the faces of Nes's troops as they looked from her to Kol, quickly and wrongfully choosing to ignore the disguised demon who had initiated all of this. Garrett separated from the crowd but kept his distance out of fear and respect.

"What is the meaning of this, General?"

Nessix held a hand back as Berann took in a breath to deliver his blunt, logical answer, wishing she could turn and snap at him that this was the exact scenario she'd been wanting to prevent. "I told you I had plans in motion to finish what was started, and this is part of them."

"You're standing beside half the reason we're all down here in the first place, and the other one was just rampaging down here, demanding to know where you went." Garrett crossed his arms to hide his insecurity in testing Nessix's intentions. "This one's half-dead by the looks of it and, if you ask me, we have a right to finish the job."

Quick barks of agreement sprang up from the crowd of akhuerai, hidden amongst each other so Nessix couldn't readily identify who was in support of killing her demon. Berann shifted his weight again, and Nessix half-turned toward him, holding an arm out both to her contentious army and the demon she had to keep cordial. "Enough!"

Her burst of authority, conditioned into her through generations of leadership and blessings from the divine realm, stunned the entire chasm floor as she made her stand, reminding her army of how she'd saved them from wallowing through life as victims, and introducing to Berann the very charisma Annin had been so concerned about. It was no wonder Kol had taken a liking to this woman; she was the natural leader he'd always dreamed of being. Berann eased his weight back on his heels and moved his hands from his weapons, and Nessix gave him an appreciative nod before turning back to her troops.

Stretching the truth to calm the masses was not a foreign concept to one born to rule a nation, and Nessix wasn't about to risk a riot—or Kol's fragile life—by letting her morals shout over what had to be done. "He is the demon responsible for our current conditions," she agreed freely. "But the time I spent with him before I raced to Zeal wasn't wasted. We were laying the foundations to remodel the hells, a feat only *we* are capable of initiating. I'm not saying he went about it the best way and I won't say I'm any more content with the road he chose to get here, but this is where we're at, and I plan to make the best of these circumstances."

"The best of these circumstances?"

"Wouldn't that be when all the demons are dead?"

"You honestly think he'd let us go if our blood can pave the way to his desires?"

Nes's heart fell at the raised arguments and she regretted that Pierson hadn't been the officer on duty when Garrett spoke next.

"You spent weeks working over these plans with him," Garrett granted, though his tone remained tight and skeptical. "Take that knowledge and use it, General, but use it for *us*, not him. Do not ask us to stand for it after what we've already been through."

Nessix's fingers twitched at her side, her deficiency of dream stop's calming effects urging her to demand this contentious subordinate who she'd given purpose to listen to her, and she was grateful she was unarmed. It was an uncomfortable feeling, this anger she had for her troops, and she crammed it as deep inside of herself as she could, lest it begin turning her into the same sort of monster she was preparing to fight. The akhuerai had every reason to doubt their security and to fear her proposal, but she had to find a way to convince them to listen. They'd been dominated by force and terror too many times for either of those approaches to be effective, even if Nessix could lower herself to utilize them. She took a deep breath, letting her shoulders drop with an exhale, and when she stepped forward, the entire gathering shifted a step back.

"Knowledge can only take us so far," she said, "and I cannot fix what has been done to us without Kol's guidance. Trust me. Please. Help is coming for us. Light is coming. But first, we need to secure Kol from the more ruthless demons he's wronged, no matter how much you hate him. We cannot accomplish our goals of restructuring the hells without him."

Her answer didn't make a whole lot of sense to the akhuerai, but neither did how they'd ended up in this unending drudgery to begin with. Nessix might have kept secrets from them and her actions might have defied their expectations of how they envisioned they'd find their freedom, but for all the doubt they threw at her, she hadn't abandoned or given up on them. She'd twice now found ways to save herself from the demons, yet she continued returning to them. She'd vowed to protect them and she hadn't quit giving her all—her safety, her welfare, her reputation—to do just that. Kol, as weak as he was right now, monitored the akhuerai with eyes no less sharp than before; if Nessix had taken liberties with any of the facts which vied to highlight a more noble side of him which no respectable demon would show, he'd have been able to correct her.

"Does this remodeling of the hells include monsters like Grell?" asked a bold voice from the crowd.

Berann drew a hasty breath to answer, but Nessix cut him off, casting a glance at her crumpled alar. "If I have my way, it will begin with him." Berann frowned at Nessix's declaration and Kol closed his eyes, a tangible pain working across his face as he turned his head from her, but neither of their grim responses matured into a debate. "I made a promise to you, to *all* of you, that I would see us to brighter days, and I have no intention of making a liar out of myself."

Nessix didn't receive the same enthusiastic cheers to her rallying as she would have from troops who truly wanted to form an army, but she succeeded in easing the caution and hostility from their rigid stances, lighting the fires of aggression for a target she approved of them carrying torches toward. Grudgingly and not without wary glares on Kol, the crowd parted as Nessix and Berann guarded the alar through the main body of the chasm and back toward the sleeping quarters. Pierson joined the growing crowd and accepted Nes's orders with much more grace and fewer arguments than Garrett had. Once she was more certain than not that she didn't have to worry about any underhanded attacks against Kol, Nessix busied herself with trying to clean the infection from the alar's swollen and seeping wings.

Just as calm began to suggest it had a place in her heart once again, a burst of concern from the group posted nearest the crumbling staircase dashed away Nes's concept of confidence, and her heart fluttered over what their alarm foretold. She'd known they'd be hunted down eventually and that those after her in particular would be motivated to make her suffer, but she hadn't expected it so soon. Briefly gripping Kol's shoulder, Nessix peeked out of the barracks to catch the glisten of a silver-toned breastplate and a flash of red hair, followed shortly by the mocking tone of Tristan's laughter, and her heart ached at the rate which ease struck her. Momentum from her relief nearly carried her forward to greet Mathias and his two companions, but a new niggling fear held her back.

Mathias had vowed in no uncertain terms to kill Kol the next time they met, and though Nessix had compromised for Kol's safety from her troops, she suspected it would take Mathias a negligent amount of effort to motivate them to take action against the battered alar. She glanced at Berann, still struggling to comprehend how such a stoic expression could exist on Talier's face. He was the only guaranteed ally she had to work with in Kol's defense, and he claimed to have some amount of Mathias's respect, but that alone wasn't enough to convince her that she'd be able to reason with the paladin on this particular matter.

It didn't take long for the murmurs of concern to warp into gasps of awe and disbelief as the first speculations of Mathias's identity began to filter through the troops and excited tales of the paladin's rumored feats were exchanged and delivered to the few who hadn't heard the legends. Sheepish glances worked back to Nessix, silently apologizing for the doubts they'd thrown at her over the past several days—and those they hadn't found the nerve to express to her face—but Nessix couldn't be troubled by them.

Tristan had casually skated and rebounded off the sheer face of the chasm wall and waited at the foot of the stairs with a cocky patience for his armored companions to navigate the perilous staircase. Sazrah struggled between her armor's bulk, and Mathias fared no better with his balance compromised by the bundle of Nes's sword and armor which he'd strapped to his back. When they made it to the chasm floor, Sazrah roughly shouldered her way past Tristan, who laughed at her disrespect, while Mathias used their little tussle to stalk ahead of them.

The paladin slung Nes's belongings from his back as he walked, expression softening for the briefest moment as he met her tired eyes before hardening again when he surveyed the chasm full of interrupted lives as the akhuerai gawked at him. His aura of power and justice, radiating strong despite his distance from Etha, parted the masses for him and his companions in a reverent silence. Sazrah's nostrils flared, lips curled as she scrutinized the akhuerai with more wariness and markedly less compassion than Mathias did, but she held her temper better than she had upon first meeting Nessix. It wasn't until the little procession had nearly made it up to Nessix that Mathias's searching gaze found Kol where he leaned against the wall behind her, still trembling from the pain of the treatment he'd been undergoing. Mathias clenched his teeth to mask his snarl as he lengthened his stride, and Nessix needed no other tells to understand his intentions.

"That's a mighty small army you were able to sway," she said, tone friendly but firm as she stepped forward to intercept his path.

Mathias stopped at her advance, eyes never straying from their focus on his target. "She's all the army we'll need." He dropped his shoulder to lower Nes's armor and sword belt to the ground. "I brought you something."

Nessix made a brief appraisal of her much-missed and fully repaired belongings from the corner of her eye but kept her attention trained just as intently on Mathias as his was on Kol. She was only slightly bolstered by Berann as he stepped up beside Kol. "I see that."

It took him marked effort, but Mathias pulled his eyes from the cursed alar just long enough to sweep them across Nes's, then down to her armor. "You should put it on, if you're still planning to go to war."

A heartbreaking promise lurked in Mathias's words and Nessix would have sent her sword and armor straight back to the surface to have been able to address it away from so many anxious eyes and eager ears. She could count on one hand the number of times Mathias had accepted orders from her but, though he might have been the more seasoned officer between them, she embraced her title of general as she never had before. "Then you will stand down, Sagewind."

He shook his head subtly, slowly, tears glistening behind his caged temper. "I can't do that, Nes, and you know it." His words came out whispered and harsh, and the akhuerai nearest him exchanged concerned glances, oblivious to the intimate conflict between their general and their salvation. Sazrah casually brought her hand to the hilt of her sword.

"You can," Nessix corrected, just as hushed. "And you will."

Before Mathias could counter, Tristan expelled an obnoxious sigh and strode up between the two forces, expression so confident and dismissive it was as if he'd been viewing an entirely different exchange. "Might I be so bold as to suggest the two of you work out the details of your little threesome after we secure what we need to get out of this miserable realm? Let us be adults and accept those who *aren't* actively trying to kill us as allies so we can prepare to meet those who *do* want us dead."

Berann raised his gaze to the lip of the chasm. "Tristan is right. If the three of you had been seen—"

"Of course we were seen," Sazrah muttered. "And we left a decent trail of bodies on the way down here."

"Did we *ever*!" Tristan laughed. "But talk in the halls—at least as much as we were able to gather before we silenced it—has been traveling fast." Tristan smirked as Mathias's fury flickered toward something that resembled defeat, though Nessix's discipline hadn't faltered. Tristan admired that in a woman. He looked to Berann. "Do you suspect your friends have woken up?"

Finally, Nessix pulled her eyes off Mathias to receive Berann's answer. Behind her, Kol shoved himself off the wall, equally interested on this information.

"I would imagine so, but I suspect they're checking on Kol's whereabouts first."

"I still think you should have let me finish them off—"

Berann spun on Tristan so fast the cocky vampire choked on his words. "Not until the sins of the gods have been righted in them. They may have become monsters, but they'd once been my brothers. If I can avoid condemning them from the purgatory I'd suffered, I will."

"And if you can't?" Mathias asked, focus still latched on Kol.

Berann frowned, swallowing a remorseful lump in his throat. "Then I can't. Either way, if we plan to stay ahead of them to locate the hammer, we should get moving as soon as possible."

Mathias clenched a fist, a low growl rumbling out of him as he filed away his desire for vengeance, just as he'd done to his morals to permit Berann to be raised in the first place, and he dropped to his knees to begin sorting through Nes's armor to aid her in dressing. "Do you know where this hammer is?" He handed the most relevant plates to Nessix and got to work on her feet and shins.

"I know its location," Berann said, "but I am not as familiar with these tunnels as those who have called them home."

"Assuming nobody kills me first," Kol said, meeting Berann's eyes to avoid Mathias's scowl, "point me in the direction you need to head, and I can navigate the halls we'll need to travel." Feeding off the building urgency, Kol overlooked Mathias's thriving hostility and joined him and Nessix in hastening her preparations. "There are few tunnels in all the region I'm not familiar with."

Nessix was about to chime in with something about Kol's contribution, but Berann beat her to it. "That sounds like a valid reason to keep Kol breathing for a few more hours, doesn't it, Mathias?"

The paladin clenched his teeth and stubbornly declined a response, but Sazrah wasn't bound by the same kinds of shame as her adopted father was. "Etha save me for trusting demons…"

"Etha save you from trusting yourself," Tristan mused, taking a prompt step back from the woman's reach as she spun on him.

"Both of you, stop it," Mathias snapped, successfully restraining the agitated woman with his words. "If I can push my grudges aside for the more immediate good, so can you."

"Wiser words have never been spoken," Tristan agreed.

Sazrah speared the smirking vampire with a toxic glare, but followed Mathias's order like the dutiful soldier she was.

As the final straps of Nes's armor were secured, the ominous rumble of a couple hundred pairs of feet rippled down the hallway overhead which led to the chasm, echoing down into the pit like a voracious wave. Tristan tisked sharply and shook his head as his contentious company let their concentration slip away from their personal grievances and to the more legitimate threat which had arrived.

267

"I don't believe that's a routine check," Nessix said, accepting her sword belt as Mathias handed it to her.

Not one occupant of the chasm—neither hero nor akhuerai—was able to disagree with Nessix's observation, and Berann put a hand on Kol's shoulder to shove him back toward the agricultural plots and their route to escape the chasm.

"That is our cue to leave," Berann said.

Aligned in motive at last, Mathias and Nessix stood firmly where they were, Sazrah stepping up beside her mentor without need of his request.

"There is an army marching on these people." Mathias's even words stopped the two demons.

Berann turned back and appraised the firmness of Mathias's stance. The demon's only knowledge of this particular paladin had come from the outwardly biased tales Tristan had yammered on about during their questing and while he wanted to commend Mathias for his act of standing in defense of others, that was not the reason they had all risked so much to come down here. "And it is my understanding this is an army, as well."

Nessix shook her head, casting a misty gaze across the men and women she'd committed herself to. Bless them, they'd tried to become soldiers, they'd tried to internalize the tactics and confidence she offered them. While they'd done their best to command those virtues and make them their own, they'd been through too much, seen too many horrible acts, and these farmers and peddlers and millworkers hadn't been able to keep up with the demands and tolls of combat. They were a drafted force and could fight if they were forced to, but not one of them had the heart of a warrior, and they looked to Nessix now for the guidance and protection she had always tried to give them.

"I told you before, Berann," she said solemnly. "I cannot leave my troops. And I will not leave them in their time of need after our actions have brought the enemy to them."

Berann fit Nessix with a disapproving glower and opened his mouth to debate, but his demand never began before Tristan stepped in the middle of this unlikely group of peacekeepers. "Leave me in charge of your troops," the vampire said. He failed to

268

disarm Nessix's building conviction to protect her troops with his charming smile, so continued to press his agenda. "Just until you achieve your objective and can safely return to them, of course." Her eyes narrowed in suspicion, and Tristan flung an irritated glare at Mathias. That pompous paladin needed a new hobby besides talking poorly about him... "You have my word as my lord has my soul, sister. I am every bit as motivated to keep this force up and functioning as you are. The enemy is getting closer." A brief moment of Tristan's silence was filled by the growing volume of charging demons, emphasizing the urgency of his observation. "Leave the safety of this hole to me."

Mathias was already shaking his head at the proposal and the akhuerai all gaped at Nessix in confusion, holding their breath as they awaited what decision she would make about their future. Though Nessix was certain she and Tristan had different motives driving them to protect the akhuerai, she couldn't completely disregard the sentiments he'd conveyed to her upon their first meeting in the Citadel's dungeon. Mathias had only given her a few vague warnings about Tristan and his nature, but the vampire continued to express a genuine sense of camaraderie toward her and had clearly helped Berann's quest for the same justice she and Mathias sought. He'd not been the most pleasant company, but he had assisted with Kol's rescue with few complaints. The growing clamor at the lip of the chasm suggested there wasn't much time left to debate this decision. Nessix was meant for something greater than simply leading armies to war; she was meant to change the world.

"Fine," she said shortly, and Tristan grinned at Mathias's jolt of disbelief. She raised her eyes past Mathias's disapproval and scouted out Pierson and Garrett, pointed eyes ordering them to support her pending command. "This is my... uh..." She looked up at Tristan, crinkling her nose as she struggled to settle on the most appropriate way to reference him. Giving up on diplomacy, she turned back to her troops and settled for the simpler truth. "This is Tristan Swift, and in my absence, I expect you to comply with his requests as you would my own."

Feeding off the growing tension among everyone in the

chasm, driven by the roar of demons closing in on them, Pierson stepped through the crowd of his peers and met Nes's eyes with the open fear she wished she could have erased from him. He ran a hand through his hair. "This will… this will work, right, General?"

Nessix's heart fell at his timid reservations. How many times now had her plans backfired on these poor people? "It—"

"Of course it will," Tristan interjected smoothly, laying a firm hand on Nes's shoulder to silence the crippling honesty of her doubts. "What sort of fools would willingly traipse down into this dismal pit from the safety of the surface for anything other than a sure bet?"

The worry drained from Pierson's eyes at Tristan's smooth words and Nessix gawked up at the vampire, horrified by the devious glint in his eyes. What sort of powers did this man command? He squeezed her shoulder and smiled at her shock in a knowing manner.

"Go on, now, General." Tristan slid his hand to Nes's back and gave her an assuring shove toward Berann and Kol. He ushered a much more resistant Mathias the same way, but stopped short of touching Sazrah. "Time is of the essence. I will allow no harm come to your people and will deliver them back to you, safe and sound, upon your return. Now, go. Go!"

Judging by the volume of their battle cries, the nearing enemy force was almost upon the chasm, and if Berann's piecemeal resistance force hoped to avoid more complications than were already guaranteed with this mission, they needed to leave here before this first wave of opposition arrived. Nessix moved first, gaining Berann's prompt approval as he turned Kol to go along with her. Outvoted on the matter, Mathias lectured Tristan with a wary glare which warned him to operate within the universally accepted lines of justice, then hastened after Nessix. Sazrah speared the vampire with an even filthier look. Scoffing as he gave her a wink, she spun to follow Mathias.

With the departure of those who had vowed to seek justice for their suffering, the akhuerai shifted about uncomfortably, eyeing the chasm lip, Tristan, and the darkened entry point of the agricultural plots in turn. Their feeble efforts to function past their fright were endearing to Tristan, a reflection on the youthfulness of these precious undead. Ceredulus had asked him only to see what he could learn about them, but it wouldn't hurt to teach them a thing or two in the process. Freshly fed on half a dozen demon guards and the sips he was able to sneak behind Mathias's back, the unaging essence warming his veins in the most exhilarating manner, Tristan looked up at the chasm lip and bore his fangs in an anticipatory grin.

"It's up to us to buy your heroes time," he told those closest to him, anxious fingers dancing along invisible piano keys at his sides.

"That's an entire army of them," came a timid reply.

Tristan hadn't known about the akhuerai's past, of their last attempt at rebelling against the demons, or the means they were forced to trudge through, but he didn't have to. He had centuries of a glorious, immortal existence to alleviate their concerns. "And there is an entire army of *you*, and you have *me*. Come, brothers and sisters. We have surpassed death. What between the heavens and the hells do we *possibly* have to fear?"

The akhuerai had been rallied into foolishness and devastation too many times before, and while they bit into Tristan's declaration, none of them were quite willing to chew and swallow. No matter. Tristan was comfortable with leading by example.

As the first of the demons reached the top of the stairs, Tristan disappeared from the head of Nessix's army, his elegant form blurring into an indistinguishable mass as he zipped straight for the chasm wall. He scaled the sheer face like a spider before the descending demons—stunned by the sudden realization that a vampire had somehow infiltrated their realm—could bark orders on how to deal with him. Tristan grabbed the arms of the two nearest him and launched them behind his back into the chasm below.

"Stop him!"

The order hadn't been the firm declaration of disciplined tactics, but a frantic scream, and Tristan's grin widened. He ducked and weaved between scrambling demons, evading grasping hands and thrusting weapons as he delivered crippling blows to the guts of those in the flimsiest armor. Demons dropped into groaning lumps as he passed through them, those on their feet scrambling about in disorder to reestablish the sense of cohesion they'd originally marched to the chasm with before they'd known the full scope of the arsenal working in Kol's defense.

Tristan pummeled a broad clearing in his opposition and turned to face the chasm full of akhuerai, holding his arms out to his sides as he raised his voice to address them. "Brothers and sisters, these foes who have tricked you into fearing them are nothing more than tender fleshbags. They cannot harm you unless you let them. Join me! This is *your* dance!"

Spurred into retaliation by Tristan's insults, the front line of demons closed in on him and he fell back to greet them. Moments later, the raising of voices crying out the injustices they'd suffered and the angst of restraining it for so long rose to back him.

TWENTY-THREE

The group saved their breath for running, allowing the conflicting interests wedged between them to stew in a silence punctuated by panting and the steady clank of armor. If an organized force of demons had already been sent to quell the akhuerai, reports of the damage Sazrah, Mathias, and Tristan had done on their way in must have circulated or, a more grim and likely option, Annin, his threads more finely tuned for recovery than average, had woken from Berann's attack and sorted out the field. The main halls wouldn't be safe for travel, but a quick survey of the resonance humming through the determined threads of those Berann counted on confirmed that they all understood and accepted that safety was no longer an expectation.

Progress continued at a steady pace through the back passages Kol guided them down, each combatant too focused on the imperative task at hand to allow their underlying thoughts to further complicate their mission, until Kol came to a reluctant stop. Nessix proactively positioned herself between the alar and the two demon hunters behind her, and Kol hissed a hushed order ahead.

"Berann, hold."

Though this was by and large Berann's quest, he obeyed the order of his former leader without hesitation, the first time he'd truly listened to one of his companions since Ceredulus had sewn his soul into Talier's body. Keeping one ear down the hall, he shifted his attention to Kol. "The path is clear," he said. "What is it you know?"

Kol grimaced at the continued sourness which accompanied admitting the truth that he'd been used all this time. "I know Annin."

Mathias cursed at the dashed hope that Sazrah's report of the oraku dropping into the ocean had meant he was dead, and Nessix sucked back her very personal fears of the measures Annin would take to correct them all for the trouble they were making for him. Despite their reservations, Berann shook his head.

"He is not nearby—"

"But he knows of these tunnels," Kol said. "And as soon as he sorts out what's happened, as soon as he realizes I'm not dead in my cell, he's going to come looking for us. There have been few days we haven't spent with each other, and he'll know I'd stick to the hidden passages to avoid notice."

"Should have known this was leading us to a trap," Sazrah muttered.

Nessix spun around at the warrior woman, bolstered by the presence of her sword and armor. "He's trying to *save* us, you self-righteous fool. Annin is the oraku who collapsed the mountain where you made your stand, and he's not to be made light of."

Sazrah made a quick jerk toward her sword, her action stopped by Mathias's firm hand at the exact same moment Kol's clasped down on Nessix's shoulder.

"Nes is right," Mathias said, crediting this revelation solely to Nessix to avoid the need to admit Kol's beneficial contribution to their odds of success. "Annin's more clever and I suspect more powerful than any oraku I've dealt with in the past. If we can avoid him, at least until we're fully armed, that will be our best course."

Mathias's advocacy didn't quite defuse the tension crackling between the two women, but it did allow them to draw back into the principles of their common goal. Berann's steady voice grounded them all to the present.

"Then let us brace ourselves for combat. If the main halls will be no more dangerous than these, lead us back to them."

Kol fit his two critics with a wary eye, gave Nessix's shoulder one last squeeze, then slipped ahead of Berann. "The nearest passage will be a tight fit," he warned, "but it will get us there the fastest and Annin will be disinclined to enter a path that would risk inhibiting his mobility."

Nobody objected to his plan, and so Kol hastened them to the narrow chute which led up to the main halls. He grimaced and hissed as the stone walls of the restrictive space clawed at the wounds in his torn wings, the scrapes of metal and grumbled curses from Mathias and Sazrah conveying they were having no easier time of squeezing through the crevice than he was. The two demon hunters were both seasoned and deadly warriors and though neither seemed inclined to risk the outcome of the battle ahead of them to pursue petty grudges, Kol never let either Mathias's vow to kill him or Sazrah's continued loyalty to her mentor slip from his mind. With the prospect of survival still a wildcard to Kol, he kept his instructions short and as infrequent as possible in an effort to minimize how much attention was brought to him, but otherwise tried to command himself to worry about these two later. He stopped and awkwardly twisted his shoulders to roll his head around to look back at the group.

"The main halls are just ahead," Kol told them. "Be prepared."

"You think we'll run into much trouble?" Nessix asked from the other side of Berann. "Their interest seemed focused on the chasm."

Kol tried to look down the line to gauge Mathias's disapproval of his correcting Nessix, but couldn't see past Berann's stoic, resolved eyes. He sighed. "Once they determine we're not down there, they'll broaden their search."

"You are assuming any of them escape Tristan to do so," Berann said. "He is repulsive for such an elegant man, but he is a voracious predator."

Kol didn't have the insight to comment on Berann's apparent respect for the vampire, but he did have intimate insight on other matters. "Do not forget that Grell's not the only inoga we might encounter. There are four separate factions in this region. Once word spreads of what's underway, Grell's won't be the only force after us."

"A noted and sound observation," Berann resigned. "How do the other inoga stack up to Grellandier?"

"One less stable, two much smarter, none of them inclined to listen to a word we have to say. If they unite and bring their elite with them…" Kol shook his head. "I will not question the skills or capabilities of any of you, but I'd bet anything I'd be the only one of us in the running for a quick death."

A choked sound which could have been either a sob or a growl came from the back of the line immediately before Sazrah's harsh demand. "It doesn't matter who they are or what they're capable of. Point me to the demons I'm allowed to kill and let's be done with this."

A solemn silence dropped on top of the group at the hitch in the seasoned woman's voice. This mission was meant to be a revolution, an act of liberation for a world which had ailed with this sickness for too long. But it very easily could be the definitive end to all of them, regardless of their superior circumstances. Mathias cleared his throat to gruffly address the others. "She's right. We've already set this field. Let's hurry and finish the charge before our opponents have more time to coordinate. Sazrah and I will maintain the rear guard."

Berann nodded. "We are ready, Chiefson."

Kol couldn't claim he was as prepared as those he was with, but this wasn't the first world-altering battle he'd been funneled into. Pulling his head forward, trusting at least half of those who had his back, Kol squeezed the rest of the way down the tunnel, hesitating once more to listen for activity in the adjoining hall.

"Nobody is presently there," Berann confirmed from behind him.

Kol had theorized in the past that Berann didn't even know how to lie, and though a new element of fear had woken inside the alar after his near-death experience and the expectation of the next bound to come for him, he trusted that Berann would not intentionally lead them into more of a losing situation than they already chased. Forcing his retained breath out to gain the extra half inch of clearance, Kol squirmed through the hole, wincing as

Berann helped position his wings to clear it.

The others extracted themselves from this crevice, anxiously milling about and keeping watchful eyes on the open ends of this more central hall until Sazrah made it through the skinny opening. Silent from wariness and dread, the group turned to Berann and his enhanced senses to resume the lead. Nessix couldn't quite decipher the nature of Mathias's strict eyes, but wasn't about to take any chances. Trusting Kol had meant it when he'd expressed thinking of her more as a peer than as property, she grabbed his arm to turn him after Berann and gave him a shove. He complied with her guidance after just a flash of a miffed glower, allowing Nessix to serve as a buffer between him and Mathias. Positions established, the party slinked along close to the walls instead of charging ahead in earnest, more acutely aware of the distant echoes of barked orders than before.

Using Berann's ability to listen for threads as a dowsing rod through these halls, they were able to carefully hold back when handfuls of reinforcements dashed across intersecting pathways. Sazrah's irritation with following the agreed upon tactic of avoiding combat pressed against Nes's back so hard she nearly doubted her own safety, but that frustration quickly dissipated when Berann froze, attention focused as sharply as a hunting dog on point. Silence pulsed around the wary group as they waited on the explanation they'd all been happier not hearing.

"Run."

Nobody dared waste the time it would take to question Berann's order, trusting that the sharpness of the oraku's tone was worth observing. The magnitude of Berann's concern became increasingly apparent as they rushed past a pair of underlings on patrol and he didn't so much as flinch to address them, too focused on his path of retreat. Sazrah hesitated to deal with those passing demons but Mathias, motivated by Berann's instincts, grabbed her sword hand and pulled her onward.

"Left!" Kol called. "Turn left!"

Berann followed Kol's instruction without question, and just as Mathias and Sazrah cleared the corner, he skidded to a stop so hard he had to branch his arms out for balance, and he wheeled around to face the others. In the varying time each of his companions had known him, Berann had proven to be of placid mind and temperament, committed to his purpose of seeking justice and salvation with a strong value placed in self-sacrifice. He was unafraid to face even the most vicious opposition for what he deemed was right, to the point that he'd died once—and would do so again, if necessary—to see his goals become reality. But Berann's eyes as he looked back down the hall reflected more horror than his companions knew what to do with.

"Berann, what's—"

Nessix's question was driven back into her throat by the sound of a thunderous roar promising the death and destruction— not necessarily in that order—of anyone who stood in its way.

"You are *dead*, Kol! *Dead*!"

The severity of Grell's fury warped his voice too much for Sazrah to place where she'd heard it before, but the three who had spent time living with the inoga recognized its brutal instability immediately. Even as her face drained of color as she recalled how easily he'd tossed around Kol, Nessix drew her sword. Grell had done a fine job expressing how much she should fear him, and she'd never before heard this degree of hyper focused madness in his voice, but this time, she wasn't alone. Even if Kol wasn't in fighting shape, she had Mathias and his crazy demon hunter and an oraku on her side now. Methodically drawing upon her chaos, surrendering to the foolishness which would let her throw herself at the monster charging their way, Nessix lifted her foot to position herself more squarely in front of Kol—and then stopped as Berann's voice cut through her racing thoughts.

"Forgive me for sparing him, Kol."

A rapid cascade of stones rained down from the hall's exit point as Berann dropped the ceiling to form a blockade, the cave-in forcing Mathias and Sazrah to hastily retreat closer to the rest of the group to avoid the bounce of stray rocks. Before the tumble was able to fill the hallway, Grell bleated a prolonged roar and charged through the barrier with braced shoulders.

He stopped before the five of them, panting from the exertion of his charge. Trails of blood from his crash through Berann's hasty obstacle flowed along the length of the scar on his face and followed the creases made by the bulging muscles of his arms. Even as his nostrils flared to recover his spent breath, his eyes were keen with focus, limbs primed and ready for use. Grell looked past Nessix, who he hated so much. He looked past the formidable opponent which was Mathias and Sazrah's potential as a plaything, past that human Annin had been so interested in. And he looked straight at Kol.

"Where do you think you're going, maggot?"

Kol sucked in a trembling breath, the residual weakness which came from his period of starvation assuring him that even with the devoted help of Berann and Nessix, he hadn't been able to outrun his death. Grell had forgotten how to handle failure after becoming a demon, and he'd failed to kill Kol several times now. None of those strokes of luck—disguised in part as Nessix's loyalty—which had let Kol escape Grell's plans for him bode well for the alar now, as the inoga's simplicity would remedy these stacked failures in a much more direct fashion. Kol was neither mentally nor physically prepared to face Grell again, but just as quickly as this doom settled over him, it became apparent he may not have to.

"This rotting sack of pig shit is mine!" Sazrah spat her claim with a ferocity the rest of the party balked at, and she separated from the group before Mathias had the chance to hold her back. Hatred propelled her charge so furiously she hadn't managed to draw her longsword full from its sheath before reaching the hideous behemoth.

"Wait your turn." Grell swept his arm toward Sazrah and swatted her aside with the back of his hand as though she was a fly to be shooed away. The strike connected soundly with her head and launched her into the cavern wall. "I'll be with you shortly."

But Sazrah would not be so easily dismissed. This beast had humiliated her. He'd been the cause of her disappointing Mathias, of failing the order she'd been given. Men she'd been responsible for—veterans she'd served beside for decades, the few honorable soldiers left on Elidae, and starry-eyed new recruits alike—had died pathetic, useless deaths because of this festering heap of garbage. And Sazrah would not wait one second longer to carve her vengeance out of his disgusting and distorted flesh. Screaming as the fury Mathias had forced her to keep bottled up these past few days erupted past caution and patience, Sazrah rebounded off the wall and charged ahead once more.

"Pesky slut," Grell growled.

He reached forward to grab her arm, but Sazrah ducked out of his reach, her smaller build and advantage of fighting left-handed allowing her sword to slide past his massive palm. As he tried to catch her, disregarding her heritage and experience in his blindness to kill them all, Grell's fingers closed down on the blade as Sazrah continued to drive closer to him.

Grell howled as his own stupidity resulted in the sword biting into his flesh, and his substantial strength against the blade's slicing edge only succeeded in closing down tight enough to cause a brief lag in Sazrah's momentum. As her sword slipped from his limp and bloodied grasp, Grell spun and caught the aggravating woman on the side of the head with the same hand, spattering his blood over them both. Sazrah scrambled to keep her feet beneath herself from the force of the blow, knowing the death sentence it would be to lose her mobility in this fight and narrowly caught herself as she turned to back against the wall she'd been thrown toward.

"Now," Grell spat, wheeling back to the rest of the group as he labeled Sazrah nothing more than a nuisance. "Answer me, Kol."

The inoga managed a single step forward before a second bite of Sazrah's blade lodged through the leather armor protecting his back, piercing through his flesh with an infuriating ease. She'd thrown herself at him silently this time, exploiting the monster's preoccupation with Kol, too blinded by her hatred of Grell to contemplate the irony of how her actions had effectively saved the life of the demon Mathias had sworn vengeance on. If she only killed one more demon in her life, it would be this one.

Grell roared in agony as the sword pried between his ribs and that anger he'd been holding onto just for Kol over the past year of tracking the alar's mistakes was dumped solely on this insolent child who wouldn't get out of his way. The inoga flung his shoulder back so quickly and with such force that it lifted Sazrah from her feet, and as she began a third flight toward the wall, she released her hold on her sword to leave it lodged in place.

Nessix had less than a passing fondness for Sazrah after the harsh reception and continued scrutiny she received from the other woman, but she did respect the warrior's focus and courage. She was grateful for Sazrah's efforts in holding Elidae together without the influence of the Teradhel name, and she trusted Sulik would not have thought so highly of this fiery human if she weren't as just and great as the paladin who had guided her this far in life. Sazrah was a capable woman who had spent lifetimes perfecting her demon-slaying skills, but Nessix knew how Grell fought. Even through his sputtering madness at having been hit by someone he viewed as inferior, he was gauging every opening, calculating where his final strike would fall, and not even Sazrah had the honed reactions needed to negate his raging power. After all Sazrah had done to carry the burdens that should have been hers, Nessix could not stand by as a brilliant warrior became one more casualty to this repulsive monster. Smaller and more agile than Sazrah, having been launched into three fewer walls than the other woman, Nessix gripped her sword and pushed off against the ground, only to be caught by Mathias.

"Do you want her dead?" Nessix seethed, unsuccessfully jerking her arm back to try to resume her rescue efforts.

"She won't die." Mathias's eyes were trained, strict and focused, on the scuffle unfolding before them, and he flicked the buckle free from his sword. "I've got her."

Nessix shook her head, bunching up her strength to try fighting Mathias's restraint as Sazrah hastily situated her feet beneath herself and Grell rumbled a deep, hungry chuckle. "I've faced this beast before. I know how—"

"Nobody can predict how an inoga will fight," Mathias said. "But we *can* predict the outcome of our mission if we all stay here." Nessix quit her struggling as Mathias's calm logic weaved through the tantrum of her instincts. "One of you knows what we're looking for, one of you knows how to get there, and one of you I actually trust."

Having left her longsword buried in the mountain of Grell's

back, Sazrah armed herself with her short one and worked a cautious path through Grell's sights, methodically turning him to expose her primary weapon clearly to Mathias. The two of them had worked together in combat thousands of times and though it frustrated Nessix to admit it, they were the most effective partnership in this group. If this mission was to be successful, the only logical option was to leave Grell to the two humans while the rest of them carried on toward the last weapon. Mathias allowed her to draw her arm away at last as she took a step back toward Kol and Berann.

"But your Etha—"

Mathias wouldn't accept Nessix's reminder that the divine had no power in the demons' realm. "Is part of me now and always. Now, go! We'll hold him."

The paladin's rally reached through Grell's focus, and dragged the inoga back to the reason he'd come down here, one far more important than to torture a rebellious Sagewind brat. He swung around again, opening his most vulnerable side to his most determined opponent, little eyes burning with insanity.

"None of you will leave this hall alive!" he roared

Mathias had only drawn his sword halfway from its sheath, Nessix falling into a preparatory crouch and Berann's arm twitching into activity when Grell belted out a bellow so loud it sifted dust from the hall's ceiling. Blood spattered from his lips from the force of his scream, carried up from the punctured lung which had done remarkably little to slow him, and he flung his arms behind himself to try ridding his back of Sazrah as she gripped tightly to the sword she'd buried there, using her bodyweight to leverage the blade higher into his body cavity.

With an inoga's resilience and tenacity, Sazrah's hasty attack may be the last distraction they'd receive. Mathias kept his eyes on the combat he was about to jump into, but directed his orders to those behind him. "Go! Now! Abaeloth depends on you!"

Kol's hand, strong and commanding, wrapped around Nessix's arm, drawing her farther away from Mathias. She had her own matters she'd hoped to settle with Grell and loathed the idea of leaving anyone to stand against the monster after the things she'd seen him do, but Mathias's encouragement stuck with her. Abaeloth depended on her stepping away from this fight so she could lead a greater one in the future. Nessix had seen Mathias face inoga before, and he wasn't alone. Surrendering her fears to a warrior's duty, Nessix allowed Kol to pull her around, and the two of them ran after Berann.

"Not today." Mathias's laughing taunt waved them a hearty farewell as they raced down the hall.

Grell sputtered an incomprehensible response followed by the rattle of crumbling stones, and Nessix did her best to focus on her assigned task.

TWENTY-FOUR

The three of them ran until Grell's roars were lost to the winding walls of stone and nothing more than terrifying memories which echoed of the danger they'd placed themselves in. Between Berann's tracking and Kol's navigation, there was very little to keep Nessix's mind off the dismal straits fate and foolishness had led her to. Her mind rebounded wildly between the peril she'd left her army in and what would become of Mathias as he faced Grell. She tried to find comfort in Tristan's apparent knowledge of the undying and that Mathias would choose death before letting Grell get past him, but what it came down to was that neither of those facts comforted her at all. Longing for the days when she'd thought Veed was her biggest problem, Nessix ordered her legs to keep pumping, concentrating on maintaining even breath so she wouldn't fall behind, until Kol's sharp growl of frustration shot up from behind her as his wasted muscles protested his efforts to use them.

Nessix slowed and looked back at him. There were fewer light orbs in these deeper halls than there were in the more frequently travelled avenues of the hells, and the shadows only enhanced the fine lines of stress and strain etched across the alar's face.

"Berann, slow down," Nessix ordered.

"We are under pursuit." In the span of those few words, the

oraku's voice grew quieter, conveying that he hadn't even slowed to assess Nessix's concern.

Kol lifted his eyes to Nessix's, nostrils flaring from exertion. The reassuring smile he tried to concoct manifested more akin to a grimace. "Keep going, little one. I'm fine."

"And I'm an ogre's mother…" Nessix muttered. Despite the chill which had accompanied the bluntness with which Berann had delivered his argument, Nessix backtracked to scoop her shoulder beneath Kol's arm. He began to recoil from her support, but for the first time in their relationship, she commanded more stamina than he did, and she pushed forward, forcing Kol to coordinate his legs alongside her or trip them both trying to resist.

Berann had paused at last due to their marked delay, turning to scold them for the time they were wasting, though when he beheld the droop of Kol's exhaustion, his expression eased with approval of Nessix's sympathy. When it became evident that the general's assistance allowed Kol to move twice as fast and only hindered the tiny woman a hair, Berann accepted this arrangement and resumed his rapid progress down the hall. Once the oraku's focus had returned to his objective, Kol's weight pressed harder against Nessix's shoulder. She was about to try hefting him more securely when she realized his shift had been an intentional lowering of his head as he nestled his lips close to her ear.

"Thank you, Nessix."

The spoken gratitude paired with the use of her proper name, even as hushed as Kol had attempted to make it, sent an untimely bout of shivers dancing across Nes's skin, threatening to steal some of the strength she needed to keep them both close on Berann's trail. It wasn't that she didn't want Kol's gratitude, but the frequency in which he'd allowed himself to openly display weakness to her over the course of this one hectic day had frayed her confidence. Yes, exhaustion barred him from certain feats of strength, but for the first time since Kol had asked Nessix for her obedience, since he'd first whispered to her that she was the only one he could truly trust, she felt the brunt of his faith in her lodge in her chest, and it was a sensation she hadn't been prepared to face.

"You don't have to thank me for loyalty, Kol." She made sure to keep her voice hushed, honoring the alar's attempt to shield this vulnerability from their modest audience. "Just reciprocate it."

Kol accepted Nessix's words in silence, saving his breath and concentration to not hinder her more than he already was. She didn't dwell on that fact, siphoning what she could from Berann's determination to keep her tremors of doubt from begging her to turn back or slow down. From the moment she'd committed to killing her guards on Elidae so she could run from Kol, Nessix had known that this road would not be a gentle one. She'd known there would be great sacrifices demanded of her when he'd quietly pled for her allegiance. But as she tracked after the soul of the long-dead demon residing in the timid dupe she'd dragged across Gelthin, entrusting her browbeaten army to the hands of a vampire, leaving Mathias and his aggressive protégé to face Grell, the ridiculous impossibility of her circumstances eagerly reached its wicked hands out to strangle her.

The reprieve Nessix's assistance had given Kol had restored enough of his coordination and stamina for him to carry himself now, the need to move reminding his body how to function with the power demanded of demons, and as he drew his weight off of Nessix, his hand gently pressed against her back every time reluctance begged her to give in to the confusion of her despair.

After all, it was too late for regrets—they would either succeed today or die for their audacity of thinking they could reform Abaeloth's most tenacious survivors. Never had Nessix's training prepared her for the magnitude of this sort of mission.

"The hall branches up ahead," Kol called to Berann. "Which direction do we need to head?"

At last, Berann slowed his gait without an underlying ripple of bitterness for being delayed. Brows furrowed in concentration, he studied the walls around them as though he couldn't comprehend their structure. "Do any of the passages lead downwards?"

"Yes. Go." Kol gave Nessix another nudge to propel her along and the party resumed their winded trek. "Second tunnel from the right leads—"

Kol's words ended in a shocked choke and all three skidded to an abrupt stop as a wall of stone shot up from the floor in front of them. Its sudden raising had come close to catching Berann, which would have put a quick end to him as he was crushed into the ceiling, but the ancient oraku had been too astute to miss the subtle tells in the warbling cries of Abaeloth's threads before the attack. He spun around, turning his sorrowful, worried eyes past Nessix's startled gaping to meet Kol's equally grim resignation.

"Is this some sort of—"

Kol's hand closed around Nessix's forearm, silencing her feeble questions as he looked to Berann. "Can you get through that?"

Berann glanced over his shoulder, eyes quickly running up and down the new wall. "I can."

"Then take Nessix and keep going. Second tunnel from the right. I'll hold the line as long as I can."

Berann spun back on Kol, a look of sheer horror much more natural to Talier's face conveying exactly what he thought of Kol's declaration. "I am the only one of us qualified to face Annin," he said firmly. "You take Nessix and—"

"You are the only one capable of tracking the hammer." There was a stony resolution in Kol's correction, marking well that he didn't look forward to the encounter he was setting himself up for, but that he was prepared to accept whatever consequences came from it. "It has to be me."

"You won't be able to stop him," Berann said.

"Probably not. But I can slow him down."

Berann's eyes welled with a deep regret, the first sign of genuine emotion Nessix had seen expressed by the logical creature. He plucked one of the last two vitality potions from his belt and tossed it to Kol, who caught it with his free hand and shoved it in a pocket. "May we meet again with the rising of the sun, Chiefson."

Nessix looked between the two demons, hardly believing what she was hearing, and shook her head. "Annin wants you dead, Kol."

The alar swallowed the surge of nausea which rose from her observation. "He wants all of us dead, little one."

She clutched his hand with fingers begging him to reconsider what he was about to do, on the verge of instinctively trying to pull rank to get her way until she remembered she had no authority over him. "I didn't save you to just to abandon you when death won't give up the chase, and I will not allow you to face Annin alone." Tears shook her voice, but discipline kept them from falling. "Berann can track the hammer and you and I—"

Berann gripped Nessix's other arm, the strength working through his fingers assuring her that he was prepared for her to resist and ready to counter any efforts she made to do so. "I can, but this will not be the last time we meet opposition. I need someone who can fight while I work. If I thought I could retrieve the weapons without endangering anyone else, I would have. We must hurry, Nessix. Annin knows we are here and he won't spare us a heartbeat more to organize."

Nessix couldn't let Kol go off to face Annin alone. She'd been unable to resign him to death back when she had no say in his welfare, and would not send him off to actively find it now that she could do something about it. Kol squeezed her arm tighter, released his hold to grasp her hand, and clenched his teeth. There was a haunting depth in his fiery eyes, a grim finality which Nessix had seen in soldiers so many times before. It was the knowledge that death was the most likely outcome of the actions which must be undertaken for the greater good, and she couldn't combat the warm sting of tears as they beat against her eyelids any longer.

"Change the hells for me, little one."

Before Nessix could voice any further protests to the madness of Kol's decision, he shoved her toward Berann. The oraku caught her in one arm, sweeping his other toward the stone wall Annin had raised against them as he spun around. The stones tumbled into rubble, and Kol used the commotion as cover to dash away from them. Berann wasted no more time in pulling himself and Nessix over the boulders to continue pressing onward.

"You heard him," Berann scolded at Nessix's subtle resistance as she tried to turn back to look after—or perhaps follow—Kol. "We must go. Do not let his sacrifice be made in vain."

"His sacrifice…" Nessix couldn't motivate herself to move past the weight of those words, frozen in place as she watched

Kol's back fade into the dimness farther down the hall. "He can't do this."

"He must do this," Berann corrected, refusing to follow Nessix's distraught gaze. "Do not shame him by wasting what he's giving us. Annin is too ruthless to simply let us go."

Every fiber of Nes's being wanted to knock Berann out so she could be free to run and assist Kol, except for the steady pulse of the wretched duty tied to the station she'd once worn with such gusto.

Change the hells for me, little one.

The urge to rescue Kol—an action she'd most likely fail to accomplish, given his opponent—was a selfish one she didn't have room to entertain. Kol was counting on her. The akhuerai were counting on her. The future of Abaeloth was counting on her. General Nessix Teradhel had been born a servant of those who needed her, and Kol had chosen his path after centuries of walking in darkness. Tucking her chin to her chest to keep it from trembling, Nessix held on to that promise she'd made Kol and forced herself to turn away from him. Berann, no less torn by the act of abandoning a friend to certain death, didn't bother acknowledging her obedience, and resumed leading the way toward the hammer's song.

* * * * *

There had been nobody for Kol to pray to since midway through the Divine Battle, but as Nessix's debates trailed after him as he increased the distance between them, he cast a desperate request out to whatever force might listen to a demon that she would continue to move forward without him and help Berann retrieve Motag's hammer. The undertones of Berann's voice answered his request, calmly rationalizing what Nessix knew must be done, and when he no longer heard either of them, Kol stopped running to work on replenishing his breath. Annin had to have been close to raise that wall.

This was a fight Kol had never wanted to think he'd have to engage in, even when in the peak of his physical strength, but one

289

which a quiet part of him had expected to come since they'd been young men. Doing his best to put aside his past dependence on Annin, his dreams of what their future could have held, and his fears of what was going to come, Kol adjusted his grip on the blades he'd salvaged from the demons slain in the chasm, testing their weight and balance as he prepared for the most trying fight of his life.

Annin, always rational and collected, seldom let tells of his urgency show, and Kol might have taken in the oraku's wide eyes and hectic dashing with some degree of humor had he not been staring down the last few moments of his life. Unfortunately for Annin, Kol had been methodically preparing himself for a torturous death since he first woke up in solitary and had forced himself to accept the fate when Annin had closed up the air sources. He'd have liked to see the future Berann and Nessix were setting up, but as far as Kol was concerned, he was already on borrowed time. It was that peace with impending death which allowed him to stand firm as Annin came to a stop in the hallway and that peace would have held had Annin not found it in himself to bury his shock and terror beneath the same sneer of expectation Kol had always associated with the oraku.

"Step aside, Kol."

Though exertion and adrenaline taxed Annin with heaving breath, he'd succeeded in delivering the order calmly and with the same demeaning patience he often used with those he considered inferior to him. It was a tone Kol had been able to brush aside all his life, excusing it away as a remnant of the harsh treatment of his youth until he'd grown so used to the underlying cruelty that he found comfort in it. It was the same tone Annin had used when discussing the fledgling theories Kol concocted, to formulate the means to bring his far-fetched dreams into reality. Kol had found an ironic form of acceptance and respect in Annin's coldness, a reliable promise that at least one part of his world would always remain stable and unchanged, but as he looked into the pale, empty eyes of his oldest and dearest friend, he could no longer find that foundation he'd built his life around. Kol gulped down the heat of his tears. He'd been prepared to die, but he'd never be prepared to

290

kill Annin.

"I can't do that," Kol answered once he was certain he had control of his voice.

Annin shook his head, no bitter laugh, no building arrogance to taunt Kol more than the circumstances already did. "Please, Kol."

Kol winced. Annin had never used that word with him.

The fact that the oraku kept his eyes angled away suggested he was no less surprised by his brief choice of words than Kol had been. "Let me pass. Let me stop them. I do not want to force this from you."

Kol's arms trembled and the betraying sting of emotions pressed against his eyes and brought a rapid tremble to his lips. "I can't," he repeated.

Annin closed his eyes and turned his face away for a moment, frown creasing tighter as his own surge of regret washed over him and drew away like an ebbing tide. When he opened his eyes and lifted them to Kol's that brief wave of remorse had disappeared completely, replaced with the callousness which had carried him everywhere he'd wanted to go in life.

"Then you must die," Annin said simply.

Kol couldn't blink, could barely move at all. The hilts of his blades grew slick in his sweaty palms as he met Annin's ultimatum. But he'd seen his friend's regret, possibly the first he'd allowed himself to experience in his entire life, and he couldn't back down. If Annin was so determined to end this, Kol would make him pay for it. "Only if you kill me."

Neither demon moved. The pound of Kol's heart raced so heavily he could have sworn it echoed off the stone walls around them. Neither of them wanted this confrontation, but they were both smart enough to know there would be no escaping it and that it likely should have happened decades ago. Kol had to make the first move if he hoped to stand a chance at crawling away when the last blow struck, but that delusion of hope clung to the thought that maybe forcing this conflict he didn't want to have was just as hard for Annin to accept, that if he held off on expressing his aggression, maybe they could lock this stalemate until Nessix and

Berann returned and he could let the more stable oraku sort out how to placate Annin so they could both survive.

Kol should have learned by now. Hope had no place in the hells.

Annin raised his hand and touched his thumb and middle finger together.

TWENTY-FIVE

Though Tristan could not call himself a priest of Ceredulus, he did consider himself the god's most devout and dedicated servant, even if he weren't the only vampire currently walking free in the world. With Ceredulus returned to the confines of the Veil and Tristan as deep as he was in the bowels of Abaeloth, the vampire had no way to raise troops of his own, but he was far from disappointed with those he was borrowing from Nessix. They were a timid and wary bunch, no doubt broken by the demons' barbaric and disgraceful practices, but they watched him carefully and with a malleable intelligence absent in the living dead which Tristan was accustomed to managing. Both he and his eager god were interested in studying these creations in action, and study them, he did.

The steady flow of demons devoted a significant portion of their efforts on trying to slow Tristan in particular, but despite their attempts to distract him, he maintained a careful eye on the akhuerai. Largely unarmed at the onset of this assault, several of the ragtag force had fallen in the first hectic minutes of combat. None of the defeated akhuerai had returned to function in the timeframe Tristan had hoped or expected they would, but without knowing the mechanics which these creations followed, he had no way of knowing how permanent death was to them. What he *did* know was that this fight was rousing something beautiful in those still standing.

Be it beholding their friends' demise or inspiration by Tristan's enthusiastic slaughter of the beasts who had oppressed them for so long, the demeanor of the akhuerai soon began to shift toward something Tristan could work with. As the army reached its tipping point between timid and furious over the injustices which had been taken against them, the demons were forced to broaden their concern from Tristan alone to the masses which he led. The tides of battle continued to sweep above and through the chasm and the akhuerai, fronted by their superhuman interim commander, seized weapons off their fallen opponents to engage in chaotic, but not entirely ineffective, combat.

The battle flowed reliably in Tristan's favor, the ratio of demon to akhuerai defeats growing steadily. As it became apparent to the demons that they were being trounced, a trilling horn sounded from above at the chasm lip and the demons on the upper level began to retreat, those who had cascaded to the chasm floor drawing back to the unstable staircase.

As much fun as Tristan had been having in this violent madness, he watched the organized haste in which the demons departed and considered his options. The force he'd guided the akhuerai through eliminating had been worn thin enough for the skilled demon hunters and their liaisons running about the upper halls to handle, should that be where his opponents planned to head, and as much as Tristan loved the idea of continuing to indulge in this fight, he'd been sent down here on a more important mission. Darting up the wall of the chasm to jump in front of the first of the akhuerai climbing the stairs in pursuit of their fleeing enemies, Tristan took that control Nessix had given him.

"We hold here," he declared, voice encompassing the power of the dozens of demons he'd sampled during this scuffle.

The young man he faced was effectively held back by the authoritative set of Tristan's brows and refined jaw, but those further from the vampire's immediate aura weren't so easily intimidated.

"We've cut down their numbers!" came a call from lower down the stairs. "Let us finish them!" Multiple voices raised in agreement.

Tristan cocked his head in contemplation of this surge of confidence, the subtle shifting of previously immobile akhuerai bodies sprawled on the chasm floor vying for his attention. He took a step closer to the ledge and pointed down. "What is happening to your fallen kin?"

"We can be killed but we cannot die," came the ready reply.

Tristan rolled his eyes and was lucky to retain an irritated scoff. "Yes. That is what it means to be undying. But what is it that *allows* you to rise again?"

His question had been patient enough but succeeded only in covering the akhuerai in a blanket of uncomfortable silence. A few of them on the stairs shuffled about as if to retreat from Tristan's curiosity, and expressions ranged from stark fear of the unknown to blatant concern of their own persistent ignorance. This was all becoming increasingly strange and quite inconvenient for Tristan; even his ghouls, as mindless as they were, had a working understanding that he was the reason they existed. That such sentient creations had no idea what gave them their invincibility meant that the demons had taken even greater liberties with Ceredulus's artistry than Tristan had first thought.

"My dear brothers and sisters, who is it that's been lying to you?"

"That damned demon, Kol!"

Tristan shook his head. "The one who just led your general and her friends out of here?" Was there *any* semblance of order or reason in this filthy realm? He looked again to the twitching bodies coming back to life, not sure if Ceredulus had counted on their problem being quite this complicated.

The answer Tristan received was muddled between excuses of Kol having manipulated their general to rationalization that she'd manipulated him before a full-bodied shout put a stop to the confusion.

"It doesn't matter who put us here, the demons are getting away!"

Tristan heaved a weary sigh as more voices raised in support of the cry and the press forward resumed. Irritated that these stubborn creatures were preventing him from the scholarly pursuits demanded of him by his god, Tristan drew upon the cursed and domineering power at his disposal, threw his arms to his sides, and bore down on the front lines with a fierce glare. "Stop!"

And the akhuerai obeyed.

"I told Nessix I would keep you safe and contained until she returned and that is what I will do, with or without your ready compliance."

"Nessix would let us pursue!" came the stubborn debate.

Once again, Tristan's attention was jerked away from studying the progress of the recovering akhuerai to address the ignorance of his functioning charges. Unexplained enthusiasm, Tristan would tolerate, but not blatant lies. "Would she? I cannot claim to know her well, but no seasoned general would allow their army to give chase into the heart of an enemy's home terrain."

The pressure backing Tristan's blunt criticism sent out another pulse of reluctance and the next wave of akhuerai slowed their press forward. Pleased with his results, wondering how to go about securing the power of demon thralls for future use, Tristan continued to talk the chaos out of this anxious army so he could get back to his more pressing interests.

"Your Nessix wants what is best for you, her people. You have demonstrated brilliant courage and…" He tilted his head to the side, balancing out how effective this force had been with the lack of organized tactics they'd actually exhibited, then shrugged. "Respectable skill, but she appointed me as your guardian while she was gone, and you will obey me. Let the demons run, and let us regroup for—"

Overconfident and too preoccupied with trying to convince the akhuerai to go back into their hole so he could poke at their wounded and dead, not even Tristan's superhuman senses and speed kept him from losing the momentum of his orders when a pair of clawed hands clasped around his chest, wiry arms and legs wrapping around his torso and waist. Balance thrown by this unexpected stowaway, he pitched forward on his precarious perch at the top of the narrow staircase and fell toward the chasm floor amid a chorus of gasps and shouts of confusion and terror. And then, a determined set of teeth sank into his neck.

Tristan considered rage an undignified emotion and always did his best to keep his suppressed, but that unsightly response flourished to life inside of him now. What sort of mockery did the demons dare to throw at him after the blasphemy they'd already shown his god? What sort of progress did they think they would make in angering him this way? Tristan snapped an arm out behind himself as he fell, raking his fingers along the stone wall to slow the speed of his descent, and as a fresh explosion of panic burst from the akhuerai above and below him, he turned his eyes up, squinting through the dust and pebbles stirred up by his hand, to find a swell of skinny demons rampaging their way like a pack of deranged wild beasts. The akhuerai desperately scrambled to get away from the madness carried in their erratic charge.

What in Ceredulus's name…?

"This is it!" Tristan cried to the troops. "You wanted to continue this fight? Now's your chance! Stand! Deliver!"

Without the influence of his direct presence, Tristan's rallying had little effect on the troops, and as the thing attached to his back unclamped its jaws to bite down on a fresh spot, an animalistic growl accompanying the shake of its head as if it was some fiercely demented rodent, Tristan understood why. Whatever creatures were pouring into the chasm now, both down the stairs and simply tumbling over the lip of it and shrieking with glee and insanity as they fell to the ground, were not demons in the sense either Tristan or the akhuerai had experienced before. Tristan shoved himself from the wall to let the weight of the thing clasped to his back hurry his descent and allowed gravity take care of crushing the breath out of his assailant.

On impact, the creature released its hold of both limbs and teeth, and Tristan sprang to his feet, kicking the wretched beast in the side as soon as he was up. He retreated from the cacophony of garbled voices which announced the arrival of this new opposing force to formulate his next plan of action.

"What nature of abomination are these things?" he asked the

horrified akhuerai beside him.

The man only gaped and shook his head as the spry creatures flung themselves at his peers, using nothing more than clawed fingers and physical strength to land their effective attacks.

Harrumphing at the lack of help as the man turned to flee from the rising threat, Tristan gave himself another moment to study these creatures' movements. They raced about like deformed apes, falling onto the support of their arms when momentum overcame their agility. They made no obvious efforts to communicate with one another and had no clear organization to their attacks. The longer Tristan observed them, the more he saw of the mindless ghouls which he'd risen in the past. Granted, these creatures bore the same twisted souls as every other demon he'd encountered, but if keeping possession of their life essence was the only advantage they had over the troops Tristan could create, the vampire was confident this fight would be won if he could work past the shock running rampant through his reinforcements.

"Do not falter!" he called to the troops. "These creatures are grotesque and fierce, but they won't be able to overcome a disciplined attack."

Without the ability to focus his words into a compulsive command, Tristan knew they would have very little influence over his stunned allies, but he had more than mere words in his arsenal. These creatures which had been sent to replace the more sensible demons had one very noteworthy difference from the mindless minions Tristan raised. They could bleed. And if they could bleed, they could die.

If Ceredulus would have told him that this mission would present this sort of perk when he'd first woken, Tristan would have driven Berann twice as hard to hurry up and get down here. Leading by example, having not realized how much he missed the gruesome rush of combat until this very moment, Tristan grinned and threw himself into the oncoming flood of enemies.

* * * * *

"You. Insolent. *Worm*!"

Grell charged at Mathias, slamming his fist into the stone wall as the human dodged out of his way. The inoga's movements had slowed due to his massive amount of blood loss and the handicap of a collapsed lung, but Mathias wouldn't allow himself to become complacent.

"That's an awful big word to come out of an idiot like you."

Though always grateful for diversions to take an inoga's attention off himself, Mathias wished Sazrah would have refrained from drawing Grell back to her. She bled from her forehead, had switched to fighting with her off hand, and her evasive actions were lagging at a far greater rate than Grell's own. Mathias's purpose of protecting her would have been much easier if she'd simply follow the natural flow of combat as opposed to digging her own channels to direct it, but she'd declared that she would claim vengeance for herself, no matter what. Sazrah stumbled as she sprang out of Grell's charge, and Mathias grimly wondered if determination would be enough to see her to victory.

In far better shape than Sazrah was, Mathias rushed forward as soon as Grell had turned, and he slapped his palm down on top of the pommel of the sword still buried in the monster's back. Grell roared, a fresh spray of blood coloring his flinging saliva as he wheeled back around to face the pesky paladin who danced a spry retreat.

"You keep leaving your back exposed," Mathias taunted, monitoring Sazrah's prowl from the corner of an eye. "It's a shame you don't have any friends to watch it for you."

Grell straightened as much as the sword in his back allowed him to and spit out a mouthful of blood. "I don't need anyone to watch my back." Attention not diverted half as much as either of his opponents had thought it was, Grell held out the log of his arm and spun to clothesline Sazrah in her charge.

She strangled a gasp for breath which was pushed out of her in a cry of agony as she once again struck the wall, and Grell turned from Mathias to stalk toward the more vulnerable prey.

"Get out of here, Mathias," Sazrah groaned. She used her legs to push herself away from Grell's approach, but her retreat was slower than he was gaining on her. "Go make sure those creatures don't betray us."

Locked in combat with a heatedly driven inoga in prime position to destroy the woman who he had fought his hardest battles alongside, the woman he loved as a daughter, Mathias wouldn't waste the time trying to explain to Sazrah, yet again, that at least Nessix could be trusted. There wasn't enough time for Sazrah to get to her feet before Grell would have his crushing grasp on her, and limited to the finite amount of Etha's blessing which he'd carried down here, Mathias couldn't call on his usual glut of might to level this field. Instead, he let Sazrah's implications guide him to Nessix, and borrowed a page from the impulsive woman's tactical manual.

What Mathias lacked in Nes's agility and small size, he made up for in strength and desperation, and he launched himself at Grell's back. Grasping the hilt of the sword for balance and security, he scrambled with his feet to climb between the monster's wings until he was able to lodge a foot atop the hilt. He stomped down, grabbing a firm hold of Grell's hair as the inoga bellowed in fury and agony, spinning violently to try to dislodge Mathias from his deadly advantage. Reinforcing his grip, Mathias stomped on the hilt again.

"Saz! Veil! Now!"

Mathias didn't know how long he'd be able to stay rooted to the inoga's back, marveling at the tenacity Nessix had to be able to ride out this sort of struggle with such outward ease, nor did he know if Sazrah had heard or understood his command over Grell's eruption of incensed curses. As stupid as Mathias wanted to think Grell was, this particular inoga had proven rather adept at adapting to his opponents' tactics—a skill likely developed as means for survival when working so closely with characters as shady as Kol and Annin—and shouting in code seemed the best chance of Mathias and Sazrah finding success. Their stand at the raising of the Veil, when Mathias had served as a decoy while the better equipped participants ended the battle, was one Sazrah would not have forgotten, no matter how beaten or hyper focused she was.

Sazrah didn't give Mathias an affirmative, and he couldn't put his eyes on her due to Grell's frenzied thrashing. His foundation on the inoga's back slipped with each turbulent spin, robbing him of the ability to find a safe opening to resituate himself. He had to hold on. Etha, he had to hold on! Arms aching, Mathias attempted to stretch his overtaxed muscles by pulling Grell's head back by the reins he'd made of the inoga's hair and then suddenly, the roaring was interrupted by a muted gurgle, and Mathias was falling backwards.

Mind still tumbling about from his wild ride, Mathias couldn't quite keep up with this development, and he pulled himself closer to Grell's body as he tipped horizontally. A wash of blood flowed over his breastplate, running down the steel and onto his face, and Mathias pressed his lips together to keep it out of his mouth. Half a second later, he was crushed between the ground and Grell's massive upper body. Gasping for breath, Mathias unclasped his fingers to push himself to his seat, shoving Grell's head, neck limp from a cleanly slit throat, off himself.

Sazrah staggered up beside him, planting her hands on her hips as she panted. "If you'd have led with that, we'd both be better off, you know."

Mathias snapped his head up to look at her, caught between rationale and excuses to explain his tactics, but Sazrah's eyes were warm with exhaustion and relief. "Yeah," he grunted, prying his way out from beneath the dead behemoth. "I'd have been happy to if you'd have given me half a second to make a move. Good timing on that strike, by the way. I'm impressed you saw an opening to avoid hitting me."

As Mathias sat to regain his bearings, Sazrah stepped the rest of the way up to Grell and crouched beside her mentor. "I hadn't seen an opening." She looked at him and smiled. "That was luck."

Mathias chuckled and shook his head, pulling his knees beneath himself to help Sazrah roll Grell's corpse over and dislodge her sword from his back. As she wiped the blood off the blade as well as she could with the soiled cloth she had access to, Mathias dutifully turned his concern to her physical condition, and she frowned.

"I'll make this easier on both of us and tell you now that I decline whatever healing you're thinking about trying to give me right now."

"Saz, you took a beating."

She gave up on cleaning the blade and slammed it back in its scabbard. "None of it's serious. Just a collection of minor injuries all added up. Give me an hour and I'll be fine. You need to save what grace you've got bottled up for more important tasks. Go. Find Nessix. I've got your rear."

If anyone else in Sazrah's condition had given Mathias such an order, he would have ignored it, but now that Grell was dead—by Sazrah's hand, as she'd sworn he would be—Mathias could safely resume trusting her judgment. He stood and found his balance.

"Don't let me down, Mathias," she said softly.

Mathias smiled, ready for this to be over. "Never. I'll not keep you waiting."

With as much faith in Sazrah's skill and determination as he had in his own, Mathias turned and ran down the hall in search of Nessix, praying he wasn't too late.

* * * * *

Kol's stomach lurched. He'd seen Annin use this insignificant gesture to incapacitate opponents a million times and had never identified a way to stop what came next. From a victim's standpoint, it was an unpredictable move capable of a vast range of unfavorable fates ranging from the humiliation of soiling oneself to a slow, tortuous death from ruptured organs. Annin had clearly stated his intention to kill Kol if he didn't stand down, and Kol was quite sure he knew the final outcome on the other end of Annin's snap. Renewed and revitalized by Berann's faith and focus, Kol had finally decided he was not ready to die. Survival instinct engaging past his lifelong fondness for Annin, Kol lifted his arm, eyes adept at aerial surveillance honing in on his target, and let his dagger fly.

Before Annin could press his fingers together, the blade sank into his bicep. He cried out in pain, the sound twisting into a livid growl as he yanked the knife out of his arm and forcibly cast it behind himself.

"That was a stupid move, Kol," Annin snarled, shifting his

focus to the second—and last—weapon the alar had. "If you'd wanted to put up a fight, you should have aimed for something vital."

From Kol's perspective, that *had* been a vital strike—it had successfully prolonged his life for at least a few more seconds. "I don't want to fight you."

Annin shook his head with a pitying frown. "I mean to kill you, Kol, and there is nothing you can do to change that."

"No," Kol said. "I suspect there's not. But there is much you could do to change it."

Annin stared blankly at Kol for the span of a dozen tense heartbeats, that silence doing all it could to give the alar hope that maybe, somewhere, Annin still remembered that they'd once been a team. The oraku's mocking laughter dashed that sentiment aside. "And why would I want to do that?"

Kol swallowed his nerves, a sharp pain lodging in his chest where his racing heart kept them from going all the way down. This wasn't even close to the first time he'd had to explain his logic to Annin, and he knew which themes to strike. "Because," he said, his voice a soft croak, "we are so close to restructuring the hells, so close to *winning*, and I need you to be part of it."

"Restructuring?" Annin asked. "*Winning*? Your pet has brought Mathias Sagewind down here. *Berann* is collecting the god weapons. None of us are going to win. This isn't a restructure. It is genocide. And *you* are fighting on the wrong side. I will be no part of it besides executing you. I'd wanted to make this painless, Kol, but here you are, destroying my plans. As always."

Kol tightened his grip on his second blade. Even if he thought he would be able to sneak in another throw with Annin monitoring every twitch he made, that would leave him completely unarmed against one of the most terrifying opponents Abaeloth had ever known. His first attack and the following debate had only bought Nessix and Berann a few moments; he had to find a way to drag out this fight.

"It can still be painless," Kol said, the faint tremor of remorse in his voice. He chose not to clear the emotion from his throat on the off chance that it might slip past Annin's cold exterior. "You don't have—"

"Oh, there will be pain," Annin swore. "Before I *let* you die, you will wish Grell had just finished the job before."

That was not the answer Kol had hoped to hear, either for his own fate or Annin's, but it also gave him a terribly brilliant idea. Annin resented insubordination worse than most, and Kol refusing to roll over and accept the fate Grell had assigned him had been what coaxed his reliable temperament down this path of petty violence. If Kol could bear the torture of extracting more of Annin's anger, if he could survive the injuries he'd receive from goading the oraku into prolonging his death long enough, he might be able to ensure Nessix and Berann had the time they needed to accomplish their mission. They might even have enough time to make it back to him. It was a horrifying gamble, but it was the best plan he could come up with in this moment.

"Yeah?" Kol asked, burying the fears of his stupidity as he'd buried those which had come with defying a goddess. "I'd like to see you try."

Annin laughed. It wasn't the same degrading laughter he'd used when trying to cover up his insecurity of being outwitted or overlooked, but a cold, mocking laughter which stated with blunt certainty that he was the only one with any influence over the situation. "Oh, Kol. It's not about what I'm going to try. It's about what I'm going to *do*."

It was clear that Annin had no intention of playing into Kol's plans, and so the alar had to pivot. Though he'd likely be able to increase Annin's eagerness to toy with him if he surrendered his last blade, the need to keep a hold of a weapon in times of peril had been ingrained too deeply in Kol for him to commit to throwing this one. Instead, he crouched low to spring forward and attempt a second attack.

Snap.

The moment Kol's leg pushed off the ground, his shin split in half. He'd expected a burst of pain from someplace upon taking action, and was able to grind his teeth against it. Using his shredded and seeping wings, he recycled the bit of power his leg had generated before the break to keep his momentum driving forward.

Annin must not have expected him to be able to ignore the pain of the fracture so readily, for Kol was almost able to sink his knife into his friend's gut before the blade was deflected by a swat to the wrist. Annin drew his hand out of Kol's reach as he backed away, but Kol, far more experienced with hand to hand combat, pressed close to Annin's movement and, before the next snap could come, he swept the knife upwards along the inside of the oraku's forearm.

Annin had already been furious. Now, he came completely unhinged. Thread manipulation had always been his greatest strength and the most terrifying talent available to him, and he'd contently passed his time by torturing people with it since he'd been a toddler. But as the warmth of his own blood ran down his arm, his fingers screaming in protest as he tried to take out the thread supporting Kol's left lung, he disregarded all of that power for the raw rage which came with Kol's sudden rejection of his sappy sense of loyalty. Needing to protect his off hand for use after this bout of fury passed, Annin did his best to ball his crippled fist and flung it with all of the might of his muscular shoulder at Kol's face. The blow connected, but glanced off due to the slickness of his blood, and Kol followed the strike's influence to shift to the side and take aim with his knife once again.

This time, Annin was ready for it, and he jammed his heel into the knee of the leg he'd just shattered. Kol might have been able to swallow the pain of the initial break, but as the bone fragments shifted in opposite directions from this blow and burrowed into surrounding tissue, nausea surpassed determination and his supporting knee buckled to drop him to the ground. So much for buying time.

Gasping for breath through the heated waves of agony lapping around him, Kol used his sound leg to push himself away from Annin, as if that would matter. A second snap shattered that ankle and Kol cried out, a third snap collapsing the lung Annin had targeted from the start and distorting Kol's cry into a shrill string of choking as the panic of not being able to breathe seized him. The wrist of his armed hand went next and all Kol could do was stare up at the rage and disgust in his old friend's eyes as he stalked up to him.

"It didn't have to be like this," Annin said, his voice menacingly quiet. "You could have listened to me."

Annin drew a leg back and kicked Kol in the ribs, launching the alar into a choked string of coughing. Trembling in pain and regret and fresh bouts of horror at the thought of what awaited dead demons, Kol reached his functioning arm over his chest with the feeble idea of retrieving the knife from his broken hand. One more snap and that shoulder rolled out of its socket. Kol let his head fall against the ground, all will to fight gone as his last means to defend himself was removed, and Annin stepped over him, sinking down on his waist as he grabbed Kol's collar and jerked his limp body upright.

"Where's your arrogance now?" Annin asked. "Where are all of your brilliant plans?"

Kol was growing dizzy from oxygen deprivation and wasn't entirely sure why he kept pushing at this point. "Please. Keep to our objecti—"

Annin's left hand clenched tighter on Kol's collar and he drew his right back to deliver a furious punch to Kol's face with each word he spoke. "Fuck your objectives!"

Without the strength to clear the shock of the blows from his head, Kol was completely at Annin's mercy as the oraku shook him until his head rolled back centrally, chin nestled between his collar bones. Annin leaned closer to Kol's face, voice lowering to a whisper in his continued interest of protecting his pride.

"I had admired you since the day we met," Annin seethed. "*What* happened to you?"

Kol didn't answer, he couldn't have even if he'd wanted to. *Hurry, little one…*

"You could have gone places," Annin continued through teeth grit tight with resentment. "And I could have taken you there. But you wouldn't. Fucking. *Listen!*"

End it all. And begin with Annin.

In the first display of emotional weakness Kol could recall the oraku ever expressing—though it was far easier to blame it on the few injuries Kol had inflicted on him—Annin's arms trembled. "Know that I mean it when I say I'm sor—"

As Kol gasped at the realization of Annin's parting words to him, the oraku's eyes flew wide, his voice cut off by a surprised choke. In his beaten state, it took the coughed expulsion of a bubble of blood from Annin's mouth for Kol to realize there was a sword projecting through his friend's chest, its tip mere inches from Kol's own heart. His tears ceased instantly in shock and disbelief, in the horror of how he'd survive in a world without Annin by his side. Death quietly withdrew the keen light from the oraku's pale eyes, his fingers releasing their hold on Kol's shirt to drop him to the ground. Annin slid down the length of the blade, pouring warm blood onto Kol's chest until his slow descent came to an abrupt stop. The blade flew back out of Annin's chest and as the oraku was shoved disgracefully to the ground, Kol dragged his gaze up to meet Mathias's righteous and rigid glare.

Finish this, little one…

He'd been so close.

Defeated and exhausted, Kol closed his eyes to quietly accept the death which had been chasing him for the past year. He'd been a fool to think he'd escape it.

TWENTY-SIX

Nessix concentrated on the steady rhythm of their running to keep from venturing too deep into her thoughts about turning back, hating her heart for the fit it threw at her commitment to duty. She'd already accepted the fact that Kol wouldn't see this new age he'd dreamed of and that he'd willingly offered to surrender his chance to do so. Logic assured her that it was a noble and necessary sacrifice, but logic couldn't override everything. Kol was injured and worn, and he was up against an opponent Nessix dreaded even more than Grell. But she'd made him a promise, and the faster she and Berann reached this last artifact, the sooner she'd be able to return to offer him backup.

It was such a sweet story to tell herself.

Winded though she was, Nessix was unable to enjoy the reprieve of Berann's rapid deceleration until he came to a full stop. Nessix slowly paced back and forth across the hall to keep her muscles warm as she watched the demon's brows tip in confusion then draw together in resolve. His eyes darkened in a refined disgust which spoke of a deep anger Nessix hadn't expected to see from him, prompting her to stop moving completely.

"What's wrong?" she asked.

Berann stared into the darkness of their path ahead a moment longer, then loosened the hook from his belt. "Reinforcements have arrived near the hammer's location. Their songs are loud and eager."

With Grell and Annin already accounted for—or so Nessix hoped—she accepted this report without fear. "The only reason I let you convince me to not stay behind with Kol was because you expected a fight. I am ready. Let's go."

Berann held his left hand, gripping the hook, to his side so his arm caught Nessix across her chest as she stepped forward. "I believe it is an inoga and an oraku—" When Nessix straightened and gasped, fear for the fates of her friends reflected past all sense of resolve in her eyes, he hastily added, "Not Grell or Annin. But with the threats such a combination can pose, it is unwise to rush in blindly."

Nessix shook her head. "It's not blind. Your assessment ensured as much." She'd seen enough of the region's hierarchy to know that the other three clans were inferior in might to Grell's, and she'd held her own against their heaviest hitters in the past to be guardedly optimistic about her odds with Berann by her side.

Berann lowered his arm and moved the hook to Nes's right hand. "This will be a fight like you've never faced before. By now, they know what we are after and why, and I suspect they are not interested in compromise. Expect them to do everything they can to avoid the fate we have decided for them. Your mortal arms will not dent their desperation. Take the hook. Help me carve a path."

The warm metal of the hook brushed against the backs of Nes's fingers as though pulsing with its own life, and for a moment, she recoiled from it. Nessix had always fought with her heirloom sword or knives; she had no idea how to wield such an awkward weapon and, even if she did, the power radiating from it even as it had barely touched her enhanced the trembling in her knees. "I… I don't know how to use that thing."

Berann was unmoved by her debate. "Then don't. Let it use you."

Of all of the answers Nessix had expected to hear, that was one she neither wanted nor knew how to handle. This weapon was ancient and powerful, a relic which had united all of demonkind so that its secrets would remain hidden. It predated Nes's people,

Mathias, and the demons themselves, having watched Abaeloth grow from its infancy, and if Berann was to be trusted, it was sentient and he wanted her to let it lead her in combat. The nature of her station had long ago conditioned Nessix to be intolerant to being given orders, but what authority did she hope to have over a weapon such as this?

The silence of her uncertainty did nothing to sway Berann's stance. "It is a tool of justice and chaos, much as you are. Speak to it your desires, then follow its lead, and the two of you will dance."

Nessix hadn't quite had time to fully process that weapons with such demon-crippling power existed, and now she was being asked to surrender herself to one? The fact that Kol hadn't so much as breathed a word to her about them after the pact they'd made assured her this wasn't a joke, as did the urgency in which the demons had organized efforts to stop Berann from reaching this last one. But how much of herself might she lose in the hands of a weapon wielded by the gods? She thought of the akhuerai who depended on her now more than ever so they could return to their lives on the surface. She thought of Mathias and Sazrah valiantly standing against Grell without Etha by their sides so she would be able to see this through. She thought of Kol resigning himself to face Annin to the death. They were all demonstrating exemplary courage, counting on her to be brave, to be victorious, and she was too cowardly to hold a damn piece of metal? Berann, the very creature these weapons were adept at killing, handled this massive hook with a natural ease, and Nessix had always fancied herself a hero. Scoffing in disappointment that she'd balked at all, Nessix reached forward and seized the hilt just beneath Berann's grasp. He nodded in approval and drew the twin sabers.

"Now, we go," Berann said. "Keep on your guard."

He dashed off again, and Nessix followed instantly, pulled along by a gentle vibration of anticipation from the hook. Its balance was awkward in her hand, the barb at the end throwing it off center and tipping it toward the ground, the grip a bit too wide to comfortably fit her small palm. Unaccustomed to this weapon in every way, Nessix fretted over whether or not she'd even be able to keep a hold of it once combat jarred it in her hands, and she tightened her fingers around the leather-wrapped hilt.

Losing it is not an option, she told herself firmly. *Too many lives are counting on me keeping this hook away from the demons.*

As she continued to trail after Berann, the hook's weight lightened with each pump of her arm, and her fingers settled in deeper around the hold as if this weapon had been made for her—and not some ancient god—all along. Her fear of being disarmed began to dissipate as the hook took on the same comforting balance as her sword, allowing her to concentrate on her forthcoming task, the focus and strength she'd need to fight a monstrous inoga and the finesse and luck required to survive a combative oraku. Her odds of overcoming such challenges quit bothering her quite so much the longer she ran, and then her mind ventured to the strangest place.

Tristan Swift. He was the most unsatisfactory, empty meal.

Confused and put off by this out of place thought, Nessix glanced down at the hook, sincerely praying this was part of Berann's implication of speaking with it, when the world around her turned black.

"Berann!" Nessix skidded to a stop. This wasn't the first time she'd had to fight after being blinded by an oraku so, backed by the hook's abundant enthusiasm and an oraku of her own, she didn't panic. "They're here!"

"Berann, you say?"

Losing her sight hadn't frightened Nessix, but the memories which came with the sound of Inek's conceited voice as he approached her from somewhere to her left, did.

"What kind of game do you think you're playing, tramp?"

The inoga's bloated confidence effectively negated the greatest advantage his oraku companion had given him, and Nessix locked on his position and turned to face him. All she had to do was keep the idiot talking and she'd be able to track where he was. Berann had proven reliable so far, and she would just have to bank on him supporting her now. "No games, you cow," she taunted, the hook vibrating with anticipation in her hand. "I've brought your doom back to the hells."

"That scrawny twig?" Inek bellowed. Depending on how loud

he was speaking, he was close, less than a dozen of Nes's dashed steps—or perhaps three of his own—away. "You're as delusional as that dead master of yours."

Without knowing Kol's current fate outside of her own dismal predictions, that taunt was the last thing Inek could have possibly wanted to throw at Nessix. Chaos melding with the hook's feisty disposition, Nessix breathed out the last of her distractions and steeled herself for combat.

Now!

"Get the oraku!" Nessix shouted, trusting Berann was still close enough to hear her. She sprang forward, pulled by the hook's desire to execute her will and claim justice, and swatted toward the sound of Inek's laughter. The hook bit into flesh, but the barb didn't sink far enough to catch before the inoga jerked free from it, his bellow of fury pitching higher with a squeal drawn out by the hook's divine properties. The force of his outrage rattled in Nes's chest.

Nessix repelled from the unspoken threats in Inek's roar and braced herself for the charge she expected from him. He was quite possibly the last inoga she wanted to face blindly, with or without an enchanted weapon. While Grell was formidable to a frightening extent, he liked to toy with those he caught, keeping the door open for escape, lucky strikes, and possible third-party interventions. To the best of Nes's observations, Inek preferred to jump right in for the kill, and he'd been after her for quite a while.

"To your left!" Berann shouted from somewhere to her right, and Nessix spun with the hook leading her movement in the indicated direction.

She didn't connect with this strike, but by the whoosh of air which stirred her hair as an unseen object passed over her head, it had succeeded in driving away Inek's attempt to clobber her. Changing tactics, deciding it better to stay as close to the brute as possible rather than risk losing insight on his location, Nessix lunged forward and dug with the hook. This time, it sank through flesh and deep into muscle and, as her vision began to show her shadows of movement, the volume of Inek's roar threatened to deafen her.

Inek's arms closed down around her upper body, holding her immobile, and all Nessix could think about was how she'd only just had her armor repaired. She redoubled her efforts to keep her fingers clamped around the hook as the crushing power of Inek's hold bore down on her. Arms pinned to her sides, she wriggled in vain to search for room to maneuver, but Inek's grip wouldn't yield. She kicked, trying to locate vulnerable body parts to target and exploit, but her feet harmlessly bounced off the meat of his stocky legs. Just as Nessix thought Inek would succeed in crumpling her armor like discarded parchment, both of his arms fell limp at his sides, and she slid down his body toward the ground.

Nes's descent was slowed by her grip on the hook, the density of Inek's obliques as the weapon tore through them countering her weight as she fell. She hadn't yet determined the nature of Inek's surrender, but didn't waste the time worrying about it. All that mattered was keeping a hold of the weapon entrusted to her and distracting this opponent until Berann was able to reach the final relic. Still unaccustomed to handling the sweeping curve and vicious barb of the hook, it took Nessix two awkward tugs—both of which Inek sputtered and flung arms limp from the shoulders at—for her to work it free from his side. Vision had returned to Nessix well enough for her to see Berann further down the tunnel, quickly looting the lump of a body on the ground. Ally's safety confirmed, Nessix spun her focus back to the pig-eyed beast before her.

He'd taken his attention off Nessix now that she'd torn the hook from his waist and he overlooked the gaping laceration draining him of blood so he could yell at the limbs he'd relied on to establish his dominance as they dangled uselessly at his sides. Removing their function had been Berann's work, Nessix was sure of it, and the only assistance he could afford to give her while still maintaining his forward momentum toward the hammer. The rest of leveling this mountain was up to her.

"Aim for the soul!" Berann shouted as he continued to press onward. "Hold him back! I'm nearly there!"

Nessix considered herself a competent and well-versed fighter. She was adaptable in her tactics and skilled at finding openings to reach the final blow. But never in her life had she contemplated dropping an opponent by aiming for an aspect as intangible as a demon's soul. Distracted by trying to make sense of the order and settle on how to accomplish this task, it took Inek growling his threats at Berann as the oraku dashed down the hall to push Nessix back into action.

If you can't find the soul, forget about it.

The thought seemed the most logical approach to their circumstances.

Your job is to stop this monstrosity from reaching Berann.

Inek plowed straight past Nessix with the power of a warhorse, shoulders tipped forward and braced to serve as a battering ram. With the strength of his overly-developed legs, there was little chance Nessix would be able to catch up with him if he succeeded in gaining ground on her. Forget the soul and stop this beast! Nessix spun around, reinforcing her grip on the hook with her left hand as she drove it into the outer side of Inek's right thigh as he passed by. She kept her swing going as Inek dragged her behind him, throwing her shoulders into the motion to finish forcing the metal through his leg. The barb sank fully into the muscle and Nessix skied behind the inoga before grinding her heels into the ground to try to slow his charge. Crying out with a great expulsion of strength and resistance, Nessix ripped the weapon through meat and flesh out the back of Inek's leg.

Inoga, the epitome of demonic power, weren't meant to scream, well above the humiliating weaknesses of those beneath them. But Inek screamed like a rabbit being mauled by a dog as cords of muscle flapped out of the gaping wound on the back of his leg, blood spattering him and Nessix both. Without the use of his hands to counterbalance, his effort to spin around and face her resulted in him collapsing onto the ground, his face slamming into the roughness of stones and dirt. Nessix accepted the pessimistic thought that even being down three limbs may not be enough to stop this particular inoga, and so she quickly severed his left hamstring to match the right and turned to assist Berann.

"Get back here, bitch, and finish the job!"

Nessix found a strained smile at Inek's sputtering. His anger didn't mask his panic nearly as well as he must have hoped for it to, but her humor didn't last long as an eruption of shouting rose from down the hall. Leaving the crippled inoga to bleed to death on the ground, Nessix lengthened her stride to find an open doorway to a room full of demons. No doubt, Berann had made it inside and the hammer's last defenders were protesting his effort to claim it. Powerful though the oraku may be, he wouldn't be able to watch all fronts at once, and if he was taken down, they'd lose the sabers and hammer both. Even running all out, it would take Nessix several seconds which Berann might not have for her to reach him.

"Berann, I'm coming!" she shouted, more to draw their opponents' attention to the fact that he was not alone than to alert him.

A boom and a crack sounded from the room and a war hammer the size of Nes's thigh flew past her head.

"End this, Nessix Demonsbane!" Berann shouted. Next, the twin sabers clattered out into the hall. "End what I'd failed to start!"

One of the opposing demons appeared in the doorway to dart after the thrown blades, but he hadn't moved fast enough. A deep groan rose from within the room and then the entirety of the stone ceiling above them collapsed, crushing all of the demons—Berann included—in the rubble.

Nessix skidded to a stop, shouting her disbelief as the doorway demon's fingers—all that was visible of him from beneath the cascade of stones and earth—twitched in the final efforts of life. Though she'd worked alongside Berann for less than a day, he'd proven himself capable and noble, the exact sort of hero Nessix would have been honored to continue fighting beside. And he'd been the only one to actually know how to use these weapons.

Nonsense. The hook radiated a soothing warmth in her grip. *Anyone with working arms can figure out how to use a god's weapon for destruction. It's the mending which needs practice.*

Nessix gulped down that ominous warning, not at all caring for this weapon's intelligence, and stuffed down the surge of remorse which came from Berann's sacrifice and the fact that he'd never get to see the results of what he'd died—twice—to achieve. That goal of his had been passed on to her, and Nessix turned to scoop up the hammer. It was heavier than the hook, especially in her off hand and after the past day of grueling trials, but the hook rested so comfortably in her right hand, trilling its satisfaction at her touch, that she couldn't fathom putting it down. Hauling the cumbersome weapon along with her, she approached the sabers more reluctantly, feeling inadequate to so much as touch the artifacts Berann had claimed as his own.

The clomp of footsteps raced her way, forcing Nessix to cast aside all of the meddlesome emotions fogging her judgement, and she scrambled to those final weapons. Alone in these cursed halls and with all of Abaeloth counting on her, she swept the swords into a pile with the hammer, clutching the hook, and prepared to protect them.

"Nessix?"

All of her fears sank away into the oblivion of relief she could hardly believe was hers at the sound of Mathias's voice and, spent, she sagged over the weapons. At least one of her comrades had survived.

"I'm here, Sagewind," she called wearily.

"What—" His footsteps slowed as he neared where Inek had likely bled out or gone into shock, and the dull flop of a body hitting the ground, accompanied by a groan, pulled Nessix's attention up to where her White Paladin, blood-stained and grim, had rounded the corner. And at his feet, instinctively curling in on himself to protect his grievous injuries, was Kol.

"The oraku's dead," Mathias told her.

The weight of both Mathias's actions and words sucked the breath out of Nessix as she looked up from her shattered alar to her paladin, and Mathias glanced away to swallow all of the terrible things his ego wanted to say. When he looked back to Nessix, her eyes possessing endless volumes of gratitude, he offered her a sad smile. No matter how much he hated Kol, he wished he could have delivered the demon to Nessix in better condition.

Time caught up to Nessix again as a great shudder wracked Kol's feeble body and she hung the hook from the hilt of her sheathed sword. Tucking one of the sabers beneath her left arm, she passed its mate to the same hand, and dragged the hammer along with her as she went to join her battered companions. After the price that was paid for them and the bounty yet to be yielded for the cost, there was no way she would let these weapons out of her sight, but neither could she waste one more second before seeing just how badly Kol had suffered for her and Berann.

"Is that all of them?" Mathias nodded to the sabers and hammer as Nessix let them fall from her grasp to crouch beside Kol.

"All of them Berann told me about." Nessix brushed blood-soaked hair from Kol's swollen face and, after his eyes cracked open to confirm his coherence, she patted down his pockets in search of the potion Berann had given him.

Mathias frowned at Nes's tender efforts but diverted his protests to them by looking around the hallway. "Where is he, anyway?"

Nessix pressed her lips tight and drew the vial of blue liquid from Kol's right pocket. "He didn't make it," she said curtly, lifting Kol's head to spill the potion into his mouth. "And Sazrah?"

Mathias blinked in shock at hearing Nessix voice her concern about the warrior woman who had been so cold to her, confirming to Mathias that her capacity for forgiveness made her a far better person than either he or Sazrah were. "Wounded, but alive last I saw her. It wasn't pretty, but we took out the inoga."

Kol coughed as his wearied responses forced him to inhale part of the potion, but he made no further attempt to weigh in on Mathias's claim. Nessix sat back once the vial was empty and assessed Mathias's hasty first aid—bloodied strips of linen bound Kol's left wrist and right ankle, a splint fashioned of two wrapped knives framing a compound fracture to his left shin. There was no doubt that Kol would have died by Annin's hands had Mathias not intervened, and there was still a chance he'd perish from these injuries if left untreated. But Mathias *had* intervened and he hadn't left Kol behind. He'd even gone as far as to stabilize the alar's most obvious injuries. Nessix looked down at the ground.

"Why did you save him?" she asked quietly.

Mathias swallowed the lump in his throat and bent down to retrieve the hammer. "We need to get going," he said, loosening his belt a notch to slip the haft of the weapon alongside his sword. "Sazrah said she had our backs, but I'd like to relieve her, especially if more trouble has shown up."

Nessix held Mathias's stubborn eyes until he pulled them away to look down the hall the way he'd come from. Fighting with him for an explanation now would not do them any good, and so Nessix was content to let it drop and simply rejoice in the fact that Mathias had chosen to act in compassion rather than vengeance. She suppressed the urge even more when Mathias, of his own volition, bent down to pick up Kol.

"Grab those sabers and hold them tight," Mathias said, still dodging her eyes.

Nessix had already been halfway through the action when Mathias spoke and was on her feet soon after. There was still so much left to be decided in this war for Abaeloth's liberation from fear, but for now, the three of them had survived, and they still had a job to do. Carrying so many burdens, Mathias and Nessix left Berann behind in his tomb, left Inek to rot on the floor, and pressed toward Sazrah's last known location.

TWENTY-SEVEN

By the time Mathias and Nessix reached Sazrah, the vitality potion had restored enough of Kol's pride and stabilized his injured joints. Though the compound fracture to his leg hadn't healed to the point that it could fully bear weight, once it was apparent that the alar was no longer courting death, Mathias was quick to reprioritize where he invested his concern.

Nessix took over the role of supporting Kol, allowing all three parties involved to internalize their thoughts on the matter for the greater good, and giving Mathias the opportunity to distance himself from his rival and go check on Sazrah. The warrior woman, enhanced by her heritage as she was, had recovered in the time it had taken Mathias to find the others, her limp having eased and the full range of motion restored to her left arm. She kept her focus trained on Kol as Nessix helped him hobble down the hall, but she directed her words to Mathias.

"Where's the last one?"

"He didn't make it."

She crossed her arms. "Does that imply we failed?"

Nessix raised her scathing glare at Sazrah's bluntness, but Mathias kept himself firmly between the two women. "Though I haven't been instructed on how to use any of them, Berann and Nessix succeeded in obtaining the last relic." He rested his wrist atop the head of the hammer. "And it was due in no small part to this alar's assistance. I'd have you remove your suspicion from him."

Nessix's breath caught in her throat and Kol tensed beside her at the sentiment Mathias had conveyed. Though the paladin still actively hid any outward gratitude by refusing to acknowledge Kol by name, he had just commended the demon's efforts in fulfilling the mission they'd all been prepared to die for. Nessix kept her delight to herself, suspecting with good reason that nobody in her company would have any interest in hearing it.

Just as Nessix held her tongue, Sazrah refused to acknowledge Mathias's words for her own reasons, and promptly pursued her greater interest. "Then give me one of those blessed weapons and let's get out of this cursed realm. Nothing's come by yet, but I can't imagine it will stay that way."

Mathias closed his fingers over the top of the hammer, doing his best to gauge the nature of what it was which motivated Sazrah to be in such a hurry. Her entire reason for coming down into the hells—against his wishes and despite her hidden reservations—had been to kill Grell, a feat which she had succeeded at. Goal accomplished, she no longer had a productive avenue in which to channel her focus. Had her memories of the demons' past tortures caught up to her? Mathias should have known, between how poorly she'd coped with his frustrating behavior and her uncharacteristic reluctance to march into danger when they'd first approached the hells, that Sazrah's mental fortitude had been exhausted. Just as he was getting ready to offer his own insight on what their next movement should be, a brief growl of displeasure left Kol to preface his agreement with the hostile woman.

"With the number of this region's heads of power we've taken out, if the underlings have retreated, it's to regroup and organize for a targeted assault. Grell and Inek might be dead, but there are two other inoga to worry about. If you want out, it's best to move now."

Nessix cut in with a sharp counter to his advice. "We're not going anywhere without my army."

All three sets of eyes turned to gawk at her, not one of them disbelieving her conviction to have her way.

"The logistics of that alone, little one—"

She turned a strict eye back on Kol, no longer allowing herself to be his subordinate, but his peer. "You sent them all to the surface once before. We can do it again."

Kol shook his head. "That had been a coordinated march driven by my kind, not complicated by them. We don't even know the status of your forces right now to be sure they're mobile enough to make the journey."

That was a valid point, but she stubbornly adhered to her stance on the matter. "Then we go and check on them. We're not marching them to some far away continent this time, just trying to reach the surface. I vowed to serve those who need me, and I promised them, specifically, that I would lead them to a brighter future. I can begin that on Elidae—"

Sazrah barked out a laugh. "With all due respect to your vows, General." The snip in Sazrah's voice adequately contradicted that offer of respect. "Elidae can barely help itself right now. It certainly doesn't have the means to welcome undead refugees from the hells."

Nessix snapped her glare to Sazrah and squared her shoulders. "Elidae may not be ready to welcome my army, but Sulik will." As Sazrah's lips tucked into a frown, Nessix turned her eyes to Mathias. "Your goddess and her most sacred temple would never turn away those in need, would they?"

Mathias cast a sheepish glance at Sazrah and he rubbed the back of his neck. Saving this army had been Nessix's primary objective for hunting him down in the first place, and he wasn't too keen on the decision she'd be honor-bound to make if their alleged saviors sentenced them to be left behind. And, in standing beside her in this duty, perhaps Mathias could resume embracing the title of paladin after his most recent fumbles of virtue. "She does have a point, Saz. There is no way the akhuerai will have any sort of future if we leave them down here, not after these recent developments. They're not soulless drones like the undead you're accustomed to. They deserve whatever protection we can offer them."

"Perhaps you're forgetting about the *vampire* you assigned to

321

their head?" Sazrah challenged Mathias. "Should he be brought up to the nation you dumped into a civil war? Does he deserve our protection?"

Mathias had reached a decision on that argument before Sazrah had even finished voicing her objections. "I'd rather pull him out of the hells and keep apprised of his actions until I can toss him into the Veil. Do not forget he knows about the Undersea Pass network and, if left unsupervised, could end up anywhere the demons can reach."

Sazrah continued to glower at Mathias's sound logic, shaking her head in dissatisfaction.

Kol sucked his teeth at the implications that would come with a second bout of agreeing with Sazrah, but couldn't keep this fact to himself. "You're forgetting one vital aspect of rescuing the akhuerai, little one."

"What's that?" Nessix asked.

Kol met and held Nessix's eyes. "Their souls."

It was a reminder both of them had been trying to forget about on a subconscious level while caught up in their more immediate trials; they still had no idea where the other half of Nessix's soul had ended up.

Mathias mistook their concern for a logistics problem and, ready to find the optimism in something for a change, chose to focus on what could be done. "Are you meaning to imply you still have possession of the fractured parts of their souls?" he asked Kol.

Kol hastily looked away from Nessix and grudgingly muttered his answer. "I am."

The tension shared between his lover and her alar was not lost on Mathias, but as many great feats as they'd already conquered today, this seemed like the easiest obstacle to take on. "Then let's grab those, too."

Kol pressed his lips together and limped a step away from the group to keep from turning back on Mathias and finding that death he kept slipping away from. "At this point, it's the souls or the bodies. We were not foolish enough to keep them all in one location, and we really do need to hurry if we want to get out of here without unnecessary complications."

"He's—" Sazrah hastily clenched her teeth, her words cut off in a snarl, but it was too late to avoid Mathias's keen eyes. She flushed and crossed her arms. "The alar's right. We should get moving."

"The bodies, it is," Nessix decided. "Who all knew of the locations of the souls?" she asked Kol.

Expression grim, Kol shook his head. "Only me and—" Kol choked on the name he wasn't ready to speak, the one which would haunt him for lifetimes to come. Nessix's eyes softened with understanding, despite the judgement bearing down on him from Mathias and Sazrah, and Kol wiped a balmy hand across the back of his neck. "I'm the only one left who knows, but—"

"We can coordinate efforts to return for the souls once we recover and better understand the variables we have to work with," Nessix said.

Sazrah removed the duty of debating from Kol by shaking her head. "We should go now and arrange a rescue effort later."

Nessix's fingers recoiled as though itching to grab a weapon, and Mathias extended his arms between the two women, facing Sazrah. "Do this without any further complaints and I will give you this hammer as soon as we secure our position on the surface."

"Sagewind—"

Mathias held a hand out to Nessix's protest. "She's more lenient and compassionate than she's letting on, Nes." He wouldn't disgrace Sazrah by delving any deeper into the reasons behind her current level of reactivity, settling for an excuse which could apply to all of them. "This has not been a gentle trial and we are all entitled to be a bit on edge. Let's get your army, detain the vampire, and return to the surface so we can escape the weight of our current danger."

Neither woman spoke another opinion on the matter, their stubbornness holding them at bay. As satisfied as he'd ever be, Mathias conjured up some patience and turned to Kol.

"Can you lead us back to the chasm?"

Kol held Mathias's eyes for a moment, balancing out their intent against their judgement. Either way, he wanted all of this behind them more than anyone else. "I can, but it will be slow."

Mathias eyed Sazrah's pout and Nes's petite build and swallowed a groan before walking over to Kol. The alar balked at his approach, not entirely trusting Mathias to not be preparing some sort of attack, and he only tensed more when the paladin grabbed his arm to throw it over his shoulder.

"Saz, get his other side." Mathias would have asked Nessix if she'd been half a foot taller. "We can make this go faster if we work together."

It was unclear if it was Sazrah or Kol who resented this arrangement more, but ultimately the entire group moved out.

Unlike the previous legs of their journey, they encountered very few demons besides the one carried along with them, the opposing underlings having run for cover or to consult with their superiors as Kol had predicted. Two inoga and the most infamous oraku in the region had been slain by this team, and Kol had apparently risen from the dead. The few surviving ancients had to have taken notice of the danger they faced. And when they settled on the means to retaliate, Mathias didn't want anyone within a hundred miles of these depths.

The halls were so bare, in fact, that the sound of fighting stretched deeper from the chasm than it otherwise would have and, despite Mathias's brief attempt to stop her, Nessix dashed ahead to assess what sort of peril Tristan had led her troops into.

It was at this point that Kol resisted the forward momentum provided by the demon hunters at his sides, and before they could question or criticize his action, he said, "Leave me and go aid Nessix."

Sazrah, disregarding her wariness of Nessix and her opposition to the idea of aiding anything undead, didn't need any other excuses to dump her end of Kol's weight on Mathias and be done with the chore of assisting a demon, but Mathias hesitated for a moment.

He'd wanted Kol dead for nearly two years. He'd lost countless nights of sleep thinking about ways to seek revenge on him, and he'd been every bit as determined to make sure this specific alar never saw an open sky again as Sazrah had been to kill

Grell, even as he'd agreed to work alongside him. Nessix had asked him why he'd saved Kol when he'd found her protecting the relics and at that time, he hadn't been able to answer her. He'd thought maybe it was because he thought Kol still had a use to him or perhaps it was simply to keep Nessix happy, but the instruction the demon had just given him was the answer.

Mathias had saved Kol and would be unable to kill him, because they both needed Nessix. Not even an insane demon would have attempted to stand against an oraku as cruel and powerful as Annin. But Kol had done so with the incredibly selfless motive of giving Nessix the chance to escape and complete the mission that would mean the end of the demons' reign over Abaeloth. Though Kol had regained most of his mobility thanks to the benefits of his racial quirks and whatever elixir Nessix had given him, his careful movement still suggested his breaks hadn't mended enough to fully hold his weight. Despite his current condition and without regard for his own safety, he was choosing to send away his support, the only backup he had access to in case of an attack, to assist Nessix's charge in defense of the men and women he'd been responsible for creating.

Accepting the notion that there could be something honorable buried in Kol was still a sour whim which Mathias actively denied, but doing so now was made easier knowing that they shared at least one common goal, to support Nessix.

Mathias pulled a dagger from his belt and flipped his hold on it to offer the hilt to Kol. "It's not much, but better than what you've got."

Kol stared at the knife then lifted his eyes to Mathias, his expression flat and unreadable as he failed to sort out what was happening. But, in the interest of seeing Nessix protected by someone more compassionate than Sazrah the Shade and of more able body than himself, he accepted the blade. Neither paladin nor demon wholly comfortable with what had just transpired between them, Kol offered no words of gratitude and Mathias neglected to deliver a heartening speech before running off to help defend Nes's army.

Mathias arrived to find Nessix and Sazrah each heatedly

engaged with a few dozen aranau. It was uniting against a common—and vicious—enemy which pushed the two women past their underlying grudges, but even as Mathias took in the scene, he watched as the spry demons routinely drove them closer to the drop which would kill at least Sazrah. Grace in limited supply, but confidence bolstered by the lack of opposing demons they'd encountered while travelling through the halls, Mathias shouted, "Nes, Saz, blink!"

Nessix dropped low to the ground for stability and Sazrah broadened her stance, bracing her sword horizontally against any coming attacks, and it was all Mathias could do to hope they'd heeded his warning. Striking the hilt of his sword off his breastplate, the paladin carefully poured from his reserve of Etha's grace to generate a brilliant flash of light. The success of his tactic was noted immediately by the number of demons screaming and clawing at their eyes, the burst of his bottled divinity blinding the creatures of this realm Etha was not meant to touch. By the time Mathias reached combat, Nessix and Sazrah had already begun executing the crippled and confused aranau as they hectically scrambled for security. As death slowly extinguished the creatures' cries, a more glorious one rang up from the chasm floor.

"As promised, your heroes have returned!"

Tristan had survived, though Mathias hadn't doubted he would, and judging by the volume of cheers which climbed with the vampire's words, so had a generous number of the akhuerai. As soon as Mathias arrived on the scene to assist Sazrah with the last of the aranau's final rights, Nessix swept her gaze behind him until she located Kol, armed with a knife and limping their way, then carefully descended the crumbling stairs.

The chasm floor was bloodier than it had been following the akhuerai's first attempt at rebelling, but most of the gore was concentrated near the wall of the chasm where a pile of dead aranau had accumulated. Several akhuerai, Garrett among them, had been taken out by their enemies, but by inspection of the first four Nessix reached, they all still had their rings where they belonged, and so she was confident they hadn't been completely lost. Tristan, fair skin speckled with sprays of red, stood amid the blood and bodies until Nessix looked his way and then held his hands wide at his sides as he strode toward her with a chivalrous smile.

"Your army, sister. Defended and thriving, just as you asked."

Nessix raised her chin, halting Tristan's advance with the suspicions Sazrah and Mathias had put in her, but as she took in how many of her troops had survived, even against the opponents which had claimed so many of her trained fleman soldiers in the past, she couldn't completely buy in to all of their doubts. Monstrous or not, Tristan had delivered on his promise and for that, Nessix was grateful.

"Then I relieve you of your duty," she said. "You... did a fine job. I'll not ask about the details."

Mathias and Sazrah stepped up to the chasm's edge and slowly, the anxious chatter of the akhuerai hushed, allowing Nessix to address her troops.

"I promised I'd bring you help from the surface, and I did," she told them, unafraid to raise her voice with the demons currently stirred into such a panic. "And now it is time for us to leave this prison behind. Use blankets to form litters to carry our fallen with us—I'll not tolerate one life left behind—and follow me. Before the day is through, we'll all feel the sun on our cheeks once again."

An exuberant cheer, so full of life and hope, lifted the gloom of the chasm for the first time, and Nessix soaked in that much-missed swell of victory which came with it. As the troops dispersed to carry out her instructions, more motivated than they'd been for anything since before their deaths, Nessix turned her eyes up to where Mathias smiled down at her. He gave her an approving nod, one which assured her the suffering was over, but the choke didn't hit her until Kol stepped up beside him and lowered his head in gratitude and acknowledgement. She jumped as a hand slapped down on her shoulder, and spun to face Tristan.

"I will be expecting new clothes."

Nessix looked over the vampire's bedraggled wardrobe and smirked. "For keeping my troops from being overrun, I'll see what I can do."

As Nessix marched off to assist her army with securing their fallen, Tristan smiled. Nessix may be but one prospective advocate, but she was influential enough to count for more.

TWENTY-EIGHT

Of all the promises Nessix had made to the akhuerai, the only one she was content breaking was that sunshine was awaiting them as they emerged from the hells in the late hours of the night. This didn't seem to disappoint the refugees, and it didn't take them long to broaden the footprint of the small campsite Mathias and Sazrah had shared to support their numbers. Sazrah, bound by her word to Mathias that she'd protect these men and women as the civilians they longed to be, distracted herself from her conflicts with the truth by standing guard near the hells' entrance in case the demons had organized against the grave odds poised against them as Kol had predicted they would. Mathias, surrendering all other management of the masses to Nessix, whisked himself away to the temple to notify Sulik of the events which had recently transpired and arrange for escort and accommodation for those they had rescued from the hells.

Kol chose to seclude himself in the quiet shadows on the fringes of the camp, hunkering down on a boulder as he watched with a shriveled impression of envy as Nessix milled about her people, checking on the wounded and recovering, ensuring everyone was as comfortable as the conditions allowed, and passing along words of encouragement that this was the first day of the rest of their lives. She'd respected his request to be left alone without argument and did well to only send the occasional glance his way to assess his status. There was a time when Kol had thought himself a leader, but as he watched Nessix, his perfect weapon, so naturally filling the role he'd been told was his, he wondered what other aspects of his life he'd lied to himself about.

"What are your plans now, demon?"

Kol's head snapped up to glare at Tristan where he leaned against a tree beside his boulder. "Mathias says you're a vampire."

Tristan cocked his head at Kol's insecure rush to change the subject. "I suppose there are times even he is right, but that didn't answer my question. Where will an exiled demon go in this realm of mortals? What will you do?"

Kol shifted his weight on the rock and looked away. Those were questions he didn't have the answers to, not anymore. His plan when he and Annin had first laid the foundation to reform the hells had involved him returning to the role of tribe leader, Annin his second in command. But now, all of that was ruined. Annin was dead, and there wasn't a demon in the hells who would even dream of following him.

He looked out across the crowd of akhuerai, following the ease with which Nessix moved through the weary crowd before ripping his gaze away again. Though there was a tangible sense of relief about those fractured souls here on the surface, they still snuck cold, resentful glances his way and he suspected if not for their continued reliance on Nessix, they'd have jumped him by now. Just as he was trapped with the consequences of what he'd done to the akhuerai, neither could Kol escape the wrongs he had done against the very flemans Nessix had told him he was welcome to live among in this new life he'd have to choreograph. And once word got out that he'd been part of recovering the demise of demonkind, not even Heiligate would be likely to offer him sanctuary. There was no place in Abaeloth Kol could go, and he had no reason to make any plans.

"I don't see how any of that is your business," Kol said at last.

Tristan's smile didn't falter, but it did grow sharper. "It doesn't mean a thing to me, but it interests my god immensely."

Kol scoffed and turned his face from Tristan. "And I don't

care what any of the gods want."

"Berann had expressed the same sentiment. I can only sympathize with your people for what the deities of old put you through, but there is a new age—"

"Of pliable children who carelessly throw about their divine gifts, calling themselves superior to those of us trapped on this disgusting world," Kol said, finishing Tristan's statement in a far more accurate fashion than the vampire could have ever intended to speak himself. "And I've no interest in positioning myself beneath any of them."

Tristan heaved a lofty sigh and raised a hand to study the cleanliness of his fingernails. "That's too bad. Because my rather focused master who has carefully honed his divine gifts for the betterment of this aching world sent me out specifically to uncover how you managed to raise the dead without his blessing." Hand staying in place, Tristan's sharp eyes snapped to Kol. "And you will tell me."

Perhaps if Kol weren't in such a dreary mood, he'd have thought it would be fun to play with Tristan, but humbled by confusion and remorse and so much uncertainty, Kol was about as far from playful as he'd ever been. "Or else what? You or your god will strike me down for my crimes like that Etha-blessed paladin has sworn to do? None of you would get your answers that way. The only other demon to understand the process of raising an akhuerai is dead and would have been even less inclined to cooperate with your petty demands than I am, and I have little reason to comply, myself. Kill me, if that will please your god. I've no care, either way."

Tristan crossed his arms. *Ceredulus? This demon's got little will to live right now and threats on his life won't sway him. How should I proceed?*

He's lonely. Befriend him.

Tristan frowned as he shifted his judgmental gaze back to the grumpy alar. He still couldn't see the charm Nessix had apparently uncovered and had thus far found only limited interest and intrigue in Kol. But an order was an order, no matter how tedious. "Very well. I can respect the trauma you've gone through and will give you your space."

Kol blew out a single beat of a laugh, eyes growing cold at Tristan's fumbled attempt at compassion. "You have no idea the trauma I've been through."

As if Tristan's pestering wasn't more than Kol could gracefully handle right now, a pair of booted feet scuffed to a stop in front of him. The demon grit his teeth and followed long legs up to the face of a yellow-eyed fleman man, contorted in a furious grimace. Even dull to his cares, the ferocity in that snarl and deadly glare stoked an instant and visceral fear in Kol which surpassed all notion of giving up, and he sat up straighter, prepared to leap to his feet.

"Are you the demon called Kol?"

Every last instinct inside Kol warned him that he hadn't come close to escaping danger yet, and he rubbed his hands on the legs of his pants, cursing the fact that Nessix had relented to Mathias's demand that he not be given any weapons. The only defense he had was Tristan.

"Good sir," the vampire said, "you must under—"

Inwan swatted a hand in Tristan's direction, abruptly cutting off the undead nobleman's words with divine force not even a vampire could counter. The god kept his glare focused on Kol, prepared to lead this wretched creature through the suffering Elidae had endured because of him. He'd always thought demons were more wily than this one was letting on, but Kol's meekness almost offended him more. Inwan jutted an arm forward to grab Kol's collar but before his fingers could close around the fabric, a small hand wrapped around his wrist. The physical strength in that grip didn't even begin to hinder Inwan, but the confidence of its hold, the familiar imprint of those fingers against the flesh of his manifestation, overpowered even his rage.

"After all these years, you were twenty feet away from me and didn't even bother to say hello?"

Inwan didn't register Kol's tentative relief or Tristan's budding curiosity as Nessix intervened, turning his shocked eyes to the waif beside him. The truth was he hadn't felt the signature of her warmth until now, hadn't been able to pick her out in this crowd of halved souls until he met the intensity of her blue eyes. She'd hardened so much from the ambitious spirit he'd last seen frolic through Elidae's fields. She'd matured into a beautiful woman, a confident one commanding enough authority to do Laes proud. Mathias had told Inwan that Nessix was living again, but somewhere in his mind, he'd let himself believe she would still be the impressionable little girl who hung on his every word. Facing the general she had been destined to become and which the cruelty of fate unguarded had forged her into, not even a god could find his tongue.

"I never quit looking for you," Nessix said, voice lowering to a harsh whisper. "I never quit waiting for you and you don't even acknowledge me now that I'm here?"

Even with the demon who had slain Nessix less than two feet from him, Inwan couldn't rip his eyes from the betrayed turmoil in hers. "Nes…" She stepped away as Inwan reached his free hand out to cradle her face, and he closed his empty fingers into a timid fist. "This… this *creature* is what took you from me—"

With a defiant shout, Nessix shoved Inwan back a step and gripped the handle of the deadly hook at her hip to hold him at bay. "Kol borrowed me from Elidae. He took me from Mathias and my people, yes. But you will leave yourself out of those hurt by his actions."

Inwan voluntarily shifted another step away from the hook's threat, jaw sagging and yellow eyes wide in shock at the disrespect his chosen daughter so calmly threw at him. "You have forgotten your place, Nessix."

That accusation earned a hard gulp from Nessix, but nothing more. "No. I've found the place I should have been all along. I'd needed you, Inwan, and you abandoned me. You left a scared little girl who knew *nothing* to navigate a terrible world without your guidance. You left me to this fate and ask me to forget about it?" She removed that step Inwan had put between them, gripping the hook tighter as years of repressed emotion surged through her. "Who are you to think—"

"Nessix!"

The sharp strain of Mathias's voice sliced through the tension building between the demon, the god and his chosen, and the muted vampire, and he ran to break up the developing catastrophe before it managed to explode and encompass the weary akhuerai. After a few sweltering breaths and tears of frustration had set in her eyes, Nessix allowed Mathias to pry her fingers from the haft of the hook as he stepped between the god and the demon, and he firmly pushed Inwan further away from her.

"We've only just escaped the hells, Inwan," he explained, voice firm with its declaration that he had no intention to grovel before this child. "There is still much we don't know for ourselves and it would be appreciated by everyone involved if you would give us time to decompress from what we've been through. Perhaps Etha will be inclined to inform you of the immediate details if she is on speaking terms with you, but now is not the time to throw about ultimatums you have no grounds to approach."

Inwan still didn't like Mathias, but he'd been humbled by the paladin enough times to know to pick battles against him with care. "I wasn't after Nessix," he sneered, "but that demon."

"He is off limits."

"You, of all people, should want him dead."

"Oh, I do," Mathias granted. "But my wants aren't the only ones that matter. Neither are yours. I'd thought that was a lesson you'd learned while away from Elidae."

Behind Mathias, Nessix lowered her eyes as she understood the unspoken message hidden within his words. If given one more reason to kill Kol, he wouldn't hesitate to do so, but he'd looked past the demon's crimes against himself and Nessix both because she had wanted him to live. In this moment, she loved Mathias even more.

Inwan didn't miss Nessix's quiet response, and he kept a frown on his face as he shoved Mathias's hand off his chest. "You can't ignore it forever," he muttered.

"I haven't ignored it one day since Nessix was killed," Mathias said. "By Etha, let us rest. Let us get these people to safety and out of the elements. Let Nessix wash the blood from herself"—Tristan loudly cleared his throat and plucked at his filthy and torn garments, and Mathias rolled his eyes—"and let the damn vampire get some new clothes. Then we can talk. You've been patient this long. Give us a few more days."

334

There wasn't a god in existence who didn't resent Mathias's power and influence on some level, and the fact that the paladin had previously asserted himself well above Inwan didn't help the god's opinion of him in the slightest. Inwan, so recently returned to freedom on the surface realm, was still on monitored status, and Mathias commanded Etha's favor. It was certainly within the god's power to level this demon and snatch Nessix away to remind her that she had only made it to adulthood due to the blessing he'd given her at birth, but it would come at the steep price of another trial by Etha and compounded hatred from the very woman he was compelled to earn the forgiveness of.

"Before any acts of vengeance are—"

"When the time is right to do so," Mathias said to the god's juvenile belligerence, "I'll offer you the first blow."

Inwan glared hard at Mathias, sneering at his inability to determine just what the cocky glint in the paladin's eyes meant. With one more glance at Nessix and a more prolonged warning glower at Kol, Inwan backed away from the little gathering, then was gone.

As Kol settled back onto his boulder, Nes's shoulders sagged. She'd lost so much faith in Inwan over the past couple years and out of all of the daydreams she'd had of how their reunion would play out and the amends they'd make, this had not been it. Her guilt never quite gained the necessary momentum to motivate her to act before Tristan cleared his throat now that he'd regained access to his voice.

"And *that*, Kol, is a prime example of everything Ceredulus is not."

"Hey, Tristan?" Mathias asked.

Tristan turned to face Mathias who, in the same moment, clapped a shackle around the vampire's right wrist. Tristan looked from the binding then up at Mathias as the paladin secured the other end of the device to his own left wrist.

"Couldn't get enough of me?" Tristan teased, doing his best to avoid testing the durability of his restraints.

"Oh, I've had quite enough of you," Mathias assured. "But, like a good, dutiful paladin, I'd like to spare everyone else from the same dreadful experience. Now." Mathias ignored the perturbed wrinkle of Tristan's brow and turned to Nessix. "See if you can get the masses to settle in for the night. I hadn't been lying when I told Inwan it's been a trying day, and it will be a long march in the morning to get to the temple. Tristan doesn't have to sleep, so he can keep watch."

That perturbed wrinkle cleaved even deeper between the vampire's eyes.

Taking his dangerous company into consideration, Mathias stationed himself far from the main body of the army after ordering Sazrah to get some rest. Though Tristan had fed generously on a steady supply of demons while in the hells and had proven at least a passing interest in the akhuerai's well-being, Mathias didn't favor the idea of him being so near the tired troops. Similarly, Nessix took a guard position sleeping near enough to Kol to be able to intercept any attempts made on his life while honoring his unspoken request for space as he labored through the task of processing the past days' events.

Morning broke with the arrival of reinforcements from the temple, and the group moved out with Kol nestled deep within their ranks, carried on one of the makeshift stretchers to mask his presence from the reactive eyes of the factions vying for control over Elidae. Sazrah took up guard of the rear, while Nessix and Mathias—Tristan bound close, of course—led the force toward the safety of the temple.

The movement of a couple thousand undisciplined and disorganized people who had never expected to see freedom again was not a stealthy operation. Though Sulik had sent a sizeable detail of knights to guide and direct the refugees, they still fanned out wider than was ideal to touch the trees and smell the flowers and stare up at the open expanse of a sky they'd assumed lost to them. It was steady progress, but slow, taxed even further by Tristan's boredom as he pried at Nessix and Mathias to stir up some drama about Nes's dealings with Kol and Mathias's dealings with the undead. Neither bit on his efforts to unearth some excitement, leaving him a trudging, brooding grump—still in unsuitable clothing he frequently reminded them of—alongside them.

The procession hadn't been marching on level ground longer than a mile before a man on horseback approached and waved them down. He wore green and gold heraldry, unfamiliar to Nessix. Though she had looked forward to enjoying at least one day of peace before getting drawn into more trouble, Nessix preemptively prepared herself for conflict at the man's arrival.

"Oh, this looks fun," Tristan said.

Nessix clenched a fist and her nostrils flared at Tristan's unnecessary provocation. Trembling against restraint she was so tired of tapping into, she raised that fist to halt the knights and order them to condense the akhuerai, then looked to Mathias and his superior patience to assess this first complication to their plan of integrating her force with Elidae's squabbling population.

"I suspect my name and title will have more clout until word gets around that you're not dead," Mathias said to Nessix.

A year ago, Nessix would have argued with Mathias that the entire reason her nation had fallen into such disgrace was due to the loss of the Teradhel line, but after her reception in Zeal and traveling with the questionable company she'd come across, she was ready to accept it. "Whatever they're after, aim for a peaceful resolution. I'm about done with combat for now."

Mathias nodded, having had the same plan from the start, and dragged Tristan out ahead of his force. "Keep your mouth shut if you want to keep using it," he muttered to the vampire.

"Consider my lips sealed, Sir Sagewind."

Regretting his decision to bind himself to Tristan, Mathias sighed and raised his voice to address the scout. "Do you have a concern Sir Mathias Sagewind can assist with?" According to Sulik, his name was still well known and at least politely respected on the island, but the recent influx of humans now that the seaports had been opened made his non-fleman features a more mundane sight than they'd been when he'd first arrived.

The scout drew his horse up short, keeping well out of the range of physical contact, and he looked down at Mathias with a flimsy authority. "My lord Elysand Arundel wishes to know the nature and destination of the force you are marching across his lands."

Well, that hadn't taken long. Mathias glanced back at Nessix to see if the name meant anything to her. When she shook her head, he sighed his misgivings about how much work would have to be done to recover the country and answered the scout's request. "The nature is refugees seeking sanctuary and the destination is the old cave temple."

A rigid frown pressed across the scout's lips at mention of the temple, but that alone didn't encompass the entirety of his discomfort. "We had been unaware of any current war efforts. Might you inform me and my lord of what city your refugees are from?"

Mathias suspected neither this scout nor the lord he served would be thrilled with the answer, but that wasn't his problem. "The hells."

"The—" Thrown back in his saddle from shock of the answer, the scout looked over the ragged group of men and women, noting as well the escort of knights of the Order and fleman warriors wearing the colors of the Teradhel line. Beneath him, his horse fidgeted from the rapid onset of his tension. "Do you mean to tell me you've brought demons to Elidae, Sir Sagewind?"

This scout didn't command the air of a seasoned veteran and neither Mathias nor Nessix had recognized the name of the man he served. In all probability, this lord was a young upstart relying on equally green forces and looking for any edge he could get in these tumultuous political times. Mathias turned to find Nessix again. He'd planned to advise they aim to keep her return to the surface quiet until they'd worked out a solid strategy for her to make a formal power grab, but saw an opportunity to stir up the odds of claiming influence over the inexperienced lesser nobles who had begun trying to lay claim over the nation.

"General Nessix Teradhel and I have brought survivors of the demons' crimes to Elidae."

The scout paled now, raising a frantic gaze to scan those Mathias spoke for until he spotted a petite woman in dark armor holding the front lines. A breathy cough left him and he raised a sweaty hand to rub his forehead. "General... Terad..." The rest of Nessix's surname died out in a wispy wheeze which satisfied

Mathias enough.

"I *had* made a promise to this country that I'd find her," the paladin continued. "Now, have I satisfied your curiosity, or are you waiting on a formal dismissal so you can run back and tell your lord what we're up to?"

"That will be…" The scout couldn't quite settle on where to ground his focus and gave a hearty gulp as he forced his eyes to meet Mathias's steady smile. "You have satisfied my lord's curiosity."

"Very good," Mathias said. "If he has any further concerns, he can send them to the temple."

A feeble nod confirmed that the scout heard and acknowledged the order, and he was quick to turn his horse around to rush his report back home.

The remainder of the march proceeded smoothly. Word of their movement must have spread through whatever channels had been implemented by Elidae's budding rulers, because three other scouts of varying heraldry were sighted along the road, all maintaining a generous distance but observing, nonetheless.

Nessix fell back from the front lines once the temple's entrance came into view, weaving through the staggered ranks of akhuerai until she located the pair grudgingly escorting Kol. They were ready and eager to be rid of him when she declared it safe for his wings to be seen, and though he barely looked at her as they walked beside each other, she stayed with him. Finding the words to express her thoughts was harder than usual; while she had finally reached the point of a long-awaited homecoming, Kol was facing an unknown future without any form of security and with only one confirmed ally, and Nessix had played a pivotal role in putting him in this bleak position.

"I would like you to stay with us," she said at last, watching the ground so she wouldn't have to face the sneer she expected to receive from him. They marched along in silence until Nessix couldn't bear it any longer, and she looked up at Kol's clenched jaw and hard eyes. "The temple's got room and I—"

"Mathias and his goddess would never permit me entry."

Nessix frowned and doubled down on her stubbornness,

lifting her gaze to where Mathias marched at the front lines, doing his best to ignore Tristan's theatrics. "Let me worry about negotiating with Mathias."

"Fine." Kol's dismissal snapped with a bitterness which made Nessix cringe, but he didn't amend it. "*I* have no desire to enter the temple."

That complication would be much more difficult for Nessix to work around than asserting her status as General over Mathias's hatred for the alar. Though she was determined to stake her claim on being Kol's equal rather than his subordinate, she'd worked with him closely enough to not even entertain the notion that she'd be able to force him to do something he was opposed to. He might adore and respect her with all that was left of his heart and soul, but that wouldn't be enough on its own to heal the wounds he'd carried to the surface. Nessix, however, adored and respected him enough to not stand by and let him resign himself to the biases of her unstable country. She looked away from him, dreading this debate.

"You'll have to go somewhere, and I don't advise you venture far from where I have influence."

"The faith you have in me is touching."

Nessix winced at his words, but the persistence of his sullen tone still hadn't changed her mind. "I may be the only person on this entire island not looking for an excuse to kill you, and your wings will need proper medical attention before you can have your way and just fly off on your own."

Kol had needed neither of those reminders. "I don't want your pity."

Nessix lengthened her stride to dart in front of him and used both arms to shove him backwards. The surrounding akhuerai fanned out to give the pair the space they'd need to sort out this disagreement, several curious eyes lingering on them to see if Nessix had finally lost her patience with the alar, but they didn't stay long enough to find out. Kol staggered back from the shove, grimacing as he spread his injured wings for balance, and he raised his hooded eyes to Nessix's fierce expression as she gripped his collar—much as Annin had the day before—and pulled him closer.

"I do not pity those who fight beside me," she seethed quietly. "I embrace them. I lend them my blade when they are in need. If I pitied you, Kol Chiefson, I'd use this hook and carve your soul to freedom right now. We've seen each other weak. We've seen each other vulnerable. And we've not once given up on one another. Now, cast aside your curse of pride—the surface has no place for it—and accept help when it's offered to you."

She shoved him away with a frustrated huff, as though waiting for Kol to protest. That part of him she'd just condemned, that pride which had kept him alive in the hells, begged to indulge her offer of debate, to dare her to take up on that threat to cleanse him, to remind her that he was a demon, not her ally, but her eyes were firm, not with the strictness of a general ordering her troops, but with that of a friend refusing to accept his self-destruction. It was a look he'd remembered from the days of the Divine Battle, a look Berann had given him just yesterday, and one which Kol didn't quite know how to accept today.

"I will stay close to the temple," he muttered to keep the tremble of his lips from showing.

Nessix sighed and backed away as she resumed walking, holding back her satisfied smile as Kol trudged after her. "I will arrange for a command tent to be provided to you for shelter and after a surgeon can properly tend to your wings, I'll do what I can to ensure you're left alone until you are ready for company."

Kol doubted he'd ever be ready for company, but he had no fire left in him to defy Nessix's optimism. Accepting her words for no other reason than not knowing what else to do with them, he carried on in a silence which Nessix respected as they completed their trek to the temple.

Sulik had issued a robust crew of guards and attendants to await the akhuerai's arrival and as the local force jumped straight into work processing the newcomers, Mathias beckoned Sazrah and Nessix over. He nearly objected when Nessix gently grasped Kol's bicep to bring him along, but had vowed to overlook their connection until it proved a genuine threat to that which he cared about. After all, that connection had very possibly spared Nes's life in those last couple tunnels of the hells.

With the refugees handled and their heroes gathered after such an exhausting week, Sulik dismissed himself from the administrative front and weaved through the crowd to fold Nessix in a tight embrace. Her recovery meant he could shed the mantle of authority he'd been forced to carry. It meant he could return to the gentle advisory role he'd always thrived in most. It meant that Elidae may yet be saved, that her most devoted guardian had returned. Having Nessix back meant Sulik could smile again. Releasing the woman from his arms, Sulik took her by the shoulders and leaned back to look her over. "Your father would have been proud."

There were many aspects of the road Nessix had travelled which would have surely devastated her father, but she accepted Sulik's praise with a bittersweet smile. "Thank you for holding the line, Commander. I am sorry to have kept you waiting."

Allowing the moment to pass before it distracted them from the matters at hand, Sulik looked between his two generals. "So, what's next?"

"I believe," Tristan spoke smoothly, "some thanks are in order to Cered—"

"What is he still doing here?" Sazrah snapped.

Tristan emitted a sharp scoff, jerked the arm cuffed to Mathias into the air and shook his shackled wrist for all to see.

Mathias, gritting his teeth, cupped his free hand over the vampire's outraged gesture and shoved their hands back down to their sides.

"Next," Nessix said, "we mend whatever nonsense has shredded Elidae so it can be a unified, standing force when the demons get around to coming after us."

Sazrah cast her eyes to the heavens and crossed her arms, shaking her head at Nessix's apparent ignorance. "We've been working on that since Mathias trotted off to go look for you and haven't achieved any noteworthy progress. I say we finish what we started and use these weapons to cleanse every demon we can get our hands on." She turned her pointed glare toward Kol, but neither moved to retrieve one of the mentioned weapons nor made any move to approach him.

Kol met Sazrah's challenge with the resignation of a man who no longer cared about his fate. "Are you still conflicted about the demon inside yourself, Shade?"

Sazrah bristled at Kol's insult, but Mathias raised a warding hand against Kol and speared Sazrah with a glare which kept her tongue—and sword—sheathed. "That's enough out of both of you. I think, before we try to impose ourselves on anyone, fleman or demon alike, we need to make sure we're actually strong enough to hold against opposition. This means everyone heals up from their injuries, we sort out how these weapons work, and Nes gets the rest of her soul."

Both Kol and Nessix hastily averted their eyes from the last part of Mathias's suggestion. Nessix snuck a glance at the alar, but the tight press of his lips told her everything she needed to hear about his willingness to be the one to initiate this confession. Still without adequate information of her own, but knowing it would be safest for her to be the one to craft an explanation, Nessix scooted a step forward to position herself between Mathias and Kol.

"Finding my soul... may not be as easy as you'd like it to be."

Mathias shook his head. "I didn't expect it to be easy, but armed with—"

Nessix laid her hand on Mathias's arm and hastily glanced away from his heavy eyes. "No, Mathias. It... will be really, *really* difficult."

Confused, Mathias looked from Nessix to Kol and back again, not much appreciating their bowed heads and steady avoidance of his prying eyes. Finally, Kol looked up to relieve Nessix from the report she only knew the bare basics of.

"Nessix's soul," he said slowly, "hadn't been kept in any of the vaults with the others."

Mathias shrugged. That news didn't surprise him, given Nes's importance to the original plans for this army. "Then we'll go to where it is."

"That's just it," Kol muttered. "I don't know where that is."

All of that hope Mathias had generated on the march to the temple, all of those dreams he'd allowed himself to finally start plucking at once again, froze at the ominous promise in Kol's words. He looked down at Nes's fingers on his arm, ignoring Tristan's impatient shuffling at his side. "Explain yourself," he ordered Kol.

Kol sighed. Regardless of Mathias's anger, he still regretted allowing Annin to convince him to part with Nes's soul, both for himself and her, and admitting to the weakness which had made him agree to do so did nothing to aid with his coping. "To keep it out of your hands when we came for the exchange, it had been left with a connection of mine in Vesper."

Mathias flung his shackled hand at Kol's wings, brows furrowing when Tristan jerked his arm back. "Then fly over there and go get it."

Kol's lip twitched and he wondered yet again how Nessix anticipated him and Mathias ever working together. "Grell killed this connection. I have no idea where it had been stashed or if it's even still in the encampment."

"So you're telling me you don't know where it is."

"Your skills of comprehension are truly legendary."

Mathias nodded in the manner of a man on the verge of snapping and pummeling in the face of whoever was nearest, and Tristan held very still as the paladin hissed his next question. "Do you have means of tracking this missing piece of her soul?" Each word plinked out with a sharp chime of tension.

Kol lowered his eyes and choked down the annoying influx of regret which surfaced as he was forced to address Annin's fate. "A couple days ago, I could have had access to a way to do so, but now?" He sneered at the limitations he now faced without his old companion around to solve his problems, and shook his head. "I believe I could locate it if it was hidden in the same room I was in, just as Nessix could, herself. But lost somewhere across an entire continent? I wouldn't even know where to begin searching for it."

Tristan cleared his throat twice as loud as was necessary and took a step closer to Nessix, grandly sweeping his free hand out to his side. "Have all of you forgotten that my god's specialty lies in tampering with souls?"

Mathias frowned and tried to cross his arms until Tristan firmly jerked his hand back down to his side. "We all know exactly the sort of business your god is involved in and he's already milked all of the lenience he will receive from me."

Tristan rolled his eyes and eased another casual step closer to Nessix. "We'll see about that," he muttered before raising his eyes to meet Nessix's hard glare. "Because you are overlooking quite possibly *the* most valuable resource you have at your disposal, Sir Sagewind."

"And what is that?"

A charming smile swept across Tristan's face, his focus still centered on Nessix as her eyes locked on his. "Me."

Mathias scoffed and shifted the tension from his stance, but before he could deliver his thoughts on Tristan's arrogance, the vampire smoothly continued his argument.

"You see, I was gifted a skill very much like your own, Mathias. I, too, can communicate with souls. Only I don't require any sort of close proximity to them the way you do. I can find the ones that aren't neatly shelved away in the heavens."

Kol stepped forward, contemplating Tristan's value in this mismatched team of immortals for the first time. "You could track it, even fractured as it is?"

Tristan shrugged and reached his graceful fingers forward to gently press against the ring hidden beneath the shield of Nessix's breastplate. She drew in a fleeting breath through parted lips at his touch, but didn't object to it. "I believe I could," Tristan said, his voice even and smooth, "provided I could familiarize myself with the other half of it, attune myself to—"

As Tristan spoke, Nes's expression grew increasingly distant, her eyes glazing over at the influence of his implied suggestions, and as she began to lean forward, Kol grasped the back of her arm to pull her away from the vampire, Sazrah reached for her sword, and Mathias forcibly jerked Tristan back.

"There will be no attuning of anything," Mathias said.

Tristan left his gaze with Nessix until coherence trickled back into her eyes and a shameful flush warmed her cheeks. "It would expedite the—"

"No. Attuning."

Tristan gauged the dedication in Mathias's eyes, ever aware of the cuffs which bound him closer to the holy man that was considered ideal for a vampire. He made careful note of the tension of the other three immortals outside the temple's entrance—two of them armed with weapons capable of slaying gods—and backed away from Nessix. "You," he said to Mathias, "of all people, cannot fault me for trying."

Nessix crossed her arms, grateful for the extra step Kol took toward her and the one Mathias took in front of her. The warmth of Tristan's influence still sat in her belly in a humiliating manner and she realized for the first time just why Mathias was so wary of this unusual man. "If the options are this one finds my soul or it remains missing, I'll take my chances of staying incomplete."

Tristan exaggerated a wounded wince which fizzled out in a much less flattering gawk as support came from the least likely source.

"He's an untrained beast, but he wasn't wrong," Mathias conceded at last. "If any of us stand a chance of tracking your soul, Nes, it would be him."

"And," Tristan added, though nobody seemed particularly pleased to accept his input. "I'll remind you all that as long as my lord's fate is hanging in the balance, I have absolutely nothing to gain from angering or endangering any of you."

As much as Nessix hated to admit it, based on her limited understanding of Ceredulus's circumstances and Mathias's ability to improve them, she found herself more inclined to believe the vampire's excuse. That didn't make her appreciate the idea of this manipulative beast holding her soul any more. Kol shifted beside her, conveying a similar—though better hidden—sentiment, and Nessix had to wonder why she was so comfortable with a demon possessing the same thing she wanted to keep from Tristan. Kol had already expressed a fervent desire, bordering on an uncontrollable need, to locate her missing soul vessel and no matter how much she had come to trust him, there was still a weighty part of Nessix which wondered if he sought to find her soul for her or himself.

Seeing Nessix's persisting doubts, Mathias pressed his left arm back to increase the distance between her and the vampire, and

346

stepped closer to her. "It's not ideal, Nes, but we need you to have all of your soul. *I* need you to have all of your soul."

She'd been about to protest that she'd been functioning just fine with the half of it she had until Mathias added that last gentle plea. Kol had never touched on the subject of if the two halves could ever be reunited and she didn't want to begin thinking of the possibility that Annin had been the only one capable of such a feat. There may be no fixing her, but if she wanted any chance to see the future she and Mathias hoped for, she had to try, even if it meant trusting Tristan.

"I've defied every god I've ever met," Nessix said. "What grounds do I have to believe Tristan is any more obedient to his?"

Sulik chuckled at Nes's logic, but covered his mouth to let Mathias be the one to correct her.

"You're one of the few inhabitants of Abaeloth willful enough to be so reckless and bold," Mathias said, suspecting his criticism would stoke her pride rather than her anger. "Besides that, Tristan's entire existence is wrapped up in whether or not his god is pleased with him. Any act of defiance he shows would result in his extermination."

Nessix flicked her attention to Tristan, still not wholly buying the dedication in his eyes past the twinkle of cunning which glowed in their forefront. "And you will return my soul directly to me as soon as you find it?"

Tristan glanced past Nessix to smirk at the eagerness in Kol's eyes, having not forgotten Ceredulus's instructions to befriend the demon. He blinked and by the time his eyes opened again, they were directed at Nessix once more. "As soon as I am able."

"And that will be before you let Ceredulus take a look at it?" Mathias asked.

Tristan frowned. "Now, Mathias. You just noted yourself how I must obey his orders—"

"Alright, Kol." Mathias looked over to the demon. "Tell me what you need to track—"

"No!" Tristan cut in. Ceredulus's orders to remain compliant with Mathias transcended any bouts of curiosity which could be sorted out at a later date. "I can do it. And as soon as I'm able to find a way to bring it here to Elidae, that will be my priority."

Mathias heaved a sigh, the last of his immediate concerns addressed. "Does this work for you, Nes?"

Nessix crossed her arms and scrutinized the grinning vampire once more. She wasn't thrilled with the arrangement, but this couldn't be the worst trial she'd been through. "Fine," she said shortly. "But make it quick."

Tristan chuckled, delighted in his victory, but another quick jerk of Mathias's arm kept him from making more of it. With plans in place and weariness and irritability falling over the hells' survivors, the gathering dispersed at last to begin the process of crafting their lives in the wake of the chaos they'd traversed.

TWENTY-NINE

Few things, Mathias decided, were more annoying than a bored vampire and by the time Ceraphlaks landed on Gelthin, he was ready to be rid of Tristan until Nessix's soul was safely obtained. Mathias's only reluctance came from his doubts as to whether or not the devious vampire, under the orders of his conniving god, could actually be trusted with such a sensitive task.

"Your mission," Mathias reminded as he fished the shackle's key from his pocket, "is to track and locate Nessix's soul."

Tristan laid his free hand to his chest and exaggerated a humble bow of his head. "After *all* we've been through, my friend, what else would you possibly expect me to do?"

Mathias didn't reward the vampire with the sort of attention he was after, and slid the key into the lock. "And if I receive any sort of report which might insinuate that you're heedlessly killing, targeting innocents for your meals, or contemplating *any* sort of arrangement involving the rise or movement of your kind or those you create, you can consider Ceredulus's sentence sealed for the extent of however long Etha deems me fit for the world."

Tristan glowered at the precise wording Mathias had chosen to deliver his terms, but trusted Ceredulus would disapprove of him pressing the matter at a time when Mathias wasn't obviously indebted to him. Besides, he truly was interested in locating the

349

other half of Nessix's soul, both for his own studies and the leverage which would be gained from achieving this impossible task.

"Yes, yes," Tristan said flippantly. "You've beat your conditions into my head well enough I could recite them in my sleep."

"You don't sleep," Mathias muttered.

Tristan's smile returned at the paladin's lack of humor. "I thought we'd worked out an understanding," he said, feigning his hurt. "What other heroic deeds beyond those which I've already displayed must I accomplish to prove my worth and intentions to you?"

Mathias hesitated with his fingers pinching the key. "Bring me the other half of Nessix's soul, safe and unharmed, and then we can discuss what I think of you."

"Fine." Tristan drew out the sentiment in a manner which openly emphasized his disappointment, giving up on extracting anything else from his grouchy companion. Perhaps he'd worked a bit too diligently at pestering the paladin over the past couple days. "I, Tristan Swift, Lord of Fallsmouth, hereby vow to provide one Sir Mathias Sagewind, esteemed White Paladin of the Order of the White Circle, with the remaining portion of the soul of his lover, the risen General Nessix Teradhel of Elidae, promptly upon my obtaining of it and without cost or detriment to any innocent party who calls this realm home." He pegged Mathias with an expectant glare.

"And the influence of your god?"

Tristan rolled his eyes. "And I will do so without the aid of any of my kind or those which I am capable of raising."

"Very good," Mathias granted. "Now—"

Tristan's brows arched strictly and he held up a finger to demand a moment more of the paladin's patience, since amendments to this arrangement were apparently still on the table. "In exchange for my tireless and generous assistance, Sir Sagewind agrees to acknowledge the role in which my lord Ceredulus has played in mitigating the recent crisis posed by demonkind to the integrity of the surface realm." He raised his finger higher when

Mathias opened his mouth. "*And* he will remain open to future negotiations regarding the welfare of said deity, in light of the good which has already been achieved by their collaboration." Tristan ended his terms with a smug smile and awaited Mathias's reply.

Considering the loose interpretation which Mathias could make of the amended closing and how eager he was to be rid of his obnoxious company, Mathias opted to accept the terms now before Tristan had a chance to refine them further. "Done."

"And to be mutually sworn as an oath beneath the eternal gazes of the most glorious Ceredulus and the great Mother Goddess Etha, herself?"

"You first."

"Mathias, truly, you insult me. It is sworn by my soul."

That was as good as Mathias was going to get. "May Etha note my vow."

Mathias held Tristan's eyes a firm moment longer, unable to help but feel like he was missing a vital aspect to the deal they'd settled on, but he always felt that way when dealing with vampires. He had another point of business in returning to Gelthin, anyway. Casting aside his reservations and punching through that wall of prejudice he had against Tristan's kind, Mathias twisted the key and the shackle dropped free of the vampire's wrist. He left Tristan with one final command.

"Behave."

Tristan didn't merit the order with anything more than a smirk, and disappeared before Mathias's second thoughts could mature into problems.

Even with his connection to Etha restored from his stint in the hells, Mathias's senses weren't quite sharp enough to catch in which direction Tristan had escaped, but what was done was done, and he tried to console himself with the reminder that dealing with Ceredulus had been Etha's idea all along.

Oh, don't you go blaming your free will on me *Mathias…*

He found a small smile at last. *I'm not sure who else I can hold responsible for such a generous gift.*

And you intend to use that gift now to speak with the Council?

I do.

351

And there is nothing this goddess can do to change the course you plan to take with them?

Mathias was still for a moment as he considered the ramifications of the stand he was prepared to make before the Council. It would shake the very foundations of the Order, but he had just witnessed firsthand how sometimes foundations had to crumble in order to forge a path toward salvation.

I am set on this course, Mother, and I believe it is the one which they've been after for some time.

When Etha offered no additional input or warnings, Mathias took it as his cue to teleport to the Citadel. He arrived in the beautiful marble halls without fanfare, quietly blending into the queue at the admissions office until he reached the front of the line, at which point he made sure to emphasize that he'd returned and was anxious to deliver the report which the Council had been demanding of him for months now. Not knowing where the day's schedule had positioned Julianna, he chose against continuing his dramatic display of having returned to Zeal and opted to let the rumor mill work its wonders. Official business underway, Mathias went straight to his room to run through how to best present the information he'd brought with him and practice his responses to the demands he expected to be made of him.

It had been so long since Mathias had been able to enjoy genuine peace and serenity. There was no shortage of worries still hanging in his mind—how to reach Nes's soul, how they'd go about restoring Elidae to the nation she'd died for, how to coordinate the purging process and if they'd be able to do so before the demons made their next organized move—but they didn't bring with them the repressive cloud which had smothered him these past several months. Past needing to aim at intimidating the Council, Mathias's new focus was to remind the general public that he was their shining beacon of justice, and he passed the time waiting for his summons by lovingly cleaning and polishing his armor and investing more than minimal effort to groom his overgrown hair to make himself look twice as respectable as the man he was preparing to go to war with.

He felt Julianna's ire press against his closed door moments before her rapid knocking and sharp demand for him to answer sounded. Mathias paused in his preparations, looked at the door for a moment, then shrugged and went back to work.

Julianna's knocking persisted. "I know you're in there, Mathias."

I always knew she was sharper than the others, Mathias said to Etha.

"Etha told me you're in there."

Mathias jerked his head up from his polishing, brows furrowing in mock irritation. *Mother, you didn't!*

Gossip travels fast with or without my assistance, and Julianna isn't going to just go away, you know.

Another round of knocking and demands confirmed Etha's premonition.

Then it's going to be an awful long day for her. Please consider this my prayer that she still has a voice when it's time to properly scold me.

The tone of Julianna's voice shifted from harsh demands to carrying strains of tense concern as she continued to order him to permit her entry, and Etha had to put her foot down on Mathias's stubbornness. Regardless of the fight he intended to pick with Henrik, Julianna had paid her own price of credibility in her brother's defense these past few months, and she deserved justice, too.

I realize you're having great fun with this, Etha said, *but I think you underestimate how worried she's been over you. You've been less than stable, dashing into danger and stirring pots that were better left untouched, leaving her to clean up after you. Be mature. At least for a couple minutes.*

Mathias pursed his lips and continued his work a while longer until Julianna's exasperated sigh pushed through the door, followed by a single thump that must have been her head or a shoulder slumping against it in defeat. Etha was right. Mathias's battle was with Henrik and those he'd coerced into his pocket, and Julianna had little more than a supporting role between them. In his desire to keep his sister innocent and uninvolved with the questionable means he'd taken part in, Mathias had ended up being terribly unfair to her. Guilt lashing him just as Etha had intended, Mathias slapped his cloth to the floor, stood, and walked over to his door.

"Mind standing up so you don't fall when I open this?" he

asked. He didn't receive an answer and, curious to know if Julianna had given up and left, he opened the door in a hurry.

Just to meet her demanding green eyes. "Out with it."

And here, Etha had convinced Mathias that Julianna was in need of his comfort... "At High Council." He moved to close the door, but Julianna slammed her palm against it to prevent him from doing so.

"Now." It wasn't often Julianna pulled on Etha's might for the purposes of intimidation and it was even less frequent that it threatened to have an effect on Mathias the way it did now. "Do not ask me to blindly build a defense for you. Not this time."

Mathias's previous assumption that Julianna had been after self-serving purposes couldn't have been more wrong, and he frowned as he saw the uncertainty glowing through the angry veneer in her eyes. "Jules... I hadn't planned to ask you to form a defense for me at all."

She shook her head, rattling that hidden fear loose so it snuck even closer to the forefront. "Henrik's been keeping score and swaying more voices—"

"Then let him."

Julianna gasped and scoured Mathias's hardened expression for signs that he'd been joking. Finding none, she took a quick, shallow breath to try appearing as the authority figure she'd been appointed to be. "Mathias, I don't think you realize how serious this is."

Despite Julianna's mounting fear, Mathias laughed. "I know exactly how serious this is, more so than you or anyone else living in this city does, and that's why I need to keep you as ignorant to everything I've been up to as I possibly can. It used to be that you thought I could handle anything, remember?"

Julianna crossed her arms, shoulders caving in toward each other. "That was when I was younger and far more naïve."

Mathias smiled gently and bent forward to kiss her forehead. "You're still plenty naïve if you think I can't see my way out of this after what I've already gone through. Now go rest up, decide which gown you want to wear to High Council since half the city's bound to be in attendance, and trust that I've got my end covered."

Julianna raised her eyes to Mathias's. "Trust you."

He nodded once. "Like you always have."

That was a bold assumption. "They are ready to speak with you."

Mathias eased back a step. "Of course they are. Henrik's been squealing about me giving reports since—"

"No." Julianna dropped her arms, one hand grabbing the opposite wrist. "They are ready to speak with you *right now.*"

"Oh." Mathias straightened, unsure what to do with this information. "Well. That was fast."

"You flippantly promised them this meeting before breaking Nessix out of jail, losing her to the demons, and launching yourself into the hells to chase after her, then showed up here, dramatically declaring to the admissions office that you'd found a way to permanently rid Abaeloth of the demons. What else did you expect besides their haste?"

When she put it that way, perhaps Mathias shouldn't have tried so hard to get their attention. "The same sort of noncommittal nonsense they usually conduct business with." Julianna's tight lips and even brow suggested that she didn't find Mathias's appraisal as entertaining as he did. "Very well. Go back down there. Tell them I'm on my way."

Julianna crossed her arms and cocked a hip in preparation to leave. "On your way once this door closes or on your way at your leisure?"

Unable to argue that he'd earned Julianna's suspicion quite well over these past few months, Mathias sighed. "As soon as I can change clothes. I won't even take the long way down."

Julianna made a couple brief gnaws on the inside of her cheek. "And you're going to be mature about your presentation this time?"

Mathias flashed her a smile and held out his arms with a shrug. "Nothing's much more mature than a knight in his armor."

Slipping a glance to the blessed armor he'd at least put effort into cleaning this time around, Julianna's hands fell to her side and she shook her head. "Mathias—"

"I've got this, Jules." He reached forward and gently grasped her hands, drawing her distrustful eyes to his. "I've been put through too many ringers the past couple weeks and the last thing I'm looking for is more trouble. I will conduct myself exactly the way I should have all along."

Julianna couldn't quite place what it was she mistrusted about Mathias's vow, but she was so tired of fighting with him over how to manage the Council. Instead, she attempted to beat him at his own game. Holding his eyes firmly, she told him, "I am trusting you, Mathias," withdrew her hands, and promptly left to descend the stairs.

Mathias watched her leave, only a little bit remorseful that she was going to be less than pleased with the decisions he'd made, but no less committed to them. Stepping back, he closed his door, and turned to dress for the meeting before him.

* * * * *

When Etha had reflected on how effectively nobles spread gossip, she hadn't been exaggerating. Word had traveled quickly through and out of the Citadel that Mathias Sagewind had come home with world-altering news to declare before the Council and, as was the Order's policy, the doors to this meeting remained open to the public. It was a policy Henrik began to regret as more and more bodies—from the most dignified of Zeal's upper class to the filthy fieldworkers who kept them all fed—crammed into the room, all seats occupied, the surplus attendees lining the walls and cramming in shoulder to shoulder. By the time haphazard rows of civilians began to sit on the floor before the podiums, he was prepared to order this flooding of bodies to stop, if not for the earsplitting roar of so many voices.

How did anyone think anything would be accomplished with so much noise?

Henrik speared a demanding glare at Julianna, holding it there until the High Priestess looked up to meet his fevered eyes. She shrugged and held her hands to her sides, palms up, and Henrik resumed glowering at the growing crowd.

Just then, a blinding flash reflected off the marble walls, silencing the commotion of the audience with stunned gasps, and as vision slowly returned to the crowd, Mathias was revealed standing before the Council. That roar which Henrik had been unable to control had been effectively squashed by the one man the Head of Court most resented having such influence, and he was ready, armed with reports of the shady behavior Mathias had been seen taking part in the days before he went missing, to put the paladin in his place at last.

"Sir Mathias Sagewind," Henrik said grandly, frowning at the way the number of bodies packed into the room robbed his voice of its imposing echo. "I was promised High Council from you."

Mathias nodded once. "And I still offer it freely.

Henrik turned to look over the panel of his peers. "And do I hear second?"

A smattering of anxious affirmatives popped up from the Council and Henrik swung around to face Mathias once again. "High Council, it is," Henrik declared. "May Etha watch over you, Sir Sagewind."

"I thank you for the prayer, Master Caldwell."

The man flushed at Mathias's return, but swallowed his outrage well. "The last time you stood before the Council, you vowed to explain to us the nature of the demons' current attacks here on the surface as they apply to one General Nessix Teradhel of Elidae, a woman allegedly brought back from the dead by the very foes you claim to detest."

"Your memory aged well," Mathias said. "And I am prepared to deliver my report in full at this time."

This was all progressing much more smoothly than Henrik had expected, and he coughed on the tick of apprehension which accompanied that observation. "Under the restrictions of High Council?"

"Every last one of them. You see"—Mathias raised his voice to carry to every ear in the great room—"during the war on Elidae, General Teradhel was slain by the demons, her soul extracted and split in half, and her physical remains stolen to be raised with the intention of leading a demon-curated undead army."

"So you admit to her ties both to the demons and the undead?" Henrik asked.

Mathias cocked his head as he thought over the best way to phrase his answer. "If by demonic ties you are referring to her enslavement by them, and her status as being undead parallel to my own, yes. I will admit that."

Henrik narrowed his eyes, ever alert for holes to exploit in Mathias's defenses. "Then continue."

"According to Zenos's records, a couple thousand souls were harvested in this manner, taken out of sight of Etha's grace, and once Nessix put this together, she vowed to keep the demons from taking any more."

This revelation resulted in a rapid burst of frantic chatter as the audience weighed in on what this frightening threat could mean for them, but Henrik was quick to quell these concerns with the pounding of his gavel and demands for silence. As the crowd subdued themselves in obedient respect of Council decorum, Mathias allowed his opponent to settle behind his podium with his awkward rendition of authority before continuing.

"General Teradhel spent that year infiltrating the demons she was able to get close to, gleaning what information she could uncover to use against them until she was able to coordinate an escape to seek Zeal's assistance in rescuing the rest of the innocents the demons had taken for their experiments."

Mathias shifted a shoulder back to deliver his next statement more to the crowd of anxious civilians than the officials who would only stomp their feet over it. "It was with these intentions that she petitioned to our own Council for aid, where it was decided by direct order that the plight she represented was of no concern to our holy city, and she was forcibly detained as a felon due to the coercion of one of the Council's own." Mathias swung back to face Henrik. "Is this about accurate, Master Caldwell?"

Hundreds of hungry eyes snapped to the Head of Court and he licked his lips nervously. "She was unable to provide adequate evidence to her nature or cause, and she drew a blade at High Council."

"What sort of evidence would you have required—or accepted, for that matter—of a refugee from the hells?" Mathias asked.

Henrik sputtered over a viable answer but couldn't find a single one. "I'd have accepted any tangible evidence she would have offered to us, but all she had was her word."

Mathias nodded. "And the word of nobility has no value to the Council? Understood."

"I never said that!" Henrik snapped, hastily directing his eyes from the judgmental and increasingly suspicious crowd around him.

The weight of Julianna's glare, reminding Mathias how he'd promised to be mature, drilled into his back, and he elected to move on without further prompting. "General Teradhel did bring evidence with her in the form of a long-dead demon's name. I don't expect many in this room to know who Berann was—most of the demons themselves don't even know of him—but he had carried with him a secret capable of ending the demons' curse."

Another round of chatter sprang up, this one far harder for Henrik to get under control, but when he did, he was quick to beat Mathias to speaking. "Not a whole lot of good can come from questioning a dead demon. I hardly see how this serves as tangible evidence in defense of this *creature* you've been rumored to be courting." The crowd didn't bite into the shock factor Henrik had aimed for with that final remark.

Mathias blew out a slow breath and snuck an apologetic glance at Julianna. This was the part he'd wanted her ignorant to, the part he wished he could dismiss her from ever hearing. But he'd made up his mind and was prepared to bear the consequences. "I didn't question a dead demon."

Confusion rippled across every face in the courtroom as Mathias's words failed to add up. It was Julianna, possibly guided by Etha, who figured it out first, and the color drained out of her pale cheeks. Mathias sighed and lowered his head as he braced himself for the pending backlash.

"Seeing as the just and fair powers of Zeal wanted nothing to do with aiding in this crisis, after the demons had taken Nessix, I made a deal with Ceredulus—"

"*A deal with Ceredulus!*" Henrik bellowed.

"Regrettably," Mathias answered.

Everyone in attendance turned their eyes to Julianna in hopes

359

that she'd be able to correct her brother's clearly incorrect interpretation of his own actions and put their minds at ease, but all she could do was stare at Mathias in stunned, pleading silence. Not even he would make this up.

"The god of the undead?" Henrik, too shocked to enunciate carefully, sputtered his request for clarification.

"If there was a different one, I'd have much preferred speaking with him."

"This is nothing to make light of, Sir Sagewind! I don't even think we *have* a punishment severe enough for such a crime!"

With the hard part of uncovering his shame past him, Mathias raised his head. "It has been noted. But perhaps while you task Lord Maynard with concocting a torture appropriate for my actions, you'd be interested in hearing what came of this deal?"

"Anything tied to that—"

"Let him speak." Julianna's voice rang through the chamber, muzzling the outrage back into Henrik's mouth. Mathias didn't thank her for the assistance, smart enough to realize she hadn't done this for his benefit. "Let him speak and then we can discuss if the ends outweighed the means."

None dared contradict Julianna's will, and so they turned their expectations on Mathias.

"Ceredulus brought the demon back to life." Mathias did suffer a pinch of guilt at the number of muffled cries of disbelief and whispered prayers for Etha to save them, but he'd not only been asked to explain himself, Zeal needed to hear it. "And Berann disclosed to me that the weapons wielded by the first three children of Etha, those responsible for the Divine Battle which gave rise to the demons in the first place, are capable of righting the damage caused by their tantrums, just as the remains of Affliction can both create and destroy."

The chamber hushed, not even the gentle flow of breath marring the silence as everyone waited for Mathias to deliver the concrete hope all of Abaeloth had waited centuries to hear.

"This led me and Nessix, along with a few carefully selected allies, on an expedition to infiltrate the hells to remove these weapons from where the demons had stowed them so that we could seek Abaeloth's salvation."

"Is it safe to assume," Julianna breathed, her soft voice carrying clearly in the comparative silence of the chamber, "that you being alive and well here on the surface means this expedition was successful?"

Mathias flashed his sister a wide grin. "It does."

Henrik didn't need much more to fuel his entitlement and cut in smoothly with the authority he'd assumed from his station. He exaggerated his efforts to look Mathias over for anything more than his usual selection of arms and displayed his dissatisfaction with an open-mouthed frown. "Where are these world-altering weapons, then, Sir Sagewind?"

"You needn't worry about the weapons' safety—"

"I am not worried about the weapons' safety," Henrik snapped. "You, Sir Sagewind, have proven less than reliable, what with your conspiring with undead demon women and making deals with Ceredulus, and I and my associates of the Council will know the location of these weapons."

Mathias bit back his desire to correct Henrik—yet again—about the nature of Nes's existence, well aware of how drawing more attention to that matter would only weaken what he was about to say. "The hammer of Motag has been assigned to Sazrah the Shade, and the hook of Eriv is with Nessix Teradhel, Lord General of Elidae."

Henrik coughed. "You've left the fate of Abaeloth in the hands of a mercenary and a felon? Where's the third weapon, then? Did you even bother to remove it from the demons? Or do you like the idea of keeping the field more balanced by giving them a chance against the mortal realm?"

"Kalina's sabers…" Mathias bought himself time to think this over in the guise of a deep breath. The fate of the sabers was a valid concern, one he and the warriors he'd served beside hadn't yet had the time to discuss, but in the interest of keeping this relic free from the bureaucratic circus that was the Council, he had to come up with an answer. "They are stowed safely in Etha's oldest temple on Elidae and will be assigned to a champion just as worthy as the first two."

"Do you have a name of this worthy champion?"

Mathias didn't even have an identity for this worthy champion, and the names of the other two survivors of their quest weren't ones anyone in this room—himself included—would accept. Either way, this was High Council, and Mathias was required to answer honestly. "I've got a couple candidates in mind."

Oh, Mathias…

There was no time for Mathias to speculate on whether or not Etha's words had expressed pride or horror before murmurs of speculations popped up among the Council members, and Mathias did briefly wonder if he would be challenged.

"I'm sure my colleagues will forgive me for saying that this simply will not do," Henrik countered smoothly, "considering those you deem trustworthy these days."

"I trust Master Aligoth," Mathias said. As color slowly drained from the Minister of Petition's face, the paladin continued. "As well as Lords Courtenay and Hildebrand, and Masters Lumley and Blaxton. Even Emory Oustland is a decent fellow when he's allowed to think for himself. Etha herself knows I trust Julianna. Are you saying, Master Caldwell, that my judgment is too skewed for these esteemed members of your very own Council to be deemed trustworthy? Or are they, perhaps, the most just and devoted of you all?"

Henrik's lips puckered in stubborn dissatisfaction as means to avoid buying into Mathias's game. "As Head of Court, I demand you recover all three of these weapons and deliver them to Zeal at once."

Mathias chuckled and shook his head. "There you go with your tyrannical orders again, overstepping any unvoiced opinions your dear colleagues might have and assuming Abaeloth's worries end outside our fair city's walls. What would *you* do with such powerful artifacts, anyway, Henrik? I'm not even sure you know which end of a sword to hold."

"I would arrange for them to be secured within the repository until the time in which the Council could assign them to champions deserving of their power."

"The same repository that was recently robbed by a vampire?"

Mathias asked.

Julianna groaned and ducked her face behind a hand.

"And," Mathias continued, as Henrik hadn't yet processed a coherent retort, "it would take this Council, as it stands today, fifteen years to agree on someone to wield these weapons, most likely decided by finances above intent, and you can bet your plush elected offices that the demons are already formulating means to try recovering what was stolen from them. No, the weapons are in the hands they belong in, and unless you intend to declare hostility against Shadeskeep and Elidae, that is where they'll stay."

"Mathias Sagewind," Henrik said slowly. "You are but one voice in this Council, one not even selected by the people, and one which a growing number of us wish to have silenced."

Mathias cast a casual glance across the crowded chamber and smirked. "My voice silenced? Careful, Henrik. That sounds a bit like a threat of violence here at High Council."

Henrik spat his regard for Mathias's counter. "You may have done some glorious things for our nation in the past, but it's not been without your own crimes against the Order. You are reckless and insubordinate, unreliable to say the least."

"I am Etha's shield," Mathias replied, "and though I am well equipped to handle such attacks, do be advised that the Mother Goddess has taken note of them, as well."

The audience hung on every word exchanged between these two men, and that final threat of Mathias's was the last thing they had to hear before whispering their fears between one another. Had Henrik gone too far? Had his hatred of Mathias led him to disgrace the goddess who protected them? Mathias squared his shoulders as he stood at the head of this room full of the voting public, the most dangerous army a politician could face, and patiently waited for Henrik to formulate his response.

"And do you see how out of line this uncivilized brute is?" Henrik swept an arm in Mathias's direction, desperately looking across the faces of peers and citizens alike. Unfortunately for him, it was only Mathias and his sister who dared to meet his eyes, neither of them moved by his attempt to demand their fear. "To threaten to use his station to manipulate this Council!"

Julianna pressed her lips together and shook her head as Mathias gleefully chuckled at the irony of Henrik's words. That last, arrogant statement had been the final nail in the coffin of this man's career, and exactly the sort of opening Mathias had been waiting for.

"Is that where this is heading? Accusing me of using my station to manipulate the Council?" Mathias asked. "Then fine. I've been a thorn in your tender flank for long enough, and you've worked harder to discredit me than I'm sure you've worked at anything else in your entire life. You want me gone so badly?"

Amid the coordinated gasp of nobles and commoners, Julianna was the only one able to speak. "Mathias—"

"You've got it," Mathias said, casting an apologetic glance at his dear sister. He did not envy her the headache his actions were about to give her. "You want my formal title? I don't need the damn thing. I've got Etha. Protect this city yourself, Henrik."

Mathias didn't wait around to hear the wails of horror from the public that had found their security in his steady presence. He didn't stay for Julianna's rush to damage control or to hear Henrik attempt to assert himself over a situation that ensured he'd never sit behind that podium again. Mathias had no intention to leave Zeal truly in peril, but it was high time the city was forced to reflect on the sacrifices he'd made to ensure they got to live an easy life.

I'm not sure you were dramatic enough, Etha said.

Mathias smirked as he fell back into the divine pathways to journey back to Elidae. *As long as I planted the seed.*

THIRTY

Nessix leaned back in her chair, no more satisfied than she'd been at the onset of this discussion. If not for Sulik's ability to gloss over Sazrah's gloomy reports of Elidae's state of affairs, she very possibly would have entertained the idea of burrowing back into the hells to find something more likely to be saved.

Instability had rattled the country apart. Brant's ascension to General had proven to observant nobles that the Teradhel line wasn't the only one able to lead, and his death had spawned a mad dash for power and influence. Of Elidae's twenty standing cities, eighteen of them had declared independence, the last two banding together or—as Sazrah claimed—had been pulled under Gareth Destain, the brother of the woman Brant had so briefly been wed to, when he claimed the old Teradhel keep as his own after Brant's death. The ogres and minotaur had recently gotten wind of the flemans' disorder and went straight to work taking advantage of the broken nation's lack of unity. The nobles were all so focused on bickering with each other, plotting assassination attempts and political marriages and how to muscle control over those beneath them, that the combined effort of the temple's residents were all that was left to take on the monsters of the island.

No, this had not been the kind of chaos Nessix had escaped the hells to accept, but she'd just proven to be an effective enough leader to force the changes she wanted to see and now that she had the cognitive availability to focus on it, she wasn't yet ready to write off Elidae as a lost cause. She'd been born a leader, had proven her worth, and was certain she could apply those skills into winning over the masses caught in the losing end of the nobles' scuffles. Before she was able to ask Sulik for a run down on the most vulnerable territories, the door of the little room they'd made their war chamber burst open. Nessix and Sazrah, fresh off surveying missions, were on their feet in an instant, but as Mathias strode inside and closed the door behind himself, Sazrah sat and Nessix shook the tension from her arms before following suit.

"How did your meeting with your idiot Council go?" Nessix asked.

Mathias squeezed his way between the back of Sulik's chair and the wall to reach the open seat between the two women. "About as well as I expected, though I didn't stick around to listen to their whining. I suspect I'll be staying here on Elidae for some time, and we're going to want to tell the knights of the Order to quit calling me sir until the likely time they're recalled to Zeal."

Sazrah shook her head, jaw twitching somewhere between a smirk and a frown. "Lost your title over this nonsense? You're telling me it went *that* bad?"

Mathias shrugged and reached forward to pick through the half-wilted grapes left on the center of the table. "I think it went great. I gave them the score, confirmed that we've got the demons covered, and told them to start solving their own problems. And I *discarded* my title, thank you. I didn't lose anything."

Sazrah drove an elbow into the tabletop and pressed a finger against her forehead. "And they just swallowed this?"

Mathias pulled a face as he bit into the first grape and promptly returned the rest of them to the plate. "More like choked it down," he said. "But what's done is done, right?"

Sazrah shook her head. "They had *nothing* to say about what happens to the weapons we found?"

"Oh, Henrik had all kinds of opinions about how they should be handled. I told him you had the hammer and Nes had the hook, and that was where they'd stay."

Not one face in the room looked entirely comfortable with Mathias's casual report, suspecting he was sparing them all from the full truth of what his actions would mean for Elidae's future relations with Zeal. It was Sulik who gathered enough of his wits to speak first. "What did you tell them about the sabers?"

Mathias shifted about in his chair, frowning at its firmness. "Those—" He drew the word out slowly as he sent a fleeting glance across the three pairs of waiting eyes. "I… said they were going to equally trustworthy hands. Not that, you know, Henrik thinks either of you are all that virtuous."

Sazrah grunted her uncensored opinion of Henrik but Nessix, far more of a diplomat than Sazrah would ever be, heard the importance of what Mathias wasn't saying.

"Whose hands did you have in mind?" she asked.

"I… ah…" Mathias blew at his overgrown bangs and looked to the corner of the room. "I didn't specify that part. But I wasn't about to let them think they hadn't been claimed."

"Do you plan to use them?" Nessix asked.

"No." Mathias rested his hand on the warm familiarity of his hilt. "My sword's been with me all of my immortal life and carries its own blessings. The sabers would be wasted on me."

Nessix accepted Mathias's answer and looked to Sulik. "You are the last decent fleman alive, so I'll ask you next. Do you have any desire to use them?"

"Nes," Sulik chuckled, his tired humor making him sound decades older than he truly was. "My greatest desire right now is to find my way *out* of the drudgery of constant combat. Besides, between you and Sazrah and Sir Sagewind, how is a mortal man supposed to withstand the perils owning such a weapon would attract?"

Nessix nodded abruptly, grateful for Sulik's assessment so she wouldn't have to delve into the details which he'd unwittingly declared for her. She crossed her arms and shifted her focus to the center of the table. "Then I suggest we turn the sabers over to Kol."

Sazrah slapped her palm on the table and looked away to mutter, "Of course you do…"

"The *demon*?" Sulik echoed.

Nessix flushed at the criticism, but even though he'd forced himself to accept that demon's place in Nes's life, Mathias couldn't quite bring himself to rush to her defense on this matter. "Nes." He tried to put compassion in his voice, but it came out as more of a strained disappointment. "I told the Council they were going to someone *trustworthy*."

"And I don't trust him," Sazrah added before Mathias's mouth had closed.

The paladin lowered his eyes to avoid the sharp glare Nessix turned his way. "And neither do I," he agreed.

"Well," Nessix snapped. "I do."

An irritated bellow from Sazrah accompanied her combative rise of tension at Nes's predictable stubbornness, and Mathias kept half his attention on monitoring the warrior woman. "This isn't really how a vote is meant to work, Nessix."

"And I hadn't opened it up to one," Nessix snipped. Sulik wisely looked away, but both of the humans sat up to take notice of Nessix's firm conduct. "By the words of everyone"—she pegged Sazrah with a pointed glare—"in this room, I am this nation's rightful General and ruler. Are you certain your will is to oppose me?"

Sazrah scoffed and spoke past the subtle raising of Mathias's hand in the effort to silence her. "You may be the rightful general, but the loyalty of those who would even care about you has been with me—"

"The loyalty of the humans and dwarves you brought over here is with you," Sulik interjected. "But every fleman heart in our ranks still beats for the Teradhel name, as does every opposing one quake in fear of Nes's return. I believe I speak for all who are good in this nation when I say we are grateful to you, Sazrah, for the aid and expertise of your forces, but you seem to have forgotten your own vow to return Elidae to what it was before Nessix died. And that includes obedience to her rule."

Perhaps it was because he'd said what she'd hoped to hear, but Nessix was the only one not gaping in shock as the typically placid man spoke so firmly in defense of her questionable desire. She wanted her way on the matter, but that wasn't enough to make her ignore the fact that she had to cushion the blows thrown at these two foreigners to her homeland before either of them felt the need to defend themselves—or throw their own titles back at her.

"I'm not asking you to trust Kol blindly," she said. "I've quite literally lived through the suffering and darkness of his mind and it still took me months to start doing so. But please believe me when I say that his only reason for creating the akhuerai was to quell the injustices of the hells. If not for his actions, Berann's secret would have remained buried and nobody able or willing to use these weapons would have ever known they existed. I'd venture to say Kol has done more to stand against his kind than any of us have in our lifetimes."

Sazrah hissed and crossed her arms, darting her glare and accompanying scowl away from Nessix's statement, and Mathias carefully leaned forward to position himself more completely between the two of them.

"Let's say we give Kol the sabers," he said. "What is your answer to what we'll do if he turns on us?"

Nessix shook her head with the firm conviction of one of Zeal's own priestesses defending Etha's name. "He won't."

Mathias sighed, closing his eyes for a reprieve from the temperamental angle of Nes's chin and the unyielding glint in her eyes. "Then humor me."

Nessix braced her hands on the table and stood. "He has nowhere else to turn to, Mathias. He gave up everything in the terms of his own home and security to forge this path, and for that sacrifice, I say we need to step up and at least offer to fill those roles for him. Isn't that the honorable thing to do? Isn't it the opportunity you presented to the demons of Heiligate when they denounced the ways of their kind?"

Sazrah, jaw clamped tight, shook her head at Mathias, and he bowed his at her silent criticism. She was one of the majority who hated everything about the demon city he'd been responsible for establishing, having warned Mathias from its founding that it would someday come back to haunt him. He'd just never fathomed it would be in this manner. It was just as hard to accept that Nessix was every bit in the right to defend Kol as Mathias had been to stand up for the lost demons who lived in Heiligate, though he couldn't quite find the humility to admit it.

Nessix slid her hand over his, her fingers working their way between his as she lowered herself back into her seat. "Don't trust him," she said, the weight of her words reflecting all of the times Mathias had begged her to go against her better judgment and blindly follow his lead. "That's fine. But trust me. Please. We could benefit greatly from his insight and experience in the days to come, and the logic which exists in every one of you in this room must know that."

Sulik bit his tongue and leaned back in his chair as he watched for the humans' responses to Nessix's words. The hells had done a fine job maturing her political mind.

"I cannot claim to know the alar well," Mathias tried once more, "but my broad assessment is that he's not of the soundest mind right now. You aren't afraid at all that he'd use the sabers on himself?"

In truth, that possibility terrified Nessix. The last time she'd witnessed a notable will to live out of Kol was when she'd arranged for a fleman surgeon to treat and stitch his wings. In the two days since, he'd withdrawn into himself, declining most of Nes's attempts at conversation and barely picking at the food which she brought him. His suffering had worn at Nessix to the point that she was grateful for Sulik's reliability and the nostalgia of what remained of her homeland to remind her that life was worth living, and she feared for every part of Kol's well-being if he continued to hide the turmoil he seemed so set on facing on his own. It was an instinct demons relied on, but it ate at the beauty Nessix had found in him. And after all he'd sacrificed and survived, he deserved better. Nessix had been through times of hopelessness and despair and had always been able to pull herself forward because of those who depended on her. Now, she prayed she could fill that purpose for Kol.

"I'd like to think if that was a road he planned to travel, he'd have taken care of it by now," she said at last. "And if you're worried about the sabers should he be unable to protect them, I plan to continue my daily visits with him until he's healed of the injuries to body and mind which have him out of sorts. It's not like the sabers would be unsupervised."

With all of the factors laid out on the table, Mathias had to accept that his greatest motive to reject Nessix's proposal was based solely on his lingering jealousy which she had made abundantly clear had no merit, and Mathias cared far too much about her to continue questioning this aspect of her life. She had worked with Kol longer than he had. She had access to his thoughts and motives like nobody else ever could. The demon had proven to distrust his own kind, and had shown a willingness to protect others as fiercely as anyone in this room. Mathias had pardoned hundreds of less chivalrous members of the fallen, and Kol deserved a similar courtesy, whether or not Mathias liked him.

"Fine," he said at last.

Sazrah's arms dropped to her sides as she sat upright. "What—"

Mathias silenced her with a firm glare. "Nessix is right. That demon has had ample opportunities to do wrong by us. I witnessed him nearly die at the hands of the oraku who attacked your troops so Nessix and Berann had a clear path to the hammer. I do not like him and can't imagine I will anytime soon, but Nes trusts him, and I trust Nes. If she says the sabers are safe in his hands, then I'm willing to offer them to him."

"You are utterly unbelievable, Mathias," Sazrah muttered.

Sulik cleared his throat, sensitive to how close the warrior woman was to blowing. "I was planning on heading down to see how our guests are settling in for the night. Perhaps you'd care to join me, Sazrah?"

She shoved her chair back, slamming it into the wall due to the tight confines of the room, and was on her feet in the same movement. "Anywhere but here."

Sulik gave Nessix a comforting smile and followed Sazrah out the door, the steadiness of his calm voice working to coax her out of her frustration. The door only swung halfway shut, but the hall gradually quieted of their movement, and before the silence became oppressive, Nes's fingers curled more snuggly around Mathias's.

"Thank you," she murmured. "Thank you for trusting me and giving Kol a chance at redemption."

"Yeah," Mathias sighed. "Just so long as he doesn't give me a reason to regret it." He was tired of politics for one day and squeezed Nes's hand in return. "We can discuss it more in the morning after you see how he responds to the offer."

Nessix allowed her stalking weariness to pounce on her at last. "To bed, then?"

Mathias smiled and stood, pulling Nes's chair back with his free hand as he helped her rise with his other. "After you, General."

For the first time in a long while, both Nessix and Mathias could clearly see the future ahead of them.

* * * * *

Nessix had forgotten what times of peace felt like. With Mathias and Sulik shouldering the groundwork for political negotiations, as it was agreed upon to ease the shock of her return over her warring people, she'd busied herself over the past few days by tending to Kol at the crude camp he'd set up for himself about a mile from the temple. He'd fussed at her halfheartedly, attempted to order her off only once before she reminded him that she was no longer his subordinate, and she had eventually succeeded in convincing him to let her keep him company in the afternoons. His mood continued to foul and Nessix only caught brief glimpses of the sly mischief she'd come to know. Despite their new balance of command, Kol had strictly forbidden her to speak of anything tied to the events they'd experienced together in the hells, and Nessix did her best to respect his wishes.

Disheartened but not discouraged, she dutifully set out on her daily trek to his little camp, sabers wrapped in linen and tucked into the satchel of fresh provisions she brought for him. The past three days, he'd insisted upon each visit that he was quite capable of hunting for his meals and protested her assistance with treating the injuries to his wings, but today, as optimistic as Nessix was, would be different.

"I finally got them to bake some rusk bread," she called ahead as she approached the crest of the gentle rise. Kol didn't answer, but she'd never known him to favor shouting. "It's my favorite and I thought you might like—"

Nessix jolted to a stop as she made it over the hill and stared at the clearing ahead of her. Kol's tent had been deconstructed, its canvas folded neatly and poles crossed atop. The modest mess kit Nessix had insisted he keep had been washed and sat in a tidy pile on top of the tent, alongside the med kit, only half stocked from what Nessix had inventoried of it yesterday. His pack and weapons were missing, as were the change of clothes Nessix had ordered made for him. The satchel of food nearly slipped from her hands.

Kol had left.

And he hadn't bothered to tell her goodbye.

Had this been the same empty confusion he'd faced when she ran from him? Was this some sort of juvenile retaliation for the heartache she'd caused him? He'd mentioned nothing about intending to leave, though he'd been talking less and less by the day, and Nessix would have wondered if he'd been run off by some opposing force, if not for the fact that he'd taken the time to carefully pack up his campsite. Satchel nearly dragging the ground, Nessix crept up to the pile of her army's belongings which she'd loaned Kol, and discovered her answer.

Rolled into the tin cup of the mess kit was a note, simply reading, *Do not come for me, little one. I have work to do.*

Nessix stared at that script for some time, the elegant sweep of the letters drawing her back to a past which seemed dreadful lifetimes ago, reminding her of all the roads she and Kol had travelled both together and apart, of the trust they'd learned to invest in each other. And it was that trust which ached in her so badly now, even as it begged her to honor his wish. Kol was hurting. Why wouldn't he let her help him?

Cramming the note into her satchel, Nessix did the only thing she could think of, and raced back to the temple.

* * * * *

Ignoring the warnings Sulik and Sazrah had given him,

Mathias was optimistic for the meeting he was scheduled to have with the standing lord of Midton. He was the first noble Mathias had found outside of the temple open to the idea of engaging in a dialogue about the future of Elidae and where Nessix fit into it, and the paladin was comfortable with his odds of reminding the old, sensible lord about the good he'd done in the country's past. He reached for the green tunic he had laying on the bed when the door of his chamber flung open. Abandoning the routine act of dressing, Mathias spun around to face the intrusion and smiled as Nessix barged into their room. The smile didn't last long, as he noted the full satchel in her hands, wrapped sabers peeking out the top, the wild glint about the blue eyes which had only just recently rediscovered the warmth of ease, and the fact that Nessix had barely been gone for half an hour to an appointment which he'd expected to take her all afternoon.

"How was Kol?" he fished. By Nes's reaction, he wondered first if the alar had met trouble and second if that might be to his own benefit.

You are terrible, Mathias…

Nessix shoved her hand in the satchel to grab the note and jutted it forward.

Mathias accepted it, briefly swept his eyes over the ancient script Nessix knew he couldn't read, then handed it back to her. "You're going to have to help me with this one."

"He's gone, Mathias." Voicing that out loud sapped much of the strength from Nessix, and Mathias pulled his tunic out of the way so she could slump on the side of the bed. The satchel plopped at her feet, spilling two fist sized rolls to the floor. "He left without saying anything." Her eyes snapped up to Mathias, hard and cold and braced to deliver the appropriate threats, pending his answer. "He didn't tell you he was leaving, did he?"

Though Mathias had no love for Kol, he'd accepted Nes's affection for and connection to him now that jealously didn't gnaw on him so aggressively. Frowning, he resumed getting dressed. "Nes, I haven't even seen him in almost a week." He nodded to the note gripped in her hands. "Did he say where he was going?"

Nessix shook her head, the fire ebbing from her eyes as

helplessness took its place. "He only said not to look for him, that he had work to do." She raised her troubled eyes to Mathias, voice shrinking as she spoke. "You don't think he went back to the hells, do you? By himself?"

This fear contrasted so sharply with the confidence Nessix had just reclaimed for herself, and it drew the sympathy out of Mathias past his unspoken hope that maybe the phase of her life which Kol had been a part of was coming to an end. Securing the last button of his tunic, he sat beside her.

"Was he of sound mind when you spoke to him yesterday?" Mathias asked.

Nessix nodded absently, staring at the way the sabers which would have been Kol's only way to survive an expedition to that cursed realm were on the floor of her bedroom and not in his hands. "Where else could he have gone?" She was already calculating the number of enemies he had made—both actively and passively—in the time she'd known him, and sank her face into her hands. "Mathias, where could he have gone…?"

The paladin's hand slid across her back as he prepared to take the biggest step he'd make in this entire ordeal of having lost and found Nessix, raising an ancient oraku from the dead to fight the demons, and preparing to reshape the structures of three entire nations.

Etha…? Can you offer any insight on his whereabouts?
I don't often keep track of solitary demons, you know.

Mathias swished the taste of his reply through his mouth for a moment before spitting it out for Etha to hear. *Yes, but he's not an average demon. You've got motive to keep your eyes on him.*

What are demons, Mathias?

The question threw him, and he didn't like how rapid and shallow Nes's breathing was growing as he waited to receive an answer he could give her. *Abominations?*

But what were they before that?

Mortals. Even if Mathias hadn't been able to recite the demons' history by rote before, he'd have been able to do so now after having met Berann.

And what is the greatest gift I gave the mortals of Abaeloth?

375

Mathias groaned at Etha's implication, shocked that she'd bother to respect a demon's free will after how removed they were from her graces. Perhaps the discovery of the god weapons and the potential to unravel the knots in the creatures' souls had shown Etha a new direction, as well. And that didn't even touch the thought that Kol *had* chosen to step onto the most difficult path toward redemption. Mathias slid his hand over Nes's shoulder to draw her against him.

He is not in danger, Mathias, Etha said gently. *If that is what Nessix needs to hear, tell her.*

"He didn't go back to the hells," Mathias murmured into the crown of Nes's hair.

She wouldn't question how or why Mathias was so certain about that, but neither would she accept it as a complete answer. "That doesn't tell me where he *did* go."

"I don't know where he went, just that it wasn't the hells. And I'm quite sure he won't stay gone forever."

Nessix pulled away from Mathias and turned to face him. He'd done a shoddy job trying to accept Kol this entire time, and she was certain he was happier playing with the idea that the demon might never return than thinking about him coming back. But instead of finding relief in Mathias's eyes, Nessix saw a distinct sorrow that didn't do much to ease her own. "How are you so sure?"

"Because you told me yourself you'd never escape him. Shouldn't that mean he can't escape you?" Mathias stood so he could retrieve the satchel. He removed the sabers and placed them with care on the modest desk in the room, then fished out a roll to hand to Nessix. "I've seen you pull off some amazing feats these past few weeks. I have faith that you'll be able to figure out where he's gone."

Nessix stared at the roll for a long moment before accepting it and holding it in her lap. "You truly think he'll come back?"

A frown fought against Mathias's smile, but the more pleasant of the two expressions won out in the end. "I think if there's any motivation in the world that would make him come back, it would be you."

His words lightened the oppressive slump of Nes's shoulders, and she looked down at her roll as she dug her fingers through its thick crust to get into the pillowy middle. "You really think so?"

"I know so. Now, Sulik has me lined up to meet with one Albion Osric of Midton, and I have to lock the room up to safeguard the sabers. Do you want to come with me or stay in here?"

With one last glance at the sabers that were meant to go to Kol, Nessix stood. "It's better to keep my mind active."

Mathias nodded at her assessment, and the two of them departed the temple to begin the tedious process of unifying Elidae under the Teradhel name once again.

THIRTY-ONE

Kol had spent days sitting on the worn outlook of Vesper's border, watching the sun set over the graves he'd dug. The act of burying Lorrin and his men—at least the parts of them he'd been able to locate in this unforgiving terrain—would have been much easier with an oraku's help, and Kol had used the aches and discomfort of the growing blisters on his palms and the fingernails he'd snapped in their beds to keep a much sharper pain at bay. He'd searched the extent of the encampments for Nessix's soul vessel three times over, hunting for it with his eyes and his mind and his heart until he broke down in his desperation and called for it out loud, as though it was capable of responding. He knew it was gone, and that made him feel even worse, because where else could he start looking for it?

A speck of darkness formed against the setting sun's glow, and like a rabbit spotted by a wolf, Kol didn't move. No other silhouettes joined this intruder and even as the steady sweep of a pair of wings became clear, he shed his fear of this lone visitor. He'd fight if he was able, if only to keep Nessix from mourning his loss for a fourth time, but wouldn't object to being granted a reprieve from this nightmare. Several minutes of trying to ignore this disruption gave way to the revelation of the golden coat of Mathias's pegasus, and Kol frowned at the prospect of his solitude being interrupted by the paladin. His frown tugged even deeper as he realized it was Nessix and not Mathias who had come to check on him.

The pegasus landed well away from the brooding alar and Nessix's booted feet crunched lightly on the loose gravel of the ground as she dismounted. She made no effort to hide her approach, and she walked up to Kol with an authority he wished she wouldn't have found, not once hesitating and confident that she would get him to talk to her. Kol swallowed his guilt in having left her behind.

"I thought I told you not to come for me," Kol said once Nessix was close enough for him to not have to shout.

Nessix took the last few steps to reach him, slung to the ground a stuffed pack with a pair of wrapped sabers peeking out the top of it, and sat, uninvited, beside Kol to watch over the quiet mounds below. "When have you known me to swallow an order I didn't like?"

Unbidden, a gentle swell of comfort reached out to Kol from Nessix's nearness, though he actively tried to deny it. It was so much easier to surrender to the void of his consumptive misery when there was nobody to pry or demand small talk of him, no illusion of devotion which would someday betray him.

Nessix pressed her hands against the ground and leaned forward. "Will you come back to Elidae?"

Kol looked at her sharply, understanding why she'd chosen to move her face from where he could easily read it. He'd known Nessix to be stubborn and defiant, but never so cruel as to torment him in such a manner. "How quickly you seem to have forgotten the trouble my kind brought to yours."

Her shoulders shrugged closer to her ears as Kol presented a valid argument she had no way to argue. The demons had terrorized Elidae, and Kol himself had slain her, ending the Teradhel line. These actions had brought upon the events which had crumbled the foundation of the country and led it to a state of civil war. And that wasn't even touching the fact that Kol had been the one to conceive the concept of the akhuerai. Kol had been instrumental in every destroyed aspect of Nessix's life, yet she

379

continued to stand by him out of a sense of loyalty and a staunch refusal to leave him behind like so much else in the world had.

Kol had methodically broken damn near everything about Nessix besides her spirit, and he hated that he seemed destined to keep chipping away at that last resilient spark which he both envied and resented. Perhaps he'd been too harsh. "I wouldn't be welcome," he clarified.

Nessix's fingers closed around the dirt and pebbles and a deep breath drew her shoulders back. "That's what my invitation was for."

Her insistence offered to warm Kol once he found a way out of his grief, but the hope her steady generosity introduced to him gnawed at his nerves and shook a sense of panic awake inside of him instead. "Your people—*all* of them—already hate demons, and with good reason. Those who know the truth about our history have an even greater one."

She snapped her glare to him, eyes vulnerable out here in the safety of the barren surface. "Not *all* of us."

Kol gave a short, spiteful laugh, hanging his head as he shook it. "You can't change everyone, little one. Not when they're so severely damaged."

"I changed you."

Nessix couldn't have meant for those words to bite his wounded heart, but Kol sucked in a quick little gasp as instinct began to hastily construct a wall around the overwhelming emotions he'd come out here to sort through in solitude. Unusual for Nessix on all accounts, she didn't say a word as he addressed these cumulative weaknesses, didn't ask him the questions he didn't want to answer, didn't try to distract him with pointless drivel. She simply sat beside him, waiting for the time when he decided he needed her, reminding him that as long as her heart still beat with his blood, he would never be able to consider himself alone. He almost preferred her chatter.

"How did you know where to find me?" he asked at last.

Nessix still didn't look at him. "You'd written often of the peace of your home, of longing for an excuse to come back here. You'd said this was the last known location of my missing soul vessel. It took me a while to figure it out, but you showed me the way."

Kol frowned and hung his head. "Through my dreams?"

"Through your dreams."

He—for Kol had forbidden himself to actively draw up Annin's name the way the inoga had once forbidden the demons from thinking about Berann—had been right to criticize Kol for binding himself to Nessix without first investigating the associated side effects. Their intimate connection had given her too much insight, too much knowledge into matters which should have been his own. Kol sent a quick glance at her from the corner of his eye, not quite sure what he expected to see in her expression, but having not anticipated the slight furrow of her brow and the tightness in her lips. She wasn't angry with him and she didn't find any sort of humor in his turmoil. Though she had no way to relate to the depth of his sorrow and loneliness, and only a vague notion of the bleakness of his confusion, she grieved with him on a deeper level than she recognized, for the gaping sore in his soul. Perhaps binding himself to Nessix hadn't been a curse on Kol so much as it had been a curse on her. He raised his head again, staring into the sun until its brilliance blinded him.

"Why did you come?" he asked quietly, part of him hoping that the mountain wind would carry the words away before Nessix heard them.

"Because I made a promise to help you," Nessix said. "You may not want it right now, but you'll need to do a lot more than disappear in the night to keep me from trying to give it to you."

While Nessix lacked the wealth of years Kol had, she commanded a raw passion for life, closer to the mortal world and the intensity of all of its beautiful chaos than Kol had been in lifetimes. He'd spent so long moving past those inhibiting traits, suppressing the aspects which so often led to weakness that he'd forgotten the power they carried. Now, with his station and his home and his oldest companion gone, all of those mortal flaws he'd overcome had burst through his walls, overwhelming his defenses and threatening to drown him if only he'd quit thrashing for the surface. How was he supposed to explain to Nessix that there was no way she could possibly help him find sense in the disaster his life had become? She was but an infant compared to him, and though he couldn't dismiss the immense loss and pain she'd experienced in her years, she hadn't invested centuries catering to a soul she'd rationalized as kindred, she hadn't survived the world-shattering disasters which could form such bonds. She hadn't even shared any amount of affection or respect for... for...

Kol bowed his head once more, pinching his eyes shut so the afterimage of the sun played through a surreal display of gradually dimming brightness against the backs of his eyelids. "I..." He dipped his chin away from Nessix. "I'd loved him from the day we first met." Snide rumors which neither he nor Annin addressed had circulated between bored demons in the hells, but this was the first time Kol had voiced the sentiment out loud, and the simplicity of the words only seemed to cheapen the emotion even more than his stubborn refusal to make it known.

Beside him, Nessix remained silent, openly receptive to his testament, neither judging nor pitying. Perhaps she, too, had known it all along; she had shared intimate insights into Kol's mind, after all.

With the confession he'd tried to hide for so long spoken, an oppressive weight slid off Kol's shoulders, loosening the binds he'd kept wound so tightly around the truth. The pain was still there but had dulled into an acute ache which stood by to strangle him when he thought about suppressing it, and he lowered his head to confide in Nessix at last. "I can't remember a time when he wasn't in my life, and I don't want to picture a future without him in it."

"He tried to kill you," Nessix said.

"Yes," Kol whispered harshly.

"And if Mathias hadn't killed him, you'd be dead."

Kol glanced up at the sun again, digging his bruised and scabbed fingers into the ground, allowing the bite of grit and gravel to sink him into the present. "That would have been for the best."

Nessix looked at the sabers jutting out of her pack, Mathias's prediction and her own fears returning to her. She still believed Kol, if he could remember what it meant to live and dream, was the only candidate for these weapons, and, ever-bound to the duty of protecting others, Nessix would lead him there.

Her head gently sank against Kol's shoulder and he jolted at her touch, turning his damp eyes to her in disbelief. Her fingers forced their way between his, easing his grip on the harsh bits of stone. "No, Kol," she told him, drawing on a new tone of authority she hadn't shown before, one of benevolence. "You are needed, more than you know. The past centuries have been unfair to you. They've stolen from you what it means to truly be alive, but I vowed to help you remember, and I will. You are allowed your grief. You are allowed your regrets. But you're not allowed to quit. Not now. Not after we've broken free. Not yet."

Kol's breath caught in his throat, stuck someplace between denial and anguish. *Not after* we've *broken free.* No matter what Kol's sorrow wanted him to believe, he was not alone. He lowered his chin against the crown of Nessix's head, his fingers clenching around hers. She tightened her grip with the promise that she had his back, no matter what complications were thrown at him while he stepped away from the security he'd known for so long and into a world which would be opposed to welcoming him, vowing she'd never let him go. With Grell and Annin gone, with Lorrin and his men buried, Kol was the last of his tribe, the last of Abaeloth's memory of the joyous people his family had once led. He'd thought he'd found an acceptable replacement for the clan he'd been meant to inherit by falling in line with Grell, but that had been before Nessix. For the first time since the conclusion of the Divine Battle and the chaos which had accompanied it, Kol wasn't simply a disposable body permitted to keep a name because he was useful. He was part of a new clan, a new family. One that actually cared.

"When do you need to return to Elidae?" he asked quietly.

"Mathias and Sulik are holding things down. I've got time," Nessix replied.

The softness of her words didn't strike Kol half as hard as the weight of their meaning did. He'd been alive for almost the entirety of Abaeloth's history, an ancient transcending the limitations of time as it affected the mortal races. But time had never been something Kol had been allowed to have. Born to lead his tribe, forced to lead an army, always fighting, always dashing one step ahead just to survive. He had carried this struggle for centuries and knew no other way to live.

But now, he had Nessix to support and fight for him in a way Annin never had, to aid him when he needed help, to give him *time*. To breathe. To heal. To *live*. This beautiful creature he had tried to rule through force had refused to be broken. As much as demons liked to think their resilience granted them superiority over the rest of the world, Nessix had withstood every trial and torture thrown at her with a dignity Kol had forgotten existed. And every time he had thought he'd fallen apart, there she was, dutiful and committed, to put him back together.

Kol withdrew his defenses now, letting his tears come to wash away his shame and loneliness, penance for the crimes he'd committed against the world in his foolish quest to prove that it hadn't beaten him. In that insecurity which fueled the core of every demon, Kol had meant to own Nessix, but she'd declined his attempts, demanding instead to stand beside him until he finally let her step ahead and lead him back into the life he'd never intended to leave. She'd shown him the way he'd forgotten, proving that if she could find her place amidst Abaeloth's cruelties, anyone could. For the first time since the Divine Battle, Kol was home.

Upcoming Series in

The Afflicted Saga

Legend of the Risen
Book I: Ballad

A HERO MUST FORGE HIS OWN DESTINY…

Return to Abaeloth, Winter of 2022, and join Mathias on his path to seize his destiny, to find Etha, and to change the very course of Abaeloth's history.

On behalf of myself and everyone who calls Abaeloth home, thank you for becoming part of this world. If you enjoyed your journey through Tale of the Fallen, please consider leaving reviews and inviting your friends to join our ranks.

To keep current with upcoming releases in The Afflicted Saga, you can follow me on Facebook, AuthorCentral, and GoodReads, sign up for my mailing list, and access more information at
www.katikaschneider.com

ABOUT THE AUTHOR

A lover of literary adventure and notorious breaker of writing rules, Katika Schneider's been an obsessive writer for most of her life. She started out writing for herself before surrendering to her characters' demands, and began pursuing publication in 2014. She's a firm believer that everyone has a story to tell.

Holding her degree in Animal Science, Kat planned on attending veterinary school until incisions started making her faint. She lives with her husband and their abundant family of critters.